THE TREVORS

Books I-IV

A Promise of Love

It Takes a Hero

One Duke or Another

Married by Twelfth Night

USA Today Bestselling Author

ELLA QUINN

THE TREVORS, Books I-IV
Copyright © 2019 Ella Quinn

978-0-578-49276-6

All rights reserved.

Except for use in any review, the reproduction or utilization of this work in whole or in part in any form by any electronic mechanical or other means, now known or hereafter invented, including, but not limited to, xerography, photocopying and recording, or in any information storage or retrieval system, is forbidden without the written permission of the author.

All characters in this book have no existence outside the imagination of the author and have no relation whatsoever to anyone bearing the same name or names. They are not even distantly inspired by any individual known or unknown to the author, and all incidents are pure invention.

Cover Design & Interior Format

© The Killion Group Inc.

BOOKS BY ELLA QUINN

The Marriage Game
THE SEDUCTION OF LADY PHOEBE
THE SECRET LIFE OF MISS ANNA MARSH
THE TEMPTATION OF LADY SERENA
DESIRING LADY CARO
ENTICING MISS EUGENIE VILLARET
A KISS FOR LADY MARY
LADY BERESFORD'S LOVER
MISS FEATHERTON'S CHRISTMAS PRINCE

The Worthingtons
THREE WEEKS TO WED
WHEN A MARQUIS CHOOSES A BRIDE
IT STARTED WITH A KISS
THE MARQUIS AND I
YOU NEVER FORGET YOUR FIRST EARL

Novellas
MADELEINE'S CHRISTMAS WISH
THE SECOND TIME AROUND
I'LL ALWAYS LOVE YOU

The Trevors (A novella series)
A PROMISE OF LOVE
IT TAKES A HERO
ONE DUKE OR ANOTHER
MARRIED BY TWELFTH NIGHT

DEDICATION

To my granddaughters Vivienne and Josephine. May you always find love and friendship. And to my husband for sticking by me and my life changes. You are my hero.

ACKNOWLEDGMENTS

For any book to come together it takes a team. My thanks to my friend, Jenna Jaxon, and my lovely mother-in-law, Margaret Baker, for beta reading the novellas, and to Doreen Knight who corrects all my Americanisms and other sundry problems.

Thanks also to my editor, Ali MacGraw, for making the book shine, and to my fellow authors for coming together for the projects that gave birth to these books.

For One Duke or Another: A special thank you to Ann Marie Friedenberg for Oberon, the name of Guy's horse, and to Candace Nagy and Charlene Whitehouse for finding the post with the name when I could not!

Last, but certainly not least, to you, my readers who make this all worthwhile! I hope you love The Trevors!

A Promise of Love

Book One in The Trevors

CHAPTER ONE

New York City, July 1817

MISS GENEVIEVE ELIZABETH MACGOWAN, JENNY to her close friends and family, poured a cup of tea and handed it to her father as he settled back against the leather chair, which was his habitual seat in the drawing room. "Have you a date for the *Elizabeth* to sail yet, Papa?"

"Tuesday next." Angus MacGowan nodded as if in approval. "But you'll have to be aboard the night before. She'll sail with the morning tide."

Tuesday next? "Papa, that's in three days!" Leave it to her father to think packing for a trip of several months can be accomplished in a matter of hours.

"That it is. But the cargo we were waiting for has arrived, and I can't delay the ship."

She studied him closely, looking for any signs he might not have recovered from his illness. "Are you sure you'll be all right?"

"Aye, lass. I'm as fit as a fiddle." Even after more than twenty years in the United States, her father still had his Scottish brogue, and his ability to hide the truth.

"So you say," she scoffed.

"I am sure he will be fine," Sarah Brodhead, Jenny's aunt said. "One cannot grow older without any problems."

"Leave it to you to mention my age," her father scowled. "I don't see you getting any younger."

Jenny hid her grin behind her tea cup. Sarah had come to live with Jenny and her father four years ago, after her mother's death. Her aunt, only a few years older than she, had her own house, her circle of friends, and was not financially reliant on anyone. Only Sarah's firm belief that Papa was not to be trusted to successfully chaperone her niece and secure a successful match had made her leave her home for theirs. Unfortunately for Sarah, despite having escorted Jenny to all the major cities from Washington, D. C. to Maine, she had yet to find even one gentleman she wished to call husband. Occasionally Jenny thought that she might be too picky, then she remembered she would have to live with the man and be intimate with him. Better to find someone she loved. It would be easier to overlook any flaws he might have, and he could overlook hers as well.

Silence had fallen over the room, prompting her to fill it. "I hear that Paris is lovely this time of year."

"It will be now that there is no more fighting," Sarah responded tartly and glanced at Papa. "It's a good thing I have already sent our measurements and a list of what Jenny and I will need to that modiste in Paris."

"Well," Papa said, clearly ignoring that last remark, "at least Napoleon kept most of the English away from our shores. It would have gone much worse for us if old George and his son hadn't had the French to keep them busy."

"Very true." Sarah's tone held a touch of bitterness which Jenny understood well. "The French are our true allies. Something many here would be well served to remember."

Between Jenny's mother's family, who had fought in the Revolutionary War, and her father, whose family had once been outlawed by the English, she had been raised with no love for the country or its people. Then a few years ago,

English soldiers had occupied her maternal grandmother's house, causing the lady to suffer a heart attack and die. Sarah had been there when it had happened.

When one of her friends had suggested London as a place to look for a husband, Sarah had given the woman a very chilly set-down.

Unable to help herself, Jenny asked, "What about that earl you once met?"

A slow blush crept up her aunt's neck into the cheeks. "He was quite nice, actually. Not at all like those Red Coats that took over our house during the war. Then again, he did not believe our country had been treated fairly, so it was easy to be in charity with him."

"That explains it." Jenny half wondered if the earl would somehow show up once she and her aunt arrived in France. She set her cup down and began to rise. If she were to leave so soon, there was much to do. After all, they would be gone almost a year.

"Isn't he the one," Papa asked, "who said that Wellesley fellow didn't think his country should have attacked us the last time?"

"Indeed he is." Her aunt puckered her brow. "Although, I believe he is the Duke of Wellington now."

"The earl?" Papa demanded.

"No, Wellesley. He pulled himself up by the bootstraps from what I understand."

"Not that I think we need the peerage, mind you, but it's good for a young man to find his own way."

Abruptly, Aunt Sarah stood. "I have a great deal to attend to tomorrow if we are to depart so soon. I shall bid you a good night."

After the door had closed behind her aunt, her father turned to Jenny. "I will miss ye, lass."

She stepped over to her father giving him a tight hug. "I'll miss you as well. If you would prefer that I—"

"No, no. I want ye to see some of the world. If ye find a man to love ye, than all the better."

"And if I do not, what will happen to the company?" Although perfectly capable of running the business herself—she had, after all, been her father's assistant for years—she knew that even men she had known and actually done business with would never accept her as the director of MacGowan Shipping Enterprises.

"I'll think of something." He lowered his bushy red brows at her. "What I don't want ye doing is marrying unless you're in love. The French are more used to that sort of thing than the English, so it's a good thing you're going there first."

"First?" Whatever could he be thinking?

"You can't tell me that Sarah hasn't decided to visit London at some point."

London was the last place Jenny wanted to be, yet she wondered if her father was right. "If she has, she has kept her plans from me."

"Aye, well, she has her own fish to fry. As long as she does right by ye first, I'll have no complaint." He hugged her tight, as if she was leaving on the morrow. "Now give me your word that if you bring back a husband, ye'll love him, and he won't be an Englishman."

"I shall promise you that if I marry, the man I come home with will have my love *and* the ability to run the company." She shuddered. "The very idea of an Englishman touching me is enough to make me feel ill."

"Ah, lass," he sighed. "From your lips to God's ears."

Rising on her tip toes, she pecked his cheek. "It will all work out the way it is supposed to. Isn't that what you always tell me?"

"There ye go again. Throwing me words back at me." He grinned. "Just keep them in mind."

Tears pricked her eyes as she hugged him once again. "I

will. Good night, Papa."

He bussed her cheek. "Sleep well, my love."

London, April 1818

"CONGRATULATIONS." JENNY GLANCED FROM HER beaming aunt to the equally happy Geoffrey, Earl of Warwick, and summoned a smile. She had known this was coming, and was a little surprised it had taken so long for them to announce their decision. The only problem was that their marriage would delay her journey home.

Shortly after they had arrived in Paris, the earl had joined them and bullied his sister, the Countess of Heathcote, whom Jenny had *not* been invited to call Penelope, to sponsor Jenny in Paris society. Paris, however, had been a disappointment. Although there were several gentlemen she thought might be eligible, they had all turned out to be indolent. In fact, it had astounded her that there were so many worthless gentlemen in what Geoff called 'Polite Society.' Even many of the younger sons were merely looking for an heiress to support them. They were more interested in living a life of leisure than working for a living like a good New Englander would do.

In her ignorance, she had mentioned moving to America to one or two likely prospects, but the men had been horrified. It was as if she had suggested they live in the jungles of South America. As for the appalling number of English in France, well, she had no desire to see any of them again. They were worse than the French and had behaved as if there was something wrong with working for a living. One of them had actually had the gall to call the

United States a country of merchants.

Against her wishes, they had arrived in England after Christmas with the intention of introducing her to the *ton* while Geoff and Sarah planned their wedding. Unfortunately, there was no escape. With gales prevalent in the northern Atlantic, winter was not the time to sail back to New York. "When do you plan to marry?"

"Sometime in the next two weeks," Aunt Sarah replied. "Geoff must obtain the special license, Penelope has decided to host the wedding breakfast, and there will be a ball."

"We do not wish to wait long though," he commended as he gazed down at his betrothed.

Sarah had blossomed under the attentions of the earl, and become a great favorite of his sister and other members of the *ton*. Jenny did want her aunt to be happy, and she was thrilled that Sarah had finally found her true love. However, it posed a slight problem for Jenny. Someone would have to be hired to accompany her back to America.

"Of course not." She hugged and kissed her aunt, then embraced Geoff. "I am exceedingly happy for you. I'll wait until you are wed before I sail home."

"Oh, my dear." She could swear her aunt was beginning to sound English. "I really think you should remain for the Season. After all, you never know whom you might meet."

Jenny wanted to argue, but she could not very well disparage Englishmen with Geoff present. Instead she raised a brow and made her only other argument. "You know as well as I do that I have already met the cream of the *ton*, and none of them meets my requirements."

"Aside from that," Sarah continued as if Jenny hadn't spoken, "it will take a while to find a suitable companion who is willing to travel to America. Geoff and I would go with you, but I shall have a great deal to do at Warwick. It has been left without a mistress for too long."

He aunt was definitely picking up an English accent. Well, that was probably for the best as she'd be living here.

Jenny would arrange for her own passage, preferably on a MacGowan ship, and find a way to, hire a companion. Then she would kiss her aunt and new uncle farewell. "I shall remain for a month, no longer."

"I know you will find the right gentleman for you." Her aunt took her hands and squeezed them. "I can feel it."

If only she had her aunt's certainty. The one thing Jenny did not want to do was fail her father. Perhaps she would meet a gentleman from Scotland she could love. They must have a Season there as well. Surely she had relatives who could help her. The only problem was that her father had not maintained in contact with them, saying it was dangerous.

April 1818, London

LORD FRANCIS (FRANK) TREVOR GLANCED around the brilliantly lit ballroom wondering what the devil he was doing there. As the second son of the Duke of Somerset, one might suppose he would be used to the *ton*. And one would be mistaken. Other than the brief period of time he had spent on the Town during a university holiday, he had been acting as his father's factor. A job that by rights belonged to his eldest brother Damon, Marquis of Hawksworth. His father's heir. One could not even state with confidence that his father had any good reasons for doing what he did. Mostly the duke's behavior was the result of sheer pigheadedness.

Frank hadn't even had a holiday from running the dukedom's estates. Not only that, but he was chafing at running in his father's harness. It was not in his nature to be constantly under another man's boot. Lately, he had been searching for a way to change his life.

He had also become a bit short tempered. Not a state of mind that pleased him. Perhaps that was the reason that as soon as Father had departed for Scotland with a few of his cronies, Mama had decided Frank could benefit from a touch of Town bronze. How the hell that was supposed to help him when he dealt mainly with crops and animals, he had no idea.

He might as well realize he was trapped in a life he did not want and had no hope of employment outside of slaving for his father. He should have been allowed to buy a commission or take a position in government as other younger sons did. Add to that, after Damon's marriage to Meg Featherton at Christmas, their father had it made very clear that in the future he would be making any necessary matches for his children.

Frank heaved a sigh. Ergo, being here was a waste of time and money, though, thankfully, not his own.

A glass of wine was pressed into his hand. "Frank, you are supposed to be having fun." His brother, Damon, had the same a lazy smile on his face he'd worn since marrying Meg. "Not looking as if you're facing a hanging."

Frank took a long pull on the wine. "I am merely having trouble knowing where to start. How did you manage to talk father into this visit?"

"Ah, well." Rather than answering his question, his brother scanned the crowd. "Your mother decided it was time you were introduced to some of the ladies. I believe she also felt you were due for a little time away from the estate."

As if he would really be allowed to choose his own bride. "Did she happen to send you a list of ladies of whom father would approve?"

"Ah, no." Damon languidly raised his hand, and they were almost immediately joined by Meg, his wife of four months, and the young lady she had in tow.

Frank pushed himself off the wall. He thought he'd already seen all of the ladies present. How had he missed her? She was beautiful with enough curves to entice a monk. Maybe being in Town wasn't such a bad idea at that. He ignored the small voice in his head telling him his father would not approve.

"My love." Damon held his hand out to Meg. "We must have forgot that Frank doesn't really know anyone one in Town."

"Aren't you fortunate that I have a remedy?" She gave Frank an innocent grin.

She was up to something. The former Miss Margaret Featherton was the only female that had ever bested his father. "Miss MacGowan, may I introduce you to my brother-in-law, Lord Francis Trevor. Frank, Miss MacGowan. She has been traveling the Continent and, like you, is not acquainted with many people here."

The woman smiled politely, but there was a hard glitter in her blue eyes as she held out her hand. As if she didn't wish to be here. "A pleasure to meet you."

The moment their hands touched Frank caught his breath. He took another look into her eyes and could now see they were the color of a Scottish lake, and not nearly as cold as they had been a moment ago. A hint of lavender and lemon wove its magic, capturing his senses, and his hand warmed where her long slim fingers rested in his palm. Her thick, auburn hair was arranged on top of her head, with tendrils curling down to frame her oval face. He imagined running his fingers through her silky tresses. He didn't know how long he just stood there, but someone coughed, and he remembered he had to bow and say something polite. Obviously, telling her he wanted to carry her off to his bed wouldn't do. His sharp desire for her didn't even sound like him. Other than a liaison or two with a widow in a neighboring town, he had not had much experience with women. Yet, this lady's mere presence brought all his senses to the fore.

"It is my pleasure, Miss MacGowan." He was surprised he could speak at all, nonetheless in a calm voice.

For a moment, she stared at him, as if she was feeling the same strange sensations that had attacked him. Then she grinned ruefully, a look of consternation on her lovely face. "Dear me, you would think I'd know this by now." She lowered her voice to a whisper, as if speaking to herself. "What do I call you?" After a moment, her brow cleared. "Oh, yes. Lord Francis."

He had the feeling she had not forgot at all, but was insulting him. The question was why when they had just met. "I actually prefer Lord Frank." Then, lost as he was by her flaming hair and flawless milky skin, he said the next thing that came into his head, "You do not sound Scottish."

She laughed. A lilting sound that made him want to laugh as well. "That is because I am not. I have Scottish antecedents on my father's side, English on my mother's side, and a great deal of Dutch mixed in." Her tone became defensive and challenging at the same time. "I, sir, am an American."

American? Frank stilled for a moment. The only American woman he had heard of was . . . "From New York?" Holding her chin high, Miss MacGowan inclined her head slightly. "The one who was in Paris last autumn?"

"Exactly." Her tone was as sour as a lemon. "The American heiress." She leaned in confidingly. "You had better watch yourself. I might whip out my tomahawk and scalp you."

The one who had been, from all accounts, exceedingly

difficult to please. His sisters kept up with any and all gossip and had regaled him with what they discovered. Even he knew the stories of the English and French peers who had traveled to Paris to seek her hand and her fortune. She was obviously not a particularly happy lady and probably wouldn't even dance with him. Still, there was something about her that called to him. She seemed as alone as he felt and no more happy to be here than he was. "I see."

"Really?" She tilted her head to one side, but her voice was as dry and brittle as an autumn leaf. "What exactly do you see?"

"Jenny." A woman a few years older than Miss MacGowan suddenly appeared. "You must not quiz a gentleman you have only just met." The admonishment was firm but kind.

Miss MacGowan pressed her lips together for a moment, then laughter filled her expressive eyes. "Thank you, Aunt." Turning to him, Miss MacGowan said, "I am sorry. I think I must be very homesick to have become so unmannerly, not to mention surly."

Frank blinked. He had met spoiled ladies, ill-mannered ladies, and ones who merely simpered, but he had never met a woman who would apologize so quickly and succinctly, with a sense of humor. "Not at all." He discovered he was still holding her hand, and decided not to return it. "The fault was mine. Will you dance with me, Miss MacGowan?"

Once again, she gave him a quizzical look. "I shall be delighted to, Lord Frank. However, first"—she glanced at the other woman who had been joined by a gentleman—"Aunt Sarah, may I introduce you to Lord Frank Trevor?" After the introductions to Miss MacGowan's aunt, Meg, and the gentleman had been made, she smiled. "My aunt and Lord Warwick are to be married next week."

The violins had begun the prelude to a waltz, and Frank found that more than anything he wanted Miss MacGowan to himself for a while. "I wish you happy." Quickly, before they could be drawn into a wedding conversation, he placed Miss MacGowan's hand on his arm. "We should join the other dancers."

She inclined her head. "Certainly." Once they were a few steps away, she whispered, "Thank you. I love my aunt, but I am sick to death of the wedding preparations."

That was an odd thing for a lady to say. At least the ones he knew. Then again, it was becoming clear that she was an unusual lady. One he wanted to know much, much better.

Taking their places, he bowed and she curtseyed, then he placed his palm on her waist. Fighting the urge to pull her body flush against his, he wished more than ever before that he was free to fall in love. Or knew a way to escape his father.

CHAPTER TWO

JENNY STIFLED A GASP AS she sucked in a breath, inhaling Lord Frank's clean scent along with it. No perfumes for him–simply an herbal soap and the musky scent of male. The palm of his hand burned through her silk gown and petticoats. The short stays she had worn gave no protection at all from his touch. The dance had begun, and he was soon expertly leading her around the floor. She had never felt so weightless or secure in a partner. Which was a very good thing as her knees felt a little like jelly. What a shame he was English. Papa would never approve.

"What is your idea of a perfect wedding?"

She gazed into his deep blue eyes. Other than his size, large and broad without a bit of fat, Lord Frank did not look much like his brother, who had dark hair, eyes, and complexion. A lock of golden blond hair fell over his forehead. Some women would want to push it back into place, but she decided it looked good there. "I would want something such as we have in our family, a simple ceremony at home and perhaps a few people to have dinner with afterward. We do not need all the parties you have here. The purpose, after all, is to marry one's true love. On my wedding day, I would not wish to share him with others."

"I understand you. I sometimes think there is more interest in the entertainments than in the ceremony itself." He seemed to pull her closer to him during the turn. "Are all weddings in America like the one you described?"

"Not all. Much depends on where a family is from. If

their former home country had large parties, they would as well." He had an almost square jaw with a dimple, and a straight nose that was not overly large for an Englishman. She tried not to look at his mouth, which was wide with perfectly formed lips. "What do you do?"

"I am in charge of my father's properties." His tone was flat, as if he was not pleased with his position.

Most likely he was another one who did not wish to work at all. How disappointing. Then again, he *was* an English gentleman. "Do you not like the job?"

"It's not the position. That is extremely gratifying when my advice is taken. It is that my older brother should have the responsibility. He is the one who will inherit from my father, not I who am the second son. My father is in good health. Therefore, the situation leaves me to find something else to do when I am no longer young and Hawksworth is duke."

At least he wanted to be occupied. If Lord Frank was being truthful, then his father was making life difficult for not only his heir, but his second born. "I fail to understand your father's decision. It does not make sense to me."

A travesty of a smile twisted his lips. "I doubt anyone understands how the Duke of Somerset thinks, not even my mother." He was silent for a few moments before he said, "He is not a pleasant topic of conversation. Perhaps we could talk about something else. Have you seen much of London?"

Despite her aversion to the English, she found herself liking Lord Frank or at least feeling for his position. She wondered if there was some way she could discover more about the duke, which, in turn, would tell her more about his second son. "Other than the shops on Bond and Bruton Streets, I have not seen much at all. Although, I have been promised a great deal if I remain in London. The most I've been able to do is to escape in the morning for a walk in the Park."

"The Park is pleasant," Frank replied. "It reminds me of the country. However, I think you would enjoy Green Park as well. It would be my honor to show you the sights. Would you care to accompany me on a carriage ride?"

She had not been to that particular park, but she had heard about it. "Is that the place that has cows with milkmaids?"

"Indeed." He smiled suddenly, and all she could think of was how handsome he was. "You may drink a cup of fresh milk."

It had been a long time since she had tasted milk directly from a cow. "I'd love to."

"Are you free tomorrow?"

"Yes." Jenny could not understand why she was so drawn to Lord Frank. Normally Englishmen did not appeal to her. Even Geoff, although very nice, was not to her taste. Yet, Lord Frank seemed to be different. Well, she would see if he was or not. "I have nothing planned in the morning."

"Can you be ready by nine o'clock?"

A smile hovered on his lips, and she wondered if she was being quizzed. "I was under the impression that gentlemen and ladies did not rise from their beds until after noon."

"Ah, but I am not a typical gentleman and will inevitably find myself up much earlier than that." His brow rose in a definite challenge. "Unless *you* are not an early riser."

"I, sir, am dressed and have broken my fast by seven in the morning." That should put him in his place. He was probably joking her. Even Geoff, who was the only good Englishman she knew, liked to linger in bed.

"Seven it is, then." He twirled them through a turn again.

She could not believe he had taken her at her word. What she had actually meant was that she was dressed in a day gown that she could put on herself. If only Rosie, her own maid, was here, but she suffered so much from sea sickness that she could not have made the journey. The London maid that had been hired for her was going to be unhappy about having to have Jenny's clothing ready by that hour. Still, she couldn't very well turn down a dare. "I shall be waiting."

Miss MacGowan's chin rose, and Frank knew he was being tested. Then again, that was fair. Even though nothing would come of it, wasn't he assaying her as well? She was beautiful, wealthy, and not likely to take a younger son as a husband. She was probably expecting a title. He should not be wasting her time dancing with her, or asking her if she would like to accompany him to Green Park, or anything else. On the other hand, she had rejected several peers. What did she want? "Are you residing at Lord Warwick's town house?"

"No, we are presently visiting Lady Heathcote." Miss MacGowan said the lady's name as if it were somehow distasteful. "However, when my aunt and Lord Warwick marry, we shall reside with him."

That sounded like another not entirely happy notion. Then he remembered her earlier comment.

"Although, I have been promised a great deal if I remain in London."

Did that mean she did not wish to remain in London? And if so, where would she go? He did not want to consider the possibility that she would depart before the Season was barely underway. Had she not, after all, come to this side of the Atlantic Ocean to find a husband? She gave him a polite smile, yet he had an uneasy feeling she was ready to return to America. And *that* was not what he wanted. It was time to find out more about Miss MacGowan, and he knew just who to ask.

When the set ended, he returned her to her aunt, who was still speaking with Meg. If he knew his sister-in-law, she would already be conversant not only with Miss Brodhead's entire history, but Miss MacGowan's as well.

They stood for several moments not saying anything as the others continued to talk, then her aunt turned to Miss MacGowan and said, "We should be getting back to our party. I am sure Lady Heathcote has arranged for several other gentlemen to stand up with you."

A militant look appeared in Miss MacGowan's eyes. "Indeed." Frank almost shivered at the chill in her voice. "I do not recall giving Lady Heathcote permission to accept engagements for me."

She was definitely strong minded. He liked that in a lady. Although, he had a feeling her aunt was none too pleased.

"Jenny," Miss Brodhead said in a voice a hint above a whisper. "She is only trying to help."

That did not seem to mollify Miss MacGowan at all. She closed her eyes for a second, before replying, "We shall discuss this matter later." As they moved to leave, she stopped in front of him. "Until tomorrow."

He inclined his head. "I shall look forward to it."

Her aunt turned back, "Jenny?"

"I'm coming." The last was said with such bad grace that he had to hide a grin. Still, he should not laugh at her. She was clearly unhappy, and he intended to discover the reason.

"Meg." He sidled closer to his sister-in-law. "What do you know about Miss MacGowan?"

She pulled a face. "The short version is that she is homesick, does not wish to marry a peer, and detests most of the English."

"Homesickness I can understand." He felt a little that way as well, and he was still in England. He had never heard of a lady who didn't want a title. "But why does she dislike us?"

"Well, not *all* of us. She has particular enmity for Lady Heathcote and the gentlemen who attempted to court her in Paris, as well as English soldiers. Apparently her grandmother died after a troop was billeted with the lady. Quite understandably, Miss MacGowan blames her grandmother's death on the soldiers. Also, many of her relations fought in both wars, and her father is from a clan that an English king declared outlawed. Other than that"—she shrugged lightly—"I haven't the faintest idea." Meg's forehead creased, and she rubbed a finger between her brows. "I almost forgot. She has no use for idle aristocrats."

That was a comprehensive list, and he could not really blame the lady for most of her feelings. He had no use for those who allowed their lands to fall into disrepair or gambled away their holdings. "Yet she came to London?"

"Against her wishes." Meg sighed. "Her goal was to find a French husband to take back to New York. The Americans are quite fond of the French, but none of the gentlemen she met were interested in leaving the Continent, and that is the extent of my knowledge. If you had been gone longer, I could have discovered more. Although, it took me long enough to glean that much as Lord Warwick and Miss Brodhead were reluctant to part with even those crumbs."

Leave it to Meg to dismiss what she had discovered as crumbs. Frank laughed. "I'd say you did very well considering the handicap you were under. Someday, you'll be as frightening as Lady Bellamny is said to be."

Before Meg and Damon's marriage, Frank had only known of Lady Bellamny because his father had several times ranted loudly about what a meddling besom she was. His mother had finally explained that Lady Bellamny, his brother Damon's godmother, was a female of definite opinions and had the ability to know almost everything about everyone. She, as well as Meg's grandmother, the

Dowager Viscountess Featherton, and that lady's longtime friend, the Duchess of Bridgewater, had assisted in Meg and Damon's courtship.

"I do hope so." Meg smiled wickedly. "How dull life would be if one could not help others."

Damon choked and snatched two glasses of champagne from a passing footman. "Please do not give her ideas. My life is interesting enough without my wife involving herself in the love affairs of friends and family, not to mention perfect strangers."

She took the glass he handed her and focused her attention on Frank. "You seem to be extremely interested in Miss MacGowan."

Oh, no! He wasn't falling for that trap. "I find her unusual. I wonder a bit at the gossip about her."

"As you probably know"—Meg raised a brow—"most think she is beyond pleasing."

Or, perhaps, no one had yet offered her what she was looking for. She did not appear to be a lady who would settle. "Why did she want a Frenchman to go to America?"

His sister-in-law's other brow rose and her eyes widened. "I have no idea. Perhaps you should ask her."

He considered Miss MacGowan's enmity for the English, and discovered he was not as shocked as he should be. Many of his countrymen and women spoke dismissively of the former colonies. That was sure to set her back up. He wondered why she had agreed to go to Green Park with him. Was it merely an excuse to leave Lady Heathcote's house, or did she think he was different? An Englishman with whom she would like to spend some time? What was she looking for in a husband, and did he truly wish to know?

He was attracted to her, but if he discovered his feelings were stronger than mere desirability, there were definite problems to overcome. After all, what sane woman would agree to live in the same house as his curmudgeonly father? None he could think of. Especially not a lady such as Miss MacGowan.

He did not even want to think of his father's reaction to him wishing to marry an American. The duke had no love for the former colonies. Now he was getting way ahead of himself. He had no idea if he and the lady would even suit, or if he would like her enough to attempt to persuade her to set aside her dislike of the English. Well, he'd find out tomorrow if his initial impressions were correct. He gave himself a shake. What the deuce was he doing? Meeting an American had obviously made him reckless. Still, he would stay the course for the immediate future.

CHAPTER THREE

JENNY'S EYES POPPED OPEN AT six o'clock exactly. Or so the clock on the mantle told her. She had an hour to be ready for her trip to Green Park. However, after having had to stand up with several gentlemen of Lady Heathcote's choosing, Jenny wasn't sure she could stomach being in the company of another Englishman. They appeared to believe that she should be honored to spend time with them. Still she had agreed to the outing, and it would be rude to back out at this late date.

She tugged on the embroidered pull then rose from the bed. Fortunately, the fire had already been stoked, so only the wash water was chilly.

Several minutes later, just as she was wondering where her maid, Jasper, was, the door opened, and the servant stepped into the bedchamber. "Miss, are you ill?"

Naturally that would be the only reason for a lady to be up this early. "No, I have an engagement and must dress."

For a moment, the maid appeared stunned, then she turned to the wardrobe. "Are you going for a walk or a drive?"

"A drive. I must hurry if I am to break my fast before I leave."

Jasper took out a carriage gown of Pomona green, laid it on the bed, and tugged the bell-pull. "I shall have breakfast brought to you immediately." A moment later, another maid knocked on the door before opening it. "Miss MacGowan requires a baked egg, toast, and tea as soon as possible."

Jenny was stunned. The lady's maid had never before seemed so eager to please. "Thank you, Jasper."

"It is a pleasure to serve you. Now, allow me to dress you and arrange your hair."

What could have gotten into the woman? "Thank you. I must be ready no later than seven."

"That early!"

In less than twenty minutes, Jenny was ready.

"I am surprised Lord Pomfry rises so early," Jasper said as she arranged the breakfast dishes on the table.

Lord Pomfry? Who was . . . Oh, yes. Jenny remembered now. Lord Pompous. The man had been good looking in a soft sort of way, spoke with a bored drawl, and talked of nothing but his family's illustrious history and horses. Horses she could understand. She liked them as well. Still, the idiot had actually had the nerve to ask her if she'd met one of his younger brothers, a captain in a unit that had been stationed in New York during the last war. "I have no idea when his lordship rises." And she did not care to know either. "I have an engagement with another gentleman."

The maid's eyes widened. "But I was told the earl had expressed an interest in you and will call today."

Like pieces of a puzzle falling in place, Jenny understood why Jasper was being so helpful. She would expect to remain with Jenny when she married, and how much more prestigious than to be lady's maid to a countess. "I hate to disappoint you, but I am not interested in Lord Pomfry. In fact, I doubt I shall be here when he arrives." If at all possible, she must make plans to remain gone until late afternoon. "Thank you, you may go."

She tucked into her breakfast as the maid practically ran out of the room. Obviously someone was going to be notified that Miss MacGowan was being difficult. She missed her own maid. It was never necessary to actually have to dismiss Rose. She just knew when to leave. She also wouldn't tell on her. Glancing at the clock, Jenny was pleased to see the hands had moved. She had less than ten minutes before Lord Frank arrived. She brushed her teeth, donned her bonnet, mantle, and gloves, then made her way to the hall, just as the front door was opened by the senior footman.

Lord Frank handed the servant his card. "I am here to collect Miss MacGowan."

"My lord the ladies are—"

"I am ready." Lord Frank smiled at her and for some strange reason, her heart began beating faster and butterflies took up residence in her stomach. He looked as handsome in his buff pantaloons and dark blue jacket as he had last night in evening wear. Even more so.

Smiling, he offered her his arm. "Shall we go?"

When she placed her fingers on his arm, her whole hand seemed to become warmer. She couldn't help but to smile back. "Yes, indeed. I am looking forward to our excursion."

"Miss," the footman said. "May I inquire as to your destination and when you plan to return?"

"I shall be perfectly safe with his lordship." Even though she didn't wish to worry her aunt, she did not want Lady Heathcote to be able to find her.

A few moments later, she was seated in a glossy dark green curricle with gold piping. He took the reins, and started the pair of horses.

"This is a very nice carriage."

"It's my brother's. I do not own one of my own."

"It was good of him to lend it to you.

"I agree." Frank glanced at Miss MacGowan. He'd never been rushed out of a house so quickly in his life. "Why do I have the feeling I am helping you escape?"

Rather than looking at him, she arranged her skirts.

"Because you are."

Despite the way his body reacted to her light touch, part of him, the responsible part, seriously considered returning her to Lady Heathcote's home. The other part asked, "Will you tell me the reason?"

"I have the distinct impression that her ladyship is attempting to arrange a match between Lord Pompous and me."

Surely he had not heard her properly. "Lord Pompous?"

She had the grace to look the slightest bit guilty. "Lord Pomfry. I make names up for most of the gentlemen with whom I am forced to dance with." Miss MacGowan was quiet for a moment then looked at Frank. "Not you. I wanted to stand up with you."

He had never had such a remarkable conversation with a lady in his life. Were all Americans so direct? Now what was he to say? "Thank you."

A sparkle entered her eyes, her lips tilted up, and she laughed. Not the type of laugh one expected to hear from a member of the *ton*, but one that came from deep inside her. "I should explain. This morning, the lady's maid who is assigned to me told me that Lord Pomfry is to call on me. I do not wish to see him. Therefore, I have decided to remain gone all day."

Extraordinary. She was the most refreshing person he had ever met. "I must confess, I would not wish to have to spend time with a man I had nicknamed Lord Pompous."

A slight blush stained her cheeks. "I should not have said that to you. I hope I have not shocked you."

"Not at all." Frank was actually surprised it was the truth. He had been raised very strictly, but he understood the need to rebel. After all, that was what he was doing in Town. Despite what his mother had said, he was positive his father had not agreed to him leaving the estate. "Will your family worry about you?"

She gave a light shrug. "My aunt knows I am with you. At some point, I will send a message that I shall not return until late this afternoon." He raised his brows, and she blushed again. "Not that I mean *you* must remain with me all day. I could not expect you to dance attendance on me for that long."

Why not? He had nothing better to do, and it would give him the opportunity to get to know her. To sort out whether the physical feelings he was having were simply caused by her beauty or if there could be more. "We can make that decision later if you wish."

A smile returned to her lovely lips, and it was as if the day was bright as summer rather than an overcast day in early spring. "Thank you."

"Have you had much experience with cows?"

"A bit. My grandmother had cows, and we used to visit her." Suddenly her joy was gone. This must have been the grandmother who died. "She is no longer with us."

He should probably leave well enough alone, but again, some force inside him needed to know more about her. "Was she quite old when she passed away?"

"No." Her lips thinned. "British soldiers occupied her house during the last war. Her heart was already bad, and she suffered an attack."

He'd been told that Cromwell's soldiers had done much the same to his family. He didn't think anyone had died, but the house had been ransacked. To this day his father hated the Roundheads. Did she detest the English that much? "I am surprised you decided to come to England."

"It was not my choice. I wanted to go home, but my aunt and Geoff decided to marry. Now I must wait until a suitable companion can be hired to return with me."

Or a husband, but would she agree to marry one of his countrymen? "You have no desire to remain here?"

She shook her head. "I cannot. My father needs me."

Then why had she traveled to Europe, and why was she looking for a husband over there rather than in America? "Miss MacGowan, I do not wish to be impertinent, but if you planned to go home, why are you husband hunting on this side of the Atlantic?"

Her head turned slowly and she stared at him for a moment. "You are the first man to ask me that. Do you really want to know the truth?"

He did, but it occurred to him that her reasons may indeed shock him. He took a deep breath and let it out. "I do."

"My plan was to find a husband who would be willing to return to New York with me and help me run our family's business. As in most places, a woman would have a hard time running a shipping line. Even our oldest customers and suppliers would not approve of me being at the helm in such a public fashion."

Now he understood why she was having difficulties finding a husband among the *ton* and the French aristocrats. Even if they were in love, very few of the men he knew would give up what they had here and live in the colonies. As a wife, she would be expected to remain in her husband's country. "That is disappointing for you."

"It is, but I am a practical woman. I shall deal with what I have."

And now for the other problem. "You have no reason to love the English. Could you even bring yourself to care for one of us?"

Yet another question no one had bothered to ask Jenny. She liked Geoff well enough, and her aunt had been able to fall in love with him. Sarah had even more reason to hate the English than Jenny did. Sarah had been there when her mother had died.

Jenny searched Lord Frank's face. Would the fact that he was English stop her from falling in love? Would that be fair? She did not even know if he agreed with either the Revolutionary War or the War of 1812. Although none of the English she had met seemed to understand that was our second war of independence. In fact, they looked at her strangely when she mentioned it. Was she rushing? After all, she had known the man for less than a day. Then again, Mama said she knew right away. "I'm not sure. I guess it would depend on the man."

"We are here." He stopped the curricle. "You lad," he called to a street urchin. "There is a yellow bob for you if you will watch the horses."

"You've got it, Guvnor." The boy grinned as he went to their heads and took charge of the pair.

The next thing she knew, Lord Frank was lifting her down. By the time her feet touched the ground, Jenny was ready to fall into his arms. Oh, dear. She had never been affected like that before. She ruthlessly shoved the attraction she was feeling down, tucked her hand in his arm, and grinned. "On to the cows."

The beasts were just being led into the park when they arrived. "Miss," Lord Frank said to the milkmaid. "We'd like two cups."

The young woman deftly milked the cow and handed them cups of still warm milk. Even on her grandmother's farm, Jenny had rarely had milk warm from the cow. She took a sip, then drank the whole cup down. "That was excellent."

"I frequently visit our dairy when the cows are being milked. Nothing can compare." He finished his cup as well, and gave it back to the milkmaid. "Shall we stroll for a while?"

"Will your horses be safe?" Once again, she tucked her hand into his arm. She had never felt as comfortable with any gentleman before. It was a shame she could not spend the whole day with him, but that would be too much to ask. After all, they had only met last night.

"Yes, the children are accustomed to watching them, and we will not be overly long. It is a small park. Where would you like to go next?"

She jerked her head around so fast it should have hurt. "Are you sure you do not wish to take me home?"

"Quite positive." His blue eyes seemed to warm as he looked at her. "You said you have not seen much of London. It would be my honor to escort you around."

For the third time this morning, her cheeks became warm. "Thank you. It would be my pleasure to accept your escort."

"I suggest that before we leave Mayfair we stop at my brother's house so that you may write a note to your aunt."

She really should tell Sarah where she was, still his suggestion surprised her. He really must be used to taking care of people. "Very well."

Not an hour later, Jenny found herself being ushered into a moderately-sized town house. Lord Frank handed his hat and gloves to a staid-looking butler, then he removed her mantle and took her gloves. "Saunders, has his lordship come down yet?"

"Yes, my lord. He and her ladyship are in the breakfast room."

"Thank you." Lord Frank took her hand. "We shall join them."

She glanced around the freshly-painted hall. "Everything seems new."

"It is. My brother and sister-in-law bought this house late last winter after he married. Our father has a house in Town, but Damon and Meg thought they would have more privacy in their own home." Lord Frank grimaced. "My father is not the easiest of persons to get along with, and he still does not approve of their marriage."

How odd. As far as Jenny had been told, Lady

Hawksworth came from an old, well thought of and respected family. "I do not understand. They seem perfectly well suited."

"They are extremely happy. I do not think my brother could have made a better choice. The duke, however, is difficult to please."

Jenny's hackles rose. The man would probably not think an American was good enough for his son. "How sad for your family."

"Damon and Meg are able to ignore him." His lips formed a line. "I wish the rest of us were as lucky."

The breakfast room was hung with pale yellow silk, making it bright and cheerful. Doors and windows to a small garden filled one wall. A sideboard held a number of chafing dishes, and Lord and Lady Hawksworth were seated at one end of the table sharing a newspaper.

Lord Frank cleared his throat. "I brought a guest."

His brother rose as his sister-in-law grinned up at Jenny and Lord Frank. "Miss MacGowan, welcome. Please have a seat. I shall ring for more tea. I am delighted to see you are an early riser as well."

"Thank you, my lady." She allowed Lord Frank to lead her to a seat on the other side of his brother.

"Can you eat again?" he asked as he pushed in her chair.

"Yes, please." She watched him as he strolled to the sideboard. No mincing steps for him, but a long, confident stride.

"Please call me Meg. My husband is Damon. I do not think there is any reason we cannot be informal when we are alone."

Jenny dragged her gaze from Lord Frank. "My name is Genevieve, but I am called Jenny."

Lord Frank glanced over his shoulder. "If we are going to be on a first name basis, I insist you call me Frank."

This was the first time since she'd met Geoff that she

had been asked to call anyone by their first name. A little thrill of pleasure at being so easily included ran through her. "Is there anything interesting in the paper?"

"Not much outside of Britain," Damon replied, handing her a sheet. "You must miss your own country's newspapers."

She took the paper as Frank—how lovely it was to be able to call him that—placed a plate filled with eggs, ham, and roast beef before her. "I do miss it. It's so hard to find a newssheet that has much about the United States in it."

Meg chewed a piece of toast then swallowed. "How long do you plan on staying in England?"

Yesterday at this time, Jenny would have said not longer than a week, but now it might be worth remaining just a little longer. . . She resolutely kept her gaze from Frank. She should not stare at him so much. "At least until my aunt marries."

Or until she discovered what her feelings for Lord Frank Trevor were, and if he could have any feelings for her.

CHAPTER FOUR

PENELOPE, COUNTESS OF HEATHCOTE, RUSHED into the breakfast room while Sarah and Geoff were enjoying an intimate, quiet breakfast. Sarah sighed. Only one more week, and she would be in her own house and not subject to Penelope's complaints about Jenny.

"She is not in the house," Penelope announced in an insulted tone.

Resisting the urge to roll her eyes, Sarah glanced up. "By *she*, I assume you mean Jenny."

"Yes, the wretched girl. I had plans for her today." Penelope took her seat at the head of the table, signaling for fresh tea to be brought. "My maid told me she left with a man at seven o'clock this morning and refused to say where she was going. It is now past eleven, and she has not returned. What am I to tell Lord Pomfry?"

Sarah had never known her niece to break plans she'd made with someone, yet she would not have put it past Jenny to ignore Penelope's plans. The two had not got along since the day they'd met. Jenny saw no reason to placate a spoiled peeress, and Penelope was not pleased with what she considered to be Jenny's lack of respect for her rank.

"Did he make arrangements to visit her?" Geoff asked. He and Sarah had just been having a conversation regarding his sister's interference with her sister.

"He asked me last evening if he could call on Miss MacGowan, and I assured him she would be delighted."

Oh, dear. Sarah closed her eyes for a moment trying to remember who Lord Pomfry was. Yet before she could respond, Geoff asked, "Did you inquire as to whether Jenny wished to entertain Pomfry?"

There was something in her betrothed's voice that made Sarah wary. At the same time, an image of a tall thin man dressed like a Dandy entered her mind. Definitely not the type of gentleman who would interest her niece. A Corinthian would be much more to her liking.

"No, why should I have?" Penelope's tone was too haughty and more than a bit defensive. "The girl must find a husband, and Percy is perfectly eligible."

"Percy is a fop. He doesn't even visit Jackson's," Geoff stated baldly. "I, for one, cannot see Jenny wanting anything to do with him. I don't want much to do with him." His brows drew together as he scowled. "Penelope, your attempts to find a husband for Jenny must cease. It is painfully obvious that you and she do not get along, nor do you have an understanding of the type of gentleman who would please her. Try looking for someone more like me."

"As long as I am sponsoring her and she is under my roof, she must follow my advice." As quickly as Penelope had flounced into the room, she flounced out.

Blowing out a breath, Sarah turned to Geoff. "I think Jenny and I should move to a hotel."

Taking her hand, he pressed a kiss on her palm. "You may be right. I shall make arrangements for you to move tomorrow."

She held her hand to his cheek. "Let us plan for today. Jenny sent me a message informing me she is with Lord Frank Trevor. I shall let her know to have him bring her to the hotel. That way we can avoid having another confrontation between Jenny and Penelope."

"Hmm, Lord Frank you say?" A calculating look came

into Geoff's eyes. "He might be the perfect match for Jenny. From what Hawksworth says, he is hardworking and has no desire to remain living with the duke. Perhaps he would not mind moving to America."

"No interference from you, either. I do not like the idea of some man attaching himself to her for the sole purpose of bettering his life." Geoff glowered at her and Sarah laughed. "Jenny must find her own heart's desire." She kissed the palm of his hand. "Just as I found you."

"MISS MACGOWAN." SAUNDERS ENTERED THE morning room where Frank, Jenny, Meg, and Damon had gathered. "I have a message for you."

Jenny took the note from the silver salver the butler held out. "Thank you, Saunders."

Using her fingernail, she popped off the seal. "My aunt and I are moving to the Pulteney Hotel today."

"Does she say why?" Frank asked. After what she had told him about the way Lady Heathcote treated her, Frank was just as happy to have Jenny living elsewhere.

"No, but I assume Lady Heathcote threw a temper tantrum when she discovered I would not be there to meet Lord Pomfry."

"Pomfry?" Damon's black brows rose. "Why the deuce would she think you might be interested in him?"

"If I recall," Meg said, her lips forming a moue as her index finger tapped the table. "he is the brother of one of her dear friends. Like many peers, he is land rich and cash poor." She glanced at Damon. "My love, there is no reason Jenny and her aunt cannot stay with us. We have the room, and it would be much more comfortable for them than a hotel."

Frank had the distinct impression that his sister-in-law was matchmaking. He and Jenny were getting along wonderfully, but this was too much too soon. He took Jenny's hand in his. "Unless you would prefer not to."

His brother and Meg moved to the desk at the other end of the room. Jenny seemed to search his face for a few long moments. "I already feel very welcome and comfortable here, but I would not wish to impose. We have not known one another long at all."

He must be going mad. Suddenly, he didn't care what Meg was doing. He wanted Jenny with him. "Very true. However, as you said, you feel at home with us. That must be better than being at a hotel." Not that he had ever stayed at a hotel. "They are so impersonal."

He waited on "tenterhooks as she furrowed her brow, clearly thinking the proposal over. He liked having her with him. It was hard to believe they had only met last night. What he didn't want to think about was his father's reaction if he discovered Frank was courting an American.

Courting. Was that what he was doing? He had never considered that he would ever woo a lady, and of his choosing no less.

Finally, she nodded to herself and said, "I would be pleased to accept your kind invitation."

"I'm glad you have decided to stay with us." Frank squeezed Jenny's hand and warmth filled her.

What had she done? Granted, her feelings for him were growing by the minute, and the small voice in her head was telling her they were meant to be together, but . . . No, she was right to accept the offer. She did not have much time, and if it turned out they were not meant to be together, then she would return to New York. At least now she'd have a chance to discover if they could fall in love, and she no longer had to worry about Lady Heathcote's interference.

"Do you have a lady's maid with you?" Meg asked.

"Only one that Lady Heathcote hired. I do not trust her. Unfortunately, my maid at home could not accompany me."

"In that case, I have a young woman here who is able to take care of you."

"Thank you." Jenny breathed a sigh of relief to be rid of Jasper and her ladyship in one fell swoop. Jenny could not abide personal servants who were not loyal. She gnawed her bottom lip. Perhaps she was making a mistake staying here. Frank's brother and sister-in-law seemed to be lovely people, but what did she know about them? This could be worse than at Lady Heathcote's house. And if Jenny decided she and Frank did not suit, who would protect her from him? She gave herself a shake. In for a penny, in for a pound, as her grandmother used to say. She would know how she felt soon enough. As for today, she planned to enjoy sightseeing.

She glanced up at Frank. "What should I see first?"

"The museum. That will take up most of the day. If you would like, we can visit the Royal Menagerie in the morning."

If he worked, she did not understand how he had so much free time. Had she been mistaken about him? "Do you not have duties to attend to?"

"Like you," he grinned, "I am on a sort of holiday. Naturally, if something urgent were to occur, I would need to take care of it. I only hope that my time here is not cut short."

"How far from London do you live?" She hoped it was not a long way. There was no way she could travel by herself out of London.

"Far enough." His jaw clenched as if the idea bothered him greatly. "It is a three day journey, and if I was called back, I would not return to Town. Let's not think of that now."

"Very well." She had the feeling there was something he was not telling her, but decided not to ask. If it was important, it would come out eventually. Although it's clear they may not have much time…

Damon glanced at her and his brother. His look was almost as grim as Frank's. There was definitely something going on.

"I'll call for the carriage."

She shook off her concerns and smiled. "Please do. If the museum will take most of the day, we should be going."

A few minutes later, he once again handed her into the curricle, and once again her fingers tingled at his touch. They would miss luncheon, but since they'd eaten breakfast twice, she wasn't hungry.

About twenty minutes later, he pulled up in front of a large brick building. As before, a young boy took care of the horses, and soon her hand was tucked in his arm.

"First, I'll show you the Elgin Marbles, then we can look at the paintings."

"Are those the statuary and frescos that Greece and some other countries want returned?" Well that was rude. She didn't know what had prompted her to say that, except that the Redcoats had tried to steal art from America. Still, she would not apologize.

"The very ones. My brother's friends are attempting to convince our government to return them, but he doesn't have much hope."

"His friends?" She glanced at Frank. "Why does he not involve himself?"

"Damon is not yet a peer. Therefore, he cannot vote in the House of Lords. The most he can hope to do is influence those who can vote. He and Meg have hosted several small dinners and other entertainments with that in mind. He also owns an estate and is able to apply some pressure on the local Member of Parliament. Fortunately, it's not a rotten seat. The problem is that the government spent a great deal of money to acquire the marbles." He glanced at her. "You are quite well informed."

For an American, he hadn't said, still the thought was there. She couldn't very well tell him that she made a point of discovering the wrongs England had done to other countries. "I try to stay *au courant*. How do you feel about the subject?"

He shrugged. "It really doesn't matter. I own no property, and, therefore, I have no vote at all."

"That is horrible!" She infused her voice with all the outrage she felt on his behalf. "In America, one does not need to own property in order to vote."

"I have often thought that the founders of your country tried to remedy some of what they thought was wrong in England."

"That is indeed the case. In fact, it is stated in our Declaration of Independence." She scowled. "Although they did not listen to Mrs. Adams and allow ladies to vote." He said nothing as they entered a large room filled with statuary. "Are these the infamous marbles?"

"They are, indeed."

"I must admit, they are impressive." She had never seen such depictions of naked and mostly naked figures, not even in a book. She wondered how Frank would compare. If the muscles in his arm were any indication . . . Oh Lord, where was a fan when she needed one, and why was she having those thoughts in the first place? It was probably seeing the boys and men swimming in the river near her grandmother's house.

"You seem a little warm." His voice was low, and a bit wicked.

Afraid of what she'd see in his face, she couldn't bring herself to look at him. Lady Heathcote had frequently made mention of how provincial Americans were. Yet it was not the marbles that made Jenny's heart beat faster and caused hummingbirds to take up residence in her stomach. It was wanting to see him naked. She had to stop thinking about that. "Do you swim?"

He leaned back. "I do."

Why had she asked? Now she felt even hotter. She had to get out of here. "It is a bit stuffy in here."

"Ah, yes. I agree." His breath tickled her ear, making her want to lean into him. "Perhaps we should view the rest of the museum."

Frank grinned to himself. The moment Jenny had seen the marbles her face had become quite rosy. He should probably have warned her about their lack of clothing. He wondered if he would ever have the opportunity to see her without her gown, petticoats, and chemise.

His member stirred at the thought. Had his growing desire for her been behind him wanting her to live at his brother and sister-in-law's house for the rest of the time she was in Town? Part of his attraction to her was lust. The question was how much was purely physical and how much was true caring. He did enjoy being with her.

Marrying her would be one way to escape his father. In fact, it would be the quickest way to be disowned by the duke. Still, if he could not love her, and she could not love him, he would be exchanging one hell for another. And that one would be an ocean away from his family. What would it be like to live in America? To be respected for working instead of pitied? To spend every night in bed with Jenny in his arms?

He guided her into a room where paintings from the Dutch masters dominated the walls. "Tell me what it's like living in America."

She gazed up at him, her head tilted to one side. "Do you mean how it is different from England?"

"Yes."

"As I see it, the main difference is that one is not as defined by his or her status at birth as much as one is here, and with hard work, one can change one's financial status. By the same consideration, one can lose everything and either wallow in failure or build one's fortune again. Using one's God-given abilities is valued more than what family one comes from." She seemed to study the paintings for several moments then said, "We have our problems. There is poverty and children begin work at an early age, but there is also opportunity. My father arrived from Scotland as a young man with almost nothing, and he has built a shipping line. He is also investing in a steamship company that runs up the coast. One day, the steamships will cross the ocean."

Another type of lust, that for a life that could participate in such ventures as ocean crossing steamships, coursed through him. "And men can vote."

He hadn't realized how much that meant to him until she had mentioned it.

"Yes, men can vote. Someday, women shall have the vote as well. Is that something you would support?"

He thought of his mother, Meg, and the other strong women he knew. "I would."

Jenny nodded. "I believe you."

Their eyes met, caught, and held. More than anything, he wanted to kiss her. Taste her lush, deep pink lips. He started to bend his head, when the clicking of heels caused him to jerk his head up.

"Lord Frank." *Oh, God. Just when I thought my luck was in.* "What are you doing in Town?" Lord Thornfield, one of his father's oldest friends, entered the room, accompanied by his wife. "I am sure the duke didn't mention it when we saw him last week." The man's white brows drew together. "I am sure he would have given me a message for you."

What he meant was that the duke would ask his friend to see what his son was up to. This was not a conversation Frank wanted to have. Yet, how was he to get rid of the older couple. He bowed. "My lord, my lady. I hope you had a pleasant stay in Scotland."

"Always do. A pity your mother couldn't remain longer."

He schooled his countenance to hide his mirth. Mama always managed to have an emergency at home that she must attend to. With fourteen children, that was not difficult. "Indeed, what happened?"

"One of your brothers or sisters. Putrid sore throat or some such thing."

Lady Thornfield gave Jenny a pointed look, and he knew he could not escape from introducing her. Then he made a decision he would no doubt pay for later. On the other hand, if Americans had no rank, then there was no reason she should be subordinate to Lady Thornfield. It would not be his fault if her ladyship mistook Jenny for a viscount's daughter. "Miss MacGowan, may I introduce Lady Thornfield and her husband, Lord Thornfield. My lord, my lady, Miss MacGowan and her aunt are visiting my brother Hawksworth and his wife.

Lord Thornfield bowed. Frank tried not to chuckle when Lady Thornfield curtseyed.

"A pleasure to meet you," Jenny said with a polite smile.

"We had better move along." Frank bowed slightly to the Thornhills. "I promised to have her back in good time for this evening's entertainment."

He had just about managed to extract her from the Thornfields when a shrill voice called out, "There you are."

Jenny's groan was so light, he barely heard it. "Lady Heathcote?"

"Who else." Jenny kept her voice low so only he could hear her.

"I suppose that popinjay with her is Pomfry?"

"In the flesh."

A strange feeling crept up his spine. He had to get her away as soon as possible, even if he did not understand the reason. "Quickly," he said. "Introduce me."

She flashed him a confused look, then did as he asked. "My lady, allow me to introduce Lord Frank Treavor. Lord Frank, this is the Countess of Heathcote."

Using all the haughtiness he had learned watching his father, he inclined his head toward her ladyship, raised his quizzing glass to Pomfry and drawled, "And you are?"

"Pomfry, my lord."

His lordship had been ogling Jenny, but now he seemed to squirm a bit under Frank's perusal. Which was exactly what he wanted.

The idea that man milliner might attempt to touch Jenny made Frank want to punch the man in the nose.

Mine.

He didn't know where the certainty of his feelings came from, but he knew it was true. If Jenny MacGowan would have him.

"Indeed." Infusing his voice with a dismissive tone, he focused on the other man's elaborately tied cravat and high shirt points for a moment before lowering his quizzer.

Next to him Jenny went still and quiet as if trying to escape notice. Although at the moment, both Pomfry and Lady Heathcote were focused on him.

"Trevor?" Her voice had risen an octave, making her tone almost painful to hear.

"The Duke of Somerset's son," he replied using his driest tone. "You must excuse us. My sister, Lady Hawksworth, is expecting Miss MacGowan and me. We are already late."

Frank tightened his grip on Jenny's arm as they walked swiftly toward the door. Once outside, he took a deep breath. "That could have been a disaster."

"I understand why it would have been one for me," she

replied tartly. "She would have insisted I accompany them. I fail to see why it affected you."

"That is because you don't know my father."

He lifted her into the carriage, then went around to the other side, flipped the boy a coin, and climbed in.

Her eyes narrowed. "Are you doing something you should not?"

"That is an excellent question. The problem is I am not sure of the answer."

Still, he had a feeling that in not much more than a week, a fortnight at the most, he would either be on his way to America with Jenny as his wife, or back in Somerset under his father's boot.

He was fairly certain she felt something for him, if only on a purely physical level. The question was, could she put aside her dislike of the English and wed him. Or perhaps, since she appeared to get on well enough with her aunt's betrothed, she might be willing to make another exception. No matter what happened, he must keep his father away from her until a decision was made.

CHAPTER FIVE

WHAT ON EARTH COULD FRANK mean by not knowing the answer? Jenny had never heard of anything so ridiculous. Maybe he thought she was unable to understand his circumstances because she was American. Quite frankly, she had experienced more than enough of that sort of disdain from the English.

She crossed her arms over her chest, then had to grab on to the side of the curricle when he made a turn. "Please explain yourself."

"My mother sent me to Damon. She said I needed some Town bronze. However, my father was, and possibly still is, away in Scotland. I am not at all sure if he knows I'm here. But I'll wager anything that Lord Thornfield will write to him about our meeting."

"You must be in your late twenties. I do not understand why he'd care."

"That is where knowing my father comes in. He keeps all of us under his thumb. Except for Damon, and my brother only made his escape this past Christmas."

"But your brother was a military officer." One Jenny had been pleased to hear did not think the regent should have sent troops to her country.

"He was, and, unlike me, he is not dependent on my father for funds. The duke threatened to cut him off from all contact with the family if he did not do as he wanted."

"Just so your father could have his way?" When Frank nodded, she gasped. "That is reprehensible. What an old reprobate."

Suddenly he laughed. Thank God she was angry and not afraid. "You are in good company with that opinion. Meg agrees with you."

Jenny liked Meg and found it almost impossible to believe that any father could not want her for a daughter-in-law. "That doesn't surprise me. She is an intelligent woman." For a few minutes she listened to the clop of the horses and the sounds of vendors hawking their goods. "Thank you for getting me out of the museum. You were very impressive."

He flashed her a quick smile. "It was my pleasure. She clearly would have stuck you with Pomfry. That wouldn't have done at all."

"No. I have little desire to spend any time at all with him." In fact, his lordship would be a great waste of her time. Even if she was interested in him, which she most decidedly was not, she would not remain here, and he would not move to America. Frank, on the other hand, had great possibilities. She had only three things to ascertain. Could he leave his family, was he willing to work for a living, and would they fall in love.

She already had strong corporeal feelings for him. Not that she could admit that to anyone. Before her mother died, she had explained the physical side of marriage to Jenny, and told her how wonderful it could be. Mama had also said that lust was not a good basis for marriage, but it did help separate the wheat from the chaff.

"Why do you not find other employment?"

She watched him carefully for any indication he did not care for her question. After a few moments he glanced at her. "I've considered it several times, but my father would make sure I was never able to. As I think I may have mentioned or alluded to, he wants to control us."

She had heard of a wealthy industrialist who attempted

to treat his children that way. One of his sons had followed frontiersman Daniel Boone west and had never returned. Then his daughter ran off with a gambler. After that, he'd changed his tune. A duke must have the same type of power. It could actually be worse. England wasn't as large as the United States, and there was that whole peerage thing. "What would you want to do if you could? Does not having an occupation appeal to you?"

"No." He gave her a rueful grin. "I'd go mad without something to keep me busy. I like organizing, and planning. I enjoy finding ways to increase the estate's income."

"You mean that you like making a profit."

"Good heavens!" He gave a dramatic shudder. "Do not, I pray, let anyone hear you discussing trade."

For the first time in a long while, she laughed. "But that is it, isn't it?

"Yes, although no one in the *ton* would use that term. Even pinching pennies is frowned upon."

"Well, that type of attitude makes no sense to me."

"I'm beginning to think it does not make a great deal of sense to me either." He kept his attention on the horses, but his voice was thoughtful.

She smiled to herself. Maybe, just maybe, she was making a convert of Frank to the good old New England way of thinking, as her mother would say. At least they'd be living in the same house. That would give her an opportunity to know him better.

"We shall be back at my brother's townhouse soon." Jenny had gone so quiet, Frank wished he could steal a look at her. Something was going on in that clever head of hers. He merely wished he knew what it was.

A few minutes later, he pulled up in front of the steps. A footman ran out and took the horses as he jumped down and went around to assist Jenny down. Yet, the moment she was in his arms, he didn't want to let her go.

His hands were still on her waist, when she smiled up at him. "I had a lovely outing. Thank you."

One digit at a time, he forced his fingers off her soft body. Finally, he had enough command of himself to place her hand on his arm. Thank God she'd be staying here. It would give them time to see if they wanted the same things. "We should discover if your trunks have arrived."

"And my aunt."

"Indeed." The door opened, and Saunders executed a stiff bow. "Miss, my lord, you are expected in the morning room."

"Have Miss MacGowan's bags been sent over?"

"His lordship wishes to speak with you." He took Jenny's coat. "I believe Miss Brodhead is present as well."

As Frank and Jenny left the hall, he glanced at her. "That's the worst thing about butlers –they won't even give you a hint. I wonder what Damon wants." Something was going on, and he had a feeling he wasn't going to like it. "Does your family have a butler?"

"We do, and before you ask, he is just as bad. Possibly worse." Her fine dark brows drew together as if something were bothering her. "Do you . . . do you help your servants find better positions?"

"As in rising through the ranks?" he asked, not sure what she meant.

"No, I mean jobs in business." She sounded confused.

This must be yet another difference between England and America. "Being in service is considered extremely good employment. Upper servants have the same respect, if not more, than a middling shopkeeper. Most of our servants have been with us for several generations. It is safe and, unless a servant is dishonest or cannot do the work, the position can be held for the rest of their lives."

She glanced at him, her eyes widening. "I had no idea. At home, being a servant is a beginning for many of the poor, but in only a few cases is it something one wishes to do for the rest of one's life." She fell silent for a moment. "Perhaps Americans and those who come to my country would rather take the risks needed to improve their lot. Opportunity is the reason many of them come over in the first place."

How different from here, where most people wished to remain the status quo. Or at least that was what the landowners wanted. He opened the door, standing back while she entered. His brother and the Earl of Warwick rose. Miss Brodhead had a tight smile on her face, and Meg didn't look at all happy.

By the time Frank and Jenny had taken a seat on the small sofa, tea arrived. After Meg had served, Miss Brodhead looked at Jenny and said, "As much as I appreciate the invitation to reside here for the next week or so, we cannot accept." Her chin took on a mulish cast, and her aunt hurried on, "I have had our possessions moved to the Pulteney Hotel. We shall be quite comfortable there until Geoff and I marry." Miss Brodhead looked at Meg. "After that, if you have decided to remain in England for a while and the invitation is still open, I will have no objection to you visiting her ladyship."

Hell and damnation! That would give every gentleman in London access to her. There is no way the hotel would be able to keep them out. Frank opened his mouth to say as much, when Damon caught his eye and gave an imperceptible shake of his head.

"Jenny," Meg smiled more warmly this time. "Our invitation stands. You are welcome here at any time, and for as long as you wish."

"Thank you." As the others began to talk, Jenny whispered furiously to Frank, "I am twenty-four years old. I do not have to abide by my aunt's decision."

"The difficulty is that if you remain here, which would

please me immensely, your aunt would not be able to stay at the hotel alone. It would also appear odd. I assume that returning to Lady Heathcote's home would be insupportable."

"It would be." Her tone was still angry, but her chin had lost its stubborn appearance.

"There is nothing to stop me from calling on you, if you would like me to do so."

Her gloved hand found his, and she squeezed his fingers. "Call as often as you wish."

It was probably too soon for his next question, but ever since he'd run into Lord Thornfield, Frank felt as if he was on borrowed time. "Whom do I ask for permission to court you?"

Jenny searched Frank's face, looking for any indication that he was not serious. He knew what she needed in a husband. Was he truly willing to leave his family and move across an ocean? A hint of fear lurked in his light blue eyes, but there was also friendship and liking that might become love. As Papa said, nothing ventured, nothing gained. She swallowed. "You ask me."

He turned so that his body blocked the others from seeing his face and hers. "Miss MacGowan, may I have permission to court you, woo you, and discover if we were meant for one another?"

Somewhere in the vicinity of her heart, a hummingbird took up residence. The fear fled his eyes, replaced by warmth that was directed entirely at her. Other men had asked to court her, but none of them had known she wanted a husband who would return home with her. Frank knew, and he asked anyway. "Yes, Lord Frank Trevor, you may."

They stared at each other, unable to drag their gazes away. If they had been alone, he would have kissed her. Then something made a strange sound, and a gray kitten jumped on his lap. Frank laughed. "How did you get in here, my lady?"

Jenny reached out to stroke the cat, but it drew back, looking at her with large yellow eyes. "Cats generally like me."

"Don't be offended. This is a Chartreux. They are known for being standoffish to strangers. She'll warm to you soon. Jenny, meet Lady Quimby."

"How do you do, my lady?" She glanced at him. "Quimby?"

"Ah, yes. We've always had a cat by the name of Quimby. Some of them were Lord Quimby. It's a name Damon came up with as a child, and the rest of us followed suit."

"I can see why. It's a fun name."

"It was also useful in other ways."

"Jenny," her aunt said as she rose, "we should be getting to the hotel. I have accepted Lady Hawksworth's invitation to dine with them before we attend the ball this evening."

Frank set the kitten on the sofa, stood and held out his hand. "Will you save me two waltzes?"

"If I had my way, I would only dance with you." None of the other men she'd stood up with had been half as entertaining or danced as well as he did. "Would you like the supper dance?"

"Do you plan to stay that long? I seem to remember you slipping out early last night."

"I shall remain if I am to dance with you." When she rose, they were standing much closer than propriety allowed, but no one said anything. "At least this evening I shall not be plagued by the *gentlemen* Lady Heathcote has selected."

"I still think you'll have to beat them off," he murmured in her ear as they entered the corridor. "Perhaps I shall stand over you the entire evening and glower at the other men."

If only he could, but Sarah and Geoff would probably

not approve. And right now, Jenny was so happy she did not want anything to interfere with her mood.

Before assisting her into the town coach, Frank kissed the palm of her hand, closing her fingers around it. "Until this evening."

She wished she did not have to leave, but at least she'd see him soon. "Until then."

Once she was settled, he shut the door, and Geoff used his cane to tap on the roof. The carriage lurched forward, and they were soon traveling through Town. She glanced out the window, wishing again that she had not had to leave, but perhaps a little distance would do her and Frank good. At his brother's house, it would have been hard to stay away from him. And, if she was honest, out of his bed. Now that temptation was gone. After all, she had only met him last night. Normally, she was slow to take to a new person, but he had captured her interest almost immediately. She also had a great deal to think about. It occurred to her that many of the wealthy land owners did work, although they would not call it that. Perhaps she had been unfair.

"You seem quite taken with Lord Frank," Sarah said.

Jenny wasn't sure if she was ready to share her feelings yet. Her aunt might think it was too soon to feel so much for a man. She gave herself an inner shrug. It was her life and her decision. "I am. He has asked if he could court me, and I gave him permission."

Across the short expanse of the coach, Geoff barked a laugh and held out his hand. "You owe me a guinea, my love."

Sarah fished a coin out of her reticule, handing it over.

"You wagered on me?" Jenny could not believe what had happened. "You *never* gamble."

A blush stole up Sarah's neck into her cheeks. "Yes, well, I did not think I would lose. Therefore, it was not wagering."

"But you did lose," Jenny pointed out, taking more than a little satisfaction from the incident.

"Genevieve Elizabeth MacGowan," her aunt said tartly, "you have been wooed by handsome wealthy Americans, equally handsome and wealthy French nobles and aristocrats, and none of them has turned your head. You meet Lord Frank Trevor, a hated Englishman I might add, and in less than twenty-four hours you are smitten. Of course I did not believe it." She shook her head. "You are perverse. I do not understand you at all."

A smile pulled at the corners of Jenny's lips. "That is just it. I think he *does* understand me. We may not agree on everything, but he listens to me, and tries to find ways to bridge our differences."

"Does he know you intend on returning home?" Geoff asked.

"I told him today. I do not think he is very happy with his situation."

"In that case"—a concerned tone colored her aunt's words—"make sure he is not courting you to run away from his life."

Jenny's happy mood fizzled. Could that be what he found so attractive about her? The fact that marrying her would give him a completely different life? She straightened her shoulders. Well, she would have to find out, and quickly. She promised her father she would marry for love, and that is what she wanted as well.

FRANK WATCHED UNTIL THE TOWN coach Jenny was in turned the corner before strolling back to the morning room where Damon and Meg were still in conversation. "Did Miss Brodhead say why she and Jenny could not stay here?"

Meg nodded. "She and Lord Warwick agreed that it would give an odd appearance for Jenny and her to leave his sister's house and move here. The hotel gives Miss Brodhead an opportunity to receive ladies for visits and more control over their wedding breakfast. I should have realized at once the plan would not work." Meg pressed her lips together. "It was just that you and Jenny seem so comfortable together. I wanted to . . . ." She shrugged and pulled a face. "So much for *my* attempts at matchmaking."

"You wanted to help." Frank went to the sideboard, poured a glass of wine and held up the decanter. When his brother and sister-in-law both nodded, he poured two more glasses. "I appreciate your gesture. I do want to know her better. My concern about the hotel is that it is not as safe as a house." Visions of men popping out from behind potted plants and laying siege at Jenny's door flooded his mind. He never knew that caring for a lady would make him so fanciful or so possessive."

Damon took the glass Frank handed him. "I don't like the idea of a hotel either." He raised a brow. "Too many ways to stage an ambush."

His brother had been in the war and frequently used military analogies. In this case, Frank agreed with him, even if it did make him sound a bit mad.

"How so?" Meg asked.

"Jenny's an heiress." Damon took a sip of wine. "There are some who would not hesitate to attempt to force her hand."

"She has no close family or connections," he continued. "And no one to scare away the fortune hunters and rogues."

Perhaps Frank wasn't being so cockled-brained after all. "Except us. No matter what ends up happening between Jenny and me"—which he hoped was a great deal—"we can take care of her."

"We will surround her with our friends," Meg added. "That way she will be safe from the Pomfrys of the *ton*."

"That will work when we are at the same entertainments, my love." Damon poured himself another glass of wine. "However, it does not address the problem of the hotel."

"I will take that watch." Frank grinned. "I asked her if I could court her, and she gave me permission."

"How wonderful!" Meg jumped up and hugged him. "You two just feel right to me."

"If only you could have seen that with us, my love," Damon drawled as she wrinkled her nose at him.

Now, all he had to do was find out how deep his feelings about Jenny were, and how deep hers were for him.

CHAPTER SIX

SHORTLY AFTER JENNY AND HER aunt arrived at the hotel, Jenny made arrangements for one of the hotel's servants named Suky to act as her maid. Geoff had also given Jenny a letter from her father.

She opened the message.

My darling Jenny,

All is well here, but we'll be glad to have you home again. As you've not written me about any young men, I am guessing that you haven't found anyone to your taste. Speaking of which, your Rose has decided to marry a man she met not long after you left. I'm sorry to say you'll have to look for another maid when you return.

Your loving Papa

P.S. The 'Elizabeth' should be in London soon. Her captain will wait on you when they arrive.

That answered one of her concerns. She knew how she was going to get home. Jenny watched as Suky put away her clothing. Perhaps if she did a good job, the woman might like to go to America.

"Which gown will you be wanting for this evening, miss?"

"The yellow one should do."

"Aye, that's a good choice. I'll just give it a bit of a press."

There was something about the woman's accent that was strange. "You're not from here?"

"Nay, I'm from up in Yorkshire, but there's not much there but working in mills and mines, so I decided to come south."

Bearing what Frank had said in mind, Jenny asked, "Is working as a lady's maid what you have always wanted to do?"

Suky shrugged. "It's what I'm good at."

"But?" Jenny smiled encouragingly.

"I had thought to save enough to get my own shop, but with having to send money home, there's not much left over."

Jenny nodded thoughtfully. Now that she knew how hard it was for people to improve themselves in England, there might be some way she could help the maid. "Perhaps your luck will change."

"My da always said hard work is better than luck."

"My father says a little luck will never go amiss."

"That's true enough, miss. Now I'd better finish up here."

A few hours later, with her hair arranged more beautifully than it ever had been before, Jenny and her aunt waited for Geoff to fetch them.

Although the time had passed quickly, she found herself missing Frank more with each passing minute. Under the guise of tugging her spangled shawl tighter, she gave herself a hug. He'd begin courting her this evening, and she could not wait. Jenny even hoped he did hover over her all night. For she truly did not wish to stand up with anyone else. Her aunt must be wrong that Frank might be interested in her because he wanted to escape his father. She had learned to recognize the look in a man's eye when he was calculating what she could give him, and she had not seen any of that in Frank. No, every sense she had told her that he really did want only her. Still, she would continue to watch him for a while longer. It wouldn't do to make a mistake.

FRANK STRODE TO JENNY THE moment her party was announced. "I missed you. Does that sound strange?"

She pulled her lower lip between her teeth, and blushed. "Not at all. I missed you as well."

"Would you like a glass of wine?" he asked, leading her into the drawing room.

"Yes, please."

Once he handed her a goblet, they moved to one of the two window seats. She sat, while he leaned against the wall. She seemed shy, something he had not noticed in her before. "Is everything alright?"

"I received a letter from my papa," she replied.

Something, the tone or quality of her voice, told him the letter was important. "And?"

"One of our ships will be in London soon. The captain is expecting to take me home."

Frank let out the breath he'd been holding. This was it then. There would be no time to see the rest of his family again. Even if his father was still in Scotland, he dare not go home. If his father had received word of Jenny, who knew the lengths the duke would take to keep him away from her. "I understand."

She rubbed her temples as if they ached. "I must know if you would do almost anything to leave home."

He studied Jenny for a moment. Something was worrying her. Sliding a look at her aunt, he found the lady staring at him. Perhaps the woman didn't approve of Jenny aligning herself with him. "The question would be easier to answer if you tell me what exactly is troubling you."

After a few strained moments of silence, she said, "It was suggested that you might be using me to escape your father."

"My love"—he paused for a moment realizing that he meant the words—"there is no escaping my father. He shall do all he is able to punish me for choosing you. He will attempt to use his influence even in America. Realizing that, I still would not change a thing. The real question is whether you would still want me knowing he will make trouble if he can." If she actually wanted him at all.

"Thank you for being honest with me." She smiled at him, and he had never seen a more beautiful look or a more exquisite lady. "And I do not care at all what your father might try to do. He has no power in my country."

He did not agree with her last remark, but decided to let it pass. There was no way he knew of to convince her how dangerous the duke could be. "I'm glad you asked instead of allowing it to continue to bother you. Still, I know it wasn't easy." In situations like this, it rarely was. There was too much of a chance to have one's feelings hurt, and the urge to protect herself must be strong. "I would like to have complete honesty between us."

"As would I." Her deep blue eyes studied him. "With our countries being at war twice and our dissimilar cultures, we already have so many differences."

"Then we are agreed." Taking her hand, he kissed her fingers. "We shall not hide our concerns or feelings."

"We are agreed." Jenny glanced up almost shyly.

He would have liked to take her out to the terrace, but his brother's butler announced dinner. Meg had very helpfully seated him and Jenny together, giving him the opportunity to select from the dishes the footmen brought around for her before they were set on the table.

"What is dinner like in America?" he asked as he placed some of the peas in lemon sauce on her plate.

"Nothing so elaborate"—she slid him a playful look—"not at my home in any event."

There would be a great deal to learn and get used to if she agreed to marry him. "I assume you have been mistress of your father's house. How would you have planned the meal?"

She finished swallowing the bite she'd taken. "As here, I would begin with a soup. The next course would be either some sort of meat, fish, or poultry, as well as vegetables or a salad. For dessert, we'd have a pie or fruit."

"Simpler more than different." He watched as she daintily dabbed her mouth with the serviette.

"Yes. I suppose that's it." They ate quietly for several moments. "I take it you have a large family."

"I have fifteen brothers and sisters including Damon."

"Are you"—her fine dark brows drew together slightly—"are you close?"

Suddenly honesty was not all it was cracked up to be. "Yes, it will be difficult not to see them again. I'm used to having the younger ones around almost every day." He wished dinner was over and he could speak to her alone. "However, if things work out between us, they will understand. What I mean to say is that my brothers and sisters would not expect me to lose you."

She gave an imperceptible nod. "I think I understand. Even though my aunt will miss her friends and family, she must follow her heart."

Damon, who was on Jenny's other side, leaned over slightly. Keeping his voice low he said, "I will assist in any way I am able." He grinned. "You never know when someone in the family might take it into his or her head to visit America."

Her shoulders dropped as if the tension Frank had seen

rising in them fled. He gave his brother a grateful smile. "I know you will."

The gentlemen decided to take their port and brandy into the drawing room when Meg rose, signaling to the ladies it was time to withdraw.

When the men entered the corridor, Frank gathered Geoff and his brother. "I fully expect trouble from the ducal member of my family." Frank's gaze focused on the earl. "If you cannot bring yourself to defy my father, I'd ask that you do not hinder our efforts."

Geoff returned Frank's look. "I have come to think of Jenny as my family. I would no sooner desert her than I would my own sister."

That was what Frank had hoped the man would say. "Thank you."

Damon then told Geoff how the duke had attempted to stop Damon and Meg from marrying first by hiring a former suitor of Meg's to abduct her, and then by trying to compromise them both by having other people enter their bedchambers the night before the wedding.

"Good God!" Geoff said. His voice full of disgust. "He really will stop at nothing."

Frank was relieved the man seemed to understand the threat to Jenny. "She must be kept safe in the hotel."

"And elsewhere," Geoff agreed. "Hawksworth, could I borrow a couple of your larger footmen?"

Frank was glad the earl was taking the threat seriously, but he couldn't convince himself that Jenny would be safe even if he told her all his father was capable of.

CHAPTER SEVEN

JENNY ENTERED THE BALLROOM ON Frank's arm and surrounded by his family. Still, she was dismayed to see not only Lady Heathcote and Lord Pomfry were present, but Lord and Lady Thornfield as well.

"This is what comes of attending early," Frank whispered in a frustrated tone. "One cannot blend into a crowd when it has not yet assembled."

Despite the irritation she had been feeling, Jenny giggled.

In front of them, Meg signaled to someone across the room. "Never fear. We shall have more than enough help to keep the wolves at bay."

In less time than Jenny had imagined possible, they were surrounded by friends of Meg and Damon.

Damon turned to Jenny and bowed. "Miss MacGowan, may I introduce you to the Earls of Stanstead and Beresford." Two tall gentlemen, one with blond curls, the other with dark hair, bowed.

"I am Nick Beresford," the dark-haired man said.

"And I am Rupert Stanstead," the blond said. Another man with almost identical hair stood next to him as well as an older man. "My cousin Robert, Viscount Beaumont, and my step-father, Lord Malfrey."

"I am pleased to meet you." Jenny smiled and held out her hand, pleased when the men in turn shook it.

Meg touched Jenny's arm, and she was suddenly face to face with an older lady dressed in the most vivid red gown she had ever seen. "My lady, this is Miss MacGowan whom I hope will soon join our family. Jenny, Lady Telford."

"Oh, no, my dear." The lady turned to a tall gentleman who appeared to be in his fifties. "I told you we should have made the announcement earlier. I am now Lady Sudbury. Miss MacGowan, I must tell you that I adore Americans. May I introduce my husband?"

Once again, Jenny had her hand shaken without the look of distaste she'd received before. "My pleasure."

"I'm not sure you should say that so quickly," Lady Sudbury said. "He's an old roué. Although I am quickly reforming him."

Jenny grinned. These people were much more entertaining than anyone else she'd met in London or in France. In a short period of time she was made known to, Vivian, Lady Stanstead, Serena, Lady Beaumont, Silvia, Lady Beresford, Marcus and Phoebe, Marquis and Marchioness of Evesham, and Lord and Lady Thornhill. To Jenny's surprise and delight, she was invited to call all the younger ladies by their first names.

Lady Thornhill shook Jenny's hand. "I understand you have already had the misfortune to meet Lord and Lady Thornfield. It's a pity our names are so similar. They are as stuffy as we are liberal."

The opening set was a country dance. Lord Pomfry got almost close enough to ask Jenny to dance, when Lord Stanstead stepped in front of the man. "Would you do me the honor of dancing with me?"

She smiled gratefully. "I'd be happy to."

For the rest of the evening, every time one of the gentlemen she had not wished to dance with approached their circle, one of Damon and Meg's friends stood up with her. Frank, of course, claimed the waltzes, and she once again felt as if she were floating on air.

This time, he did hold her too tightly and too closely.

"You are going to cause talk."

A wicked looked entered his dark blue eyes. "It is hard to be chastened when I enjoy holding you so much."

"Devil." She tried not to smile, but felt the corners of her lips turning up. "Flattery?"

"No, the truth." His warm breath brushed her ear. "There *is* a reason I am courting you, and it has nothing to do with my circumstances."

So he thought now, but what of later? Would he truly be able to leave his large and close family? Or would he begin to resent her for not being able to live in England? If only it did not feel so right to be in his arms, and be able to talk easily with him. No matter that they had met only a little over a day ago, she felt as if she had known him all her life. If only she could be certain that if he asked her to marry him and she agreed, that they would be happy. Then again, even if they were from the same county, there were no guarantees all would be well.

Perhaps she should do as her father had advised and follow her heart. On the other hand, Papa also told her not to bring home an Englishman. She winced inwardly. Frank had been so concerned about his father she had not wanted to tell him about hers.

"Jenny, my love, what is bothering you?"

She wished they had not agreed to be completely honest. "Aside from the possibility of me taking you away from your family if we wed, nothing. Except that my father told me not to bring home an Englishman."

He lifted his gaze to the ceiling. "And here I thought all our problems were on this side of the ocean."

They danced without speaking for a few minutes as Frank pondered Jenny's concerns. He would miss his family. There was no doubt about it. Yet, his father would not live forever, and all but the youngest ones would understand. Even his mother would want him to marry for love, and he did love Jenny. As to being an Englishman, well, America could give him several things Britain could not, chief among them, the right to vote. The ability to make a difference. "What must one do to become an American?"

She stumbled, but he held her steady. "You would give up your citizenship?"

"I dearly want to be able to vote, and I doubt I could do it without becoming an American." Jenny stared up at him as if in shock. "Am I correct?"

"Yes—yes, you are." A faint line appeared in her forehead. "All that is necessary is for you to declare yourself an American, once you arrive, that is."

Then that is exactly what he would do, if she agreed to marry him. That also solved the problem of her bringing home an Englishman.

The set ended and he led her back to their circle. Glancing around, he noticed Jenny's aunt and Geoff were not present. A shrill voice caused him to look toward the stairs where Lady Heathcote stood next to her brother and Sarah. "I have the feeling Geoff is bearing the brunt of Damon and Meg's maneuvering."

"Oh, dear." Jenny turned and frowned. "I do feel sorry for him. She can be such a shrew." She clapped her hand over her mouth. "I should not have said that. I am probably just as much at fault for us not getting along."

"Somehow I do not think her temperament has anything to do with you." Frank watched as the earl said something to his sister, and the lady's expression changed from petulant to interested. But interested in what? He shook his head. "I believe it is warm enough to brave the terrace, if you would like to stroll."

"I would be delighted." Jenny tucked her hand into the crook of his arm. "Lead on."

They wove their way through the now crowded ballroom toward the French windows. Once outside, he noticed that he and Jenny weren't the only ones seeking relief from the heat of the room. Torches lit the way down the steps and out into the garden where lanterns hung from tree limbs and from stands. Birds, Nightingales most likely, sang, and white flowers sent their perfume into the air.

"It's beautiful," Jenny said, leaning more heavily on his arm. "Almost like a fairy world."

"What do you know of fairies?" He stopped and stared down at her in surprise.

"You must remember my father is from Scotland." She laughed. "Fairies may be beautiful, but they can be dangerous and sometimes cruel. I have always preferred to focus on their beauty and forget the rest."

"Could that not be dangerous?" A smile played around the edges of his strong well-shaped lips.

She tucked her arm more securely in his, and began to stroll. "More dangerous than ambling down a dark garden path with a gentleman?"

"I suppose that depends on how far down the path you intend to go." His voice, deep and rich as warm maple syrup, caused her to shiver with anticipation. Would he kiss her?

They had reached an arbor and he drew her into the shelter and his arms.

"Jenny?" His breath warmed her cheek, and one finger gently caressed her jaw. She lifted her chin, staring into his dark eyes, and his lips brushed hers.

"Yes." She didn't know if she was giving him permission or asking what he wanted, yet it didn't matter. His lips touched hers again, this time more firmly, and she kissed him back.

Time stopped. She slid her hands up his strong shoulders, tangling her fingers in his hair. His tongue swept along the seam of her mouth, and she opened, allowing him to take possession of her in a way she had never experienced before. Frank slanted his head, deepening the kiss, holding her closer. Her breasts rubbed against the finely embroidered satin of his waistcoat. Tingles turned to fire as her skin heated, drawing her toward his flame. Oh, God. She rubbed against him, like a cat seeking more attention.

He started to pull back. "Jenny, my love, we must—"

"No." Cupping his face, she drew him back to her. This . . . his touch . . . their kiss, her first one, felt so good. Like nothing she had ever experienced before. "I don't want to stop." Then music floated out into the garden. Another set must be starting. She could not even remember who she was promised to.

His chuckle was wicked, as he nibbled her lower lip. "If it was up to me, I would remain here all night, yet someone will notice we are missing. Unless you wish to be compromised into marrying me, we must return."

Was this one of those differences between their countries, or perhaps Frank did not wish to have to marry her. The idea was unsettling and a little hurtful, particularly as he had asked to court her. Then again, he may have done that to see if they would fall in love and have enough in common to have a good marriage. It wasn't as if she was interested in any other man. They had only known each other for a very short time. Although, she knew some people fell in love at first sight and had splendid marriages.

She stifled a sigh. "No, I would not want that."

Frank heard what sounded like a small breathy sigh. Was he wrong to take such care of her reputation? No. He did not wish anyone to think they were marrying because they had to. Perhaps he should declare himself to Jenny now. Yet if he did, and she refused him, that would make it difficult for them to continue. He might lose her, and that was not an outcome he could or would accept. If he discovered his father knew of her or his plans for her, Frank would get her shackled to him in short order. But for now they should merely enjoy one another and find other places to kiss. She clearly had never been with a man before and that pleased him more than he'd thought possible. Maybe they could remain in the garden a little longer. Beaumont was to have partnered with her for this set, and he would not mind dancing with his wife instead.

Frank leaned down and kissed Jenny again. When she yielded to him, he wanted to crow. A soft moan escaped her lips as he caressed her back, stopping just before her tempting bottom found its way under his palm. He swept his tongue into the warm cavern of her mouth. She tasted of wine and woman. His body tightened as desire, the need to make her his, rushed through his veins. God how he wanted her! Wanted to see her fiery hair spread out against his pillow, to have her naked beneath him. He brushed his thumb against her breast and she shivered, sinking even deeper into their kiss. If he didn't stop now, he wouldn't return her to the ballroom at all.

His breath beat the same tattoo as his heart. If they didn't stop now—"Sweetheart, we should go back."

"Yes." Her voice was breathy as if she had trouble speaking. "You are probably right."

He kept his arm around Jenny's waist, holding her close for a few moments longer, before placing her hand on his arm. "Lest you think otherwise, I could easily have remained until the ball ended."

Her eyes widened as if in surprise, but her lips, still swollen from his kisses, curved up. "I'm glad you told me."

"You should know I would not have minded being caught with you. However, you would be subjected to unwanted gossip." Nor did he want others to gossip about her more than they were already doing. She was his to protect. His to love.

"And I have had more than enough of that."

"The next set is our second waltz, after which we go down to supper." He paused at the door, not wanting to rejoin the ball. "If you were staying at my brother's, I would suggest we depart after eating."

Jenny searched his face, and he wondered what she found there. "I don't think we'll be allowed another stroll in the gardens. Perhaps we could just amble around the room and talk."

If only he could kiss her one last time, but eyes were already turning their way. "I would enjoy that."

What she did not seem to understand was that by allowing him to keep her by his side, they were already making their preference for each other clear. Then again, she may know and not care, or things could be different in America. If only he knew what she was thinking.

Their friends, standing near the windows, formed a circle around them. Jenny's aunt looked ready to ring a peal over their heads.

Meg tucked her arm in Jenny's, a show of support Frank silently applauded. "I had to stop your aunt from going after you."

"I had no idea we'd been gone so long."

"No, I dare say you didn't." She grinned. "Yet unless you are ready to announce your immediate betrothal, a half hour is enough to cause talk."

"For a mere thirty minutes?" At first, Jenny appeared surprised, then her countenance took on a militant cast. "I've never heard the like, and I—"

"It's my fault." Frank cut in before she could continue. She would not take the blame for their being together. "I know the customs here. Jenny does not."

"Nevertheless," Miss Brodhead said in a frustrated whisper, "it must not happen again. There are some people"—she cut her eyes briefly at Lady Heathcote who was staring at them—"who are waiting for you to make a misstep."

The overture to the next set began, and he took Jenny away from his sister-in-law. "Let's forget this and enjoy the dance."

Or, in his case, enjoy being able to hold her once more.

"Thank you." She smiled gratefully. "That would be perfect."

She had always fitted him whenever they stood up together. But since they'd kissed, and he knew what she felt like when her body touched his, he couldn't stop himself from holding her a bit closer. He glanced around watching for anyone who might be paying them too much attention, but saw nothing and relaxed. Miss Brodhead had likely overreacted, and Meg was simply attempting to be diplomatic.

"A penny for your thoughts." He looked down, and Jenny grinned.

"I was just thinking how well we fit together . . . when we dance."

A tinkling of light laughter bubbled from her. "Is that what you call it?"

For the first time in years his neck grew warm, and he knew he was flushed.

"They do say Americans are forward," a young lady near them murmured just loud enough for him to hear.

Jenny must have heard the girl as well. She stiffened, and her lips were drawn into a thin line. "She insulted me."

"I would not make too much of it. She is probably jealous." He smiled. "Did you see the coxcomb she's with?"

"I'll take your word for it." Jenny relaxed again. "If he is anything like Lord Pompous, she's welcome to him."

This time it was Frank who laughed too loudly, causing soft comments. "I fear we are neither of us as well behaved as we should be."

Her eyes twinkled with mirth, and he was glad she was happy again. Would that he could save her from all her troubles, but she was a strong woman and would not appreciate being smothered by him or any man.

At the end of the set, as he was escorting her to supper, Damon put his hand on Frank's arm. "Meg is tired. She suggested that we all adjourn to the house. Cook can find something for us to eat."

Jenny cast a concerned look where Meg sat on a chair. "Yes, of course we will come."

A few minutes later they had bid adieu to their hostess and were in the town coach. Sarah and Warwick had decided to remain at the ball.

Jenny laid her hand on Meg's knee. "You may take me back to the hotel if you'd like."

"Oh, no. I shall feel much better once I'm home." She paused, but it was too dark for Frank to see her expression. "The noise and heat were bothering me. Nothing more. I am feeling better already."

"I abhor disagreeing with you, my love," Damon said. "But Jenny brings up a possible solution. If there is a prospect of a cold collation at the Pulteney, then we would not have to worry over someone seeing Frank escorting her to the hotel in a closed coach."

"I am quite sure the kitchens are open at all hours," Jenny said.

"It is decided then. I have always wondered if the food was as good as it is reputed to be."

Damon and Meg had neatly danced around the subject, but Frank had the distinct feeling that he and Jenny had been the subject of talk. *Well, hell!* They would simply have to be more circumspect when in public. He would not allow her to be pushed into marriage. That was a choice she would be free to make. Even if he did not like her decision.

Suddenly, what Jenny had said earlier came crashing back to him. *Perdition!* They did not have much time at all. One of her father's ships would be here soon ready to take her back to New York, and Frank had every intention of being on that ship with her when she left. Five days more. That would have to be enough. On the sixth day, he would ask her to marry him, and hoped the ship didn't arrive before then.

CHAPTER EIGHT

FOUR DAYS AFTER THE ILL-FATED ball, Jenny left the book store, stepping onto the sidewalk. Brian, her footman, was behind her carrying the rest of the books she had purchased in preparation for her journey home. She turned right toward Geoff's town coach that had been loaned to her for the excursion. She really had had no idea she and Frank could have caused such a stir by having fun with each other. These people obviously did not have enough to keep them busy.

On the other hand, except for Pomfry attempting to accost her at the hotel, the other gentlemen Geoff's sister had introduced her to had stopped bothering her. Unfortunately, she and Frank had not been alone since. One would think that he could have arranged *something*.

Does he or doesn't he? Jenny sighed softly so that no one would hear her. Perhaps it should be does she or doesn't she? Lord Frank was everything she had been looking for in a husband. Funny, handsome, nice, and he kissed extremely well. And danced well. She mustn't forget that. And she was afraid she was falling in love with him. Actually, if she was honest, which she did not truly wish to be at the moment, she had already fallen. Hard.

If only he wasn't English. Papa would not be at all happy about that. Then again, he did trust her judgment. If not, he would never have agreed to her proposals regarding the settlement agreement she brought with her. Papa was a dear, and she loved him with all her heart, but he could be a bit old fashioned when it came to women and property. He had not agreed that she could keep everything that was hers, until she had pointed out that it would keep fortune hunters away. Now that that was no longer a problem, she had to make up her mind.

The question was whether Frank loved her. He was attentive and seemed to have a great deal of fun in her company, but others had pretended to as well . . . until she had mentioned living in New York. Something *he* appeared to have no concern about. Nor had another man kissed her. God, how he'd kissed her. And he was courting her. If only he would say the three little words she wanted to hear, everything would be settled.

Then again, despite feeling as if she had known him all her life, it had been less than a week since they'd met. Her aunt would be marrying in another two days. He was courting her, she reminded herself again. If Frank did not declare himself by the time Sarah wed, Jenny could not move to his brother's house. In that case, she would simply propose to him. She nodded to herself, happy to have made the decision.

Her new maid stood in front of the millinery shop and signaled by lifting her chin. She probably would have waved if her hands had not been full. Suddenly, a boy bumped into her and her books began to fall. Before she could lunge to save them, a large, meaty hand grabbed her arm. Jenny screamed, the man's hand covered her mouth and she bit down, tasting blood.

"You'll pay for that, bitch!"

Digging her feet into the cobblestones, she was able to slow down him down. Where was he taking her? The next thing she knew, he shoved her in to a coach. She took a breath, intending to scream again, but the boot she landed on caught her stomach, making it difficult to breath, much less shout.

Strong hands gripped her shoulders, lifting her, and setting her on the seat opposite the boots.

"Take shallow breaths and you'll be fine in a minute," a cultured, but unknown voice said. "I should have told the brute not to treat you roughly."

The carriage had started, and Jenny couldn't do anything until she could breathe again, so she did as instructed, and in a few moments was able to suck a deep breath of air. Once she felt in possession of herself, or as much as possible considering her heart was still clanging inside her chest, she faced her captor. He was tall with brown hair and eyes. He had a straight, almost military bearing. "Who are you and what do you want with me?"

His eyes crinkled as he smiled. "I should have thought that was clear by now. I plan to marry you."

Insane! The man is insane! "I don't even know you."

"That will be remedied soon enough." He glanced out the window as if having explained everything he thought she should know, that was the end of the discussion.

She tamped down her rising fear. "What is your name, and where are you taking me?"

He looked at her, a bored expression on his face. "You do ask a great many questions."

Insufferable Englishman. She tried to copy the haughty tone Frank used at times, but couldn't keep the rage infusing her body from her voice. "It is my life. I have a right to know."

The man sighed. "I suppose it won't hurt. There is nothing you can do about it in any event. You are already irreparably compromised by being in the coach with me, not to mention the abduction took place on Bond Street. We shall travel to a tavern at the edge of Town, where I shall arrange a separate room for you." He gave a sardonic grin. "Naturally, the door will be locked. Don't think to try to talk the innkeeper around. I have concocted a plausible story for him. He will not assist you."

"Naturally." Jenny wanted to spit at his smug expression. No matter what happened, or what she had to do, he would not win. "Please continue."

"I shall inform your aunt, that I intend to wed you. She will be forced to agree. After all, Warwick will not want a scandal tainting his wife." He raised a brow. "Have you any more questions?"

Too many, but first . . . "Who are you, and why me? I am absolutely positive we have never met."

"I am Major Reginald Upton, late of His Majesty's House Guards." He may not have been in one of the units that had invaded her country, but she would *never* allow an English soldier to touch her, much less marry him. "You are correct," he continued in the same bored tone. "We have not been introduced. As to the reason you were chosen, it appears you have become much too friendly with a certain duke's son, and his grace wants you out of the way."

Frank's father. She . . . they . . . had expected him to do something, but not this soon. There was, however, one thing neither the duke nor the major had considered. She didn't care about her reputation in the *ton*, and neither Sarah nor Geoff could force her to marry this blackguard. If only she had made an arrangement to meet Frank this morning, he could save her. But she hadn't. Well, she simply needed to find a way to get back to the Mayfair herself.

Fortunately, unlike the usual unmarried English lady, she had a fair amount of money with her and wouldn't hesitate to bribe her way out of the inn. If only she had brought her pistol. Yet who took a weapon to Bond Street?

The major had returned to his perusal of passing scenery. Obviously, he wasn't concerned about her causing him any trouble. Therefore, she surmised, as long as she appeared to go along with his plan or act as if she had no choices, she was in no immediate danger. She looked out the other window, noting landmarks that would assist her on her way back to Town.

"WHAT THE DEVIL JUST HAPPENED?" Frank bellowed, not caring who heard him. Jenny's safety was more important than street gawkers.

"Miss, she was taken." Jenny's maid wrung her hands. Books lay on the pavement and in the street.

"Yes, but who took her?"

"I don't know, my lord. I got a quick look, but I never seen him before."

A young man came running up carrying several more tomes. "What can I do to help?"

Ah, the footman Jenny had brought from America. "Help her"—he pointed at the maid and noticed a group of people had begun form—"back to the hotel. Tell Miss Brodhead what has occurred, and ask her to notify my brother. I am going after your mistress."

Thank God he stopped at the Pulteney to see Jenny and been told she was shopping. Otherwise, who knew how long it would have taken to discover she was missing.

Frank gave the horses their office and set out after the coach. Keeping it in sight but not attempting to stop the conveyance. Whoever had her would not want her harmed. At least not until they had her tied right and tight. He'd dawdled long enough. As soon as he could manage it, they were getting married. He only hoped she loved him as much as he loved her.

About forty minutes later, the coach turned off into the yard of a busy inn, and Frank drove in right behind it, throwing the ribbons to an ostler, as he jumped down. "Walk them. I won't be long."

A tall, dark haired main climbed down from the coach, then turned, but Jenny had already hopped down. Ignoring the offer of his arm, she glared up at the cur. Thank God she was no missish lady.

Frank strode up to her, took possession of her arm, and addressed the bounder who abducted her in a loud voice. "Thank you very much for accompanying my betrothed this far. I shall take it from here."

For a moment the cur seemed confused, then his brows snapped together. "Betrothed?"

Smiling brightly, Jenny leaned into Frank. "Had you given me an opportunity, I would have told you he was meeting us here." She gazed up at him, fluttering her lashes. "I cannot wait to become Lady Quimby."

Frank almost choked. Clever of her to have remembered the story he'd told her about his family's cats. "Indeed, my love. It will not be long now."

"Quimby?" the other man asked incredulously, as his eyes narrowed.

If looks could kill, the blackguard would be dead. Although Jenny's expression was calm, her eyes shot daggers. "You see, there was no need for your employer to worry."

Before the other man could react, Frank had her in the curricle, and headed back to Town at a much faster pace then he'd arrived. "Are you all right?"

"I am now." She pressed her lips together. "But you are not going to be happy."

"Who was that man?"

"He is Major Reginald Upton, late of His Majesty's House Guards. Your father hired him to abduct and marry me."

It was as if Jackson himself had punched Frank in the gut. His vision blurred, and a red haze colored the landscape. He had never wanted to murder anyone before, but this time his father had gone too far. Upton was probably a half-pay officer who'd needed the money and had willingly become his father's tool. "Blo—blasted bas—old man!"

"Please feel free to curse him as much as you please. I assure you, I have heard worse around the docks."

Bloody, bloody, hell. "You may have heard it, but I am not going to . . . rubbishing commoner."

She cracked a laugh. "That is probably the worst insult you could give him."

He slid a glance at her and was amazed to find her grinning. She had just gone through what would have terrorized any other lady of his acquaintance, with the possible exception of his sister-in-law, and she was laughing. "Jenny MacGowan, you are the most remarkable woman I've ever met, and—and I love you."

She swung her head around, so quickly her long slender neck might have snapped. "What did you just say?"

"I said I love you, and I want to marry you if you'll have me. I'd get down on one knee, but I'd rather put some distance between the good major and us. If he's got any brains at all, he'll figure out who I am before long." Frank turned off the main road toward the market town his brother Quartus had recently moved to.

"Where are we going?"

"To one of my brothers whom I believe will help us."

"And defy your father?"

"Quartus and my father are not speaking at the moment." Frank thought about the argument his brother and father had had before the duke had gone to Scotland. "My brother is a vicar, and had one of my father's livings. When my father wanted him to use his position to support a bill in the House of Commons my father was attempting to further, Quartus refused. The duke threatened to remove Quartus from the living, then departed for the north, obviously thinking he would come around. About a week ago, Damon received a letter informing him that our brother had taken another living and was residing not far from London." Frank wished he could study Jenny's face but, unfortunately, the pair needed his attention.

"At the rate your father is going," she commented drily, "he might find himself alone."

"There are fifteen of us. One can only hope he'll become more intelligent with time."

They reached a toll booth and Frank blew the horn. As soon as Jenny handed the keeper the two pence, they were on their way. If the major was following, they would not be hard to find. He just prayed the man didn't find out until he had her safe.

After two or three miles, Frank slowed the horses. He didn't want to stop to take the time to change them, and blowing them would do no good at all. The sun was directly overhead. With luck, they'd reach the town in another hour.

Then he remembered that instead of giving him an answer, she'd changed the topic. Tension and fear infused him. He had never thought he'd love anyone as much as he did her, and didn't know what he'd do if she rejected him. "Jenny, will you marry me?"

Her jaw dropped, and she began to laugh again.

What in all of damnation was so funny about his proposal that she'd—

"No, no, don't scowl so. Yes, I'll marry you." She placed her slim fingers on his arm, and he started to relax. "I love you, too, and I want nothing more than to spend the rest of my life with you. It is just that this fleeing business has muddled my brain a bit." She kissed her fingers, placing them on his cheek. "Now, what is your plan?"

"When we get to my brother's house, I'll write Damon and Meg. He will be able to secure a special license so that we can be married immediately." Jenny nodded. "Meg can go to the hotel and fetch some clothing for you."

"Then what?"

"Then . . . then we can reside with Damon until we make other plans or your father's ship arrives."

"I agree we must tell Damon and Meg what has happened, but I think the message should go to my aunt." Frank opened his mouth to argue, and she held up her hand. "What if your father is having your brother's house watched? You said the major might figure out that you are not Lord Quimby."

"In fact, both the house and hotel might be watched."

"I agree, but Geoff can come and go as he pleases, and he has more of a reason to procure a special license than Damon has. Sarah can contact the office that handles my father's ships' schedules in London, and ask if the *Elizabeth* has arrived. If not, she can book passage for us on another vessel."

For some reason, this was the first time Frank had thought about actually sailing away. It was a strange feeling, and he did not quite know what to do with it. He'd be leaving everything he knew. Yet, if he wanted Jenny, and he did, that was exactly what he was agreeing to, had already agreed to. It would be a new start for him. A chance to discover if he had what it took to make a go of a business. In America no one would defer to him because of his father's rank. In fact, having a title would do him little good at all. "You are right. We should contact your aunt first. However, the messenger must remain in Town until we are wed."

"Yes, that way no one can follow him to us. After we marry we can slip into the hotel."

He mulled the plans over again. "I'll have my trunks sent there."

"There are so many guests coming and going, no one

will notice." She chewed on her bottom lip for a moment. "This is a perfect plan."

And everyone knows what happens to perfect plans. Frank sent a prayer to the deity.

AN HOUR LATER, FRANK AND Jenny arrived at the rectory to find his brother surrounded by boxes. Yet, instead of removing items, he was putting them in the crates. This was not good. Jenny glanced at him and he shrugged.

"Shouldn't you be unpacking?" he asked after the door had been closed.

His brother glanced up scowling. "You, of all people, ought to know what has occurred."

Frank raised his hands warding off his younger brother's ire. "I have been in London for the past two or more weeks. I only knew you were here because of the letter you sent Damon."

"Then someone else told Father." Quartus swiped a hand down his face. "I've been sacked from my new position and ordered back home."

For a few seconds, Jenny was silent, then she scowled. "No one should be allowed to have that much power. Your father should be horsewhipped."

There was his democratic American! Tugging her against him, Frank barked a laugh.

His brother stared at her for a moment before a slow smile formed on Quartus's face. "Horsewhip a duke. What an interesting idea. Frank, would you care to make the introductions?"

Taking her hand, he said, "My love, allow me to introduce my brother Quartus. Quartus, this is my betrothed, Miss

Jenny MacGowan of New York."

"Oh, Lord." He plopped himself on a crate. "It needed only that. Does our father know?"

"Yes. Unfortunately. Probably not that we are actually engaged, but he has expressed his disapproval of the idea." Frank grimaced. "I had to rescue Jenny from a man who said that our father had ordered him to abduct and wed her. We came directly here. I had hoped we could remain here with you until I was able to obtain a special license and you could see us married."

"Are you mad? What would you do?" Quartus's brows had drawn together as he scowled, and Frank prayed his brother was not going to oppose them. A rift with one family member was enough. "How would you live?"

"That is the easy part," Jenny said. "We are going back to New York."

Quartus gazed at her for a moment, a grim look on his face. Then he glanced at Frank. "How did you arrive?"

"I have Damon's curricle and pair." Frank slipped his arm around Jenny's waist, and she stepped closer to him.

This was so much worse than he had ever thought it could be. His father was treating peoples' lives as if they were his to play with. He had always known the duke could be ruthless, but had never seen it directed at him or his younger brothers and sisters. Damon had always seemed to be their father's sole focus.

"I have to leave in the morning." Quartus raked his fingers through his hair. "I suggest you take the mail coach to London. You are less likely to be followed. I'll bring the carriage and horses to Town tomorrow. There is nothing suspicious about me visiting my brother before heading west again. As soon as you are able to get the special license, I shall be honored to perform the ceremony."

Frank let out the breath he'd been holding. "Thank you, but won't it make your situation harder?"

Quartus grinned. "If it becomes insupportable, I shall merely hop a ship and come to you."

"You could join us, if you'd like," Jenny said unexpectedly. "I'm sure your credentials will be honored in America."

"Thank you. It is a generous offer." He shook his head and stood. "Come, I'll make sure the horses are settled, and walk with you to the inn where you can catch the mail."

CHAPTER NINE

AN HOUR AND A HALF later, after eating a hasty meal at the tavern, Jenny and Frank were on the crowded coach heading toward London. She had been able to obtain a seat inside the conveyance, but Frank was on the roof. Taking his advice, she sat next to the window, but was still crowded by a large man who smelled strongly of onions. The woman across from her held a basket with a chicken in it, which would not have been bad if the animal had not felt it necessary to relieve itself. Perhaps when they stopped, she would join her betrothed. A little fresh air would be nice.

She grinned to herself as she thought of Frank's ruffled feathers when she insisted on paying for their fair.

"I should be taking care of you," he said in a hushed tone as they finished their meal.

"You are protecting me. I just happen to have the ready funds. Pay me back when we get to London."

"I won't continue to take your money. I have some put aside, and I shall earn enough to support us."

"I know you will." She softened her tone. Male pride could be hurt so easily.

He'd harrumphed, but stopped arguing. She prayed that the money issue would not be a problem for them in the future.

Tucking her reticule between her skirt next to the side of the coach, she closed her eyes, and to her surprise, slept.

The next thing she knew, the coach was stopped and

Frank was there.

"Jenny." His hand cupped her jaw. "Come on, sweetheart. We've arrived."

She rubbed her eyes. "I can't believe I slept so soundly." Touching her skirt, she found her reticule. "Where are we?"

"The Bull and Mouth in the City. We'll take a hackney from here."

"To the Pulteney?"

"Yes." He helped her out of the coach and into an odoriferous old carriage that had most definitely seen better days. "The Pulteney Hotel," he ordered, before getting into the coach. "Around in back."

"You got the fare?" the driver shouted.

"Oh, for the love of God," she grumbled. "Yes, now go!"

The hackney lurched forward, jerking her back against the seat. Frank, who had taken the bench across from her, fell, landing almost on top of her. She moved to one side of the coach. "Sit next to me. He doesn't seem to be a very good driver."

"As long as he gets us where we're going, I'll be satisfied." He placed his hand over hers. "I never imagined getting married would be quite this fraught with danger."

"Danger?" Surely the hackney driver wasn't that bad.

Turning his head, he glared at her. "Need I remind you that a mere few hours ago, you were abducted?"

"Oh." There was that. She cuddled next to him. "I have decided that I don't like your father."

"I don't like him much at the moment either." He snaked his arm around her waist, pulling her closer.

Jenny enjoyed his warmth and being held by him. She'd like being kissed even more, but that would mean removing her bonnet. She sighed. Kissing would have to wait. She felt a slight tug, and the ribbon under her chin loosened. The hat lifted from her head and stopped.

"What's holding it on?"

"A hat pin." She pulled it out, affixing it to her bodice. A moment later, her bonnet landed on the opposite bench.

Just as she was about to ask how much time they had before arriving, Frank's warm, firm lips covered hers, teasing and nibbling until she opened to him. His tongue tangled with hers. Her blood heated as he lifted her onto his lap. When he cupped her breast, she gasped with pleasure, wanting more. Wanting him.

"We're here," the jarvey called.

Jenny scrambled off Frank's lap, jammed her hat on, and tied the ribbon. "That will teach us."

Tossing the hackney driver some coins, he lost no time getting them out of the carriage and in the back door to the hotel. "Where do we go from here?"

Biting her lip, she glanced around, seeing a plain set of stairs. Much better than going up the main staircase. "This way. Sarah and I have rooms on the third floor."

"That's almost in the attic," he said, as if he'd been insulted.

"My third, your second." She grabbed his hand as they ran up the steps. Yet another difference for him to become used to. They might both speak relatively the same language, but there was still room for many misunderstandings. It was a good thing they'd decided to always be truthful with each other.

When they reached the floor her rooms were on, Jenny glanced around. "I don't see anyone."

"Perhaps Fate has chosen to be on our side after all." His voice was barely a whisper.

"It's the third door on the other side of the main stairs."

This time he took the lead, moving so slowly she thought she'd scream. "I hear someone below. Run. Quietly."

She opened the door to the parlor she shared with her

aunt and pulled Frank through, closing the door behind them. "Thank God, we made it without being seen."

Frank leaned against the door, bringing her against him. They'd not run far, but their hearts beat rapidly, and their breath ragged.

"Jenny, Lord Frank, what is going on?" Geoff rose, striding toward them.

"Oh, thank heavens." Aunt Sarah reached Jenny before Geoff could and embraced her. "Your maid came back saying you had been abducted. "Then"—she waved her hand in the direction of the fireplace where Meg and Damon had risen—"Lord and Lady Hawksworth arrived. We were just about ready to call the Bow Street Runners."

"Lord Frank." Geoff pressed a glass into his hand. "The two of you look as if you've had quite a time of it."

Jenny took the other glass in Geoff's hand. "You might need one as well."

"Meg, Damon," Frank said after taking a sip of wine. "Father had Jenny abducted with a plan to marry her off."

Within a few minutes, they'd told their relatives what had occurred and what they planned on doing.

"Quimby?" Damon laughed. "That was brilliant thinking, Jenny. Though you realize as soon as Father hears the name he'll know you were rescued and by whom." He leaned against the mantel. "Thank you for not abandoning my cattle. I'll ensure we have a room ready for Quartus." He held his hand out to his wife. "Meg?"

"Give me a moment." She glanced at Sarah. "May I write a note?"

"Yes, of course."

A few minutes later, Meg handed Geoff the letter. "Have this delivered to Featherton House. My father will be able to notify the *Elizabeth's* captain or make other arrangements for the passage more easily than Sarah can." She glanced at Jenny. "I'm glad you are safe. I wish the circumstances were better, but we are dealing with Somerset."

"There is no problem in securing a special license." Geoff drained his glass. "I'll go now."

"If you take my advice," Damon said, "you will not wait for our brother to arrive. I have someone in mind that could perform the ceremony almost immediately."

"And who will not suffer later for it," Frank replied. Quartus was going to have enough problems as it was. "I'd like to go with you."

His brother seemed to study him for a few seconds. "Very well. It will also give you an opportunity to change. Your clothing is rather worse for wear."

"The only seat I could procure was the top of the mail coach."

"That explains it." Damon grinned. "Ladies." He bowed to Jenny and her aunt. "We'll see you in about three hours. If not less."

"I shall remain here," Meg said. "That gives you an excuse to return, in the event your father is having our house watched."

"And give us just enough time to prepare," Sarah said as she ushered the men out the door.

"What are you thinking?" Frank asked his brother as they made their way down the corridor.

"How did you enter the hotel?" Damon asked.

"From the mews."

"Good. We shall depart that way as well."

"Even me?" Warwick asked.

"Yes. If my father is having us watched, they will most likely be looking for us to leave from the front. The longer we can keep the old man guessing, the better." When they reached the mews, Damon and Warwick called for their carriages. Luckily, Damon had brought his town coach, enabling Frank to hide his presence.

THE MID-AFTERNOON SUN STREAMED THROUGH the window of the Duke of Somerset's study as he tapped his fingers on the massive old walnut table that had been handed down through six generations of dukes. He narrowed his eyes at the filthy specimen before him. "You are certain that neither of my sons is aware that chit from the colonies has been abducted?"

"Ain't seen Lord Francis, Yer Grace, but the marquis didn't seem to be in any hurry when him and her ladyship left their house."

"Good. Then all is going as planned. Return to your post. I shall expect another report later this evening."

"Yes, Yer Grace. I'll keep me peepers pealed on that door."

Once his hired tool had left, Somerset leaned back against the leather chair. His duchess had been correct. It was time to find a wife for his second son and ensure that this time no one interfered with his choice. Reaching out, he tugged the bell-pull. A second later, the door opened and his butler bowed. "Yes, Your Grace?"

"Tell Belling I wish him to attend me."

"Yes, Your Grace."

A few moments later, Somerset's secretary entered carrying a notebook. "You wished to see me, Your Grace?"

"Take a seat. I shall dictate the requirements needed for the proper mate for Lord Francis, then I want you to provide me a list of likely candidates. As long as he is in Town, he may begin courting the lady." He pressed his fingertips together. "Passably pretty. A great beauty will have higher expectations, and I cannot expect my son to marry a lady with any obvious defects. Malleable. I will not have a woman taking my son's side against me. She must have the usual accomplishments, and her father must be willing to support me in the Lords."

After a few moments, Belling stopped scribbling. "Anything else, Your Grace? Fortune?"

"Not a large fortune. She and her family must be grateful to have her marry a younger son."

"I shall have a list to you by the end of the day tomorrow."

"You may go."

The door closed, and once again Somerset turned his thoughts to his second son. What the devil had Francis been thinking to take up with an American? It was a damn good thing that old gossip, Thornfield, couldn't keep anything to himself. When Somerset had arrived two days ago, his neighbor had had the infernal gall to ask when the wedding would be. Well, the answer was never. At least not to that woman and never to an American. No son of Somerset would bind himself to a heathen traitor.

ONCE BACK AT HIS BROTHER'S home, Frank had sent his valet on an errand that would take at least two hours, possibly more. He had no doubt, the servant would report anything he was doing to his father in the most expeditious way possible.

Frank entered Damon's study. "I have an unexpected problem."

"What is it?"

"I cannot imagine my valet agreeing to remove to America, and I am not at all proficient at taking care of my own clothing."

Leaning back in his chair, Damon said thoughtfully, "What you require at present is someone akin to a batman."

Frank mulled the idea over. A servant who could care

for not only clothing, but a multitude of other things as well. "Where am I going to find one at this late date?"

"I have a man here. A former soldier who's officer was killed. He's working as a footman, but he might be interested. Shall I call for him?"

"Please do." He sat in one of the chairs next to the fireplace.

Several minutes later, a man in his late twenties arrived. "You wanted me, my lord?

"I did indeed. Frank, this is Perkins. Perkins, my brother is getting ready to sail to America. He needs a batman. Would you be interested?"

A slow smile spread over the footman's face. "I'd be more than happy to take the position, my lord."

One more problem settled. Frank grinned. "In that case, I am more than happy to have you. Your first tasks will be to help me change, change out of your livery, and pack my trunks. We shall be departing soon." He started to leave the room and stopped. "Not a word to anyone, especially my old valet. Hawksworth, I'd appreciate it if you found a way to send the man home. He will only cause problems if he remains here."

"I'm sure I can come up with something."

Less than an hour later, Frank was bathed and dressed as any gentleman making a call would be. He'd wanted to wear something more suited to the occasion of his marriage, but Damon had been right. If Frank was seen, it might cause questions to be asked. With luck, it would not take long for Warwick to obtain the special license.

Just as he left his bedchamber, a footman topped the main staircase. "My lord, his lordship asked that you come right away."

"Thank you." He quickened his steps, arriving at Damon's study in time to see him hand a glass of claret to a gentleman around his age. "Is everything all right?"

"It is. Frank, meet Mr. Henley. He will be performing your wedding ceremony."

The man rose, facing Frank. Lines, such as his brother had, formed at the corners of Henley's eyes and mouth. "I've heard a lot about you over the years. All to the good, I might add."

Frank stuck out his hand. "You must have served in the army with Hawksworth."

"Indeed I did, and I'm happy to do him a service."

"I don't want to rush you." Damon nodded at the glass of wine. "But I'd rather see my brother married sooner than later."

Henley tossed off his wine. "In that case, we should depart."

Once again, they left from the mews behind Damon's house. Frank sat on the rear-facing seat out of respect for his brother's friend. "Thank you for agreeing to officiate."

The man cocked a brow. "If old soldiers don't stick together, who will? Aside from that, I will enjoy poking a stick in the duke's wheel. Any man who can treat his children as he has does not deserve my respect." A sly grin tipped his lips. "And he does not have the power to hurt me in any manner whatsoever."

Unlike how Father could make Quartus suffer for helping Frank and Jenny. They fell silent for several moments, and he reviewed their plans. His biggest fear was that his father would discover they intended to leave England and attempt to stop them. The duke would be furious to be thwarted in the matter of their marriage, but Father would be enraged when he discovered they'd left the country. An image of him red-faced and shouting down the house came to Frank. Yet, for the first time, he simply did not care. He would no longer be ruled and dictated to by an ill-tempered old despot who thought nothing of anyone but himself. And Jenny was worth everything to him. She was the most determined, intelligent, beautiful, funny woman he had ever met, and he thanked God she was his.

"You're smiling," Damon remarked drily. "It's not over yet. Trust me when I tell you our father will stop at nothing to have his way."

"I am well aware of what he tried to do to you and Meg." He glanced out the sliver of the window available to him. "Still, I can't help but feel as if I've been freed."

"I know what you mean. Even after I learned of my inheritance from my mother, I was still under the old man's boot. Then I met Meg, and nothing else mattered. I had to have her in my life."

That was exactly how Frank felt about Jenny. He couldn't imagine living without her. He already had visions of red-haired children. Children who would be free to choose their own paths.

When the coach came to a stop, he jumped down. Soon they were in the corridor outside of Jenny's apartments. The door flew open, and a moment later, Jenny was in his arms.

"Geoff just returned with the license." Her voice was breathy, but she had a wide smile on her lips.

"We brought the clergyman." Frank brushed a kiss against her lips. "Are you ready to be married?"

"Yes. More than ready."

"In that case, there is no reason to delay."

Soon she would be his forever, and nothing his father could do would stop that. Yet once they left England, he would still have her father with whom to contend. A man who did not love the English.

CHAPTER TEN

JENNY'S CHEEKS HURT FROM SMILING so much, but she couldn't help it. Before the men had returned, Sarah had arranged for champagne and light foods from the kitchen. Suky had dressed Jenny's hair in a knot high on her head, with ringlets framing her face.

"Give us one minute," Sarah said, pushing Jenny into her bedchamber.

Meg took off a broach that had been pinned to her bodice. "It will not do to ignore tradition. Wear this for something borrowed."

Sarah placed an old sapphire necklace around Jenny's neck, then handed her the earrings. "Your mother wanted you to wear these at your wedding."

Tears pricked her eyes. "They are beautiful. It never entered my mind that she would think of it.

"It was her heart's desire to see you marry a man you loved." Sarah gave Jenny a quick hug. "No crying now. I had meant to buy you something special for this day. Unfortunately, the handkerchief I just purchased will have to do."

Jenny took the fine linen trimmed with lace. "It's lovely."

A knock came on the door. "Are you about finished?" Damon asked. "It appears we have forgotten something important."

"What is it?" Jenny asked.

"The settlement agreements."

"Give me a moment." She opened a small trunk which

held a few books, her jewelry, and the documents she'd brought from home."

Jenny, her aunt, and friend walked into the parlor.

She handed Frank the papers. "This is the settlement agreement my father and I decided upon before I left New York. Please take a look at it, then tell me if you agree with it."

He broke the seal, and with Damon and Geoff crowded around Frank, perused the documents. After several minutes, he glanced up. "This is perfect. It protects you, which is all I care about."

"It also ensures that if anything were to happen to Frank, our father could not touch any of Jenny's fortune."

Frank grinned. "Even better."

"Which is the reason Papa and I drafted it." Jenny linked her arm with his. "Shall we?"

Frank's warm blue gaze held her breathless for a moment, before he murmured, "Yes."

"If you will gather here, we will begin." Mr. Henley took his place between two vases of flowers.

With everything she and Frank had been through today, she was amazed at how calm they were as they said their vows. When the vicar got to the part about Frank worshiping her body, a wicked gleam entered his eyes, warming her from her cheeks to her toes. Tonight, they would be together for the first time, and she found that she was a little nervous, but looking forward to it. The only question was where they would be.

A half an hour later, as their little party was drinking champagne and eating lobster patties, a knock came on the door. Geoff opened it, and a tall gentleman who looked to be in his early thirties entered.

"Kit!" Meg rushed over and hugged the man. "Jenny and Sarah, allow me to introduce my brother Mr. Kit Featherton. Kit, my new sister, Lady Frank Trevor—"

"If you don't mind," Frank cut in, "I believe she would rather be known as Mrs. Frank Trevor-MacGowan."

For a brief second, Jenny couldn't speak. She opened her mouth, but nothing came out. That he would want to take her name was more than she could have imagined. Her father would be beside himself with joy. "Are you sure?"

He circled his arms around her, holding her tight. "I've given this a great deal of thought. Your father has no male heirs. I believe that even in America a man would wish for his name to continue."

"Yes. Yes, he would." For the second time that day, tears threatened to fall. Her throat tightened, making it hard to speak. "I love you."

"I love you, too."

Someone cleared their throat, recalling them to the others in the room.

"Now that that's settled," Damon drawled. "Featherton, this is Mrs. Frank Trevor-MacGowan."

Mr. Featherton's lips twitched as he bowed. "It is about your passage that I have come. The *Elizabeth* is in London Pool. I caught the captain as he was getting ready to search for you. She is taking on cargo and will be ready to depart tomorrow on the evening tide. I explained to the captain that you are anticipating a departure from England as soon as possible. He will expect your baggage to be delivered early tomorrow morning and be ready to receive you and your husband aboard tomorrow afternoon. The tide changes at five fifty-one."

Jenny clapped her hands. "Perfect! Everything is working out exactly as it should."

"My dear," Sarah said. "It might be best if you do not count your chickens before they are hatched. You must still manage to board the boat without Frank's father trying to stop you."

Jenny was sure she and Frank would be able to trick the old man. "I have faith he will not find out we're gone before we've sailed."

Or at least, they'd do their very best to get aboard without him knowing. Still, nothing would stop them from going home.

SOMERSET'S SECRETARY TOOK THE SEAT in front of his desk. "I have the list almost completed."

"Do you have the information on that American?" Not that he would need it. The chit was well on her way to being wed by now.

"Yes, Your Grace. Would you like to read the dossier, or shall I recite it?"

"Tell me. I shall read it if I have to."

"Her father is originally from Scotland. He built up a shipping company with trade mainly between the Continent and the Americas and the Caribbean. Although he does trade in Britain, it is only a small part of his business. I received word yesterday that one of his ships has arrived to take on goods. Once that is accomplished, the ship will return to the colonies."

Somerset tapped his fingers on the desk. "Have you seen or heard from Lord Francis?"

"No, Your Grace. The persons watching the house have not seen him enter or leave. Neither has Lord Hawksworth returned home."

It was almost dinner time. If Francis cared about the girl, surely Hawksworth would have sent to inform Francis she was missing. All seemed to be going as planned, but Somerset had the feeling something was not right, and he always followed his feelings in these matters.

A scratch came on the door, and Somerset's butler opened the door. "Your Grace, Major Upton wishes to see you."

What the hell was Upton doing here? He should be off making sure he was shackled to that woman. He's better have a damn good excuse for being in Town. "Show him in."

The dratted man strolled into the room, and bowed. "Your Grace. Apparently we were mistaken about where Miss MacGowan's attentions lie. When I stopped at the inn, a gentleman by the name of Quimby drove up. She is betrothed to him."

Somerset clenched his jaw. "Lord Quimby?"

"Yes, Your Grace. When he arrived she went on about how she wanted to be Lady Quimby."

The damn cats!! Of course Francis had told her about the cats! *Bloody hell.*

"*Imbecile!*" It was a blasted shame he was too old to jump over the desk and strangle the major. "That was my son."

"Belling."

"Your Grace?"

"Find Lord Francis."

WHEN JENNY WALKED INTO THE parlor, Frank knew she was the most beautiful woman in the world, and he the luckiest man. The pale yellow silk made her skin look like rich cream. The sapphire neckless was the same color as her eyes. And when he'd said his vows, the one about worshiping her with his body brought up an image of her on his bed, her hair a riot of color against pristine white pillows.

He was glad Featherton had arrived with the news Frank and Jenny could depart on the morrow. The festivities seemed to go on forever, but once their families had left the hotel, and Sarah had retired to her room, he'd ushered Jenny into their bedchamber.

He couldn't wait to unwrap her. He wanted to kiss and caress every inch of her gloriously naked body. "We wouldn't be married without their help, but thank God they've finally left." He'd expected one of her witty retorts, instead when he glanced at her, a pale face and nervous eyes met him. Taking her in his arms, he kissed her. "I'm sorry. The idea of sharing a bed with me must be a bit frightening."

She rested her head on his chest. "I'm not afraid, precisely. It's just that we have not been alone very often." A smile trembled on her lips. "Except lately when we've been running around the countryside."

"I . . . we shall take this as slowly as you wish. Will that make you feel better?"

"I think so," she replied. Her tone still hesitant.

Hell. Why hadn't he thought about this possibility before? He did not have vast amounts of experience, but she had none at all. Not to mention that they'd only known each other for a week. Even if it did seem as if she was the lady he'd been waiting all his life for.

"Let's begin with what I know you like."

He kissed the top of her head, and when she raised her face to him, he feathered kisses from one corner of her mouth to the other, praising the deity when she opened her lips to him. Their tongues tangled, and she speared her fingers through his hair. He pulled out one hair pin, dropping it on the thick carpet when soft curl escaped, falling past her shoulder.

"Jenny, love," he murmured, pulling out the rest of the hair pins, unable to wait to see her shining red tresses flowing free.

Slanting his head, he deepened the kiss, and she moaned. Surely that was progress. He carefully allowed his hands to slowly move from her waist to her breasts, caressing the full mounds. She inhaled sharply, and just as he wondered if that was a sound of enjoyment, she rubbed her hands over his chest.

"So hard. May I remove your jacket?"

Yes, yes, a thousand times yes!

"If you wish," he replied with credible calm.

He helped her tug the garment off then removed his cravat and waistcoat. Her clever fingers lost no time pulling his shirt out of his pantaloons. Soon his shirt joined her hair pins on the floor, and her fingers played with the curls on his chest.

"My love, may I unlace your gown a bit?"

"Umm." Her voice was muffled as she placed kisses on his chest. "I adore your chest."

Deciding to take that as permission, Frank quickly unlaced her dress, enjoying the view as the bodice and petticoat began to sag, then fall, with a little help from him, to the carpet. She rose onto her tip-toes, rubbing her body against him. Next, he untied her stays that followed the growing pile of clothing, then her chemise.

He touched his tongue to her breasts, and she stilled.

"What are you doing?" Her tone slightly hesitant.

"Worshiping you with my body," he said, reminding her of his vows.

"Oh. That's all right then." Her voice not entirely steady.

He probably should have asked her how much she knew, but he didn't want to give her time to become even more nervous. Kissing her, he slowly walked her back until they were close enough to the bed for him to pick her up and lay her on the thick mattress. She was just as exquisite as he'd thought she would be. Generous breasts led to a slender waist that flared into full hips and a rounded stomach.

"You are beautiful."

"As are you." Jenny could not believe how natural it felt to be almost naked with him. "I should remove my stocking."

"Allow me." For the second time that day, his smile was wicked.

He placed light kisses up her leg, creating flames wherever he touched her. Then he moved over her, possessing her mouth again. She felt his hard ridge against her, and heat coursed through her, making her want—no, need—him.

When he licked her breasts, she arched up, encouragingly. "So good."

Flames licked at the apex of her thighs, and his hand moved to cover and caress her mons. He inserted one finger into her passage, then another, stroking when she pushed her hips up wanting more.

"I want to see all of you."

Holding her eyes with his, he removed his pantaloons. His member jutted out large and stiff from a mass of golden curls. Before she could think much more about it, Frank was kissing her again, and she was ready to become his in body as well as in mind.

His member pushed against her sheath. "I'll be as gentle as I can be."

"I know you will, and I love you."

"I love you."

Taking her in a searing kiss, he entered her, filling her. Then he pushed hard, and she felt a sharp pain.

When she tensed, he stopped. "Let me know when you're ready."

Jenny nodded. "It's better now."

He moved slowly, allowing her to get used to having

him inside her. Then the flames were back, heating her, coiling the tension until it exploded and coursed through her, making her cry out.

Frank tensed and pumped in one last time before she felt his seed fill her. Falling off to her side, he hugged her close, nuzzling her hair. Her mother had been correct. When one makes love with the right man, it is heaven.

"Jenny, my love. Are you all right?"

Cuddling closer to him, she smiled against his chest. "I am perfect. After searching for so many years, I had given up even hoping I'd find love. I didn't even want to come to London."

"I didn't want to either." He pulled the covers over them. "I saw no point in it. Yet I'm glad I did."

"When I think of how chance our meeting was . . ." She gazed up at him.

"And how uninterested you were at meeting another Englishman . . ."

"And the way you found me so quickly when I was abducted . . ."

He kissed her tenderly, as if she was the most precious thing in the world to him, as he was to her.

"It was Fate," Frank muttered against her mouth. "I should, however, send Lord Pomfry a letter thanking him for being so pompous."

"We mustn't forget one to Lady Heathcote for being so hateful to me." She started to laugh. "Oh, I agree. It must have been Fate. Think of all that could have gone wrong."

"But it didn't and now we're together."

Jenny gave him what she hoped was a leer. "Yes, and I would very much like to do something about that."

"Who am I to deny my wife's wishes?" He rolled her beneath him. "Particularly when they coincide so nicely with my own."

She had been timid before, now she had the confidence

to show her passion for him. This time when they made love, there was no pain, only love and joy.

CHAPTER ELEVEN

THE FOLLOWING AFTERNOON, JENNY, FRANK, Damon, and Meg arrived in the Hawksworth coach to the part of London's massive port used by the *Elizabeth's* crew and captain. Sarah and Geoff followed in his smaller town coach. Jenny and Frank's trunks had been sent earlier in the day, accompanied by their personal servants.

It seemed like such a long time since she'd been at a dock. She was used to the scent of fish, brine, and tar, but the Thames was reputed to be used for dumping not only refuse, but dead bodies as well, and the warmer weather hadn't helped. Competing with the stench of the river were the spices, tobacco, and other cargo.

"How can you stand it?" Meg held a scented handkerchief to her nose.

"I've been around docks all my life. Although, I will say that the Hudson River is not nearly as odorific."

Sarah joined them, also pressing a handkerchief to her nose. "I need not pretend I enjoy the smell any longer."

"Don't tell me you were afraid of Papa teasing you?" Jenny asked, hardly believing that her aunt had hid her distaste all these years.

"Not your father. Your mother." Sarah pulled a face. "She would have been merciless. Where are we to meet the captain?"

"Here at the London Dock." The ship was anchored in what was called London Pool. After several moments, she spotted the distinctive bow of the MacGowan ships.

"Frank," she pointed, "do you see the ship with the long high bow and the American flag on the stern?"

"Yes. Is that the *Elizabeth*?"

"It is. She is named after my mother." Jenny's voice caught as she remembered how her mother had loved that ship.

Frank raised her hand to his lips. "We'll be on her soon. I must speak to my brother before we leave."

Blinking back her tears, she nodded. A few minutes later, a short man with salt and pepper hair in his mid-forties approached. "Captain Jones, how good to see you. I thought you were going to take the *Scotia* to China?"

He gave a curt bow. "My plans changed. I have been commissioned to bring you home, Miss Jenny."

"Not Miss any more." She grinned. Glancing around, she saw Frank with the other gentlemen. He looked up at the same time, and she beckoned to him. Once he was next to her, she tucked her hand in the crook of his arm. "Captain, this is my husband, Frank Trevor-MacGowan. Frank, this is an old and dear friend, Captain Jones."

Frank held out his hand, and the captain shook it. "Pleased to meet you, sir."

"Trevor-MacGowan is it?" the captain said thoughtfully. "Your father will like that. It's a pleasure to meet you, young man. We all wondered if our girl would finally settle down. Well, we'd best be off. My cook is making something special for this evening." The man winked at Frank. "A celebration as it were."

"You fraud." Jenny gasped. "You knew all along I was married."

"It was the valet for his former lordship here that gave it away." He chuckled. "I couldn't let you get one over on me."

Shaking her head, she turned to hug her aunt and Meg farewell and saw instead a rough looking thug grab Frank.

He slammed his fist into the cur's face, and another man wrapped his arm around Frank from behind, dragging him away toward a black carriage.

Damon, Geoff, and Captain Jones dashed in to help, when a loud whistle broke the air.

"Cease!" A tall, broad shouldered, elderly man stepped down from the coach. "I told you to bring him to me. If he is damaged, you will suffer."

Frank shook off his attacker. "Father."

Jenny glanced from her husband to the old man. So this was the Duke of Somerset.

His cold blue eyes cut to Frank. "Did you think I would allow you to marry a colonial? A heathen?"

Frank stood as still as a statute. Only the tick in Frank's jaw betrayed how angry he was. His gaze was as icy as his father's and his voice even colder. "My *wife*"—he let the word hang for a moment—"is every bit as educated and cultured as any lady of the *ton*. I will not allow you to disparage her."

The two men stood staring at each other for several moments.

"*You* will not allow *me*—?" his father finally said. "I can see you are being corrupted already. Get in the carriage," the duke commanded. "I'm taking you home where you cannot get into any more mischief."

"No." Frank's hands curled into fists, but Jenny knew he would not strike his father.

When he didn't move to obey, Somerset nodded to one of the men, and the bounder seized Frank's arm.

"Father," Damon cut in. "He needs to live his own life."

"*You* stay out of this." The duke glowered. "You are not the head of this house yet."

The confrontation had caused a group of dock workers and bar patrons to gather around them. No doubt enjoying the show. Yet, even though money could be seen exchanging hands, no one spoke.

Well, this wasn't accomplishing anything. If she didn't do something soon, she'd have to chase her husband across England. Not only that, but the Duke of Somerset had just gotten on Jenny's very last nerve. Frank had saved her from an abduction. It was her turn to rescue him.

Frank filled with pride as Jenny strode to his side. She took his free hand, and faced the duke. "As my husband has already told you, we are married. You have no right to interfere with the decisions we make."

The old man's jaw moved, as if he was grinding his teeth. His gaze moved slowly from Frank to Jenny.

The duke perused her from her bonnet to her shoes, as if she were a piece of filth he'd like to scrape off his boots. "*I* have every right. *I* am a peer of the realm. *You*, however, have no right to speak to me at all."

She raised her chin, glaring right back at the duke. "Not in my country, you're not. In my country, you are naught."

At that moment, Frank could see the generations of her family who had fought for their freedom from a system that would allow men such as his father so much power by the mere chance of birth. He admired her and all she stood for.

"You are a tyrant," she continued in a hard voice, "who has nothing better to do than make your children miserable."

Frank shook his arm free from the thug and started to move them away from his father. "Come, my love. We have a ship to catch."

The blackguard grabbed him again. In a flash, Jenny had pulled a pistol from her reticule, leveling it at the duke. "Release him."

There was a shocked silence, and for a few seconds the only sound was the gulls screeching and horses' hooves clopping on the cobblestone. Even Father seemed to be having trouble taking in the fact that a young woman held a gun directed at him.

"You won't shoot me," he sneered.

Jenny raised one dark brown brow, meeting the duke's cold gaze with one of her own. "Are you sure about that?" she taunted. Frank was proud of how calm her voice was when he could feel her pulse beat so quickly he was afraid she'd swoon. "I am, after all, an American heathen. Do you truly wish to test me?"

Father moved his gaze to Frank. "If you leave with her, you are dead to me."

Knowing that would be the threat, he was glad his father had finally made it. He hoped his mother and brothers and sisters understood his decision. Damon would explain it to them. "So be it." He took her hand, cold even encased in a glove, in his warm one and whispered, "Don't put the pistol away until we've reached the dory."

"I won't. He really isn't trustworthy, is he?"

"Not in the least. If he wasn't a duke, he'd have been hung by now."

Quartus strode up to them, wrapping his arms Frank and Jenny. "I'm sorry I was unable to attend the wedding. We'll miss you, but you have made the right choice. Have a good voyage."

"Quartus," their father said, "I'll not have another son in Town. You are coming with me.

Grinning, he winked at Frank and Jenny before responding, "I believe I'll stay with Damon and Meg for the Season. I am quite sure you can go on without me."

While Quartus continued to argue with his father, Frank and Jenny quickly said adieu to their families. Just as quickly, Captain Jones got them on to the dory, and then out to the ship.

"Good God, girl." The captain's voice boomed. "Remind me never to tangle with you."

She grinned, a blush making her cheeks rosy. "Sometimes one must fight for those one loves."

Frank had known she was strong, perhaps even stronger than he, and he'd never been prouder of her. They had only one more hurdle to jump, that of her father.

TWO MONTHS LATER, AFTER HAVING sailed down Cape Verde, across the Atlantic to the West Indies where the ship took on cargo, then north, they pulled into the MacGowan docks in New York City.

Frank's first thought was that this river smelled much better than the Thames. During the passage, the captain and crew had taught him how to sail and navigate. Jenny taught him about the business side of shipping. He'd been surprised at the position she held, unofficially, in her father's company.

"Aren't you angry that although you are perfectly capable of running the business, you are not allowed to because of your sex?"

She heaved a sigh. "Yes. Of course I am." Then she grinned. "But with you at the head after Papa, I can still be involved."

"More than merely involved. Full partners. I do not know what I would do without you."

Tears filled her eyes. "I am so glad I married you."

He took her in his arms. "I'm glad I married you, too." They were in the luxurious owner's cabin they'd been assigned, making sure the rest of their belongings were packed. "Will you father greet us?"

"I expect so." She looked anxious. "He can be a bit gruff at times, but he has a good heart."

Unlike the duke.

After speaking with Captain Jones, Frank had already decided on his course.

"Mrs. MacGowan, Mr. MacGowan"—it hadn't taken long for the crew to shorten the double name to one familiar to them—"the captain said he's ready for you to disembark." The man lowered his voice to a whisper. "Your father's waiting."

Frank took Jenny's hand. "I'm looking forward to meeting the man who gave me such a beautiful and brilliant wife."

"He will also be glad to have a grandchild on the way." Touching her still flat stomach, she smiled.

She walked down the gangboard ahead of him to a huge, bear of a man with red hair, who folded her into a hug. "Jenny, me love! I've missed ye."

For a moment, Frank wondered how he would fit into this already close family, then he remembered how Meg's family had embraced Damon, making him one of their own. Frank hoped he would be as lucky.

"Papa, I've missed you as well." She extracted herself and turned to Frank. "I've brought you two presents. This is my husband, Mr. Frank Trevor-MacGowan." Her father's eyes narrowed slightly, and she hurried on. "And in about seven months, you will be a grandfather."

The man's eyes rounded with pleasure. "A grandfather? Jenny lass, you're with child?"

"Yes." She grinned widely. "Aren't we clever?"

"I'll see how clever ye are when I've met this man ye've married."

Frank stuck out his hand, but dropped it almost immediately when it didn't look as if MacGowan was ready to shake hands. "I am, or was, Lord Frank Trevor, second son of the Duke of Somerset."

"You're English?"

He glanced down, making sure he was on dry land as

he had been told he must be. "Not any more. I am now an American."

"And you let my Jenny talk you into taking my family name, even though we were outlawed for years by the English."

"Papa—"

"You hush, lass. Let your man speak for himself."

A mulish look formed on Jenny's face, but she said nothing.

"She did not ask or mention it. The decision was mine and she agreed."

Her father stroked his chin. "So you think you'll sit back and let her and me do all the work like the fine laird ye are?"

"Not at all, sir." Meeting the older man's eyes, Frank resisted the urge to shuffle his feet. Being under his father-in-law's scrutiny was much different than being called to account for himself before his father, where he was always found to be lacking. "I have spent the last two months learning to sail the ship and run a company. I was in charge of my father's estates and know a good deal about managing a large business as that is what the estates are. I am ready to take any position you wish to offer me, or find another job on my own."

After what seemed like an eternity, Mr. MacGowan nodded and held out his hand. "Welcome to the family, son."

Frank's throat closed painfully as he gripped the older man's hand. Jenny's tears rolled down her cheeks as she hugged them both, bringing them all together.

"Now, Jenny love, you're not supposed to be crying," her father said.

"You know they are tears of happiness." She took the handkerchief Frank handed her, and blew her nose. "You have no idea what Frank went through to be with me. His father cast him off."

"From what I've heard about the Duke of Somerset, that might not be all bad."

Frank's jaw began to drop, and he clamped it shut. "You know of my father, sir?"

"I know about the part he played in the House of Lords during the War of 1812. That was enough for me."

He grimaced. His father truly disliked Americans, and now Frank was one of them.

"Let's go home," Jenny said, taking them both by the arm.

"Good idea." Her father beamed. "I'll let you two get settled. Next week will be soon enough for me to start introducing my new son around." A few yards away the captain stood talking to another man. "Jones," Mr. MacGowan called. "You were right. She did us proud."

"First Captain Jones and now you," Jenny grumbled to her father. "I might have known you would have talked to him before putting poor Frank through an inquisition."

Her father shrugged unapologetically. "I had to know if he could stand up to me, lass."

Until Frank had met Jenny, he'd never let himself dream of the life he had wanted. But if he had, it would be this, a wife he loved, a child on the way, and a father who would be proud of him.

EPILOGUE

Seven months later.

SNOW DRIFTED ONTO THE WINDOW sill outside, but a fire roared in the fireplace, making the bedchamber warm enough for the two babies Jenny held in her arms. A boy and a girl. Apparently, twins ran in Frank's family.

The birth, the mid-wife said, was not hard, but you couldn't have proven it by her father and husband. The first time she screamed, they both burst through the door, only to be soundly routed by the doctor and mid-wife. Now she and the babies were clean, she'd nursed them, and they were sleeping peacefully like little angels.

The door opened and, almost sheepishly, the two men she loved the most entered the room.

"Jenny." Frank kissed her before stroking the cheek of the child nearest him. "Are you well?"

"I'm fine, as are the babies."

Her father kissed her head, then the top of the baby on that side of the bed. "I know we've gone round and round with names. Have you settled on them yet?"

She looked down at the little girl who had a light covering of red hair on her head. "I would like her to be named Elizabeth Catherine. After our mothers."

Frank nodded. "I agree. What about our son?

That was harder. When she'd broached the idea of naming a possible boy after her father he'd replied, "Nay, Angus. I'm honored, but it's not an easy name to have."

Naming a son after Frank's father never came up in discussion, although his brother Damon's name had.

"I would like to call him Daniel, after Mama's father."

"What would be his second name?" Frank asked.

"I thought Andrew, after your maternal grandfather."

"Daniel Andrew it is." Her father beamed. "By the way, I received a letter from Frank's mother"—for reasons completely unknown to Frank and Jenny, her father and his mother had begun a correspondence—"It seems your brother Quartus's bride is going to present her with a grandchild in the spring."

"Quartus?" Frank's mouth dropped open.

"But who did he marry?" Jenny asked, remembering their departure from London.

Book Two in The Trevors

CHAPTER ONE

London Docks, May 1818.

"QUARTUS," HIS FATHER, THE DUKE of Somerset, growled. "I'll not have another son in Town. You are coming with me."

Quartus winked at his brother, Frank, and Frank's new bride, Jenny, before responding, "I believe I'll stay with Hawksworth and Meg for the Season. I am quite sure you can go on without me."

"Quartus, get in this coach." Father's tone was as hard . . . harder, than Quartus had ever heard it before.

From the corner of his eye, he saw his brother and Jenny had boarded the dory that would take them to the ship sailing for America. Once he was sure the duke could no longer stop them, he glanced at his eldest brother and their father's heir, Damon, Marquis of Hawksworth, who inclined his head toward Quartus slightly.

"As I said, I have decided to remain in Town for the nonce. I am certain you have no need of me."

"May I remind *you*, young man, that you have a parish to see to?"

"May I remind you, that I resigned my position?" His father's face assumed an alarming purplish hue. He might not like the duke very much, but he certainly didn't want to be responsible for his death. Still, he had to be his own man. "Perhaps, Octavius would like the living."

Quartus met the duke's icy gaze with one of his own.

Minutes seemed to pass before the older man nodded. "Very well remain here for the Season, but be warned, I will not increase your allowance, nor will I pay your debts."

"Agreed." He stood where he was until the ducal coach rolled down the street and was out of sight. "I hope you don't mind putting up with me?"

"Not at all," Meg, Hawksworth's wife, said warmly. "We are delighted you will be staying with us for a while." She linked her arm with Quartus's turning him toward her carriage. "And do not worry about the expense. We are well able to support you for your Season."

"Speaking of that, I think a trip to Weston's is in order." Hawksworth leveled his quizzing glass at Quartus. "As soon as possible."

"I can't be that bad."

His brother raised one black brow, and Meg laughed lightly. "It is clear you have a great deal to learn."

TEN DAYS LATER, QUARTUS LOUNGED against one of several Grecian columns in Lady Merton's ballroom, his legs crossed. The first set had just begun and he watched as ladies dressed in every color of the rainbow, from soft pastels to brilliant hues, danced a Scottish reel. Despite the lessons and tutors his brother had hired for him, he was a little at loss as to how to go on. Being in the *haut ton* was much more complicated than he'd thought. "This is a bit . . . overwhelming."

"Only at first," Hawksworth replied. "You will soon become used to it."

"Just take some time to become comfortable." Meg had a sharp eye on the crowd, and Quartus wondered for what or whom she was looking. "Most of the ladies in white, cream or other pastel colored gowns are just out or in their second Season. The others are married, widowed, or have been out for a few years."

"That's helpful, thank you." Not that he actually expected to find a lady he could conveniently fall in love with and marry. American heiresses, such as Jenny, were thin on the ground. During the past few weeks his status as a penniless younger son, thus his ineligibility for marriage, had been made clear to him by the match-making mamas of the *ton*. Nicely, of course. No one wished to alienate his brother, the future Duke of Somerset.

Yet, nothing Quartus had said would discourage Hawksworth and Meg. Between them, they had arranged dancing lessons, tailor's appointments, an introduction to Damon's club, Brooks's, and managed to get Quartus kitted out and socially ready for his first introduction to the *haut ton*.

Meg, ever the optimist, was convinced that he would be able to find a wife who was independent and wealthy enough to withstand his dastard of a father. Another tick in the eligible column.

A stir started toward the front of the ballroom near the stairs, catching his attention. The butler made an announcement, but with the music and the whispering that had begun, he couldn't hear what it was. Then a petite young woman with warm brown hair, accompanied by an older man, and a tall slender matron with red hair covered by a purple turban stepped forward.

For a moment it seemed as if everyone in the ballroom was holding their collective breaths, then the chattering began again, much louder than the first time.

"Who are they?" he asked without taking his eyes off the lady as she moved gracefully down the steps, candles catching golden strands in her hair.

"That is the new Duchess of Wharton." Meg arched a

brow. "At least, I assume you are asking about the younger lady."

For some reason, Quartus felt disappointed by the news. "I take it that the gentleman with her is the duke."

"Not at all." Meg's eyes had a sly look in them and the corners of her lips began to tremble a bit. "That is her father, Mr. Calder."

"Is she widowed?" Quartus asked. Good Lord, was he going to have to pull every piece of information out of her? What a maddening woman his brother had wed.

"No. The older lady on her other side is Lady Tatiana Harrington an aunt of some sort."

That didn't make any sense. But at the rate this was going, he'd have to shake the information out of his sister-in-law. "*Meg!*"

She glanced at Damon who quickly concealed his grin by taking a sip of champagne. "If you must know, she is a duchess in her own right."

Quartus pushed himself off the pillar. He could not have heard her properly. "There is no such thing."

"Indeed there is," Meg pronounced. "There may be only one of them, and the situation is rare, but the title is real none the less."

Damon raised his quizzing glass. "Is she not the lady your mother took you to visit the other day?"

"Just so," Meg confirmed. "She appears to be very down to earth, and I liked her a great deal." Linking her arm with Quartus's she stepped in the direction of the duchess. "Come, I shall introduce you."

"For what reason?" Good Lord, if mothers of baronet's daughters did not think him eligible, how the deuce would he be suitable for a duchess? "She'll be looking to marry as high as she can."

"I am not suggesting you propose to her," Meg retorted, casting her eyes to the ceiling. "You might ask her to dance though."

Her grace's sets were most likely all taken. After all, the lady was lovely. Small and round in all the right places. She reminded him of a plump partridge. As they approached he could see her eyes were an interesting shade of blue, more like turquoise. When she laughed at something her aunt said it was not a false titter, but a full sound that came from deep within her.

"Your Grace." Meg curtseyed.

"Oh please. I asked you to call me Anna," the duchess said, her blue eyes twinkling.

"What have I told you," the aunt said in a repressive tone. "Not in public."

"Ah, yes. My lady, so good to see you again." Her voice was regal, but her pert nose scrunched up.

Meg rose. "Please allow me to introduce my husband, Lord Hawksworth, and his younger brother, Lord Quartus Trevor."

The duchess held her hand out first to his brother. "I am very happy to meet you, my lord."

"I'm pleased to meet you as well, Your Grace." Damon bowed dutifully.

She offered her hand to Quartus. "And you Lord Quartus. How do you do?"

"Very well, Your Grace." He took her small slender hand and a sense of well-being infused him. Glancing up he could swear her eyes widened at their contact. And he threw caution and good sense to the wind. "Do you happen to have a dance available?"

Meg cleared her throat. "Lady Tatiana, please allow me to introduce Lord Quartus."

"Forgive me, Lady Tatiana. My mother would have my head to see me so rag mannered."

Anna remembered seeing him when she entered the ballroom. By the look on his face, she'd thought he was bored. Yet now, she would swear Lord Quartus was blushing. How interesting.

Aunt Tatiana curtseyed, but not only did she not offer her hand, her body was ridged with disapproval, and Anna decided to cover for her aunt's lack of welcome. "Almost all of them, my lord. This is my first evening event." He appeared surprised, then smiled, and she decided to take matters into her own hands. "Perhaps the next set, if you are free."

"I am indeed. This is my first evening event as well."

"In that case, we should have much to discuss." Anna gave him a warm smile. If he had been put through what she'd been, he had her sympathies.

Her aunt she sniffed as if a foul odor was in the air. She had never known the woman to be so disagreeable.

"Your name is very unusual, my lord," Anna said. "Does it stand for anything in particular?"

"I am the fourth son. There was a still born baby before me—"

"Suffice it to say, Your Grace," Lord Hawksworth cut in. "That our father lacks the temperament to find suitable names for the children he sires. Nor will he allow anyone else to do it."

"My understanding is that he lacks temperament at all." Lady Tatiana said.

"Aunt—" Anna began, mortified at the woman's want of tact and kindness.

"Her ladyship does not offend me"—Lord Hawksworth nodded toward his brother—"or, I am sure, my brother. However, your aunt is incorrect. Our father does indeed have a temperament, all bad. It is a bane to his family."

The sound of violins being tuned floated across the ballroom ending the discussion, for which Anna was grateful. If anything was more awkward than this conversation, she had never experienced it.

"The set will be forming soon," Meg Hawksworth murmured, taking her husband's arm. "My lord?"

"My lady." Her husband bowed. "As always, it is my pleasure to stand up with you."

Her eyes sparkled, and Anna could see the deep love the Hawksworths had for each other. Despite everything her great aunt had tried to teach her over the past several months, that was what she wanted for herself. A man she could love who would love her in return.

Lord Quartus held out his arm to her. "Your Grace?"

"Thank you." She placed her hand on his arm, and he led her to where the other dancers were taking their places.

"This will be the first time I have waltzed with anyone other than my poor sister-in-law." He grimaced. "She took to wearing her riding boots until I stopped stepping on her toes."

Anna couldn't help but laugh. "This will be the first time I've danced the waltz with anyone other than my father and the dancing master. I believe that makes us even, my lord."

"The blind leading the blind' I shall try not to disgrace either of us."

They bowed and curtseyed. He placed one large palm on her waist, and held her hand with the other, as she placed her fingers on his shoulder. She was astonished at how comfortable she felt with his hands on her. Oh dear. She probably should not think of it in quite that way. She would most likely feel the same with any other gentleman. This was simply a new experience.

When they began to move, she was able to easily follow him. In fact, it was a little like floating on a cloud. A moving cloud. Then again, clouds did move.

For several moments, they did not speak. Each of them concentrating on their steps, then he grinned. "I think we're doing quite well for our first time."

"Yes, indeed." Anna let out the breath she'd been holding. "I shall have to thank your sister for the pain she suffered."

Lord Quartus barked a laugh, and heads turned toward them, but Anna didn't care. Not when his light blue eyes lit with so much joy, an emotion that seemed to be lacking in the *ton*.

"Tell me, my lord, why is this your first ball? I thought all young men spent time in London after their studies were completed."

"Most do," he replied in a dry tone that rang of what? Disapproval perhaps? "On the other hand, most are lucky enough not to have my father as their sire."

He did not elaborate as she hoped. That was the second reference to the duke, and neither of them had been good. Her interest was definitely piqued.

"I suppose it would be considered rude of me to ask more about the duke?"

"He is not a pleasant topic of conversation." Lord Quartus smiled but it was one of the forced polite smiles she detested. "Let us change the subject," he said. "Where are you from?"

Perhaps if she got to know him better he would confide in her. "The West Indies. Tortola to be precise."

"Truly?" Once again his countenance was alight. "How interesting. Did you always know you would become a duchess?"

Anna waited until they completed the turn before answering, "Not at all. It came as a complete shock, and I'm still not quite sure it was a welcome one."

"Do you mean you do not wish to be a duchess?"

"Well, there is not much sense in *not* wishing to be a duchess." She shrugged lightly. "It is not as if I have a choice. If I do not perform my duties"—one of which was to marry, but she would not tell him that—"my people and properties would suffer."

"You make a good point." Lord Quartus's forehead creased faintly. "I'm interested in how it came about. When Meg first mentioned your rank, I thought she was mistaken."

"Ah, well"—Anna began to pull her bottom lip between her teeth, but thought better of it as he twirled her around—"The title has been around since the time of the War of the Roses. Once of my ancestress performed a duty or favor—I am not sure I wish to know what it was—to the crown and she was made a duchess in her own right. Through the years, most of the children have been born female, and the title passed down through the ladies. Apparently, my great aunt had three girls. My grandmother, who was the next oldest, married and had my mother. To make a long story short, everyone on my side of the family seemed to have forgotten about the title. Strange I know. Although, to be fair, my mother died when I was a child. Perhaps if she had lived, she would have mentioned it. At the end of the day, the other heirs died without issue. Aunt Tatiana, the youngest of my grandmother's sisters, tracked me down, and here I am."

"Fascinating." His tone was quiet, thoughtful. "I suppose England is rather different from the West Indies."

"It is and much colder." Anna gave a dramatic shiver even though the ballroom was quite warm. "The society is different as well. Everyone knew me and, in turn, I knew everyone. There were no surprises. No worries that one misstep could harm one."

"I would love to visit the West Indies at some point." His voice was wistful, as if traveling could only be a dream.

"In that case, you should do so," Anna replied bracingly. It disturbed her that he seemed melancholy at times. Ladies always seemed to be constrained, but she had never met a gentleman who was so burdened. The music ended and he brought them to a stop with a flourish. "Nicely done, my lord. I greatly enjoyed dancing with you."

"And I you, Your Grace." For a long moment, his eyes seemed to search hers. "May I request the supper dance?"

"I would be delighted." A feeling of satisfaction welled inside her. She had not embarrassed herself with Lord Quartus, or he with her. She had been more than a bit concerned about this Season she was having, but all appeared to be smooth sailing. As long as a squall didn't come along to disrupt her, all would be well. She simply needed to fall in love with a man and wed him. The question she must start considering was what type of man would be the best match for her.

CHAPTER TWO

"COME, I'LL ESCORT YOU BACK to your aunt." Lord Quartus offered her his arm.

"Of course." Generally, Anna chafed at the close chaperonage she was under, she was not a young lady, yet this evening she had no desire to go wandering off by herself. That would likely change once she began to make friends.

When she and Lord Quartus reached her aunt, several gentlemen Anna had not previously met were standing about.

His lordship had no sooner taken his leave, when her aunt said, "Your Grace, may I introduce you to Lord Capell of Tewkesbury"—a baron then as the title was not mentioned—"My lord, my great-niece, the Duchess of Wharton."

"My lord." She held out her hand wondering why her aunt thought she would be interested in a portly older gentleman.

"His lordship has a son who was unable to attend this evening," Aunt commented.

Well, that explained that. Anna was about to respond when Aunt Tatiana continued. "You will be able to meet Mr. Capell at their ball later this week."

The next gentleman was much younger and tall with an ascetic look about him.

As he bowed, her aunt said, "Viscount Hatton."

Again she held out her hand. "A pleasure."

"May I hope you have a country dance available, Your Grace?"

"I do indeed," she replied as she retrieved her hand.

By the time the fifth gentleman, the Marquis of Markville, had been introduced, Anna was glad she had worn gloves. At least two of the men had left wet marks on her fingers, but, at least, not on her bare skin. All but Lord Capell claimed a set, and even though they danced well, she missed the easy conversation she'd had with Lord Quartus.

"May I have the next set?" Lord Markville regarded her with an almost proprietary air.

Anna gave a cursory glance at her dance card. As she suspected, the next set was the supper dance. "Unfortunately my card is full, my lord. Perhaps another time."

"You may count on it, Your Grace." His tone was hard, and although he bowed gracefully, he seemed angry.

Well, good. She did not like his attitude and made up her mind to stand up with his lordship as little as possible. What right had he to assume she would save a dance for a gentleman she did not even know?

"Who has claimed that one?" her aunt asked in a sharp tone once the marquis was out of hearing.

"Lord Quartus," she replied, trying not to look to see if she could see him.

Aunt Tatiana's lips scrunched up as if she had eaten a particularly sour lemon. "You'd do well to stay away from him.

"Good heavens, whatever for?" Anna tried not to let her exasperation show. Though she had not known her aunt for long, she had never seen the woman take an immediate dislike to anyone. Generally she was an extraordinarily fair woman. "He is an excellent dance partner."

"As long as that's all you want him for. There is bad blood in the Trevors. Mother's family is good enough.

Cunninghams. But the Dukes of Somerset act as if they are royalty."

Chances are they sprung from one king or another or a close association with one. Most dukes did. She would have liked to ask for more information, but Lord Quartus was almost upon them. "I would not worry yourself, Aunt. I have no designs upon him other than a waltz."

At four and twenty, she was old enough not to let a man turn her head. Even if he was handsome with curling blond hair, and summer blue eyes, and lips that curled nicely when he smiled.

He kept his eyes on her as he wove his way through the crowd.

"Lord Quartus"—she smiled as he approached—"you are in good time." Placing her hand on his arm, she glanced at her aunt. "I shall see you after supper."

The older lady harrumphed, but did not argue.

"I have the distinct impression that she does not care for me," he murmured.

"I believe it is your sire that she doesn't like." And all the other dukes before him.

A wicked grin appeared on his firm lips. "In that case, she is in excellent company. I can name a score of people from duchesses on down who loath my father. And, from what I can see and have been told, he brings it all upon himself. The problem seems to be being tarred with the same brush. I simply hope that those I meet understand I am much more like my older brother than my father."

"Yes, indeed. Well, if anyone should ask me, I shall speak up for you. What do you do when you are not in Town?"

"I am or was the rector of the church in the market town near one of my father's estates. As soon as I completed my education in the clergy, he placed me in one of his livings. I had not even attained the age of three and twenty."

She fought to keep her jaw from dropping. How could

such a strong, virile man be in the clergy? Well, there was the Pirate Priest on Tortola. Still, that was back home. None of the rectors and vicars she had met here looked like Lord Quartus. But what was he saying about age? "I beg your pardon? What does your age have to do with it?"

"Only that under the rules I was too young for the position. My father used his influence to get what he wanted."

"Do you like being a clergyman?"

He was silent for so long she thought he would not answer, then he said, "In many ways I do. I enjoy taking care of others. Nevertheless, I feel as if I am meant to do more." His fingers tightened on her waist, and for a moment she wished she could simply sink into him. That would cause her aunt to suffer apoplexy, and cause a scandal. Perhaps if she pretended to stumble she could feel how strong his arms actually were. "In what way?

"All of our lives my father's narrow view of politics has been force fed to us. Yet when I was at university, I became aware that I do not believe as my father does. Only Hawksworth is in a position to defy the duke by holding political parties. I would like to do more." His sharp blue eyes focused intently on her. "To help more people."

"That is an admirable ambition—" Anna would have said more, but the music stopped.

For a few moments longer, Lord Quartus held her as if he was not ready for the set to end. Truth be told, neither was she. And, although she had given her aunt to understand that she would sup with his lordship. He had not asked her.

"I believe," he said slowly, "it is customary for one to have supper with one's partner for the supper dance."

What a relief. "I believe you are correct." She tucked her arm in his. "Are we joining your brother and sister-in-law?"

"That would be best. From what Meg tells me, Hawksworth is an expert at ensuring they have the best of the delicacies on offer."

The duchess's eyes twinkled and a lovely smile graced her lips, and Quartus wished that he was in a position to see what could grow between them. But it could not be. He had heard what his father had done to both his brothers and their wives. Making a woman he loved go through possible abductions or being placed in compromising positions was not something he was willing to do. Not that he thought any lady could or would overlook his lack of wealth and property. Although he did not care for the idea, he would most likely end up single or married to a lady of his father's choosing. With luck, that would give him some measure of independence.

Once again he glanced at the duchess, and wanted to drag her into his arms. Whoever captured her heart would be a lucky man. Perhaps he had been born a few centuries too late. There was a time when younger sons could capture the lady of their choice.

They caught up with Meg and Hawksworth as they made their way down the stairs. "There you are. I was beginning to wonder if I would lose you in this crush."

"Knowing your appetite," Hawksworth said, "I did not doubt for a moment you would find us."

"Ah, yes. All this dancing has made me a bit peckish."

"I as well," her grace added, looking at Hawksworth. "I have been told that no one can best you at finding sustenance."

Meg laughed. "And I can attest that no one will go hungry with Hawksworth near them."

She launched into a story about the Christmas house party they had attended, and how, ever since his time in the Army, he made sure he had provisions.

Quartus was glad to see the duchess was enjoying

herself. Several moments later, he and his brother had found a table for them all. After the ladies were seated, they went off to the supper table.

"She appears to like your company," his brother commented in a low tone.

He glanced at Hawksworth who was regarding Quartus with that intent stare of his. "I am enjoying her company as well, but that is all there can be. She will look for a much more advantageous match than one to a penniless younger son."

"Perhaps she wishes to marry for love. That seems to be all the crack these days."

Love matches *had* gained in popularity. Although, many still believed they were vulgar and only for the lower classes. Certainly, his father did. Yes, after seeing his brother and Meg together, Quartus was beginning to think he would like a love match as well, but he wasn't counting on it. "You know as well as I that few of us will be able to wed whom we wish. Especially after you and Frank defied Father."

"Once you fall in love, you will understand we had no choice. But here is the supper table. Come, you'll feel better once you've eaten."

Quartus followed Hawksworth's lead in selecting the best of the offerings. Soon they were making their way, two footmen in tow, back to the table where the ladies had their heads close together.

"The conquering heroes have returned," Hawksworth said in a jovial tone.

"Excellent!" Meg sat back from the table allowing the footmen to place the various dishes down. "I am famished."

"As am I." The duchess's eyes grew wider as each plate was positioned. "Goodness, what a lot of food!"

"I did tell you that Hawksworth lives in dread of starving." Meg motioned for her husband to sit next to her as if he would really take any other chair.

Quartus sat next to her grace and commenced to help her find the foods she would most enjoy before filling his own plate. "Somehow, I do not think there will be much left."

While they dined, the duchess entertained them with stories of living in the West Indies. Hawksworth talked of his travels to Greece where he had met his mother's family for the first time.

"I have been nowhere of interest." Meg pulled a face. "What about you Quartus?"

"I suffer from the same fate. Once Hawksworth was gone, father kept the rest of us close until Nonus began acting up. He was the only one other than Hawksworth to be sent to the Army."

"Nonus?" Her grace's brows rose. "You were serious about your father numbering his children."

"Only the boys." Quartus took a sip of the excellent champagne. "I think our mother would have defied him if he had attempted to number the girls. Although, the first three are named for the three graces. Nonus is Octavius's twin, but their temperaments are vastly different."

"Do you see him often?"

"Not as much as we would like. Now that the war is over, he has got himself attached to the embassy in Paris." Quartus seldom found himself talking about his family, but it seemed natural to tell her about them. "I think he would like to go farther afield, but the duke would have a fit, and Nonus does not want our father interfering in his career."

"Not as much of a fit as if he found a French lady to marry," Hawksworth added drily.

"If Father even suspected something of that sort of thing occurring," Quartus said, "Our brother would find himself firmly on British soil. And Nonus is well aware of that fact."

The duchess set her glass down. "I must say, I am not at all sure I can blame my aunt for disliking him as she does. He seems to be a thoroughly disagreeable man."

"If only you know the half of it," Meg muttered, mostly under her breath. "What"—her voice rose cheerily—"have you seen of London?"

Oh, no! That was how Meg managed to throw his brother Frank together with Jenny. She was not going to try her matchmaking on him. "I'm sure her grace has more important things to do than sightsee."

"I am quite busy, but I would love to see the marbles I have heard so much about. In fact, I believe it is my duty to visit them." She slid a look toward him. "If only not to be considered provincial."

"Excellent." Meg clapped her hands together. "Perhaps the day after tomorrow you will be available for a tour of the museum."

The duchess tilted her head to the side for a few moments, then said, "I am indeed free at eleven in the morning."

"Quartus, you may take my curricle." He could not read anything in his brother's face, but the meaning was clear. Start getting to know the lady. "I trust you remember how to drive it."

"It hasn't been that long." Frank had shown up in the carriage when he was looking for help rescuing Jenny from one of their father's abduction attempts. Quartus had put them on the stage coach to London. The next day, he had driven the curricle to Hawksworth's house.

"It is all settled then." Meg had a satisfied look on her face. "You should visit Gunter's for an ice afterward."

"What a fabulous idea!" her grace cried. "I have been wanting to taste them."

Quartus almost groaned. How could his brother and sister-in-law not see how impossible a match between the duchess and him would be? Yet, there was nothing else to do but smile politely. "I would be delighted."

"BELLING, BRING ME THE LIST. Thornfield was at a ball last evening and noticed Lord Quartus in the company of a woman who will do me no good at all. He waltzed with her twice."

"Two waltzes." Belling's eyes widened. "Extraordinary. I shall have it in a moment."

Somerset waited while his secretary trotted off to find the folder. The Whitestones had caused enough trouble for his family. None of the women acted properly, especially the duchesses. If they had, the Wharton duchy would have been part of the Somerset holdings. Seething at the insult, the Duke of Somerset waited as his secretary fetched the folder containing the names of ladies he considered suitable for Quartus. A lady who knew her place and brought something to increase the wealth or the dukedom. Damn the Duchesses of Wharton. The last one had been a thorn in his side. Women had no right being peeresses in their own right. It went against the natural order of things.

Once the folder lay open before him he settled in to make his choice and saw what he wanted to find. A lady who was content to remain in the country, approaching her last prayers, and had something he wanted. Ah, there. He placed his finger on a name. She came with a property that bordered his Surrey holding. "Lady Sarah Martin should be suitable."

"Isn't she a bit quiet to be a rector's wife, Your Grace?"

"Quite. However, I have decided Quartus should take over Francis's old duties as my steward."

"Ah, yes. In that case she is perfect. I understand that

she does not care to be in company."

"I shall approach Markville. He'll probably be glad to have the girl off his hands."

Less than an hour later, Somerset received the reply he'd wanted. "Send a note to Lord Quartus that he is to call on Lady Sarah tomorrow at ten o'clock."

"Straightaway, Your Grace."

His secretary left the study, and Somerset leaned back in his chair. Markville's missive had been short and to the point. Foreseeing a mutual benefit to both families, he would be happy to entertain a union between their two houses provided Lord Quartus and Lady Sarah agreed.

Somerset scowled. He'd make damn sure Quartus agreed. Markville would have to bring his sister around.

A few minutes later, Belling placed a piece of pressed paper in front of Somerset.

His Grace, the Duke of Somerset
Somerset House
Mayfair
My dear Quartus,
I have found a suitable wife for you.
You shall meet with her tomorrow at ten in the morning at Markville House in St. James Square.
Do not disappointment me.

Somerset signed the letter. "Have a footman take this around. Then contact Mrs. Grayson."

"The actress, Your Grace?" Belling's tone indicated his shock. "I thought you had decided not to keep a mistress this Season. I am positive we let the house you used."

"Not as my lady-bird. I'm too old to have need of another one. I have a role for her to play." One that would guarantee his fourth son married where Somerset wished.

Chapter Three

"HAVE YOU EVEN BEEN INTRODUCED to Lady Sarah?" Concern colored Meg's voice as she held a note from his father in her hand. "She is said to be quite reclusive."

They had been sitting down to tea when the letter arrived. After Quartus had read it, he'd handed it to Meg and Damon. Her glower had managed to dim even the bright yellow morning room, and Quartus had no doubt that she was holding back some very colorful descriptions of his father.

"No, never." She handed the heavy pressed paper back to him, and he glanced down at his father's command. "I suppose I should be happy he has not ordered me to propose on the spot." He suppressed a sigh. It was not as if he hadn't expected the duke to do something of this sort. His father had been furious that Damon and Frank had chosen their own brides. Yet, ladies such as Meg and Jenny, an American heiress, were few and far between.

"Well." His sister-in-law huffed. "I think it is quite gothic."

"Meg, my love." Damon placed a restraining hand on her arm. "Quartus is only going to meet the lady, and arranged matches are still made all the time."

"That may very well be, but Quartus has an engagement to take Anna Wharton to the museum at eleven. The least your father could have done was to have asked what time was convenient for him." He opened his lips to tell his sister-in-law that he intended to cancel that meeting, but Meg held up a finger, forestalling him. "Do not even think about crying off. You will simply have to explain to Lady Sarah that you had prior plans and cannot stay long."

That would actually work well. Particularly in the event that she took an immediate dislike to him or he to her. "An excellent idea, Meg. I shall do precisely that." Wishing to change the subject, he asked, "Do we have an event to attend this evening?"

"My mother's ball." She shook her head in disgust. "I have, repeatedly, told you and Hawksworth we shall attend, and that you, both of you, will be required to help ensure that all the ladies who wish to dance have partners."

"That, my dear, is your brother, Kit's, forte." Hawksworth slipped his arm around her shoulders. "I intend to remain next to my beautiful wife."

Her lips tipped up, but she gave him narrow-eyed look just the same. "Flattery will not help you this evening my love."

"In that case, I insist I be allowed to save my waltzes for you."

"If you must." Her voice held a note of exasperation, but she was smiling.

What would it be like to have a love that deep? And not only love but a friendship with one's spouse? A tightness formed in Quartus's chest. Unfortunately, he would probably never know. Without his father's financial support, he could not afford to marry.

"You said she was reclusive?" he asked, wanting to figure out why his father had chosen Lady Sarah.

Meg's brow scrunched up. "The last time I saw her in Town was when she first came out." With her finger, she tapped her chin. "Very nice and not at all shy, which is the reason I was surprised when she did not come up for the Little Season or the next Season. There was no mention of her marriage. I was astonished when you said she was here now for I have not seen her anywhere, not even during morning visits. I wonder what the reason could be."

"I would like to know what benefit the duke will receive from the match," Damon added dryly.

Meg gave a sharp nod. "As would I. He must be benefiting from it in some way."

Clearly Quartus's brother and sister-in-law were much more up to snuff than he was. "What do you mean? I am so far down the line when it comes to inheritance there is nothing to be gained from my marriage. I am almost surprised that Father is arranging one for me."

Damon rose, holding his hand out for Meg. "Mark my words. He stands to gain. Whether it is political influence, or something else, he does nothing that does not cause an advantage for himself."

"Markville as well," Meg said as she shook out her skirts. "From what I have seen, they are cut from the same cloth. I agree. I would dearly like to know what it is." She picked up the last ginger biscuit from the tray. "In the meantime, we must dress. We are due at my parents' house in two hours."

Quartus found that he was actually looking forward to dinner and the ball. His brother had assured him her family was easy to be around, and he had reserved a dance with the Duchess of Wharton as well. Although, marriage was out of the question, he did enjoy speaking with her and standing up with her. He even looked forward to tweaking her aunt. Although, he couldn't say why he did. Possibly because no one had ever thought of him as dangerous before. One could not gain a reputation as a rake or an out and outer as a rector, and he rather liked that she did not see him as a safe clergyman. As long as the woman didn't liken him to his father again, he would be happy.

Then again, it could be because his father had settled on

a match for him, his time to do as he wished was drawing short.

Whatever the reason, Quartus was determined to take advantage of his freedom while it lasted.

ANNA, ACCOMPANIED BY HER FATHER and aunt, was bowed into Featherton House by their butler. "Your Grace."

Once he'd taken her outerwear—she was still chilly in England—as well as her father's hat and cane, and her aunt's evening cloak, they were shown into a drawing room.

"The Duchess of Wharton, Lady Tatiana Whitestone, and Mr. Calder."

"Welcome, Your Grace." Lady Featherton glided forward to greet them. "Lady Tatiana, I am delighted to see you again. My mother-in-law will be present this evening, and Mr. Calder, how lovely to meet you." Lady Featherton took Anna's arm. "I believe you know everyone who is here at the moment. Would you like a glass of sherry?"

"Yes, please." Anna glanced around the room as she accepted the small goblet of wine.

The gathering was smaller than she had expected, and she did, indeed, know all the women. She smiled to the others, but, for some reason, her gaze was drawn to Lord Quartus. He was dressed in a navy blue jacket and breeches, and snowy white linen. His red vest was embroidered in silver, and the only fobs he wore were a quizzing glass and a pocket watch.

The man was standing by one of two window seats, speaking with Lady Evesham and Lady Rutherford. She had met the women during morning visits.

He turned, and his eyes met hers making her heart

flutter. It was the first time since Aaron, her former betrothed, had died that she felt warm toward a man. Once more, she decided to take the initiative, and strolled toward the small coterie.

The ladies curtseyed deeply, and Lord Quartus bowed. "Oh dear." Anna didn't know if she would ever become used to ladies curtseying to her in that manner. "Good evening."

Lady Evesham's blue eyes twinkled. "I understand it will be a while before you are at ease accepting you due. It will come." She signaled to someone across the room. "For now, I believe I have a surprise for you."

A tall broad-shouldered man sauntered toward them, and Anna gasped. "Lord Marcus! How wonderful to see you again."

"Lord Evesham now, Your Grace." Taking Lady Evesham's hand he grinned. "I have been told you already met my wife."

"Yes, indeed." A memory or rather a ship stirred in Anna's mind. "This is Lady Phoebe?"

"As you see." The lady herself blushed as Marcus brought her hand to his lips. "But tell me, why did I not hear about you being heir to a duchy before now?"

Anna told him what had occurred. "I have to say, I feel much more . . . Oh, I don't know, at home seeing you here."

"In that case, you will be happy to know there is one other of our friends from Tortola in England as well."

"I heard Emma Spencer-Jones married a Harry Marsh, but I haven't seen her."

"The youngest child was not feeling well," Lady Rutherford said. "Causing them to delay their travel to Town. Harry and Emma should be here tomorrow or the next day." A playful smile hovered on Lady Rutherford's lips. "Emma is my sister-in-law."

Tears of joy pricked Anna's eyelids. "Despite what my aunt tells me, I think it is appropriate for us all to be on a first name basis. I sincerely hope that Marcus and Emma will *not* remember to call me 'your grace.' Which will make it awkward for everyone else."

"An excellent idea, in gatherings such as this," Phoebe Evesham said gently. "However, you are too new to the role to let down your defenses as it were."

A few minutes after the exchange of first names, a striking lady with deep auburn hair accompanied by a gentleman with a face that reminded Anna of a Greek or Roman bust entered the room, followed by two more couples.

"Robert and Serena, Viscount and Vicountess Beaumont, Caro and Gervais, Earl and Countess of Huntley, and Will and Eugénie, Viscount and Viscountess Wivenly," Meg, who was standing next to Anna, whispered. "The only ones of our group unable to attend are Matt and Grace, the Earl and Countess of Worthington, and Rupert and Vivian, the Earl and Countess of Stanstead."

Anna could not keep a broad smile from her face as the others were introduced. It appeared as if she was being drawn into a close group of friends, something she desperately needed and wanted. "Did you all grow up together?"

"The gentlemen knew each other, and many of the ladies did as well," Meg explained. "Eugénie and Emma were imported from the West Indies. Eugénie is of French origin, but had been living in St. Thomas . . ."

By the time dinner was announced, Anna felt as if she had made fast friends with the ladies, and was delighted she no longer felt alone in England.

"Will you allow me to escort you into dinner?" Quartus winged out his arm. "I have discovered it is the custom among this group to dine informally. I believe that is the reason we are so few."

"Thank you." She glanced up as he looked down. Her heart jumped again. *Could I truly be falling in love with him?* No, it was much too soon. "I . . . I am glad to be included."

"As am I." She searched his face. Was it longing she saw there? "I haven't had so many companions since I left Oxford." Something else that could probably be laid at the Duke of Somerset's door. "Leaving your family behind permanently could not have been easy for you. I am happy Meg and Hawksworth have introduced you to their friends."

The warmth she felt for him grew hotter. "And you as well. You have made me feel very welcome."

"That was easy," he said in a voice only for her. "Not only are you a beautiful lady, you are a delight to dance and speak with."

It had been a long time since a gentleman had told her she was beautiful. The last man was Aaron. "Thank you. May I say you look vastly handsome."

Lord Quartus smiled down at her as if she was the only person in the room. The only woman who mattered to him. "And thank you."

"Grandmamma and Duchess!" Meg exclaimed, as Anna and Quartus were nearing the dining room.

"I think"—Quartus placed his fingers over her hand—"we are about to be entertained."

After everything Aunt Tatiana had said about duchesses being regal and staid, Anna was at a loss as to how a duchess could be entertaining. "I do not understand."

"You are about to meet the Dowager Lady Featherton, Meg's grandmother, and the Duchess of Bridgewater, Lady Featherton's bosom friend." He'd placed his lips close to Anna's ear, causing a pleasurable tingle on her neck. "They were instrumental in Meg and Damon being able to wed."

That would be an interesting tale. "How so?"

"It is not really my story to tell. Suffice it to say that they foiled my father's plot."

A very interesting tale. Perhaps Meg would tell her. "I look forward to meeting them."

He guided Anna to two chairs near his brother and sister-in-law, yet before she was able to take her seat, a lady who was sixty if she was a day, pointed at her. "You must be the new Duchess of Wharton. You are the image of your mother."

"That she is, Your Grace." Father held out a chair for Aunt. "The years have treated you well."

"John Calder." The Duchess of Bridgewater held out a be-ringed hand. "I never thought to see you again."

Going to the older woman, he bowed. "You wouldn't have if things had turned out differently. I'm very happy in Tortola. As soon as I have Anna settled, I'll return."

"I had no idea that my parents moved in such exalted circles," she said in a low voice.

Quartus led her to two chairs near the head of the table. "I have a feeling that if we simply listen, we'll learn a great deal."

"There is nothing those two old ladies don't know about the ton," Damon said from her other side.

"Anna, my dear." Her father's voice brought her attention back to the older ladies. "May I introduce her grace the Duchess of Bridgewater, and the Dowager Vicountess Featherton? Your Grace, Lady Featherton, my daughter Anna, as you correctly surmised, Duchess of Wharton."

"I look forward to getting to know you," the duchess said. "If you ever need help with anything, feel free to call on me."

The elder Lady Featherton's eyes warmed. "I do as well, my dear." She glanced at Papa and chuckled. "We'll tell you all the secrets you'll need to know."

Anna's aunt closed her eyes as if she was in pain, and her father groaned, she couldn't hold back a giggle. "I shall look forward to it, my lady."

If only she had met all these new gentlemen before she had accepted Lord Markville's request for a set this evening. However, when he had arrived during visiting hours the other day, she had not been certain her card would be full by this evening. Anna sighed to herself. She still could not like the man. He appeared cold, and preoccupied, as if nothing was going the way he wished it would. Even his blue eyes reminded her of the ice pond she had seen at Wharton. Nothing at all like the warm light blue of Quartus's eyes. Still, there was no real harm in him. She did wonder if he was as stiff on the dance floor as he had been in her drawing room. Then again, she was only standing up with the man. It was not as if she was inundated with gentleman clamoring to dance with her. There must be something about being a duchess that was off putting. She would enjoy herself this evening, and look forward to her outing with Lord Quartus tomorrow. If her feelings for him continued to grow, her hunt for a husband might be short indeed.

CHAPTER FOUR

A FIRM KNOCK ON THE DOOR of Lady Sarah Martin's parlor, heralded her brother's imminent entrance, she tucked the letter she had received from her betrothed between the cushions of the small sofa.

"Sarah."

Rising quickly, she turned to face Markville, who was several years her senior. "Good morning. What brings you here, and why are you unable to wait until I give you leave to come in?"

Oh dear. Now he was scowling.

"It is my house, and what would you be doing that requires privacy?" He glanced around the room as if she had a lover hidden somewhere.

"Never mind." If he was not going to make the effort to be polite, she saw no reason to placate him. He had not even explained his reasoning for uprooting her from the country and bringing her to Town. Which was the last place she wished to be. Instead of being allowed to ramble where she wished, and swim in the stream, and breathe clean air, she was forced to be escorted everywhere or remain in the house. "What is it you want?"

"You will have a visitor at ten this morning."

She gave her head a little shake. "No one knows I'm in Town. How could I possibly have a visitor?"

"I have received an offer of marriage from the Duke of Somerset to his son, Lord Quartus. He is coming to meet you."

Biting down hard on the inside of her lip, Sarah resisted the urge to throw something large and hard at her brother's head. She could not, however, hide her exasperation. "Has it escaped your memory that I am already betrothed and have been for almost four years?"

"Not at all." Markville gave her his I-am-in-charge-of-you-now-look. "You, though, appear to have forgotten that unless your erstwhile *fiancé* marries you on or before your twenty-first birthday, you agreed to marry where your family chooses. *I* am that family, and I have decided you will wed Lord Quartus."

Plopping back down on the sofa, she crossed her arms over her chest. "You are being medieval."

"No. I am doing exactly as I promised our father I would do." Flipping his pocket watch open, her brother strolled back to the door. "And if you want your inheritance, you must wed within one month of attaining your majority." Ah, yes. The inheritance her father and now her brother said she would have, but gave her no other information. Hence, she had no idea what this wonderful inheritance entailed. "I might have taken a different tack if you had come to Town over the years for the Season, or tried to find another husband. You have not. Not to mention that Jeremy Bellingham has not contacted me at all. Aside from that, I plan to wed in the very near future, and I do not desire my wife to have to chaperone you. I met Lord Quartus last evening. He is a very good match for a lady who has made herself a recluse."

"Does he wish to wed me?" She could not believe that in these modern times a gentleman would consent to marry a woman sight unseen, and at his father's behest. Even if the father was a duke.

"He will do as he is told." In that case, this Lord Quartus did not sound like a gentleman she wished to marry. A spineless man was not for her.

Markville lifted the door latch. She had meant to be silent. Instead she blurted out. "Jeremy and I love each other. He *will* be back in time."

"Oh?" Her brother said in a voice that made a cold shiver run down her back. "And have you heard from him recently?"

Ignoring the missive hidden in the sofa, she lied, "No, but I know he will come."

"It may be better for him if he does not. You, of all people know I did not favor this arrangement."

The door closed behind him, and Sarah placed her hand on her chest, trying to still the beating. All these years she had never given it much thought, but now she was glad that when her father had died she told Jeremy to write to her in care of her old nurse. Taking the letter out, she reviewed the short note.

My darling Sarah,
I have arrived back in England. I must remain in Plymouth for the next week or so sorting out business, but I will be with you before your birthday. Special license in hand. Write to me at the Ship as soon as you receive this letter.
All my love forever,
Yr servant,
Jeremy

Somehow she must send a letter to him warning him not to approach her brother and informing him that she was no longer on her family's estate in the country. But who could she trust? Not poor Mrs. Potter, her companion. Sarah would have to find someone else to help her escape Markville and marry Jeremy.

She glanced at the gilded mantel clock. There was not much time. She had just over an hour to figure out how to let Lord Quartus down before he arrived.

Quartus presented himself at number twelve St. James Square a few minutes before ten. It was not until he had talked with Meg this morning that he knew it was the residence of Lord Markville. That then, begged the question why the man had not discussed the proposed marriage between Lady Sarah and Quartus last evening when they had been introduced.

The door swung open immediately, and he was faced with a butler every bit as imposing as his father's. "Lord Quartus, I presume."

He inclined his head the slightest bit. "Indeed."

The butler bowed. "If you will follow me, my lord, Lord Markville is waiting for you."

The servant led Quartus into a front drawing room where Markville stood, hands clasped behind his back, staring out the window overlooking the square.

"Lord Quartus Trevor, my lord." Bowing, the butler withdrew, closing the door behind him.

The man turned and looked at him, but he could tell nothing from Markville's expression. "Lord Quartus, welcome. Lady Sarah will be down shortly. However, there is a matter I would like to discuss first."

Was it possible that the marquis did not want his sister to marry him? Quartus raised one brow. "That would be?"

"I have noticed that you are spending a good deal of time with the Duchess of Wharton."

Now he knew what was bothering Markville. He must think that Quartus would hurt Lady Sarah. "She is a friend of my sister-in-law's. Naturally, I am frequently in her company."

"It is good that there is nothing more. I intend to marry the duchess."

He wondered if Anna knew about Markville's plans,

but before he could respond a lady who looked to be in her late sixties fluttered into the room, positioning and repositioning the several shawls she wore. "Don't mind me, my lord."

Markville looked as if he wanted to roll his eyes. "Mrs. Potter, may I introduce Lord Quartus. My lord, my cousin, Mrs. Potter. She is Lady Sarah's companion."

"Lady Sarah will be here straightaway, my lord." The woman gave Markville a look that reminded Quartus of a wary horse before settling into a chair in the far corner of the room that seemed to have been positioned there just for her.

A moment later, a tall, slender lady with dark brown hair joined them casting a glare at her brother as she walked by him.

"Sarah," Markville said in a bored tone. "I'm glad you could finally join us. May I introduce Lord Quartus Trevor?"

She held out her hand and he bowed over it, barely touching her fingers with his. Yet he felt none of the warmth or pleasure that he felt when he touched the Duchess of Wharton's hands. Perhaps it would come. He hoped it would. If not, this would be a very cold and unsatisfying union.

"It is a pleasure to meet you, my lord."

"I will leave you now." Markville lost no time striding out of the room.

"Well," Lady Sarah huffed. "It appears I must apologize for my brother."

His behavior was odd. One would think Markville would wish to become acquainted with his sister's prospective husband. But Quartus was not about to point out to the lady what she already knew. Calling on his years of being a rector, he set about smoothing her obviously ruffled feathers. "Think nothing of it. I have several brothers and can attest to their forgetting the most important things at the most inappropriate times."

She smiled briefly, then glanced to her cousin in the corner. "It is a lovely day. Would you like to walk in the square?"

"That sounds wonderful." He resisted the urge to look at his pocket watch. "But I am afraid I cannot—I apologize. This is very awkward. I had already made an appointment for eleven this morning when I was told to be here at ten."

"A short stroll, then." She ducked her head into the hall. "Please bring my spencer, gloves, and bonnet."

Something was going on, for in no time at all, she practically dragged him out the door and into the square. Once they were far enough away from her brother's house and from any others who could hear their conversation she came to a halt. "My lord, I am terribly sorry to have wasted your time, but I cannot marry you."

Unless she had taken him into immediate dislike, which did not seem to be the case, something else was indeed going on. "May I ask the reason?"

She studied him for a few moments. "Can you keep a confidence?"

Quartus would have grinned if she had not appeared so worried. "I am a clergyman, Lady Sarah. Keeping secrets is my . . . stock-in-trade, as it were. Your secret is safe with me."

"I did not know." Nodding, she took a breath. "But thank you for telling me. This is very awkward for you see I am already betrothed and have been for four years. But, my brother has never liked the match." In very short order, she explained how her engagement had come about and the terms of it. "I recently received a letter from my betrothed—"

"However, you are concerned that your brother may attempt to interfere."

"Precisely. Particularly after what he said this morning. I am even afraid that he will do something to harm . . . my betrothed."

After hearing the warmth in her voice when she spoke of her as yet unnamed intended, Quartus felt as if he had made an escape. Not from anything in particular, but an escape nonetheless. Perhaps he was not as resolved to a match made by his father as he thought he was. One thing was for certain. He would do everything in his power to help this lady and her lover. "Tell me what I can do to aid you."

"Well"—her brows drew together for an instant—"I must get a letter to my betrothed as soon as possible. He does not know I am in Town."

That was easily taken care of. "Consider it done. I shall take you driving tomorrow morning. Bring the missive with you."

For the first time a smile graced her face. She was very pretty, but nothing in her features affected him the way Anna Wharton did. "What a good idea. That will make my brother think that you are courting me as well."

It would make the duke think the same thing, which could only be of benefit to Quartus. "That will most likely help."

They continued to stroll, but this time he did look at his watch. "I only have a few minutes left. Shall I see you home?"

"If you please, and when we return, you may kiss my hand." She had a wicked twinkle in her eyes. "Markville is sure to hear of it."

It was clear she did not trust her brother. Yet was there more than his dislike of the match that made her feel threatened? "What do you think your brother would do if he discovered your betrothed was already back in England?"

"I am not sure." She shook her head. "It is more of a feeling really. As I said, he does not wish me to marry Jeremy, and I believe he will do anything to stop the wedding. I must find a way to either meet Jeremy here or go elsewhere."

Quartus had heard too many people, particularly women, talk about the 'feelings' they got which turned out to be facts to question her conclusions. "By the way, when is your birthday?"

"In three weeks. It is imperative that we work fast."

"Let me give it some thought." At this point, he did not have a clue what he would do. Still . . . "Do you mind if I take my sister-in-law into our confidence? She is very good at thinking of solutions."

Lady Sarah bit her bottom lip. "Are you sure she can be trusted?"

He gave a bark of laughter. "Absolutely. She is convinced everyone should have a love match."

"Very well." She glanced at him, a shy smile on her face. "Thank you. Even though you are a rector, I took a chance in trusting you. I find it hard to believe our vicar at home would have kept this to himself."

She was likely correct. Many vicars did not wish to anger the peers who held their livings. Quartus had always held the belief that a member of the clergy should answer only to God, his conscience, and, perhaps, his bishop. "And I thank you for it."

Quartus escorted Lady Sarah to her door, and dutifully kissed her fingers in full sight of the butler. "I shall see you in the morning, my lady."

"Until then, my lord."

He waited until she was in the house before retrieving Damon's curricle from the groom walking the horses. As soon as he was finished taking the duchess to the museum, he would speak with Meg about Lady Sarah.

He arrived in Grosvenor's Square as the church bells struck eleven o'clock. Thanking the Fates that he'd made it in time to take Anna to the museum.

Before he could knock on the door it opened. Anna stood in the hall drawing on a pair of tan leather gloves. She glanced up at him and her smile made him wish she would always look at him as if she would never require another gentleman.

"Good morning." He bowed as she strolled to him, and he could not resist giving her an answering grin.

"Good day to you." She placed her hand on his arm, and he had to fight the urge to kiss her and keep on kissing her.

Whatever was happening to him he had to stop before she found the gentleman who would be her husband. He just hoped she did not choose Markville. For some reason, Quartus could not see her being happy with him, and her happiness was all he wanted.

"I cannot wait to see the marbles."

He just wanted to spend more time with her. Which was a problem he did not know how to solve. Perhaps he should simply enjoy the time they had together. Soon, he would be back at his father's estate. Then again, he really did not wish to be there or anywhere around the duke. Maybe he could approach his bishop about being recommended for a living overseas. He would not mind traveling. He could even go to America where Frank and Jenny were. All he had to do was to keep thinking of options to being under his father's boot.

He helped her up into the seat, then went around to the other side.

CHAPTER FIVE

"YOU LOOK TO BE IN an excellent mood, Quartus," Anna commented as she situated herself in the carriage.

After threading the ribbons around his fingers he gave the horses their office to start. "I have been put in the way of doing someone a good deed, and that always makes me happy."

"I can see that." She tried not to frown. Anna would have been much happier if he had said she was the reason he was in such a good mood. "Is it something you are able to talk about?"

"Unfortunately, it is not my tale to tell."

That was disappointing, but it was more important that he keep a confidence than speak to her about it. Perhaps someday he would trust her not to repeat anything he told her. "In that case, I may discuss the weather. It is a very fine day."

"The weather?" When he glanced at her he had such a boyish grin on his face, her heart stopped for a moment. "It is a lovely day. It is a shame we must spend it in doors."

"If it was not for the marbles, I would happily go elsewhere." She waited for him to make a suggestion, when he did not she said, "Perhaps we may plan a drive to Richmond. I hear it has beautiful grounds."

His grip on the reins seemed to tighten. "I have not been."

Anna pursed her lips. It seemed as if she always had

to make the first move with him. Totally unlike Lord Markville. "There are so many things neither of us have seen. Would you like to take in the sights together?"

"Are you sure?" His look of surprise almost made her laugh. "I thought you—well Meg seemed to be . . ."

Did he not know how appealing he was? Not only was he handsome, with his blond curls and clear blue eyes, but he was kind as well. She knew how hard that could be to find in a strong man. "Very sure. Your sister may have made the suggestion, but I was in full agreement."

"I did purchase a guidebook. Perhaps we could read through it and decide which attractions we would like to see."

Anna smiled to herself. This was much more promising. What confused her was why Quartus did not have more confidence—no that wasn't right. He had confidence in himself and his accomplishments. Only when it came to her did he seem a bit shy. It was almost as if he did not seem to think he had much to offer a lady. And truthfully, if she was a normal lady, one who needed to be supported, he might be correct. However, she was not, and she did not want a husband who would decide to subsume her duchy in his holdings. Or believe that as a mere woman, she was incapable of running her holdings. She had read the settlement agreements of the previous two duchesses, and it was made very clear that her future husband would have no part in her estates that she did not wish to give.

That was what bothered her about Markville. From the comments he had made last evening, he thought she *needed* a man to look after her. It was almost as if he expected her to be grateful that he was interested in her. Fortunately, her new friends had effectively hindered the man's apparent determination to stay by her side all evening.

What Anna needed was a gentleman who was strong enough and self-confident enough to support her as she performed her duties. Not take them from her.

They had arrived at the museum, and Quartus flipped a coin to the boy who came running over. "Take care of these fellows and there is another one for you when we return."

"Is he trustworthy?"

"So my brother told me when I asked him what to do with the rig when I got here." He lifted her down from the carriage as if she weighed nothing, which she knew wasn't true. She might be short, but she was not skinny. "I think it would be better for the child if he could be trained as a groom."

"I agree." Anna placed her hand on Quartus's arm. "There is much I would like to do."

"You are in a position to make changes," he replied rather wistfully.

Now was her chance to find out more about his ideals. "Given the opportunity, what would you do?"

"Save the world, or, at least, my small part of it." He gave her a rueful look. "Seriously?"

She nodded.

"I would make sure that no family under my care went hungry or lived in squalor. I also believe in education for the masses." He handed the fee to the porter. "That is not a very popular idea in some circles."

From what she had heard last night, Quartus's views marched with the people Meg had introduced her to at Lady Featherton's. He must be referring to his father. "On the other hand, it is very popular in other circles."

He set her carefully on her feet, placing her hand on his arm. "I think you'll like the Elgin Marbles. They are all everyone has been talking about."

"So I have heard. One is made to appear provincial if one has not visited them at least once." She rested her fingers lightly on his arm, even though she would have preferred to hold on with both hands.

He paid the small fee at the entrance before guiding her unerringly to the famous artifacts. "I never thought there were so many!"

"Yes, it's as if Lord Elgin shipped back most of the artifacts in Europe. The Greeks are already asking that those belonging to their country be returned."

Anna studied the sculptures and other pieces that clearly came off buildings. "Do you think they will be sent back?"

"Not after the price our government paid for them."

"I have to say, some of my enjoyment in seeing them is lost. It is as if I'm looking at stolen goods."

Lord Quartus leaned closer to her and now her stomach behaved like butterflies had taken up permanent residence. "I agree, but we mustn't say anything. It would be considered not *the thing*. They are here to be admired, not criticized."

As she and Quartus made their way out of the exhibit, she somehow bumped into a woman, causing the lady's book to fall. "Oh. I am terribly sorry." Before Anna could bend down, Quartus had already retrieved the book and handed it back to the woman.

"It is no bother at all." The lady gave them a friendly smile. "As a matter of fact, I am sure I was to blame. I was paying too much attention to the guidebook and not enough to where I was going."

The woman glanced briefly at Quartus, then back to Anna. "Allow me to introduce myself. I am Mrs. Grayson."

"I am the Duchess of Wharton, and this"—she motioned to Quartus—"is Lord Quartus Trevor."

"Your Grace." Mrs. Grayson curtseyed deeply. "It is a pleasure to meet you."

"You as well," Anna replied. "Perhaps we shall see each other again."

"I do hope so," Mrs. Grayson said then walked into the

room.

Anna and Quartus began ambling back toward the entrance. "She was very nice."

"Yes," he answered absently.

"Is anything wrong?"

"No, no. Not at all. It is just that the name sounded familiar." He paused as if to figure out a puzzle. "Yet there are no Graysons living near my home, so I don't know where I could have heard of the name."

"Maybe while you've been here?" she suggested.

He gave a relieved grin. "You must be right."

"Now"—giving in to her desire to touch him more intimately she wrapped her hands around his arm, drawing closer to him—"What shall we do tomorrow?"

"WELL?" MEG SAT ON THE edge of the loveseat as Quartus strolled through the morning room door behind a footman delivering a large tray with tea and other sustenance.

"You'd better tell her quickly," Hawksworth drawled. "She has been on tenterhooks all morning."

He ducked as the cushion his wife threw sailed by his head.

Quartus chuckled, but quickly grew serious. With any luck, his problem with Lady Sarah would distract his sister from Anna Wharton. "Meg, I need your help. Or rather Lady Sarah does."

Meg began to pour, and he noticed there were not three cups on the tray, but five. The door to the garden opened, and in walked her grandmother and the Duchess of Bridgewater.

"You have done a lovely job with the garden, my dear."

Lady Featherton smiled beatifically.

"Mary gave me a great many ideas when she and Kit were in Town." Meg handed the older ladies cups of tea before placing some small sandwiches and biscuits on two plates for them. "Quartus, what does Lady Sarah need?"

"The problem was told to me in confidence." He glanced at Lady Featherton and the duchess. "I should not speak of it to anyone but you."

Hawksworth gave a short laugh, and Meg grinned. "If anyone knows how to keep a secret it is my grandmother and the duchess."

"They are also experts in arranging matches," Hawksworth added.

"Indeed, my dear Quartus," Lady Feather said. "We are completely reliable. Now, how can we assist you?"

Quartus regarded the older ladies. It was true that Lady Sarah had not given him permission to include them in her confidence, but Meg was correct. If not for these two ladies, she and his brother would not be wed. Yet, was it his decision to make?

"Open your budget, brother." Damon lowered himself onto the love seat next to Meg. "You will not receive better advice or help from anyone including my lovely wife."

"He's right, Quartus. They are completely trustworthy." She offered him a cup.

"Very well." Sitting on a chair in between the sofas, he related what Lady Sarah had told him. "As you can see, a marriage between she and I would not work. I do not wish for a wife who is in love with another. Therefore—"

"You offered to help her wed her betrothed," the duchess finished. "But who is he?"

"His name is Mr. Jeremy Bellingham. He has just returned from the East Indies. Lady Sarah is giving me a letter to send to him in the morning." Quartus glanced at his brother. "I hope you do not mind if he sends his reply here."

"Not at all." Hawksworth refilled his plate. "What I do not understand is why Markville would abrogate an agreement his father made for the lady."

Quartus did not understand it either. His attention was distracted from the food his brother had piled on the plate. He had never seen anyone who could eat as much as Hawksworth could and remain fit.

"Bellingham . . . Bellingham," the duchess muttered to herself.

"Lovely family. Very good *ton*," Lady Featherton said. "Not noble, but related to half the houses in England."

"Yes, yes, but I remember something." The duchess bit into a small lemon curd tart.

"You will think of it in a moment." Lady Featherton patted her friend's arm before looking at Quartus. "I do not understand what Lord Markville has against Mr. Bellingham."

"Miranda or was it Maria." The duchess pounded her cane on the floor. "I remember now, Lucinda."

Lady Featherton glanced at her friend. "Remember what, Constance?"

"Markville, when he was still Viscount Martin had expected to wed Maria Bellingham, and she accepted another gentleman."

"Miranda Bellingham, you mean," Lady Featherton corrected in a gentle voice. "Maria was her grandmother. Goodness, I had forgotten all about that. Yet it must be the reason Markville does not like his sister's betrothal."

Hawksworth had emptied his plate and set it on the table to the side of him. "Did he actually put it about that he was going to marry her before he proposed?"

The duchess raised an imperious brow. "The clodpole put it in the betting book at White's."

"This morning, he warned me away from Anna

Wharton," Quartus said. Not that there had been any need to. He admired her greatly—well more than that it seemed—but she should most likely wed someone like Lord Markville.

"Markville and the Duchess of Wharton?" Lady Featherton appeared shocked.

"It will not do at all!" The Duchess of Bridgewater thumped her cane on the floor again. "Not. At. All. It appears, Lucinda, we will have to take action."

"That is all very well"—Lady Featherton's brows drew together slightly—"but first we must have a plan to allow Lady Sarah time to actually wed the Mr. Bellingham."

With the duchess and Lady Featherton involved, it appeared as if Quartus would not have much to do at all. Other than ferry letters back and forth. "Hawksworth, may I borrow your curricle again tomorrow? I am taking Lady Sarah for a drive and then Anna and I are going to the Tower of London."

"You are?" Meg's eyes widened. Drat it all. He should not have mentioned it. Outings with Anna would just encourage his sister-in-law's match making tendencies.

"Well, yes. Lady Sarah would rather give me the letter away from her brother's house. We have also agreed that we should look as if I am courting her. To put her brother and my father at ease."

"And Anna?" Meg asked.

"She thought that since we are both new to Town, we would have more fun seeing the attractions together." He would have said more but Shakespeare's line about protesting too much made him keep his mouth shut.

"What an excellent idea." Meg sat back on the sofa with a smug look on her face.

The problem was that he didn't know if it was because he was helping Lady Sarah thwart her brother and his father or if she thought he was actually courting Anna Wharton.

He also wondered how they would arrange for Lady Sarah to be away from her house long enough to marry her betrothed without Markville becoming suspicious.

"I have a question, Grandmamma, and I hope you know the answer."

"What is it, my dear?"

"When Lady Tatiana was introduced to Quartus, she became quite rude"—Meg scrunched her nose up—"well to Hawksworth as well. I know many people do not like Somerset, but she seemed to truly detest the man."

"Oh, that is easy. Tatiana and one of the duke's younger brothers fell in love. His name escapes me at the moment. It was a very long time ago. She thought the former duke would come around, but for the current duke's influence. To make a long story short, the younger brother decided to seek his fortune so that he could marry her and he died. She blames Somerset."

"I do not understand why either duke would object."

"There has been a long history of, shall we say, difficulties, between the Trevors and the Whitestones. It was rumored—"

"But never confirmed," the duchess interrupted.

"Confirmation would have ruined the family," Lady Featherton nodded.

Sensing that the older ladies were going off the subject, and very interested in the story, Quartus said, "What would have ruined her?"

"Oh, yes. It was said, that one of the earlier dukes thoroughly compromised one of the duchesses."

"Forced her, you mean." The duchess thumped her cane.

"So she would have to marry him?" Quartus asked.

"Well, that was his plan. The duchess and her ladies claimed that he was never alone with her. Needless to say, she carried the day."

"Dear God." Quartus was almost at a loss for words. "Who knew my father wasn't the only dastardly duke."

It was no wonder Anna's aunt didn't like the family. One instance would have been enough, but it appeared the Dukes of Somerset made a habit of bad behavior. It was just as well he had decided she would never marry him.

CHAPTER SIX

"GOING SOMEWHERE?"

Markville's hard tone almost made Sarah pat her reticule to ensure that her letter to Jeremy was still there.

Looking into the hall mirror, she tied the wide bow of her bonnet under her ear. "Lord Quartus is taking me driving in the Park."

Markville narrowed his eyes. "Why so early? He should be taking you out during the fashionable hour."

Sarah turned, meeting her brother's glare with one of her own. "I did not wish to be made a spectacle. He asked what time I preferred to go, and I told him this morning." She shrugged. "We may drive to Green Park instead. I hear drinking the fresh milk is wonderful." A sharp rap sounded on the door. "That will be Quartus now. You should be happy that we are getting along."

"Are you?"

"Yes, I just told you so. I find him charming and easy to talk to." That wasn't a lie. Quartus just wasn't Jeremy.

"Excellent. I shall inform his father that we may begin the marriage settlement negotiations."

Instead of mentioning Jeremy, she merely smiled politely. "As you wish. Remember, my inheritance is mine alone."

"How long will you be out?"

She gave him her most innocent look. "I have no idea. If I am not back by dinner, feel free to inquire about me"

Her brother opened his mouth, but at the same time

his butler opened the door. "My lady. Lord Quartus has arrived."

"Have a pleasant day." She wiggled her fingers at Markville, causing him to seethe a bit more. Well good. He deserved it. "I shall be back later."

She could feel Markville's stare on her back as she took Quartus's arm and strolled out the door.

"Lady Sarah?" Quartus asked. "Are you all right?"

"I shall be perfect as soon as we are away."

He helped her into the curricle and quickly climbed into the other side. "My sister-in-law, Meg, would like to meet you, and my brother promised to frank your letter. Shall we drive the carriage way in the Park first?"

For a moment, Sarah wished to crawl under the seat and hide. She hated to involve so many people in the plotting, but needs must. If Markville had simply left her in the country, she and Jeremy could have easily been married by her village's vicar. But in Town, she was allowed no freedom at all, nor did she have the resources she did at home. "Yes, please. I must have some time to calm myself from my encounter with Markville and steel myself to meet your family. When I asked for your help, I did not know how many people would become involved."

"You have no idea," Quartus muttered cryptically. Then the corners of his lips curled up. "Neither did I. But it occurred to me that I do not even know where the nearest post office is located."

"Oh dear. I have no idea either." This was becoming more and more complicated. "I am very glad they offered to help."

"Er, yes. As am I." He slid her a look, but this time he appeared worried. "I hope you do not mind, but before Meg told me she wished to meet with your today, I had made other plans. I will leave you with her and fetch you later."

He was abandoning her! Sarah took several deep breaths trying to calm her fears. Get a hold of yourself. You are not marrying him, so he deserves to court another lady. "I shall be fine."

Twenty minutes later, Quartus drew up in front of a modest, but elegant house.

"Here we are." He jumped down, and a footman helped her out of the carriage. "You will like Meg. Everyone does. Well, almost everyone. My father is probably the sole exception."

Soon Sarah was being shown into a sunny morning room decorated in shades of cream and yellow. A young matron not much older than she came forward. "Lady Sarah. I do not know if you remember me. We met when you first came out. Meg Featherton. I am now Lady Hawksworth."

An inkling of a memory came forth. "You were wearing pink."

"Bright pink if I remember." She laughed. "I do not wear that color now. I am surprised my mother allowed me out of the house in that gown."

"Well"—Sarah pulled a face—"it was better than white."

"Indeed it was." Lady Hawksworth led Sarah to a small sofa. "Tea shall be served directly."

"Thank you, my lady."

"Please call me, Meg, and I shall call you Sarah." She nodded. "I have two other ladies I would like to involve in your dilemma, my grandmother, the Dowager Lady Featherton, and her friend, the Duchess of Bridgewater. They are very, very good at this type of planning."

A shiver of trepidation ran through, Sarah. "Are you certain they will wish to help frustrate my brother's attempts to stop me from marrying my betrothed?"

"Quite certain." Meg's firm assurance made Sarah feel

better. "They are in the garden and should be here any moment. If you will give your letter to Quartus"—Meg glanced at him—"Hawksworth is in his study waiting to frank it for you. Make sure you have our butler send it express."

She gave him the missive as two elderly ladies entered the room.

"Grandmamma, duchess," Meg grinned, "this is Lady Sarah Martin. Sarah, my grandmother, and the Duchess of Bridgewater."

"A pleasure to meet you, my dear," Lady Featherton said in a voice so sweet and kind that Sarah wanted to throw herself in to the woman's arms and tell her all her troubles.

"Lady Sarah, we knew your parents and grandparents." The duchess sat in a chair next to the sofa where Meg began to pour tea. "We will get this all straightened out as it should be."

"Yes, indeed." Lady Featherton nodded. "Helping young people is our *forté*. Quartus told us some of what was going on, but we would like to hear the whole story from you."

After being served a cup of tea, and taking a large sip, Sarah began, "I was seventeen and just out when I met Jeremy. He said he knew immediately he wanted to marry me"—she couldn't stop her cheeks from becoming warm—"but I am of a more cautious nature. After a few weeks, though, it became clear to me that I loved him. He was getting ready to sail to the East Indies, and asked my father if we could wed so that I could accompany him. My father refused. I suppose now that I think about it that should not have surprised me. Yet, at the time I was devastated. That was when the agreement was made that if we still wished to marry when he returned, we could become betrothed. However, we had to wed by my twenty-first birthday. My father insisted that I would wait no longer." She stared at the biscuit for a moment then took a bite and swallowed. "We were given permission to write to each other, and with each letter we became closer and more in love. Two years ago, my father died and my mother went to live in Bath, and a cousin came to act as my companion. My brother wanted me to come to Town for the Season, and I refused. At the same time, I missed at least one or two of Jeremy's letters. I wrote him immediately asking him to address his missives to me to my old nurse. She lives in a cottage on the estate. Once he began using her address, the letters came as they always had." Sarah glanced at all three women. "I am certain Markville tried to stop me from receiving Jeremy's correspondence. Just yesterday, my brother told me if my betrothed does not arrive by my birthday, he will choose my husband."

"Well, of all the high-handed, imbecilic things to do. All due to his disappointment." Lady Featherton huffed. Sarah waited for her to elaborate on that last part, but Lady Featherton stopped and frowned. "Never fear, my dear. We will see you and your Jeremy wed."

"The question is," the duchess said, "how do we manage to get Sarah away from her house long enough to marry her betrothed?"

An hour and a half later, Meg rose. "I am going to send a note around to your brother that you are joining us for luncheon."

In a few minutes the missive was dispatched, and the ladies went back to discussing options.

"The problem is that we are in the middle of the Season," she said. "If it was not for that, I would suggest a house party." A pretty blush stained her cheeks. "It worked well for Hawksworth and me."

"Margaret Hawksworth"—the duchess pounded her cane on the floor—"you have your grandmother's brains.

A house party is just the thing. The question is where to have it?"

Sarah listened as names flew back and forth. Finally Meg said, "Caro Huntley's house would be perfect. It is not so far from Town that people would wonder at it, and it is far enough away that one would not wish to simply drop in. If one were rude enough to appear uninvited."

Such as Markville. She had met the Earl and Countess of Huntley this morning during her short drive with Quartus. They had stopped and chatted with the couple as they were strolling. But would Lady Huntley agree to host a party on such short notice? Sarah sat forward on her seat. "Where is their estate?"

"Suffolk, near Long Melford," Meg replied. "I shall send a note around asking if we may have a private discussion after luncheon."

Within a few minutes, the message was dispatched with orders that the footman wait for a reply. Less than an hour later, a beautiful lady with pale blond hair and startling blue eyes was announced and ushered into the room.

Lady Huntley halted near the door, her eyes scanning the company, and smiled. "I sense a conspiracy." She took the chair Meg indicated. "Now, tell me all about it."

A little while later, she pursed her lips and nodded. "Yes, I think this will work. I shall make up a guest list and send it here for you to look over. We do not want anyone who will report back to either Somerset or Lord Markville or any of their friends."

In the meantime . . .

"IT IS EXQUISITE!" ANNA EXCLAIMED as Quartus and she explored the grounds of the Tower of London. "Such a shame that such a beautiful place would be turned into a prison."

"I agree. Though, it was used as a prison at different periods since the twelfth century."

They turned back to where the Royal Menagerie was to be found. "Did you know that all the animals here were given to the king?"

"Of course. I think every English school child knows that." She slid him one of wicked looks she had been giving him since he'd fetched her. "Even in Tortola, we are still English."

He could have groaned. "Forgive me. I did not think."

"No, no. I am or was, completely ignorant about the *ton* and most of London. It was a reasonable supposition that I would not know how the beasts came to be here."

The side of her soft breast pressed into his arm, and he stifled a groan. She could not possibly know what she was doing to him. Despite his best efforts to keep a distance between them, he felt himself becoming closer to her. And that would not do. For a number of reasons. Firstly, she needed to marry a peer. Someone who could help her manage her holdings and vote in the Lords as she could not. All he could give her was his support and love.

Blast it all! Where had that thought come from? He was not falling in love. He would not.

Yet, he couldn't help but wonder how soft the rest of Anna would be. How silky her skin and hair. How would her lips and mouth taste when they kissed. His member hardened, and he ruthlessly shoved down his desire to satisfy his curiosity. That was all it was. A man's desire for a woman. He had never had a regular mistress and did not think it right to have relations with any of the women in his parish, nor would he go to a brothel. His desire was nothing more than not having lain with a woman for a while.

"Quartus, is something wrong? You look as if you are in pain? Do your boots pinch?"

Caught. At least she had thought of his boots and not other body parts. Although, no well-bred lady would have mentioned *those*, even if she had thought about them. "Not at all and boots from Hoby had best not pinch. Not for the price he charges."

They were visiting the cells of the many prisoners kept in the Tower. "Look at this writing. That is Latin, is it not? Can you read it?"

"Of course," Quartus said before reading it out loud.

"The more affliction we endure for Christ in this world, the more glory we shall get with Christ in the world to come."

"It was done by Philip Howard, Earl of Arundel in 1587. I wonder how far back they go?"

She turned to a page in her guidebook, and her brow puckered with annoyance. "It does not say."

His stomach made itself known. It must be close to luncheon. "I should probably take you home."

"Yes." Anna made a noise that sounded like a sigh. "I suppose it is time. It is my 'at home' day."

He remembered his sister-in-law's 'at home.' There had been a constant stream of ladies and some gentlemen all afternoon. "I do not envy you that. Even my brother heads for his club when Meg has her 'at homes.'"

"There are times when I wish I could escape as well. At least there were. After having met Meg and Hawksworth's friends, I no longer dread them quite as much."

Anna still clung to his arm as they made their way out of the gate and to the pavement beyond. Once more, his body began to express a less than innocent interest in her. She could not possibly know what she was doing to him.

He had to get her home and fast. The other option was to find a secluded place in the Park where he could kiss her if nothing more.

Quartus called to the boy holding the horses. He arrived at Anna's house faster than he ever had before. It hadn't helped that her leg kept touching his thigh all the way to Grosvenor Square. He helped her down and walked her to the door. "Thank you for an excellent excursion."

"Thank you as well. Do you have any ideas about what you would like to do tomorrow? Richmond perhaps?"

Richmond was out of the question. She would never come back untouched. "Unfortunately, I am still helping the other person which will not give us time to travel to Richmond and return before your afternoon visits."

"In that case, I shall ask my guest this afternoon where they would suggest and let you know in the morning."

He kissed the gloved hand she held out to him. His lips seemed to burn through the kid leather. If only he could touch her bare skin to bare skin. "Until tomorrow."

Quartus drove off, doing his best not to look back at Anna. If only she was not a duchess. If only he was a peer or heir to one, or if one of his mother's elderly relatives had made him their heir. But none of that had happened. And the fact remained that she needed a man who could offer her more.

When he reached his brother's house, he was directed to the breakfast room where his brother, Meg, her grandmother, the duchess, and Lady Sarah were partaking of luncheon. Quartus took the empty chair next to Meg. "How is it going?"

"Very well. We have decided to have a weeklong house party."

He had been reaching for a platter of ham that was positioned within arm's reach when a footman beat him too it and held the plate for him to make his selection.

"But you said your estate was not ready yet."

"It is not. It is also too far from Town. Caro Huntley has offered to host the party. The Huntley's estate is too far for a day trip, but not so far that it makes it difficult during the Season."

"I think it is a brilliant idea." Sarah smiled broadly. "I have already written to Jeremy. He will be able to obtain our special license on his way from Plymouth to Suffolk."

He cut into the ham. "When do we leave?"

"In a week," Sarah answered. "I cannot wait."

CHAPTER SEVEN

ANNA HAD FUMED QUIETLY TO herself as she'd watched Quartus drive off. Was the man made of stone? Any other gentleman would be trying to find a place to kiss her if not more. Markville, she was sure, would actively attempt to compromise her. Perhaps Quartus was not as interested in her as she was in him. Yet—yet his eyes softened when he gazed down at her. He laughed at her jokes, and his already hard body tightened when she'd purposefully brushed against him. Pantaloons did not hide much at all.

If she did anything more, he'd think she was a fallen woman. And in a way she was. Neither she nor the man she had been betrothed to thought he would die two days before the wedding. She would have to confess her lack of maidenhead to whomever she married, and she would much prefer to make that confession to Quartus than to someone like Lord Markville.

Surely there was a way she could find out how he felt about her, short of asking, naturally. Hmm, this might take a bit of thought.

LATER THAT AFTERNOON, THE BUTLER announced Caro Huntley, one of the friends she had met through Meg. Anna took in who was in the drawing room and found, for a change, there were only those considered friends. "Caro, thank you for coming."

Anna motioned for the newcomer to sit next to her as she poured tea.

"How could I not." Caro sank gracefully onto the sofa. "I know what it is like to have to sit here for hours. Aside from that"—she lowered her voice so that only Anna could here—"I wish to invite you to a small house party I am having in about a week."

Anna glanced at her aunt. "In the middle of the Season?"

"I know it is not the usual thing to do." Caro grinned ruefully. "But Huntley must attend to some business at our estate, and I do not wish for him to go alone. So, I decided to have a party. It will only last a week, then we'll all be back in Town."

Aunt Tatiana would not approve, but it might do Anna good to have a break from the Season. There was only one problem. "I would hate to leave my father alone with only my aunt for company. Although they do try to get along, they are like chalk and cheese."

"Bring him. With parliament in session, I have a feeling we will have more ladies than gentlemen. He can help make up the numbers."

That was perfect. Anna was certain her father would enjoy the house party as well. "Thank you. I would love to attend."

"Is there anyone else you would like to have invited?"

Anna thought about Quartus, but decided to leave the possibility of his attendance up to chance. "No one. I shall look forward to a holiday from the Season."

"Wonderful." Caro smiled brightly. "I'll send round an invitation with the directions. I know I call it a rambling old pile, but it does have its charm, and the countryside is beautiful."

"If there is any fishing to be had, my father will be a

happy man. He has told us story after story of fishing from a lake or stream."

"I am glad we will be able to accommodate him. Huntley says the fishing is excellent. I can attest to the quality and quantity that is brought to the cook."

Anna was happily contemplating the party, and the conversation turned to fashions and the speed with which the Royal dukes were attempting to fill the void left by Princess Charlotte's death last year.

"The difficulty they appear to have is siring legitimate children," Lady Fotherby said. "Although, I would not normally mention that to an unmarried lady, you are a duchess."

It was just as well she was privy to this sort of talk. Married or not, in her position she would need to know what was going on.

Mrs. Darling, the daughter of an earl who was married to a member of the parliament, set down her cup. "My husband asked me the other day if you had chosen a successor for one of your members of parliament who has taken a royal sinecure."

"I have heard nothing about it." Anna glanced at Lady Tatiana. "Aunt?"

"The by-election will not take place until June. There is plenty of time to discuss it."

"Naturally," Mrs. Darling said. "If you marry soon, your husband will make the selection."

The devil he would. Anna fought to keep a pleasant mien. That was the precise reason Anna was resolved not to marry a peer or any man who tried to take control of her duties. She was the duchess, and she would run her duchy. Taking a sip of her now tepid tea, she hid her frown. It might be time to take a more direct approach with Lord Quartus.

That evening when her party entered Lady Merton's

ballroom, Anna had still not told her aunt about the house party. The only reason she could think of as to why she had not was that she didn't wish to listen to the older woman natter incessantly about the propriety of Anna attending a house party without a companion other than her father. Yet, she had been assured by Caro that only people Anna had already met would attend. Which meant there were sufficient matrons to watch over her. As if she needed watching over at Caro's house.

A few minutes later, the evening took a decided turn for the worse.

"Your Grace." Lord Markville bowed. "I trust I am not too late to claim a dance. Preferably a waltz."

What was the man doing here this early? He always arrived late, much later than she or her friends did. Aunt was adamant that Anna be on time. The exception was at her first ball when she was meant to make an entrance. And, now that she thought about it, Quartus had not requested the first waltz and the supper dance as he normally did.

Still, she'd been caught, and there was only one answer. She affixed a polite smile on her face. "Of course, my lord."

By the time Quartus arrived, she only had one dance left. A country dance. He claimed it, but it appeared he did so reluctantly. What was the matter with the man? Neither gentleman was doing what she wanted them to do. Markville had too many dances and Quartus not enough. Maybe she should plead a headache and leave early. First she would find out what was the matter with Quartus.

She made her way over to Meg. If anyone would know what was going on with him, it would be her. Anna greeted Hawksworth before pulling Meg aside. "Is Quartus feeling quite the thing?"

"There is something wrong." Meg made a face, scrunching up her nose. "Unfortunately, I have no idea what it is. He was so late getting ready that we almost left him at home."

That *was* odd. "He is normally so prompt."

"It may just be that the Season is taking its toll. He's not used to so much gadding about."

Anna wondered if he had been invited to the house party. Yet, she could not ask Meg in the event that she had not been invited.

An hour later, after almost fighting to keep a proper distance between herself and Lord Markville during the waltz, she skirted the ballroom, making her way back to her aunt and father. If she was careful not to be seen coming from the direction of the retiring room, there would be no lecture of going off on her own.

Just as she stepped behind a large potted palm, two gentlemen stopped in front of it.

"I see that you still have requested a set with the duchess," Markville commented in an angry tone. "I told you to stay away from her."

"You will have to take that up with my sister-in-law. I, for one, would rather upset you than her."

"Speaking of sisters, when you wed mine, you shall leave Town immediately."

"That will not be a problem."

Wed Markville's sister? Anna fought the tears pricking her eyes. All this time, she thought Quartus was coming to care about her, and he was betrothed to another woman. It was not that he only had short bits of time to spend with her, he needed to dance attendance on another lady as well.

A sick feeling lodged in her stomach. What a fool she'd been, practically throwing herself at Quartus. She straightened her shoulders. Well, she would be one no longer.

As for Markville, he could go jump in the Thames and drown. She would not stand up with him again.

Once the men had gone their separate ways, Anna found a footman and ordered her carriage. She could send it back for her father and aunt. Right now, she just needed to be alone.

"WHAT HAVE YOU HEARD?" SOMERSET asked his secretary.

"Nothing as yet, Your Grace. However, Mrs. Grayson sent a note saying she had decided the rumor would be better spread by servants instead of her. When she saw Lord Quartus and the Duchess of Wharton at the museum earlier, she thought he might have remembered her name."

"The damned fool. What possessed the stupid slut to use her own name?"

"Her idea about using the servants might work," Belling said. "It is well known that most of the *ton's* secrets are spread below stairs. A maid is much more likely to spread an unfounded rumor than a lady."

"That's all." Somerset turned back to his correspondence.

Belling cleared his throat. "There is one other matter."

"Go on."

"Lord Markville wishes to set the date of the wedding for two weeks hence. He also wishes to be assured that the property Lady Sarah brings to the marriage will be used by her and Lord Quartus as their home."

"Tell him it will be as he wishes."

"Have you decided to have someone else take over Lord Francis's duties."

"I have not. What Markville wants does not concern me. Once Quartus is married, his lordship shall have no say in the matter."

"As you say, Your Grace. I shall draft a letter immediately."

Three days after the disastrous and last ball Anna attended, Annot, the maid who had been hired for Anna when she had arrived in England, entered her study.

"Your Grace, I need to tell you something, and you're not going to like it."

That wasn't surprising. She hadn't liked most of what she had heard this week. "What is it?" The maid wrung her hands together for so long, she finally said, "Just tell me. If it is that important, it's better that I know."

"It is about Lord Quartus, Your Grace."

Anna tried to keep the look off her countenance that scared even her brothers. "Go on."

"There is talk going around that he is a womanizer. A man who likes innocent ladies, ruins them, and leaves them."

Could that be the reason he had not been interested in her? She wasn't young enough for him? And what of the young lady he was to wed. Markville's sister would be devastated. Clutching for the chair behind her, she sat down hard. "What proof do you have? Is there the name of a young lady he harmed?"

"No, Your Grace. No lady has been mentioned. It's said he does it up in his home county."

That did not make any sense. He was a rector at home. Surely he would have been called to account. Unless no one believed the young women because he was the rector. Or, perhaps, they were afraid of the duke. She hoped no one would be so afraid of her that they would fail to tell of such a crime.

Did Meg and Hawksworth know about Quartus's reputation? No, they could not have. Meg said that her husband had not been home in years, and she had never been there.

But Quartus of all people. He was so kind and easy to

talk to. She firmed her lips. Yet that was exactly the kind of person who *could* take advantage of a young lady. And her maid had said 'lady.' Servants did not use that term indiscriminately. A lady was a woman of Quality. If this rumor was true, some father would have demanded that Quartus marry his daughter.

Anna stood and began to pace. If the allegations were correct, Quartus should be punished in some way. But what if the rumors were false. Who would benefit from spreading such an unspeakable lie about a clergyman?

Well, someone had to ferret out the truth, and she had just been handed the duty. "I want to know everything. From whom did you hear the rumor?"

The woman sniffed. "As you know, Your Grace, I would not stoop to gossip with the lower servants. Mr. Puller told it to me in confidence. I believe he had it from the under-butler, who had it from Cook, who heard it from one of the maids, who was told by someone she met at the market."

That the butler had carried the story to Anna's maid was significant. Tortola might be small, but she was well aware how a story could change with many tellings. "I wish to speak with the maid who originally heard the talk."

Annot's eyes flew open. "Your Grace, you'd scare the poor girl to death. It might be better for Cook or Mrs. Flowers to speak with her."

Well, drat. Annot was right. Anna was still not used to how her rise in status affected others. "Does she work in the kitchen or in the household?" And to whom the maid answered to, Cook or her housekeeper, Mrs. Flowers, was important in the hierarchy of the household.

"I believe Mrs. Flowers sent her to Cook after one of the kitchen maids was unable to work this morning." Annot added helpfully.

"I shall leave it to you." Anna rubbed her forehead

attempting to relieve the aching that had begun. "I wish to know all I can discover about the teller of this tale."

"I'll see it done, Your Grace." Annot left the room, and Anna sank onto a sofa.

When she'd discovered all she could, she would send a message to Meg. Her friend needed to know whether she harbored a criminal or an innocent man someone was attempting to discredit. Although, who would spread such detrimental gossip was beyond Anna's comprehension.

Sometime later, Annot handed Anna a note written in her housekeeper's neat hand giving her the direction of the servant who had related the tale to her maid.

Sally, the tweenie went to the market this morning as one of Cook's girls was not feeling well, and the other was already making breakfast. When she was buying potatoes, a maid comes up and asks where Ruth, the regular maid, was. Sally told her and this other maid starts telling Sally about a Lord Quartus and how he was dangerous to young ladies and other young females. She must have heard his name mentioned, because she came straight to me and told me what she'd heard. As was my duty, I discussed with Mr. Puller what was to be done and he spoke with Miss Annot. Sally made sure to get the maid's name, Susie, and the address, Number Six Hill Street.

Sally has been assured that you are not angry. If you have any other questions, Your Grace, she will answer them.

Mrs. J. Flowers

Anna was thankful she had decided to have the upper servants talk to the tweenie. It was not nearly as complicated as her maid had originally made it sound. Still, she must tell Meg Hawksworth about this immediately.

"I shall want my carriage as soon as possible."

"Yes, Your Grace."

As she was in the hall pulling on her gloves, someone plied the knocker.

CHAPTER EIGHT

MEG LOST NO TIME ENTERING the hall. "May we speak in private?"

"Yes. Indeed, I was just about to have a missive sent to you." Anna said. It was probably better that the lady was here. That way she could answer her questions. There were sure to be several. The tweenie was here as well.

"Your Grace, will you still require the coach?"

"If we need to go anywhere, mine is waiting," Meg handed her gloves to the butler.

"Come with me." Anna led the way to her study in the back of the house, overlooking the garden. "I have some disturbing news."

"First, tell me." Meg's forehead pleated with concern. "Have you been ill? No one has seen you since the Flowers's ball. At first I thought you might be a little fagged from all the parties, but Quartus said that he has not seen you either."

"As if he would want to bother with me when he is marrying another." Anna did not wish to have the conversation. "Nevertheless, it is about Lord Quartus I had written to you."

"Marrying another? Oh, good Lord!" Meg folded her lips together and shook her head. "And of course my sapskull brother-in-law did not tell you about Lady Sarah."

Anna's legs threatened to give way, and she quickly lowered herself onto the sofa, motioning Meg to sit as well. "Lady Sarah. That is her name?"

"Yes, but he is not going to wed her. She has been betrothed for years to another gentleman."

The headache that had threatened earlier moved to her temples and started to thrum. This was worse than she had thought. He was playing with a woman who was already taken. "Does Markville know?"

"Markville and my father-in-law planned it."

But Markville had said . . . Wait, none of this was making any sense at all. "I think you had best tell me all of it from the beginning. But first, wine or tea?"

"Wine, please." She glanced at the door. "We will not want to be interrupted."

Wishing it was rum, Anna poured two glasses of the red burgundy her predecessor preferred over claret.

"Excellent," Meg said after she had a sip. "Now, let me tell you what this is about. Somerset decided to see Quartus married to a lady he chose. Markville agreed that his sister and Quartus would suit. The only problem is that she is already betrothed, and has been for four years . . ."

Before Meg had finished, Anna had drained her glass and refilled it. She was definitely ordering a supply of rum. She had been right about not encouraging the marquis. How could he be so cruel to his sister? "So when I heard Markville talking to Quartus, it was not what it seemed. Well as far as Markville knew it was, but Quartus is actually assisting Lady Sarah to marry her intended."

"Precisely." Meg nodded. "We are in the process of working out a way for them to wed without either the duke or her brother discovering what we are doing until after the deed is accomplished. Everyone agrees that one or both of them would attempt to stop the wedding."

How Machiavellian. Anna's esteem for Meg grew. "How will you do that? If you can tell me, that is."

"We have arranged a house party where Lady Sarah and her betrothed will marry. He will arrive with a special license. It is all perfectly legal as her father signed the agreements before he died."

A house party? The only event of that sort Anna knew of was . . . "At the Huntley's estate?"

"Yes." Meg glanced at her almost empty glass and grinned. "I know you were invited. Do you plan to attend?"

"My maid is packing as we speak." This might work out very well. She would have a whole week with Quartus and without her aunt and Markville interfering. "I'd better tell you my news, and as my maid said to me, 'you are not going to like it.' This morning . . ."

As she related what she'd heard, Meg's eyes narrowed and her lips formed a thin line as she grew angrier and angrier. "That is all I know."

"That insufferable commoner." She set her glass down with a loud snap. "That care-for-nobody here-and-therian."

"The duke, I take it."

Meg nodded. "If Quartus doesn't murder him, Hawksworth will."

Anna poured her friend another glass of wine. "I am loath to mention it, but patricide as well as killing a duke is against the law."

"After all that devil has done, no one could possibly be blamed." Her friend took a large drink of wine.

"Are you so sure it is Somerset?"

"Who else could it be? There is no way Quartus could have engaged in that sort of behavior and his mother not discover it, and she would have told my husband. Not only that, but my grandmother Featherton would have heard about it as well."

"I agree, it is damning, however, what must be done immediately is to scotch the rumors."

"We have enough friends and allies to accomplish that in short order. By the time we return from the house party, all will be right." Meg rose. "Now, where were we going?"

"To a house on Hill Street where the maid works."

"Hill Street?" Her jaw dropped for a second then snapped shut. "There is one house on that street that neither of us will wish to be seen visiting. Unfortunately, I do not know the address." Meg placed the bonnet she'd removed back on her head, tying the bow off under her ear. "We should speak to my husband and brother-in-law first. Quartus deserves to know what is being said about him."

Anna did not even bother to argue. If her friend said that the house might not be an appropriate place for a lady to be seen, it must be notorious. Duchess she may be, but it would not be prudent to risk her reputation. "Very well, but I'm coming with you."

"I would not attempt to stop you." Suddenly, Meg gave Anna a conspiratorial smile. "You might even be able to meet Lady Sarah. She has been spending a great deal of time at our house sending and receiving letters from her betrothed."

"I imagine the visits also serve to convince her brother and the duke of Quartus's interest in her." And make Markville believe that his sister and Quartus would actually wed.

"That is part of the scheme."

If everything Meg had said was true, and Anna had no reason to believe it was not, then she would have to find a way to convince Quartus that she was not going to marry Markville. The problem was how to do that and not look as if she were asking for a proposal. And could she do it in the space of a week?

AS QUARTUS BROUGHT THE CURRICLE to a halt in front of Lord Markville's house, he noticed Sarah's hands clenched together. Beneath the gloves her knuckles were most likely white with apprehension. "Your brother has said you could attend the house party, has he not?"

"Yes." She nodded slowly. "Yes. As long as I bring Mrs. Potter and my maid, of course, he does not object." Sarah glanced at him. "I am just so afraid that something will go wrong."

Quartus tied the ribbons off and covered her hands with one of his. "You must trust us. We will see you and Jeremy through this."

"You are right. I'm being nervous for nothing." Her grip relaxed and her lips tilted up slightly even if they wobbled a bit. "After all, he will be better able to further his suit with the duchess if he does not have to concern himself with me."

And that was the one thing that worried Quartus. Despite all of Markville's advantages, or what appeared to be his advantages, Quartus could no longer see Anna wed to a man who would run roughshod over her as he was trying to do with Sarah. Yet, for the nonce, there was nothing he could do about it. When he returned from the country, and if she was not already engaged, he would do his best to tempt Fate and court her in earnest.

For now, he had to help Sarah and Jeremy. "It will all work out. It always does."

After escorting her to the door, and making a show of bowing over her hands, he said in a low voice. "We will be by at eight o'clock to fetch you and Mrs. Potter. Your maids will be picked up by Meg and Hawksworth's personal servants about a half an hour earlier."

"We shall be ready," Sarah assured him with more confidence than she'd had a few minutes ago. "With luck, my brother will still be asleep."

Several minutes later Quartus entered Hawksworth's house, and was almost to the morning room when his brother's bellow seemed to bounce off the walls. "I am going to roast the blasted scoundrel over a spit!"

What the devil? He entered the room stopping by the door on the off chance he was the one in trouble. "Roast whom over a spit?"

"Our father." Damon bit out, resembling nothing so much as an enraged bull.

"What has he done now?" The duke should be under the impression that everything was working out as he had arranged.

"He is attempting to blacken your name," he replied through clenched teeth.

"But why?" Meg took Quartus's arm, leading him to the sofa. "I do not understand. He cannot possibly know that Lady Sarah and I will not wed."

"Thank God for that," his brother snapped. "The Lord only knows what he would do if he suspected his scheme was in danger of coming to naught. It must be his way of ensuring your marriage takes place. If you do not marry Sarah, then no other woman will have you."

Quartus knew his father had behaved in a dastardly manner to Hawksworth, Frank, and their wives, but he had a difficult time believing the duke could be so reprehensible for no apparent reason.

"But how do you know he is responsible?" Not that Quartus could think of anyone else that would start rumors, unless it was Markville, but he thought Quartus was marrying Sarah. He took the glass of wine Meg handed him.

"Aside from no one else wanting to cause you harm? Anna Wharton told me that a maid who works at a certain house on Hill Street started the rumors at the market this morning. The house is currently occupied by a Mrs.

Grayson"—his brother glanced at Meg for a moment—"the duke's former mistress."

"Grayson?" Air rushed out of him as if he'd been punched in the gut. "If she is a lady around thirty or so, she introduced herself to Anna and me at the museum."

"The effrontery of the woman." Damon scowled. "She probably thought to ingratiate herself with the duchess and spread her lies in private." He headed swiftly toward the door. "I'll take care of this immediately."

"If you are going to confront her, I'm coming with you." Quartus followed his brother into the corridor. "It is me she is trying to slander."

Damon stopped and turned, a wicked look graced his face. "And have her lie to me? I am going to speak with her current protector, and the conversation will be short in the extreme."

"Oh. I see." The idea of women being bought and traded sickened Quartus, and he was not at all sure he wished to be part of the discussion. That his father had betrayed his mother was even worse. Yet, now he knew where he must have heard the name Grayson. Frank had to have mentioned the woman when paying the duke's expenses. Shrugging, Quartus straightened his shoulders. Nevertheless it was his reputation at stake and he would not stand by and watch everyone else protect him. "I am still accompanying you."

"While you do that—" Meg rose from the writing desk—"I shall pay a visit to my grandmother. She will know exactly how to stop this talk from going any further."

The next day, Anna met the Hawksworths, Quartus, and Lady Sarah at an inn for luncheon, the journey to the Huntley's estate near Long Medford in Suffolk took on an almost festive atmosphere. As the weather was fine, the gentlemen decided to ride and the ladies invited Anna to join them in Meg's coach. Mrs. Potter, Lady Sarah's companion, snoozed against the corner of the coach, and the afternoon passed quickly. Sooner than Anna had thought possible, they were stopping at the inn Caro Huntley had recommended to break their journey.

Mrs. Potter retired to her chamber after they had finished an excellent dinner, and shortly thereafter Sarah began to fret. "What if something has happened to Jeremy?" She wrung her hands together as her brow pleated with worry.

"I am sure everything will be fine," Meg responded. "You should not borrow trouble."

"But I have not heard from him in several days." Sarah's tone wrung Anna's heart. She knew what it was like not to hear from the man she loved and to fear the worst. Though, in her case the worst had happened. Aaron had died. Anna doubted the same fate would befall Jeremy.

The younger woman looked to be working herself into a passion when Quartus took her fingers in his much larger hands. "Sarah, if he has been following the plan, he will have been traveling hard during the past few days." His serene, sympathetic tone seemed to immediately calm her nerves, and Anna was impressed at his ability to so quickly reassure the lady. "It would have been difficult to write to you. I am sure he will arrive at Lord and Lady Huntley's estate shortly after we do."

"Do you truly think so?"

"Yes. Else I would not have said it."

Lady Sarah nodded, appearing to accept Quartus's assertions. "I should not worry myself so."

"I think your feelings are normal. After all, you and your Jeremy have not traveled an easy road."

She nodded again, the strain slipping from her features as she gave a slight smile.

Quartus patted her hands and rose. "Shall we seek our

beds? A good night's sleep will help us to arrive rested in the morning."

Anna waited until there was only she and Quartus in the parlor. "You did a very good job of comforting Sarah."

He tucked Anna's hand in the crook of his arm. "I have always been able to calm people and situations." He shrugged. "I believe that is the reason my father thought I would be a good clergyman."

It was also a skill useful for a politician and in a man who would help her run her duchy. And although he seemed drawn to her, the difficulty might be in convincing him that he was the right gentleman for her. "There are many ways to put such talent to work."

He looked surprised. "I have never really thought about it."

"Perhaps you should. Being a rector is only one option you have in life." Should she mention the parliamentary position she had coming open? Would she want him around if they were not to marry? She did not think she could stand the idea of him being with another woman. "There might be an opportunity for you to run for the House of Commons."

"I appreciate you trying to help me, but one must have property in order to run for the Commons. Even if I found a peer to support me for the office, I have no property."

He would if they married. "Forgive me. I did not know."

They strolled to the stairs and climbed them. When they got to her room she reached up on her toes and kissed him softly on the lips. "Good night, Quartus."

His arm circled her waist, and he pressed his lips to hers. "Good night, Anna."

He opened the door and she walked in backwards, watching him as he made his way down the corridor. Touching her lips she sighed. She was definitely kissing him again.

CHAPTER NINE

THEIR PARTY ARRIVED AT STOUT Manor, named for the river marking one boundary of the Huntleys' estate, just before noon the next day. As their coaches drew up before the large portico, Caro and her husband came down the steps to greet them.

She appeared perplexed. "Are you missing someone?"

"My father." Anna felt like rolling her eyes. "He discovered he has a friend not far from here and has ridden over to visit for a while."

"Ah. It is not a bother. He can arrive when he chooses." Caro's smile widened as Sarah was assisted from the carriage. "This must be Lady Sarah. My lady, there is a gentleman who has been anxiously awaiting your arrival. I believe he told me his name is Mr. Bellingham."

Sarah's eyes widened as her jaw dropped. "Jeremy? Here? How did he arrive so soon?"

"Come with me." Taking her arm, Caro led the younger lady into the house as the rest of them followed. "I was once told that there is nothing a gentleman in love will not do for his lady."

A man with burnished brown hair who looked to be in his middle to late twenties stood in the hall.

"Sarah," he breathed as if his breath had been stolen. "You are even more beautiful than I remembered."

"Jeremy, how I have missed you!" The next moment she was in his arms. "You are much broader than I remember and as brown as a nut."

"I was afraid your brother would do something to keep you from coming."

"I, as well. Yesterday, I was so worried, but"—she firmed her chin—"I never would have let him. I would have disguised myself and climbed out of a window."

"Thank God *that* didn't happen," Meg murmured.

Thank the Lord indeed. Anna glanced at Quartus. "I am so glad you helped her."

The corner of his lips tilted up, and she felt as if he held her more closely than before.

Slipping one arm around Sarah's waist, Jeremy guided her to a front parlor. "I would have stolen you away before I let you put yourself at risk."

She glanced over her shoulder. "Jeremy, we are being rude."

His eyes followed her gaze, he gave a rueful smile. "And after Lord and Lady Huntley have been so kind to me. I beg your pardon, my lady, my lord."

Caro's fingers fluttered as if to dismiss his need to apologize. "Ladies, allow me to introduce Mr. Jeremy Bellingham. The second son of Mr. Bellingham of Bellingham Court Northumberland."

"Mr. Bellingham, the Duchess of Wharton, and Lady Hawksworth."

Without letting go of Sarah, he managed to bow. "Lord Quartus, Lord and Lady Hawksworth, I cannot thank you enough for your assistance. We will be beholding to you for the rest of our lives." He turned to his betrothed. "My love, Lady Huntley has arranged for us to wed tomorrow if it is not too soon."

"After all the years we have waited, this very moment would not be too soon."

"Especially if she was ready to climb out a window," Quartus whispered in Anna's ear.

"In disguise," she whispered back.

"Well then," Caro said. "I shall confirm our appointment with Mr. Fulton, the vicar. The ceremony will take place here, if you do not mind."

"Not at all," Sarah said, her eyes suddenly shining with unshed tears. "Here is perfect."

Huntley closed the door behind them and looked at Hawksworth. "He brought the settlement agreements and the proof of his income that was required in them. I understand that he also provided you with the information, but since the wedding will take place here, I did not want to be in a position where I could be accused of misguiding a minor. I am happy to say all is in order."

"Did he happen to mention where they would go after they have wed?" Quartus asked.

"To his parents," Huntley replied. "Apparently Bellingham's father is not at all happy about Markville's behavior and thinks the pair would be better off with family if there is any talk. Naturally, the Bellinghams would have preferred that the wedding take place there, but it is a long way for an unwed couple to travel."

"Much better that they wed sooner than later." Anna was more than pleased that Huntley and Hawksworth had taken it upon themselves to ensure Sarah's safety, but she did not understand why the wedding would be at the house. "Is there a reason they should not marry in church?"

"We are not all that far from Town"—Caro led them down a corridor to the back of the house—"and we have some very well-connected gossips living close by. They could not fail to note a wedding. Huntley and I agreed with Mr. Bellingham that they will need as much time as possible to get north before Sarah's brother discovers they have defied him."

"I understand." Then another thought occurred to her, and she glanced at Quartus. "Your father will be unhappy as well."

Hawksworth made a harsh harrumph. "That, I believe, is an understatement. Not only will he be enraged, but he has spiked his own guns by attempting to ruin my brother's reputation."

"What did happen to the maid?" Anna did not approve of gossip, but, at the same time, she did not wish to see a servant harmed.

"The maid was only doing what she was told to do," Hawksworth responded. "Her employer had a stern talking to with his mistress who was hired to spread the rumor. It will not happen again."

"I am not quite sure I understand."

Quartus thought Anna's confusion, the way she drew her brows together, was adorable. Yet he would not be the one to tell her that a high-flyer had shamelessly approached her, and he hoped his brother did not do so either. She may be a duchess, but she was still an unmarried lady.

He and Hawksworth stole glances at each other. Finally, Meg huffed. "One of the duke's former mistresses was hired to do the deed."

"You told me he was behind the slander. Yet, how horrid!" Anna gasped. "I have to say that it never occurred to me that a father could treat a child in such a terrible fashion."

"That is not all." Quartus decided it was time for Anna to know the whole truth. If they were to have a future together, and after the two, albeit short kisses last night he thought they might. She must know everything. After finishing he said, "Now you know why your aunt detests him so much." Quartus kept his tone dry, but she was correct. What did it say about his father that the duke would attempt to ruin one of his children, and for no good reason? It wasn't as if Quartus had always defied him. He had rebelled when his father had tried to force him to coerce some of his parishioners. And what did it say about his family that his father was not the only Duke of Somerset to behave in an unconscionable manner?

"What do you suppose he will do now that his scheme has failed?" She worried her bottom lip as she always did when she was thinking about something.

"He does not know yet." Not wanting to think too much about his future if it didn't include Anna, he shrugged. "We have no idea what he'll do when he does discover he was tricked."

"But what will you do?" She had halted, causing him to stop walking as well. "He will not be pleased that you helped Sarah marry another."

"I am not yet sure. I will not go back and allow him to play with my life again." They had reached a sunny room where tea and trays of food were laid out. It had been a long time since breakfast. And situations always seemed better on a full stomach. "I'm famished."

"Yes, of course." Her voice was quiet as if her attention was elsewhere.

Doubts about her feelings toward him assailed Quartus again. He wondered what she was thinking. Was she upset simply because the duke had tried to harm someone, or was she truly concerned about him because she cared what happened to him?

If only he had not pulled back from her thus encouraging Markville to pay attentions to her. Yet, that was the only way he could help Sarah, and, after seeing her with Jeremy Bellingham, Quartus was more than happy he had aided the lovers.

He had a week. Something was bound to occur to him. Suddenly it was the most important thing in the world that she fall in love with him the way he was falling in love with her.

The following morning, the Huntleys, Eveshams, Beaumonts, Rutherfords, Anna and Quartus stood as witnesses to the marriage of Lady Sarah Martin and Mr. Jeremy Bellingham. Two hours later, the newlywed couple was bid a safe journey to Northumberland.

Three days later, Quartus strode into the small front parlor where Sarah's brother was wearing a path in a plush Turkey carpet. "How may I help you?"

Markville turned, grim lines that had not been there previously scored his face. "Where is my sister?"

"On her way to the Bellinghams. She and Jeremy Bellingham were married three days ago. They left immediately after the wedding breakfast."

Covering his face, Markville dropped onto a hard looking couch. After several moments, he raised his head. "Why did she not tell me he was back?"

Quartus refused to let himself feel sorry for the man. "So you could do what you could to stop them from wedding?"

"No. So that I could be there when she married." He leveled a perplexed look at Quartus. "Did she truly believe that I did not wish her to wed the man she chose?"

"Yes. Why else would you agree that she marry me?"

Groaning, Markville ran a hand down his face. "Because I did not believe he, Bellingham, would make it back before her twenty-first birthday. He never attempted to contact me. I knew your reputation as a kind and caring man, and when the duke approached me I thought I could secure her future for her with someone for whom she could come to have affection. Her entire inheritance, including a tidy property in Surrey, is tied up in marrying by the time she turns one and twenty. As her guardian, I could not countenance Sarah losing everything for a man who would never return." Hanging his head, he shook it. "I do not understand how she could have thought . . . did she tell you?"

Quartus poured two glasses of claret and handed one

to the marquis. "From the first day, she told me she was already betrothed and that you did not wish her to marry Jeremy. She said letters had gone missing, and she thought you had something to do with it." He took a sip of wine. "I had no reason to disbelieve her. She had a copy of the settlement agreements signed by him, his father, and your father. There also appeared to be some bad feelings on your part concerning one of his older sisters. I discussed the problem with my sister-in-law, and we agreed to help Sarah. Quite frankly, it did not occur to any of us to speak to you about the matter."

"No." Markville grimaced. "I can see why you would not. I promise you, I did not interfere with her mail. Ships go missing and the post is lost. I would not have attempted to hide Bellingham's letters from her. I did not even know she was receiving letters. Had I known he had been faithful to her, I would not have agreed to the match with you."

"How did you know to come here?"

"I thought to surprise Sarah by buying her some new gowns and had one of the maids go to her room to find one. All of her clothing was gone. I rode to your brother's estate in Bechingstoke where I discovered you had all come here." Tilting his head back he seemed to study the ceiling. "I made a mess of this. I should have just left her in the country and trusted her. This is a lesson I shall not forget." He drained his glass and rose. "If you will excuse me, I must head north and make this right with my sister and her husband."

Quartus rose, preparing to escort the marquis to the door. "Does my father know?"

"I have not seen or spoken with the duke. As far as I'm concerned he is not in dire need of the news."

"Very well then, I wish you safe travels."

Once his lordship had gone, he poured himself another glass of wine. He had been more than a little shocked by what Markville had related. Without a second thought, Quartus had tarred the man. Not publicly, but he had wronged the marquis just the same. It had affected how suitable he thought Markville was for Anna, but Quartus had not been correct. Had he been so eager to find fault with the man because he was in love with Anna?

During the past few days they had ridden and strolled over the countryside. They agreed on almost everything from family to politics. He had come very close to proclaiming his love for her, and he thought she loved him as well. But what if love was not enough? What if she needed a peer who could vote in the House of Lords and perform other acts on her behalf? There was also the problem, not in his or Anna's eyes, that he could be considered a fortune hunter. He would not want the *ton* to think she had married someone far beneath her. Not in rank, of course, but in what he could bring to the marriage. No one would think less of her for marrying Markville, or even a wealthy earl, but a younger son might raise some brows and cause talk.

For Anna's sake, he had to give her the choice. Present Markville to her as a better option for a husband than he was. When she picked the marquis, Quartus would go to Frank and Jenny in America and begin anew in a place where he could prove himself.

He knew where she was and it was time for him to speak.

Tossing back his glass of wine, he left the parlor and strode down the corridor to the door to the garden.

Spying her ambling along the path in Caro's rose garden he called out, "Anna, please we must talk."

CHAPTER TEN

QUARTUS TOOK ANNA'S HANDS IN his. Her fingers warmed, and a shiver at his gentle touch ran through her.

The scent of the roses perfumed the air, and the scene would have been romantic if he had not done it to keep her from coming closer.

His strong throat worked with emotion, and his sky blue eyes were sadder, more defeated than she had ever seen them. And she waited. Waited to see what loving folly would spout from the lips she so desperately wanted to kiss.

"Anna"—when he paused, she nodded encouragingly—"I love you."

He stopped again, waiting for her to respond. "And I love you."

"Yet, I have nothing to offer you." He turned away for a moment as if he was unable to speak. "Not social or political connections. And after what my father did, not even a good name. Markville has everything I do not, and—"

"He may go to the devil." She almost grinned when Quartus's brows slammed together. "In the nicest possible way, of course." He opened his mouth, but before he could speak, she continued, "I do not need wealth. I already have social position. Together we will gain political connections. Indeed, with your brother and Meg, we have already begun helping me."

"But—"

Anna's heart broke for him. No one deserved to be maligned as his father had tried to do to Quartus. "I do understand how distressing your father's blackening of your name is. However, Lady Featherton and her friends, as well as others, will not allow the lies to continue."

"Still, you have a duty to your title, and your people." He spoke softly, but the firmness in his tone echoed the Dukes of Somerset. Past, that was. No one could find much to like about the current holder of the title. "Markville will know how to help you run the estates and do what needs to be done."

"To Markville, my duchy will always be secondary. His main concern is the marquisate." Why could Quartus not understand that the only man she wanted standing beside her was him? "My love, I need a husband who will put me and my dependents first. Who is strong enough to be married to a duchess without being a duke or even a peer. Neither of us may be allowed to sit in the House of Lords, but you, if you like, may have a seat in the Commons. Together we can do what Hawksworth and Meg are doing to influence others to our causes. And I don't care about your lack of wealth. I have never given it a thought."

Quartus's fingers tightened on hers, but his arms bent, allowing her to step closer to him. "Anna, I am a man. I would come to you with something to contribute, to offer to a marriage. It may not matter to you, but it does to me."

"Oh, my darling." Taking her hands from his she cupped his lean cheeks. "You have offered me the most important thing I sought. You have offered me your heart."

She searched his eyes as they darkened and warmed. Finally, the lines that had marred his forehead softened, and he drew her to him. His mouth only inches away from hers. "In that case, Your Grace," he said in a voice rich with love and desire. "Will you do me the honor of being my wife?"

"I would like nothing better, my lord." His lips descended the short distance and melded with hers.

She molded her body to his, wanted to feel every inch of him as their tongues tangled in an age old dance of love.

Sometime later, he lifted his head, and Anna contented herself with placing her cheek against his hard broad chest. "Do you think I should have been the one to propose? I mean—"

"No. I have wanted to ask you to be mine for days, and I will not be cheated out of the opportunity."

"That's nice. I did not truly want to be the one to propose." Slipping her hands under his jacket, she explored the contours of his back. "Would you really have stood aside for Markville?"

Quartus gave a short laugh. "I promised myself I would try." He touched his forehead to hers. "But I prayed that you would talk me out of it."

"You, my lord, are too noble for my own good." She would love to stay here kissing him forever, but soon the world in the form of his brother and sister-in-law and their friends would find them, and they had better have some pertinent. "How and where are we going to wed?"

"Quickly and quietly?" His brows had drawn together again and his lips formed a thin line.

"I would like to have the ceremony in the Wharton church. That way all the local people who would like to attend may do so."

Quartus considered her desire. It made sense. Yet the question was how to keep his father from discovering their plan. Her aunt might present a problem as well. The lady still did not like him. Yet if he could get past the ceremony, he was sure he could bring her round, given time. An idea began to take shape in his mind. "How many people know we are here at the same house party?"

Anna was quiet for several moments, her fingers tapping on his chest. "Only those who are here." She furrowed her lovely brow. "I think that is correct." The tapping on his chest increased. "That must be it. I came with you with your family." Suddenly she grinned. "Clearly, there was some match making going on as my aunt was not included in the invitation."

He thought so as well. In fact, the house party consisted of only his family and her. Thank the Fates all had fallen in place. "If I remember my geography correctly, we are about four to five days from Wharton."

"I believe you're right. But if we are to avoid the banns, we'd have to travel back to London for a Special License. So, that doesn't do us any good at all."

"Ah"—she had started biting her lips and he kissed them—"but we may obtain a regular license in York. We must pass through there in any event. The license requires us to wait seven days, but with the rest of the travel, and planning for the celebration you will want for your dependents, the wait will be short."

"A regular license. I've never heard of it before, but I am sure you are correct." She reached up and kissed him. "You see, there is a very good reason I am marrying you. Look at all the useful things you know and think of."

Smiling, he held her against him. "The only problem is how to plan the wedding without word getting out."

"If Meg will agree to help, we can make it all happen in a thrice." Anna nodded decisively. "I do not care if we have a huge wedding breakfast or if the *ton* attends. Our close friends, the villagers, and those who rely on me are all I need."

"Brilliant suggestion." Quartus was loath to leave the folly, but surely he and Anna would not be left to their own devices too much longer. "Shall we announce our betrothal to the others and beg their assistance?"

Her smile was all he could have hoped for. "Yes, lets." Then she frowned. "I really do need to find Papa. I thought he'd be here days ago. He'd be very disappointed if he missed my wedding."

"Absolutely." At least one of them should have a father present, and Quartus liked the older man. "We shall contrive."

When they strolled into the morning room, it seemed as if everyone was waiting for them.

"Well?" Meg asked.

Anna laughed and he knew he had the largest grin he'd ever had. "We shall marry in Wharton."

"An excellent choice." Caro smiled at her husband. "A wedding for you and a new carriage for me."

"Caro!" Anna's eyes flew open in a wide stare. "I cannot believe you wagered on whether Quartus and I would marry."

"Oh, no." Her tone all innocence. "Not on whether you would wed. That would be vulgar."

"Tell that to my aunt," Huntley mumbled.

She continued as if he hadn't commented. "On where it would take place. My beloved husband was certain you would wed here in all due haste."

Quartus wanted to laugh. "Except that *I* was not at all certain she would agree to become my wife, and did not arrange for a special license."

"What will you do?" Meg asked. "Certainly you'll not wait until the banns are called."

"That would present another difficulty as they would have to be called in both our parishes."

"Meaning our father would receive word of the nuptials in a matter of days, if not hours," Hawksworth said.

"Exactly what we do not want. We will stop in York and obtain a regular license from the archbishop."

Huntley called for champagne to be served, toasts were

made, then Anna sat with Caro and Meg discussing the wedding breakfast until it was time to dress for dinner.

Talk of the ceremony and celebrations continued over the meal.

"I wish my aunt could be happy about Quartus and me marrying," Anna said to the table at large. "I fear she is allowing her bad opinion of Somerset to influence her feelings about Quartus. It would be a shame for her to miss the ceremony."

Meg scrunched up her face as she usually did when she was thinking. "I'll write to my grandmother Featherton. I am positive that between her and the Duchess of Bridgewater they will be able to influence your aunt."

Even with the short time he had spent with the ladies, he agreed that if anyone could change Tatiana Harrington's mind those ladies could. "It is worth the attempt, in any case."

Anna smiled softly at him. "Yes, it is."

"What are we going to do with Mrs. Potter?" Quartus asked. As long as they were dealing with loose ends, they may as well take care of everything.

"Sarah asked me to keep her as my companion," Anna said. "It seems she irritates Lord Markville, and Sarah wanted her to have a home. I assured her she would be welcome." Anna slid a look at Quartus. "In any event, I shall want a companion on the way to Wharton. If nothing else it will raise my status when we stop along the way."

"That is absolutely true," Caro said. "My godmother, who is an earl's daughter, was treated like a princess when she traveled with her servants."

That prompted the telling of Caro's, Huntley's, and, her godmother, Lady Horatia's flight from Venice.

Soon after, they all repaired to the terrace to enjoy the dry and still sunny weather.

He whispered in her ear. "Would you like to take a

stroll?"

"I would love to. This might be our last chance to relax for the next few weeks."

Slipping his arm around her waist, he turned her toward the path beyond. When they entered the wood, she turned to him. "There is something I must tell you. In fact, I should have told you before." She took a large breath. "Several years ago, I was betrothed several years. We anticipated our vows. He died two days before the wedding. If—if you do not wish to—"

He brushed his lips gently across hers. "You are not the only one to have done so. The ton is full of seven and eight month babies. However, I believe we shall wait until our vows have been said. I would not wish to tempt Fate."

"Yes," she murmured. "That would be for the best. Thank you."

"No, thank you for agreeing to be my love and my wife." He sent up a quick prayer that his father would not hear about their nuptials until he and Anna were safely wed. Not that he believed his father would injure him, but at times his tools were not as cautious. And the thought of Anna bearing an illegitimate child, his illegitimate child, did not bear thinking of.

They ambled down the path a little farther when she stopped again. "There is one other thing," she said chewing her lush bottom lip. "Because there have been so many ladies holding the title, it was decided that the family name should remain Whitestone. It doesn't make much sense considering none of the duchesses used anything other than Wharton as a last name—"

Again, he stopped her with a kiss. "It makes perfect sense. I do not think the Trevor name needs to be associated with another dukedom."

"Are you sure you do not mind?" Her eyes filled with concern.

"Absolutely. My brother, Frank, changed his name when he wed the only child of a shipping owner.

What Quartus would have to do is find out if by changing his name he lost his title. His brother did not use his title, but he was living in America. Keeping the title and his rank could only help Anna. It did not seem likely, yet if so, he would simply add Whitestone to Trevor.

Early the next morning, he helped Anna into Meg's carriage. They had decided to travel as fast as they could, considering Caro and Huntley and the others were bringing their young children with them.

"It looks as if it might rain," Anna commented peering up at the sky. "Are you sure you wish to ride?"

The fat fluffy clouds that had been with them for the past few days had thinned out to horse tails, and were becoming darker. With luck, they'd out run any bad weather. "If it starts to rain I'll join you in the carriage."

"Very well." She gave him a peck on his cheek.

Her maid handed her a traveling desk. "Thank you. As long as the ride is not too rough, I should be able to complete some of my correspondence." Frowning slightly she looked at him. "I know Lord Markville had hopes in my direction. I trust he will not be too disappointed to discover I have found another gentleman. Perhaps I should write him a note."

Quartus stifled a groan. There was a reason knights used to ride off with their ladies, and this must have been one of them. "Write him all you wish . . . after the ceremony."

By then, he'd make damn sure she was thinking about him and not bloody Markville!

"BELLING!" SOMERSET TAPPED HIS FINGERS against his desk. "Where the devil has that young care-for-nobody got to?"

His secretary entered the room calmly, as if nothing was wrong. Well he'd soon find out that was not the case.

"Lord Quartus, Your Grace?"

"Yes, Lord Quartus. Who else would I want to know about? Thornfield hasn't seen him at any of the entertainments this week. Is he ill or has he gone home just when I arranged a match for him?"

"I have been informed that he is attending a house party not far from Town, Your Grace."

"House party, eh? Is Lady Sarah attending too?"

"Yes. My information is that she traveled with Lady Hawksworth to the party."

"Markville's gone out of town as well. Don't tell me he's at a house party."

"I do not know that to be a fact, Your Grace."

What the devil was wrong with these people? "Damned lot of hieing off in the middle of the Season going on." It would be deuced odd if there were more than one house party right now. That might work to his advantage, but only if . . . "Find out if Markville's at a house party."

"Yes, Your Grace."

That must be the reason the marquis was not in Town. The man wouldn't allow his sister to go off on her own.

Fate had been playing him a rotten hand lately. Somerset was due for his luck to change. Still . . . "Keep an eye on both houses, and tell me when Quartus and Lady Sarah return."

That young couple needed to be married as soon as possible. He had plans for her property in Surrey.

"Naturally, Your Grace. I shall inform you the moment I receive word that either Lord Quartus or Lady Sarah are back in Town."

"You may go."

"Your Grace."

Somerset pressed the tips of his fingers together. House parties were excellent places for young gentlemen and ladies to meet and develop the fonder feelings they wanted these days. As long as the ladies were someone else's daughters. None of his were going to attend a house party, not even if he was there as well. As soon as Quartus was taken care of, he'd have to find a match for, Faith, his eldest daughter. She'd been upset that she had not been allowed a Season yet. Even Somerset's duchess was not happy with his decisions about Faith. Not that he understood why the girl needed a Season when he would be choosing her husband. Then again, his wife might have a point when she argued that Faith needed to learn how to go on in Polite Society, and a Season would give her that. Perhaps his duchess was right. He'd think about letting her go in autumn for the Little Season.

CHAPTER ELEVEN

BY THE END OF THE second day of their journey they had reached York, and Anna was hardily glad to be able to stop early. She had never traveled so hard or so fast. Still, she should not complain. The weather had remained dry if overcast making their travel easy. She had decided to accompany Quartus when they visited the Archbishop of York's office for the license, and they set out early the next morning.

"Do you think he will remember you?" As they strolled along the street toward the Vicar General's office, Anna gazed around at all the ancient buildings. Nowhere she'd been had seemed as old as York. Though, Quartus had told her that most of the earliest buildings in London were now in sections of town that were not safe.

"The bishop?" He guided her across a busy street, heading confidently through a square.

"Yes. You mentioned that you had met him at Oxford and again when you were ordained."

"I cannot think he would. I was one of several young men." Glancing up at a street sign he turned right. "He is most likely not even in York. His residence and office is south of the city in Bishopsthorpe, when he is there."

They entered a building, walked down a corridor, and he knocked before entering.

"Good afternoon." Quartus spoke to a man sitting behind a desk. "I am Lord Quartus Trevor." She almost laughed as the gentleman popped to his feet. "I require an ordinary license to marry."

"The Vicar-General is busy at the moment, but if you will give me the information I shall fill out the license."

Once they were seated, Quartus provided his name and birth information, then said, "Anna Elizabeth Amelia, Duchess of Wharton, born in Tortola, British West Indies on . . ."

The clerk jumped up. "Excuse me Your Grace, my lord. I will be right back." And dashed through the door to their left.

"That was surprising." Anna had never had anyone react to her in quite that manner. "I wonder if I should be concerned."

"I think"—Quartus smirked—"he decided that getting the Vicar-General might be a good idea after all." Quartus smirked.

A few short moments later, two men entered the room from the same door the clerk had run through.

"Lord Quartus." A gentleman above average height with a straight patrician nose and heavy black brows addressed her betrothed.

"Your Grace, it is a pleasure to meet you again." He bowed holding his hand out to Anna as she rose. "Anna, allow me to introduce his grace, the Archbishop of York. Your Grace, my betrothed, the Duchess of Wharton."

"I'm afraid you startled Mr. Younger, the young cleric who was here." The archbishop chuckled. "If you will have a seat, I shall sign the license. When and where is the wedding to take place?"

"In about a week at Wharton," Anna replied, pleased that Quartus had made such an impression on the archbishop.

"I believe Mr. Sutton is your rector. Am I correct?"

"You are, indeed."

"If you do not mind"—the archbishop glanced at Quartus then Anna—"I would like to assist in the service."

Even though he gave no obvious indication of his surprise, Quartus's hand tightened around her fingers, and she nodded. "Thank you. Your presence will make our wedding that much more special to us."

The archbishop slid the license across the desk to Quartus. "Very well. A week from today. Shall we say ten o'clock?"

"Thank you sir. Ten o'clock will suit us well."

The man spoke as if he would simply pop in for the service, but her home was still a two day drive from York. "We will have a room prepared for you, Your Grace."

"Thank you, Your Grace." The corner of one lip lifted and he bowed. "If you will excuse me?"

Quartus took a large breath and blew it out. He had never dreamed that he would come across the archbishop or that the man would remember him, never mind offer to help officiate at his wedding. For the past few days, he'd felt the need to keep looking over his shoulder, but now that fear was gone. With the archbishop at his wedding to Anna, nothing could stop them.

"That was unexpected," she said taking his arm.

"It was. I'm honored by his offer." Quartus drew her a little closer. His need to have her in his arms had been growing by leaps and bounds. Making riding his horse difficult at times. Still, the decision not to make love with her was the right one, even if his body didn't agree.

"As am I." She smiled at him, and it was as if a ray of sunshine was breaking through the clouds. "I cannot wait to get home. I do hope Mr. Sutton will not be made nervous by the archbishop coming."

"Does he normally have an anxious disposition?"

"Not that I have seen. He was a sea of calm when I was there learning how to be a duchess."

"In that case, there is no need to worry." Quartus quickened his pace just a bit. "We must be on our way again."

TWO DAYS LATER THEIR PARTY arrived in the Lake District. Earlier, he had joined Anna in her coach rather than appear before their dependents on horseback.

People came out of stores and houses as they passed through the village. Many of them waved and Anna returned their greetings.

"You must wave as well."

Quartus felt foolish, but he did as he was told and soon people began to cheer.

After the town, they passed a large lake that gave views over the gently rolling countryside, and he immediately fell in love with the area. "It is more beautiful than I expected it to be."

She ordered the coach halted on an old bridge. "Look out this window and you can see the house. This stream runs by the house. My gamekeeper tells me the fishing is excellent."

He glanced out and was stunned. Built out of a pinkish-gray stone, it resembled something out of a fairy tale. Even his father's house was not as large or grand. "You didn't tell me it was a castle."

"I wanted to surprise you. Isn't it marvelous?" she grinned. "At sunrise and sunset the windows seem to be made of fire. Is your home anything like this?"

"Ours is newer, only dating back a little over a hundred years. It is full of Greek symmetry. So, no. Nothing as wonderful as this." He wanted to explore, as if he was a boy again.

"You cannot tell it from this view, but the house has been added on to over the years. Wait until you see the gardens. I do hope you like them as much as I do."

"I am sure I will." He stared out the window a bit longer. This would be a change for him, but he had lived in England, and in a great house, and had visited even older houses. But for Anna all this had been completely new. "It must have been even more of a change for you than I'd thought."

"Yes, at first." She nodded thoughtfully. "Our house in Tortola was of wood and not even a tenth as large. I was concerned about the castle being cold and drafty, but one of my ancestors hated being cold as well and insured it could be kept warm. The duchess before me, added new windows, and bathrooms. The one we'll share even has piping. She did not entertain much, and thought it would be a waste to add piping though out. We shall have to see if we think it will be worth the expense."

And the inconvenience of the remodeling. Though, he supposed, they could arrange to be elsewhere during that time.

By the time they drew in front of the house, the servants were lined up to greet their mistress. He wondered what they'd think of him.

Anna's jaw dropped. "How did they know to expect us?"

He scanned the area near the front door. "Your aunt is here."

"But . . . but she couldn't be."

Kissing her on the cheek he grinned. "Yet, she is."

"I feel like a naughty child about to get her knuckles rapped."

Grimacing inwardly, Quartus agreed. "Just remember, you are the duchess."

"Then why don't I feel like one now," she retorted, pulling a face.

He gave a bark of laughter. "Come, Your Grace. It's time

to pay the piper."

The door opened and steps were let down. Quartus jumped out, then took Anna's hand as she came down the steps.

When they turned to face the servants, he saw two elderly ladies flanking Anna's aunt. "I think I know how Tatiana came to be here.You are about to meet the Dowager Lady Featherton and the Duchess of Bridgewater."

"Meg's grandmother?"

"One and the same." The concern about how Aunt Tatiana would respond to his obvious place in Anna's life dissolved. If anyone was on their side, it was her ladyship and the duchess. He straightened his shoulders and rose to his full, not inconsiderable, height. "Ready?"

She smiled and nodded. "Never more so."

"Your Grace." Her butler bowed.

"My love"—her smile broadened as she looked at him—"I'd like to you meet Corbet, our butler. Corbet, Lord Quartus Trevor, soon to be my husband."

"My lord, it is the staff's pleasure to welcome you home."

"Thank you, Corbet. I am pleased to be here."

The butler continued, "This is Mrs. Pennymore, our housekeeper."

"Mrs. Pennymore, my pleasure. I am quite sure the children will call you Penny."

"And that's fine with me, my lord. This house needs children running around it, if I may say so."

"Indeed you may." He glanced at Anna and found her eyes sparkling.

His time as a rector proved to be of aid as he met the other servants. Out of long habit, he remembered their names and bits of information about each one of the maids and footmen. Finally they reached the end where Tatiana was waiting with her ladyship and the duchess on the steps.

To his utter surprise, she smiled at them both, but addressed Anna. "I understand why you did not choose to tell me of your feelings for Lord Quartus. Lady Featherton and the duchess explained the matter to me." She turned to him. "I misjudged you, my lord. Please forgive me."

"There is nothing to forgive. You only knew my father. Many think the apple does not fall far from the tree."

"Thank you. My old friends have also related to me some of the actions of the duke with regard to his sons. Be assured that if he tries any of his tricks here, he will not succeed."

"Thank you." He felt as if a pile of stones had fallen from his shoulders. "Lady Tatiana."

"You may as well call me Aunt Tatiana." She smiled at him for the first time and he returned it with one of his own. "Anna, I do not believe you have met her ladyship and her grace. This is Lady Featherton, and the Duchess of Bridgewater."

Anna held out her hands. "I have heard so much about both of you that I feel as if I know you already. Thank you for coming and bringing my aunt. The wedding will be in five days. Will you be able to stay?"

"Oh yes, my dear," Lady Featherton replied. "We would not miss it for anything."

While they had been speaking, the servants had resumed their duties and their friends joined them on the stairs.

Taking his hand, Anna called out. "Please come in. Tea will no doubt arrive shortly. It will be a few minutes before your rooms are ready." She motioned to Corbet. "There are three young children with us and more to arrive in the next day or two."

"Pennymore has already sent maids to the nursery, Your Grace."

Quartus couldn't wait until his and Anna's children filled the nursery, the house, and their lives. Waiting to make love to her was going to be the death of him.

SOON AFTER ANNA, QUARTUS, AND their friends arrived, it seemed as if the castle had turned into a mad house. Rooms were turned out, already clean floors, chandeliers, and banisters were so highly polished she felt as if she was in a house full of mirrors. Quartus did his best to help, but Anna ended up telling him to keep the men out of everyone's way. The benefit of that was the amount of fresh fish the gentlemen caught.

Two days before the wedding, Viscount and Viscountess Wivenly along with Lord and Lady Stanstead, two couples she had met in Town arrived, as well as Meg's mother, father, and her brother, Kit and his wife, Mary. Aunt Tatiana remarked that the castle had not been this full in decades. Still, there was plenty of room which turned out to be fortunate.

"Anna." Quartus came striding into her parlor.

They had hardly had a moment together and she missed him, but he seemed agitated for some reason. "What is it?"

"My mother and the younger children are here. She apologized, but said she could not stay away. She missed Frank's wedding and she would not miss mine."

"How did she find out about us?"

"The Duchess of Bridgewater and she correspond."

Anna could sympathize with Quartus's mother. She would likely feel the same. Yet if the duchess and his brothers and sisters knew did that mean . . . "The duke?"

"No." He let out a breath. "Catherine would never tell him. But he will undoubtedly have discovered that we are getting married. The only questions are what he will do and how long will it take for him to set his schemes in place."

She had heard of the horrible things the duke had done—from abduction to attempted compromise—to Meg, Hawksworth, and Quartus's other brother and his wife.

Anna tried to think of ways to keep the duke and his thugs away from her and Quartus. Naturally, they would ensure all the windows and doors were locked at night, but what in Heaven's name had induced the previous duchesses to fill in the moat and remove the portcullis?

Something had to be done to make them safe, but she had no idea what. "Make any arrangements you think necessary."

"I shall." He pulled her up, pressing his lips to hers he encouraged her to open to him. Their tongues danced and explored, and caressed with a desperation she had not known before. "Don't worry." He rubbed her back, obviously trying to soothe her. "No one is going to stop us from marrying. Meet me in my study an hour before we are to gather in the drawing room. I'll have a plan in place by then."

That was in only two hours. She prayed he was right. Surely neither God nor Fate could be so cruel as to rip them apart now that they had found each other. Breathing in and out slowly, she tried to calm her fears. By tomorrow at this time she and her beloved would have said their vows, and there was nothing the duke would be able to do to stop them.

At the appointed time, she entered the study she had offered Quartus as his own sanctuary. Hawksworth, Meg, the Eveshams, Huntleys, and Rutherford's were just settling in with glasses of sherry. Quartus handed a goblet to her, and she noted new lines seemed to have formed on his handsome countenance. He sat behind his desk, and she took her place in the chair he'd placed next to his.

"Anna and I have a potential problem. My father knows we shall marry. I am not sure he is aware of the date or time, but there is every possibility that he will attempt to stop the wedding." He motioned toward his brother. "Hawksworth suggested we inform you in addition to the security we have already arranged."

She appreciated the way Quartus included her even if she was ignorant about what he had done or what she could do. "You might want to tell them of the plans you have set in place."

He smiled at her. "The footmen, grooms, and gardeners are patrolling and will continue to patrol the inside of the house and the grounds on varying schedules. The idea is to make it difficult for an intruder to figure out when the guards change." He took a sip of sherry. "All the servants have been told to immediately notify their superiors if they see anyone they do not know or who would not normally be at the castle. I would not put it past my father to try to hire locals. People who would not normally be suspect." Quartus looked at their guests. "Does anyone have any other suggestions?"

"I assume the guards are armed." Phoebe Evesham said. "What have you put in place to guard the coaches for tomorrow and on the way to the church?"

"The younger grooms are sleeping on top and under the carriages, not just Anna's, but the others as well."

"Marcus and I will loan you our servants as well, if you have the need."

The lines that had formed in Quartus's face began to ease. "Thank you. That will help."

The others offered their servants as well, assuring him and Anna that they would be armed.

"I have a question." Meg focused on both of them. "Where will you put anyone you capture?"

"The dungeon." Quartus grinned.

"We have dungeons?" Anna had never considered the matter before, but the castle was certainly old enough. "I had no idea."

"I've even had them swept out," He added. "We may tour them if you'd like."

"No thank you." She shuddered. "Whenever I think of dungeons, I think of mice and other unsavory creatures."

"I also notified the magistrate. He was not best pleased to hear there could be a problem."

"Surely he does not blame you?" If that was the case, she would have a talk with the man.

"No, Sir William is upset that anyone would interfere with the nuptials of their duchess."

That was more like it. "I think we should tell the archbishop."

Raising a brow, Quartus said, "That is a very good idea. Especially if the duke tries to disrupt the service."

"What are the plans for the ride to church," Hawksworth asked.

"Outriders. Armed, of course. Do you have any other ideas?"

He leaned forward placing his elbows on his knees. "I assume it is common knowledge that the ceremony will take place at ten o'clock." Anna nodded. "I suggest that a small party of us, including you and Anna arrive at least an hour early. During our explorations, Quartus and I discovered a secondary road from the castle to the town. We could use that."

They spent the next few minutes adding to Quartus's plan, before joining the other guests in the drawing room.

Anna sent up another prayer, thanking the deity for her almost husband's keen intellect and decisiveness, and for their friends and family. This would all work out. It had to.

CHAPTER TWELVE

SOMETIME AFTER THE HOUSE HAD quieted, and Quartus had lulled himself into thinking his father would leave he and Anna alone, he was awakened by a knock on his door.

"My lord." The sharp, urgent voice of the butler came to him.

"Enter." There was a reason he'd left his breeches on.

He was pulling on a shirt when the door opened.

"Three scoundrels attacked the house, my lord, and one attempted to sabotage her grace's coach. We caught two of the thugs attempting to enter the house and the one in the stables." Corbett sniffed. "Unfortunately, the fourth got away. The malfeasors are in the dungeons."

Three out of four was a damn good job for servants that had never done this kind of thing before.

"Excellent work. Give my compliments to those who detained the culprits." Quartus pulled on his stockings and shoes. "Have Lord Hawksworth meet me in the dungeons."

"Yes, my lord. Will there be anything else?"

"I'll need candles, five mugs, and a pitcher of ale."

"As you wish, my lord." The butler bowed before hurrying off.

Quartus was standing in what was probably a guard's room at one time when Hawksworth arrived.

He raised a brow. "I was told they got three. It appears that our father does not intend to lose you."

"The duke has already lost me. It doesn't matter if he

meant to abduct me or harm Anna. I'm done with him." Quartus took the keys down from a hook embedded into the stone wall. "I thought you might like to help me interrogate our prisoners."

"Gladly." His brother gave a humorless smile. "Lead on."

They found two guards outside the cells. "Are you and Charlie the ones who captured these thugs?"

"No, my lord," the older of the two, George, answered. "That were Howard, Ben, Luke, and Billy. Howard and Luke are back on guard, and Luke and Billy are in the kitchen getting plaster put on their faces." He motioned with his chin to the heavy wood plank door in front of him. "That one got knocked out, but I heered him moving just now."

"Do any of them appear to be the leader?"

"Aye, the one in that cell." He pointed to the right.

Quartus glanced through the barred window into the small room. The man was laying on a pallet facing the back wall. "Bring him to me."

He and his brother returned to the guardroom and a few minutes later George entered, carrying a coaching pistol pointed at the leader. Quartus was not surprised to see the thug's hands bound and his feet hobbled by a rope. "Put him in this chair."

None too gently George pushed the prisoner into the chair. "Do you want me to stay with you, my lord?"

Quartus placed his pistol on the table in front of him. His brother did the same. "No, thank you."

The thug eyed the weapons. "What ye goin' ta do?"

Raising his brow, he responded in a bored drawl. "That depends on you, Mr.?

The scoundrel sifted in his chair. "Wheery. That's all ye need to know."

"Is it indeed? In that case, you will be bound over to the magistrate for hanging. They do not take well to having their duchess threatened."

"Dook won't let 'em."

"My father, the duke will have nothing to say about it. I, on the other hand, could help you continue to live."

"Ye'd let me go?"

"I would have you transported." Quartus shrugged. "At least you'd be alive."

The man clapped his lips together. "I got nothin to say."

"In that case, you may return to your accommodations, such as they are."

Wheery's mouth dropped open. "Ye mean ye're quittn' just like that?"

"I am tired and have a wedding to attend in—he took out his pocket watch—four hours. I have neither the time nor inclination to play games with someone who would rather hang than save his own life." Quartus rose. "I bid you a good night. I am sure one of your friends will see the value of confiding in me. My father does not keep tools who fail him."

The man's eyes widened even more, and a look of panic replaced incredulity. "Wait! I'll talk."

Hawksworth slid Quartus a look. "Well played."

Less than an hour later, they had confessions from all three prisoners. "Their stories almost match." Quartus ran his hands through this hair. It would be getting light soon. "What do you think?"

"They're telling the truth. No two people tell the same story the same way. The question is what will you do about the planned attack on the coaches?"

"I would love to see one of the duke's scoundrels get cracked in the head with the Duchess's of Bridgewater's cane, but the safer course is to have everyone take the back road. It's not as good, but it will be safer. We have enough grooms and outriders to protect the coaches." He covered his mouth as he yawned. "I'll send a runner to the magistrate. Once everyone has arrived at the church, he can take the servants to capture the other criminals."

"Go to bed.You'll need all your strength in a few hours."

"You get some sleep as well. We must be prepared for anything."

"You're learning fast, little brother."

Quartus punched Hawksworth in the arm. "Not so little anymore."

He made his way to his chamber, glad that Anna's rest was not disturbed. Before he slept, he'd write a note telling her what happened. He'd love to be able to gloat over tonight's success, but it wasn't over yet.

Anna woke the next morning and stretched. Sounds came from the dressing room, and she sat up, pulled back the curtains, and looked out to find her maid laying out her best gown as well as various other garments. "Tea please. I think I shall break my fast here."

Handing her a missive her maid said. "I'll send down to the kitchens. Eggs, toast, and tea?" She nodded. "Your bath will be up soon."

"What is this?"

"From Lord Quartus, Your Grace."

She popped open the plain wax seal. Was there a crest or ring the duchesses' husbands wore? She'd have to ask her aunt.

My darling Anna,

We had some trouble last night caused, as you might have supposed, by Somerset. Hawksworth and I, as well as several of our servants took care of it, and managed to discover further plans the duke made to stop or delay our wedding.

There is an attack planned on the main road to the Town. I have taken it upon myself to order all the coaches to depart one half hour early and take the lesser used back road. I have also notified the magistrate of the attack on our house and the one planned for the road.

I pray you slept well, as that was my intent.

With much love always,

Quartus

A thrill of joy ran though her. He had taken care of all of it and thought to inform her. All without them even discussing what the procedure would be. She could not have asked for a better husband or partner.

Just over an hour later, she was dressed. Tatiana had suggested she wear the Wharton sapphires. "Something old and blue."

The older woman kissed her cheek for the first time, surprising Anna.

Meg came in with a gold bracelet. "Something borrowed. Welcome to our small family."

"Thank you." Anna hugged her soon to be sister-in-law. "I am proud to be a member of your family."

After Meg left, a soft knock came on the door, and Anna's maid opened it. Catherine, Duchess of Somerset stood at the entrance.

"Please." Anna held out her hands to the older woman. "Come in."

Catherine smiled softly, as she glided forward. "I know we have not had an opportunity to really get to know each other. I wish it could be otherwise."

Anna wondered if she knew her husband was in the area and what he had done. The first time she met her soon to be mother-in-law, she had absolved her of complicity in the duke's behavior. She was as Meg confirmed, soft, gentle, and incapable of controlling, or even influencing,

Somerset.

"I had this made for you." It was a finely wrought gold broach in the shape of her coat of arms. "I hope you like it."

"But how did you know?" Catherine could only have heard about the wedding a few days ago.

She smiled that gentle smile again. "I just know certain things." She kissed Anna's cheek. "I will not be able to see you as often as I'd like, but know that I love you, and I am more than happy that Quartus has found his mate."

Anna's eyes filled with tears. Some of them she was sure were happy, but others were sad. How much she would like to get to know this lady.

A handkerchief was pushed into her hand. "No crying. All will be as it should be."

LESS THAN AN HOUR LATER, Anna and Quartus faced the archbishop as he began the ceremony. Barely listening, she glanced at Quartus who looked at her and smiled. Despite the attempts of his father, they would soon be man and wife.

"Therefore"—the archbishop said—"if any man can show any just cause why they may not lawfully be joined together, let him speak now, or else here after forever hold his peace."

"I object." The words were spoken loudly from the back of the church and with a certain amount of pique. "Stop this service immediately."

Her hands began to shake as she heard Quartus groan. "I have had more than enough of my father."

"For what cause?" the archbishop asked in a calm tone.

"I am Somerset. Lord Quartus Trevor is my son and I

will not have him wed to that woman."

Anna could see the archbishop take a breath. That seemed to be the most frequent reaction to the Duke of Somerset.

The archbishop raised a brow. "I was unaware that Lord Quartus was a minor."

"He is not. I have other plans for him. You will stop this wedding now."

"As you have not stated a valid reason. The service shall continue." The archbishop looked at her and Quartus. "I require and charge you both that if either of you know of any impediment why yet may not be lawfully joined together in Matrimony, ye to now confess it . . ."

"No." Anna and Quartus said at the same time.

"Quartus!"

He closed his eyes for a moment. "I'll be right back."

"I'm going with you."

He nodded, yet when they turned, the crowd of people in the church had started moving into the aisles. Somerset was still shouting, but his voice was becoming fainter as the townspeople and those from the area filled in the open areas, forcing him to move back out of the church.

"They are protecting us," Quartus said, his voice filled with awe.

"I never even imagined they would do such a thing."

"Nor did I."

A soft melodic humming filled the space near the church doors drowning out the duke's tirade.

She and Quartus glanced at the archbishop, who smiled and said, "Shall we continue?"

Quartus took her hands as they repeated their vows, and when the archbishop finally proclaimed them husband and wife, a large sigh filled the church as if everyone had been holding their collective breaths.

She felt like sighing as well. They walked quickly to the

register and signed their names as did their witnesses.

"I will guard this book well, Your Grace," Mr. Sutton said firmly. "I shall also make a copy."

The man was right. She would put nothing past Somerset. "Thank you."

"Come, my wife." Quartus tucked her hand in the crook of his arm. "There are a great many people who want to wish us happy."

And there were. Part of the celebration began in the Town where tables laden with food had been set up. Children were kept busy playing games that someone had organized. He did not see his father, but the magistrate lifted a mug of the ale that had been provided to them, and grinned. The footmen, grooms, and others who'd been pressed into duty as guards were present as well.

"Are we safe now?" Anna asked.

"Yes. He knows once the ceremony is over, he has lost. If he did anything at this point, he'd be prosecuted, Hawksworth would be named co-guardian of our children. My father will do anything to keep that from occurring." Quartus glanced around again and noticed that they were always accompanied by at least three or four men. "Although, our people are not as sanguine."

"We won."

"We did indeed." He began smiling broadly.

She slid a look around and grinned. "I could not be prouder of them, and how they joined ranks against your father."

"I know what you mean."

"Anna, Quartus." Meg saluted them with a glass of wine. "It is time to go home."

It turned out that tradition mandated they walk the mile from the village to the castle. The villagers and their other dependents following behind, singing.

When they arrived the great hall was filled with the

local gentry and their friends. Toasts were made, even Aunt Tatiana joined in, and Anna and he were led to an enormous cake.

"Go on," his brother instructed handing him a large knife. "You make the first cut. The rest will be handed out to everyone else."

LATER THAT EVENING, HER MAID dressed her in some sort of silk gown that would most likely not last the night. Yet it had been a gift from Caro, and Anna decided to wear it.

The door opened and Quartus, dressed in an elaborate robe, entered their bedchamber. His eyes warmed with desire as he gazed at her. "I don't know what that is you are wearing, but it is enough to tempt a stronger man than I."

"Is it really?" Rising slowly so that the silk fell smoothly into place she snoodled toward him. "And what, my lord husband, do you intend to do about it."

He met her halfway and lifted her hair, and caressed the back of her neck. "Love you as you deserve to be loved for the rest of your life."

Anna thought she would be nervous, but she was not. Could it be because she was older, or was her love for Quartus deeper, more mature, than when she was younger. "I wish to love you as well."

He drew her carefully into his arms as if she would break if he was not careful. "You will let me know if I do anything you do not like."

"I will." She slanted her head, touching her tongue to his lips and trailing it along the seam of his mouth. "Kiss me."

"Gladly, my love."

He opened to her allowing her to take control. Then the back of her legs hit the bed. Oh, the devious man. Slipping her hand inside his robe, she discovered his chest was as hard as she had hoped and was covered with soft curls. He groaned as she reached down and stroked his member, then kissed him. Over his chest, up to his neck, finally reaching his lips again.

"I think I was the one who vowed to worship you with my body."

Slowly, so slowly she wanted to scream, he trailed open mouthed kisses over her chest and breasts. When he took first one furled nipple then the other in his mouth, Anna grabbed the linens, clenching them as she took a shuddery breath. Lord, she was going to expire before he finished. His fingers fluttered down her body as light as butterflies, then over her stomach, and finally dipping into the curls hiding the tiny pearl that could cause such pleasure, he rubbed softly with the heel of his hand, as he slid his finger into her passage.

"Don't stop." She pressed into him wanting more. "That feels so good."

"Are you ready for me?" Quartus's eyes glinted wickedly. "You must tell me before I go on.

How could she not be? Had she ever been so wet in her life? And oh God, he was serious. "Yes, my love, yes."

He entered her slowly, as if she was a virgin, and he was trying to feel her responses to his invasion.

"I need to make this right for you. Tell me if it hurts."

"No pain," Anne gasped as she wrapped her legs around him pressing her heels into his bottom, urging him to go faster. Withdrawing, he plunged back into her, and the tension that had held her captive burst out like the sudden appearance of the sun after a storm.

"Anna, Anna, my love." As he pumped his seed into her, she continued to tremble. He held onto her, stroking her back, murmuring words of love. "Are you all right?"

Her fingers caressed his cheek, and she pressed soft kisses over his jaw. "I have never been better."

Thank God. "Neither have I."

EPILOGUE

Ten months later.

ANNA CLENCHED HER TEETH AS another contraction gripped her body. "Is it time yet?"

The mid-wife lifted the sheets. "Push, Your Grace, push."

She bore down as if her life depended upon it. "Arghhh." The pain passed. "Well?"

Meg pressed a cold cloth on Anna's head as she had been doing for the past eight hours. "It won't be long now."

She'd been more than grateful that her sister-in-law had arrived for the birth.

Another contraction took hold. God would this ever end? "Now?"

"Now."

Again, she pushed hard.

"That's it, Your Grace. I see the head. Once more, and we'll have the little mite."

Her womb contracted, and she could feel the child slipping from her.

"It's a boy!" the mid-wife cried. "The first one in a century. Well done, Your Grace!"

"Oh, Lord. I'm glad that's over." Then another contraction hit. Anna tried to sit up. "What the devil?"

"That'll be the after birth, Your Grace. We must get it out." The woman looked under the sheet again. "It can't be," she said in a hushed voice. "This has never happened before.

"What is it?" Meg ran to the end of the bed.

Anna pushed, and the mid-wife screamed. "Two boys, Your Grace! Two!"

The door slammed open hitting the wall, and Quartus rushed into the room. "What is going on? Is Anna all right?"

The mid-wife was practically dancing as she cleaned up the first one and handed the child to him. "Two boys, my lord." She cleaned the second one, giving him that baby as well. "Now stay out of the way."

The afterbirth came, and then things began to happen quickly. A maid lifted Anna as they changed her bed linens. Meg and Annot helped Anna into a clean nightgown. The babies were set to nurse. Each as hungry as if they'd waited months for this moment, and perhaps they had.

After they were satisfied, Quartus propped himself on the bed, gently caressing her face and neck. "Are you well?"

"I am." Sore, tired, but healthy. "Although I feel as if I've made up for a hundred years of male heirs."

"I did mention that twins run in my family, did I not." God in Heaven. What had she got herself into? Twins ran in her family as well, although they had never appeared in the direct Wharton line.

"In that case, Wharton will never again have a lack of male heirs, and I am not going to number them in Latin."

"Thank God for that." He grinned.

AUTHOR NOTE

While researching peeresses in their own right, I discovered that there had, indeed, been duchesses in their own right. Granted there hadn't been one since around the seventh century, but there could have been if lines had not been so disobliging as to die out.

There really was a 'Pirate Priest' in Tortola during the Regency. He (his name has been lost to history) was the vicar of St. Michael's church, which, sadly, no longer exists other than a ring of rubble. Earlier in his life, he was a look out for the pirates going into Cane Garden Bay. He has a much larger role in my book *Enticing Miss Eugénie Villaret.*

You will notice that characters from both my series, *The Marriage Game* and *The Worthingtons* make appearances.

I hope you enjoyed the story.

One Duke or Another

Book Three in The Trevors

CHAPTER ONE

THE SEVENTH OF JUNE, 1818

My dear Somerset,

As you may have heard, my wife had an unfortunate illness and passed away several months ago, leaving me as childless as I was before.

I understand that your eldest daughter is of an age to wed. I would be pleased if you would consider a union between our two families.

Yr servant,

Bolton

THE TENTH OF JUNE, 1818

My dear Bolton,

You are correct in your understanding. My eldest daughter, Aglaia, is of an age to be married. Her mother, my duchess, is a good breeder. There is no reason she should disappoint you with regard to an heir.

She will bring a sufficient dowry. However, I should like the title to the land you own that marches with my estate near Bath.

Yr servant,

Somerset

THE THIRTEENTH OF JUNE, 1818

My dear Somerset,

Consider it done. If you send me your requirements, I shall have my solicitor look them over.

I would like the ceremony to be at the end of July.

Yr servant,

Bolton

LADY AGLAIA TREVOR, ELDEST DAUGHTER of the Duke of Somerset, entered her father's study and stood in front of the large, elegant, walnut burl desk. Her hands clasped, she surreptitiously took in the room she hardly ever saw as she waited for him to acknowledge her presence.

The study itself wasn't particularly large. Not like the drawing rooms or even the morning room. It was, however, as elegant and cold as her father.

Ornate plaster glittering in silver surrounded colorful paintings of mythological scenes. The walls were lined with grayish-blue silk in a subtle stripe of the same color. One crystal chandelier hung in the center of the room directly behind her. Heavy, light blue, velvet curtains with silver trim framed the many windows in the room. All but the curtains directly behind the duke were open, allowing the sun to shine through. Unlike in the cozy morning room, no cat lazed in the sun's path along the light blue and white Turkey carpets. No dust motes dared invade the space.

Laia knew better than to speak. That would bring a sharp rebuke. Instead, she studied the man himself. Even though he was past seventy, he was still tall and broad shouldered, traits he had passed down to all of her brothers.

Most of them, though, had not inherited his blade-like nose. None of them, thankfully, had his testy temperament.

The duke's blond hair was turning to silver, but his pale-blue eyes, the same color as the walls, were still sharp. His face was always stern. No laugh lines showed at the corners of his eyes or mouth. In all her almost one and twenty years, she had rarely seen him smile.

She wondered why she had been summoned. She could not think of anything she had done to displease him. Then again, that was not difficult to accomplish. No matter how well educated or talented she or her brothers and sisters were, he never seemed to be happy with them. Although, he saved most of his ire for her eldest brother, the Marquis of Hawksworth. For his part, Damon did not appear to care what their father thought. He had an inheritance from his mother, the duke's first wife, and did exactly what he pleased. Laia was tempted to sigh. To have such independence was something to which she could never aspire. At the rate she was going, she'd live and die an old maid.

"Sit down, girl."

The barked command was so sudden she almost jumped.

"Yes, Father." Laia sank into the chair behind her, knees together, her hands folded in her lap, eyes cast modestly down.

"I have found you a husband."

A shiver of trepidation slithered down her back. She was not to be a spinster after all. She should have expected it. After all, he had arranged matches for two of her brothers. Not that either Damon or Frank had wed the women Father had chosen. Still, the news was such a shock she could think of nothing to say. He had so little to do with her she had almost believed he had forgotten she existed. That he had gone out of his way and arranged a marriage for her was more than she had hoped for.

"He is the Duke of Bolton." Her father tapped his pen on the desk as if in a hurry. "You will be married at his estate in Hampshire in July."

Bolton? Wasn't he already wed? Or had she confused him with another duke? Not that there were many of them. Yet, she must have. After all, she could not be marrying him if he already had a wife.

Somerset speared Laia with a look reminding her that he probably wanted a response even though she could say only one thing. "Yes, Father."

"You may go." He picked up a document and began to read it.

She rose and almost fled the room. Still . . . was that all he thought she needed to know? Steeling herself for a rebuke, she asked, "When will I met him?"

The duke raised one thin white brow, and Laia fought the urge to escape as quickly as she could. Yet, this was the rest of her life they were discussing, and it was the nineteenth century not the fifteenth century. She would like to get to know her prospective husband before actually saying her vows. "I have arranged for a house in Bath. Your mother is convinced that you need to be in society before taking your position as the wife of a peer. If he can take the time, you will meet Bolton while you are there, I assume."

"Yes, Father. Thank you."

Skirting the chair, she walked as swiftly as she was able from the study and headed straight to the library. She had apparently forgotten who the Duke of Bolton was, but *Debrett's* would answer many of her questions, and her mother the rest. Laia hoped.

But *Bath*! That was above all things absolutely wonderful! It was true that Bath was no longer as popular as it once had been, but there were assemblies, and other parties, and the famous Pump Room, where people met, not only to take the waters, but to see others and be seen. Neither Laia nor her sisters had been allowed to attend even their local assemblies. The promise of Bath was wonderful indeed. And then she was to be wed! What a momentous day this was turning out to be.

A quarter hour later, uncertain what to make of her discovery, she closed the latest copy of *Debrett's*. How could the Duke of Bolton be so careless as to have lost *four* wives? One or two might be understandable, but four seemed a bit excessive. Particularly as he did not even have any children to show for his unions. Then again, perhaps they and their mothers had died in childbirth. Unfortunately, it happened more often than one would like. Thankfully, Laia's mother had never had a problem in that respect. Perhaps that was the reason the duke wished to wed Laia.

He was rather old. Yet Father was much older than Mama, and they seemed to get on well. Laia wished he had chosen a younger man. A handsome man who wasn't four and sixty. If one was to dream, one might as well wish for everything, and no one could argue that four and sixty was not old. If only the duke was four and thirty or even four and forty . . . Still, having children and her own houses to manage was a dream come true. She and her sisters had become convinced that their brother Damon would have to ascend to their father's title before they would be allowed to wed.

Laia would have liked to marry for love like her brothers Damon, Frank, and Quartus had done. But they had all defied Father in their choices. He was still extremely upset about that. The wives' names were not even to be spoken aloud. At least not in Father's hearing.

Laia sighed. There was absolutely no possibility he would even consider allowing her or her sisters to find their own husbands. Then again, it was hard to look for a spouse when one was never allowed to meet *any* gentlemen at all except the elderly dancing master and the servants.

Nevertheless, she should be happy. Her father had gone out of his way for her, and she must trust he had chosen a gentleman who would treat her well.

Rising, she shook out her skirts before making her way to the morning room, where her mother could usually be found. Packing must be done, and Laia wanted to ask when they were leaving for Bath. Fighting the urge to skip, she hastened her step. Just the thought of visiting the spa town made Laia giddy.

As she expected, her mother was with the cats in the morning room reading. A tea service was on a low table in easy reach of her chair.

"Mama." Laia waited while her mother placed a marker in the book and closed it.

Her mother searched Laia's face. "Is something wrong?"

"I do not believe so. Father has informed me that I am to wed the Duke of Bolton."

Mama's already straight back seemed to straighten even more and her brows lowered. "Bolton?"

"Yes." Laia nodded. He also said we were to visit Bath."

Her mother's lips tightened for a moment, but then she smiled and rose. "We are indeed. You should inform your maid. There is much to do before we depart. I must write a letter."

"Yes, of course." She followed her mother out of the room. "When do we leave?"

"In a few days." Mama's voice sounded distracted. "Yes, that will do." She glanced up as if surprised to find Laia still next to her. "Run along now."

She left her mother muttering to herself. What could be the matter?

GUY PAULET, FORMER ARMY OFFICER, current Member of Parliament, and nephew and putative heir to the Duke of Bolton, had just sat down to tea with his good friends, Damon, Marquis of Hawksworth, and his wife, Meg, when their butler entered the well-appointed, sunny parlor carrying a silver salver.

"My lady"—the butler bowed—A letter from her grace has just arrived via messenger. I gather it is urgent."

"Thank you, Saunders." Plucking the missive from the salver, she popped the seal, and shook the paper open. A fine line formed between her brows. "It appears we are going to Bath for the summer," she told Hawksworth

"Indeed?" he asked after a few stunned seconds. When she did not respond he continued, "I suppose at some point you will get around to telling me *why* exactly we must go to Bath."

Meg Hawksworth's frown deepened as she re-read the note. "Somerset has decided that your sister Laia is to marry the Duke of Bolton—I would love to know how that came about—and Catherine has convinced your father that Laia must be brought up to snuff socially before the wedding if she is not to embarrass the family. Of course, if he had let her come out like a normal lady. . ." Meg shook her head in disgust. "The Season has only another week to go, and your father will not allow her to come to Town or Brighton in any event, so Bath it is."

Pain radiating from Guy's back teeth became intolerable, and he tried to loosen his jaw. If this union occurred, it would be his uncle's fifth marriage. And Guy had no doubt at all that it would end the same as the others. In the death of his wife. In this case, the sister of his friend.

Bolton, with his massive sense of self-worth, would not even consider the fact that *he* might be the cause of his wives' failure to breed.

Well, Guy was damned if he'd allow another lady to die

for failing to give the duke an heir.

Especially an innocent such as Lady Laia Trevor.

One way or another, this engagement must come to an end. Guy would see to it.

Before he could voice his objections, Hawksworth spoke. "What the devil is the old man thinking? Bolton will never see sixty again."

"Not to mention the tendency of his wives to depart this earth in an appallingly consistent fashion," Meg murmured in a dry tone. "However, to answer your question, my love, he is thinking that his eldest daughter should wed a duke."

"And as Bolton is in need of a wife, he'll do." Hawksworth scowled. "That's too simple. There is something Somerset wants from Bolton, and he's using Laia to get it."

"I believe you are correct. Somerset doesn't *give* anything away, even his children." Meg placed the letter on a small cherry table next to her. "Well, there is nothing for it. We must think of a way to stop the marriage."

"The question is, short of putting my sister on a ship to Frank and Jenny in New York, what are we going to do?" Hawksworth glanced at his wife.

Guy favored the idea of Hawksworth sending his sister to his brother and sister-in-law. Even Somerset couldn't get to her in America. Or could he? From what Guy had heard of the duke, he'd go to any lengths to get his way. Meg was right. Stopping the marriage was the only sure way of saving Lady Laia.

The conversation paused as the butler carried in a tea tray complete with tarts, biscuits, and small sandwiches. Once Meg had ensured Guy and her husband had cups of tea, and even fuller plates, she said, "We shall find another gentleman for Laia to wed."

An excellent idea. Guy wondered if Meg had someone in mind.

"The gentleman must be at least marginally acceptable

to Somerset." Hawksworth bit off half of his biscuit, chewed, and swallowed. "Unlike my brothers, my sisters are well under Somerset's thumb. And if Laia marries someone of whom he will not eventually approve, it will go worse for the other girls."

"You have a good point." Meg nodded thoughtfully and took a sip of tea as Guy applied himself with gusto to the offerings on his plate. "Guy, I think you would be the perfect solution."

CHAPTER TWO

GUY CHOKED AND HASTILY COVERED his mouth to keep food from spewing over himself and the furniture. Laughing, Hawksworth slapped Guy on the back. "Me?" Guy croaked, barely getting the words out. "But I'm not ready to be leg-shackled yet."

"Since Meg and I married, I've never been happier," Hawksworth assured Guy in a manner he assumed was meant to be helpful.

"Aside from that," Meg added, "if you wish to progress in your career, you must wed."

Yes, but not this minute or even this year. "Why me?" Not only that, but her suggestion was preposterous. He did not even know the lady. He had to find a way to change Meg's mind. "There must be dozens of gentlemen more eligible than I. Somerset will never approve of me. I don't even have a title."

"Not in Bath." Meg's tone brooked no argument.

"I beg your pardon, my dear," Hawksworth said. "But I believe you have jumped ahead in the conversation. Not *what* in Bath?"

"Gentlemen." Her eyes widened as if she were amazed her husband and Guy were confused. "Most of them will be in Brighton." Well, *that* was distressingly accurate. "Aside from the obvious, Somerset wants a duke, and when Bolton dies, Guy will ascend to his title."

"Our family is amazingly long lived," Guy said. "It will be years before I become a duke."

He glanced at Hawksworth in a vain hope of finding support.

"She is right, you know." Hawksworth smirked. "You are the perfect candidate."

"I have never even met your sister." Guy hoped the desperation he felt did not show. Meg Hawksworth was like a dog with a bone when she got one of her ideas.

"No one has. All the girls have been kept close." Hawksworth seemed to consider his words for a moment before saying, "If it comes to that, I had never met Meg before I was introduced to her." Hawksworth gave his wife a smoldering glance. "After that, I couldn't get her out of my mind."

Meg grinned. "And you were the last person I wished to fall in love with." Her gaze lingered on her husband before she turned back to Guy. "The very least you can do is allow us to introduce you to Laia. If you take a violent dislike to each other, we shall attempt to find another gentleman."

"You cannot judge by that, my love." A slow smile dawned on Hawksworth's face. "Look what happened when you decided you couldn't stand me."

She met Hawksworth's smile with one of her own. "Quite right, my love."

This was getting Guy absolutely nowhere. But if he met the lady, he might be able to find some gentleman more suitable to her than he was. After all, the main goal was to stop her marriage to his uncle. "Very well. I agree to meet her."

"Excellent." Hawksworth wandered to the bell pull and tugged. A moment later, Saunders appeared. "Inform Mr. Cummings that I have need of a house in Bath . . ." He looked at Meg.

"Near or in Laura Place," she said.

"Near or in Laura Place," Hawksworth parroted as if

the butler couldn't hear Meg.

"Very good, my lord. I shall inform him immediately."

One of Hawksworth's black brows inched toward his hair line as he considered Guy. "Will you require a house there as well?"

"No. I have one. Believe it or not, one of my great-aunts has given me a house in Great Pultney Street, not far from Laura Place. I was going to rent it out, but wished to inspect the condition first."

"How generous of her," Meg exclaimed.

"Not really. Her bosom friend, with whom she has lived for many years, died not long ago, and she did not want to pay for the upkeep." Guy frowned to himself. "For a reason I do not understand, I have been the recipient of a number of properties either by bequest or gift." He shrugged. "Fortunately, they are all self-supporting and provide me with more than sufficient income to maintain my position in the government."

"In that case," Meg said, setting down her cup, "you will have no problem supporting a family."

Guy wanted to groan. He should have known that part of the conversation had not ended. He had to make them understand that he would not commit himself to the lady. "I promised to meet her, nothing more."

Her eyes widened innocently. "Naturally."

"I shall make arrangements to post to Bath in the next few days." He stood to say his farewells. "Please advise me when you will arrive."

"We shall." Meg rose as well. "According to my stepmother-in-law, they will be in Bath next week sometime."

He bowed to Meg and shook Hawksworth's hand. "No need to show me out. I know the way by now."

As Guy strolled down the corridor to the front door, a thought came to him. His uncle would not be at all happy if Guy managed to filch the man's bride. Still, even though neither he nor his friends thought the young lady should wed Bolton, Guy wondered whether they could turn *her* from the betrothal. Assuming she even wished to escape it. Most ladies dreamed of marrying a duke. Not only that, but from what Hawksworth had said, Lady Laia was very much under her father's control. Would she refuse to honor a betrothal Somerset had made?

The situation was not nearly as straightforward as his friends appeared to think it was.

Dear Bolton,

I shall inform my daughter of her July wedding.

My solicitors will send you the settlement agreements. I trust you will make time to visit Bath before the wedding. My duchess has taken a house on Laura Place.

Yr. servant

Somerset

ALTHOUGH BATH WAS NOT A great distance from their father's principal estate, Mama refused to allow anyone to remain there while she was in the town. But not everyone would fit comfortably in the town house. The children, Thalia, the seventeen-year-old third sister, and Mary, the youngest at eleven, were too young for the entertainments in Bath. They were left at Roselands, a modest family estate only a half hour from Bath. They were accompanied by their nurse, nursemaids, and governess. Their twin brothers, Decimus and William, both thirteen and back from Eton for a holiday were at Roselands as well.

Gazing at the town house in Laura Place, one in a long row, Laia understood her mother's decision about room for them and her nineteen-year-old sister Euphrosyne. The house had four floors and what appeared to be an attic, but was not very wide.

"Let us find our rooms and prepare for dinner." Mama smiled. "Then I have a surprise for you."

Laia couldn't think what would make her mother so happy. It certainly wouldn't be a visit from the Duke of Bolton. Her mother clearly hadn't been pleased with the betrothal when she had muttered something about the news and excused herself to write a letter. Laia had spent the next week expecting to hear she was no longer engaged. Instead, preparations for their journey to Bath had consumed all their time.

On the day before they had departed, her father gave her a betrothal ring and a miniature of her betrothed sent by the Duke of Bolton. One would think his grace could have sent them directly to her.

She glanced down at the thick gold band set with a large ruby flanked by diamonds of almost the same size. The ring would have looked much better on a dark-haired lady. Laia had inherited her mother's pale complexion and her father's nearly white hair and would have much preferred sapphires. Perhaps she should have sent a miniature of herself to the duke so that he would have known what would look well on her.

The ring also hung loosely on her finger, and if she was not careful, she would lose it before she could have it altered.

She studied the painting once again. Bolton was handsome enough, with russet hair and blue eyes. Yet there was something about those very same eyes that appeared almost feral. She gave herself a shake. That could have been a mistake by the artist. She hoped it was.

If the portrait was accurate, he was either in very good health, or the painter had—except for the eyes—flattered him. He did not look like a man of four and sixty years, but once again, she wished he were younger.

Laia shrugged her shoulders lightly. She was becoming fanciful. Father had said she would meet her betrothed here, and once she did, everything would be fine, she was certain. She just wished she knew when that would be.

A half hour later, she sat before her mirror as her maid, Smithers, deftly twisted Laia's normally unruly curls into a fashionable confection of braids, a knot, and tendrils, before weaving a Prussian blue ribbon through it all.

After donning a white, spangled shawl, she picked up her reticule and fan and proceeded to the drawing room. Unlike in the two other houses she had visited, Meg's family's home and Anna's—her other sister-in-law, the Duchess of Wharton—Laia did not require a footman to show her the way. The Laura Place house was not only small, but straightforward.

As she approached the parlor, low voices filtered into the corridor. One of them was male and very familiar.

"Damon!" The next moment, she spied her sister-in-law. "Meg! How come you to be in Bath? I would have thought you would spend the summer in Brighton." Laia glanced at her sister-in-law's stomach. Meg was five months pregnant, but she was barely showing in the high-waisted gown. "How are you feeling?"

"Excellent." Meg bussed Laia's cheek. "I have not been ill once. Why would we go to Brighton when you are in Bath? We have so little opportunity to spend time with you."

Meg laughed as Damon scooped Laia up into a tight hug and exclaimed, "I swear you have grown prettier since

I last saw you."

"Do not crush me. Smithers just spent thirty minutes on my hair."

"This"—Damon released her—"is what happens when the children grow up. They become too old for hugs from their brother."

Mama shook her head and Meg embraced Laia, careful of her hair. "We have taken a house and plan to spend as much time as possible with you and your sisters and brothers. Catherine told us you would be here."

Ever since Damon's falling out with their father, her brother had not been home to visit. Laia still did not know how her mother had persuaded her father to agree her brothers and sisters could attend the wedding breakfasts of Damon and her second-eldest brother, Frank.

"I'm glad for it." Rising up on her toes, she pecked Damon's cheek. "We do not see enough of you. Have you heard I am to marry?"

"Yes." Meg's smile was more polite than real and did not reach her normally expressive eyes. First Mama, now Meg. For some reason, neither of them was happy about Laia's wedding. "Your mother wrote to us about the betrothal."

That answered the question of who Mama had written that day, but why was no one but Laia and her father pleased with her engagement? It was as if her mother, brother, and sister-in-law chose to completely ignore Laia's new status. And that irked her. She was about to mention the subject when Euphrosyne entered the room and practically threw herself into their brother's arms.

"Meg, Damon! This is wonderful. I never dreamt you would be our surprise."

"Now, that's what I call a proper welcome!" He twirled Euphrosyne around before setting her feet back on the floor.

"We miss you." She gave Meg a quick hug. "Thalia,

Mary, and the twins are at Roselands. Will you visit them as well?"

"Of course we will." Meg kissed Euphrosyne's cheek. "We have missed all of you as well."

The small drawing room already seemed crowded with people when her mother's butler, Perkins, intoned, "Mr. Guy Paulet."

Paulet? That was the Duke of Bolton's family name. She tried to envision the information in *Debrett's* concerning the Paulets. If she was not mistaken, Guy Paulet was the son of the duke's younger, twin brother and currently heir to the dukedom.

Mr. Paulet was as tall as Damon and had the same military bearing. Dressed in a well-cut dark-blue jacket with a waistcoat in lighter blue and gold, Mr. Paulet was the epitome of what Laia imagined a fashionable gentleman to look like. His breeches were of the same dark blue, and his cravat was tied neatly. His only ornaments were a pocket watch, quizzing glass, and sapphire cravat pin.

Yet, what captured Laia's attention most was his reddish-brown hair. It was very much like the duke's. In fact, he looked very much like the man in the miniature. She was too far away to get a good look at his eyes, but she would wager her new pearl necklace they were blue.

"Guy." Mama glided forward, her hands held out in greeting. "How good of you to come."

"Your grace. You flatter me." His lips tilted up in what Laia decided was a ready smile. "I could not have turned down an invitation to see you again." Lightly grasping her fingers, he bowed. "My mother sends her love and wishes she could be here as well. However, she is with my sister, Constance, who has just given birth to her third child."

Mama placed her hand on his sleeve, drawing him into the room. "I received a letter from her before we left Somerset. A healthy boy, is it not?"

"Yes, indeed. Haverstone has been telling everyone who would listen how clever my sister is."

That would be the Earl of Haverstone if Laia remembered correctly.

Had Mr. Paulet come here to inspect her before she met the duke? If so, she did not like that idea. On the other hand, he might have come to welcome her to the family, as it were.

Her mother smiled. "Guy, I understand you have been making a name for yourself in the Commons."

"So I am told." Mr. Paulet was close enough now that she could see his eyes were blue and, unlike his uncle's, seemed to sparkle with good humor. "It is not much different than moving troops around. Once one has the trick of it, that is."

She remained where she was, but set her glass of wine down on a small table as Mr. Paulet greeted Damon and Meg as friends.

"Laia, my dear," her mother said. "I would like to make you known to Mr. Paulet. His mother is an old and close friend of mine. I have known him since he was in leading strings. He also served in the Army with Hawksworth." Mama cast the man a twinkling glance. "At present he is a Member of Parliament and doing quite a good job from all accounts. I was delighted to hear he meant to spend some time in Bath this summer."

Goodness, he seemed to know everyone and was liked by them as well. Perhaps his being here had nothing at all to do with the duke.

Laia curtseyed slightly and held out her hand. "A pleasure to meet you, Mr. Paulet."

CHAPTER THREE

GUY BARELY STOPPED HIS JAW from dropping. *She* was Hawksworth's younger sister? Why had no one told him she was . . . was . . . so beautiful? The word hardly did her justice.

Thick curls of the palest blond framed her oval face. Her eyes reminded him of the sky in winter. Not the deep blue of summer, but warmer than the ice that covered the lake at his home. Her brows and lashes of dark brown and the roses in her cheeks set off the white of her demure muslin gown. Her nose was straight, but not sharp, and her deep-pink lips were nicely shaped, the bottom slightly plumper than the top.

A mouth made for kissing.

For a moment, Guy was so dumbstruck he almost forgot to bow, bringing her fingers to his lips at the last minute.

She was the lady Meg and Hawksworth wanted him to wed?

"Guy"—he could hear the merriment in the duchess's voice and thought Meg and Hawksworth were laughing as well. Still, he could not marry a lady based on beauty alone. There must be common interests and a confluence of minds—"My eldest daughter, Lady Aglaia Trevor."

"The pleasure is entirely mine, my lady." Guy straightened and remembered to give her hand back.

Before he could draw her into conversation, the duchess brought forward a younger lady. "Euphrosyne, I would like to introduce Mr. Paulet. Guy, my second daughter, Lady

Euphrosyne."

Once again, he bowed and the lady curtseyed. "Delighted, my lady."

"Thank you." She glanced at her brother. "I am always happy to meet my brother's friends." Leaning toward him a bit, she said in a saucy tone, "We do not often get to do so."

A minx as well. Hawksworth would have to keep an eye on her.

Meg handed Lady Euphrosyne a glass of lemonade, drawing her away and enabling him to speak with the older sister.

"Do you remain in Bath long?" he asked Lady Laia even though he knew the answer.

She gave him a quizzical look. "Only until my marriage. Surely you are aware that I am to wed the Duke of Bolton." A delicate pink painted her cheeks. "Before I knew of your friendships with my family, I had assumed you were here at his behest."

Little did she know that Guy was the last person Bolton would send to meet his new betrothed. Guy would have to skirt the truth if he wasn't to give the plan away. A plan to which he was starting to become agreeable. "My uncle has told me nothing. In truth, I am rather surprised he has decided to marry again. Thus far, marriage has not gone well for him."

She pulled her plump lower lip between a set of white teeth. "I understand that he has lost four wives. I had assumed it was to do with complications surrounding their delicate conditions."

Her blush deepened, and she took a drink of wine. She was even more innocent than he had realized.

Then again, she was brave enough not to shy away from the subject. Guy was surprised she had asked at all. It was not a topic an unmarried lady usually broached with a gentleman.

Her courage convinced him to give her a more direct answer than he had planned to offer. "Not at all. None of his wives were"—drat, how was he to put this so as not to embarrass her? None of the ladies had been pregnant. They had not even had a hope of giving birth unless they played his uncle false—"were in an interesting condition. He had been married to his first wife for fifteen years when she succumbed to a lung condition. He has been wed considerably shorter times to his subsequent wives. All of them surrendered to similar ailments. You might have noticed"—surely she had read about them in *Debrett's*—"the length of his marriages have decreased with each wife."

The corners of her lips turned down and her smooth forehead creased. "Are you trying to tell me he has had something to do with their deaths?"

"Unless one has absolute proof, to do so would be slander." This was the ticklesome part. He arched one brow. "I am merely saying that his brides are not long-lived." Avoiding her gaze, he flicked a piece of lint off his sleeve. "Aside from that, I would not want him convicted of murder."—that would give Prinny an excuse to take the dukedom—"I am his heir, you see." Better to get that piece of information out before Lady Laia discovered it herself. Although, what she would do with the knowledge he had no idea.

She gazed at him for several moments before saying, "I believe I do understand. It would do you no good if he were to produce an heir."

"Nothing could be further from the truth. If he could do so, I would be extremely happy for him and for myself." He fixed her with a look of his own. "I have my own property, wealth, and career. I do not require Bolton's. That said, I do not believe an heir will be forthcoming no matter how many wives he acquires."

"Thank you for your candor, Mr. Paulet. However, I cannot believe my father would betroth me to a gentleman in whose hands my life would be at risk."

She regally inclined her head and went off to her sister-in-law, leaving him standing there wondering if it would even be possible to turn her from Bolton. Honesty about the possibility of children and hints about the fate of his wives had obviously not worked.

Hawksworth sidled up to Guy, two glasses of wine in his hand. "I believe we forgot to ask if you would like refreshment."

"Thank you." He took the claret, and tossed back half the glass.

"I take it your conversation with Laia did not go well?"

"In a word, no. I told her as much as I could without accusing my uncle of murder, but she has a firm belief that your father would not put her life in danger."

His friend scoffed. "He would do anything to accomplish what he wants. Since we last met, I discovered your uncle has a minor property that marches along Roselands. I do not think he would have approached your uncle with the plan, but . . . ."

"But if my uncle was searching for a good breeder, he need look no further than the duchess's daughters."

"Indeed." Hawksworth sipped his wine. "Out of fifteen she has lost only one and that was not in childbirth. My grandmother Somerset also had an impressive number of healthy children."

Guy tried to think of a way to change Lady Laia's mind about his uncle. The problem, as he saw it, was that it would be easier for someone else, a member of her family, for example, to do it. He was obviously suspect. "Could your stepmother help?"

"No." Hawksworth shook his head. "Catherine is in a precarious position. She dare not be seen taking a position opposite of my father's. If he had an inkling that she was defying him, she'd be banished to one of the minor estates without the children. Needless to say, that would break her heart. The only thing she can do is help guide."

Devil it all.

His friend grinned wickedly. "I, on the other hand, and Meg, will do everything we are able to in order to ensure my sister does not wed Bolton."

Meg left Laia's side and joined them. "We still need a strategy. Laia has no idea what her father truly is. Nevertheless, Guy, from what she just told me, your honesty has made her question, at least a little, the betrothal. We may never convince her that Somerset doesn't care about her, or anyone else for that matter, but we can make sure she comes to know you better." Meg's eyes twinkled. "You do not dare to be seen with her in the Pump Room. If any intimates of my father-in-law are in town, that is where they will be. My Grandmother Featherton says Bath is a hot-bed of gossip. I have no doubt we shall soon know who is here and where it is safe to be seen with her."

"But will Laia not be in the company of her mother here in Bath?" How would he ever be alone with the beauty?

"I shall accompany Catherine to the Pump Room, subscription libraries, and the Assembly Rooms to give our names to the Masters of Ceremony so that we receive cards to the assemblies. Whilst we're doing that, you and Hawksworth shall take Laia and Euphrosyne to the Gardens. Or"—Meg glanced at Hawksworth—"you could order the horses to be brought round from the stables and go riding on Lansdowne. I leave it to you to arrange." Meg tapped her lips with her index finger. "Talk about anything except the betrothal. Your first step is to earn her trust."

"I'll ask her which she would like best," Hawksworth said.

Guy's shoulders lightened. He was still not sure he wished to marry Lady Laia. Yes, she was beautiful and seemed to be intelligent, and he desired her, but he wanted more. He wanted the type of marriage his parents had, one filled with trust and love.

Yet, at the moment he was going to make sure she did not fall victim to his uncle's maniacal search for an heir. If Guy and she were not meant to spend their lives together, she would find another gentleman.

Her tinkling laugh floated across the room. Or perhaps they would suit.

The Duke of Bolton crumpled up his latest missive from Somerset and threw it in the fire. What in blazes was the blasted old man thinking about in sending Lady Aglaia to Bath, of all the God-forsaken places?

Her being there was going to cause Bolton problems. He could feel it in his bones.

A grandmother of Margaret, the last Duchess of Bolton, lived there. And the old besom blamed him for Margaret's death. Well, it was the chit's own damn fault. She should have accepted his offer of a divorce.

He had arranged for two gentlemen to testify that she had been unfaithful.

Not that she could have remained in England. The scandal would have ruined her. But he had offered to set her up nicely somewhere in Italy. His lip curled. Instead of agreeing, she had enacted him a Cheltenham tragedy and threatened to tell her grandmother, the Dowager Lady Engle. That old lady would have taken pleasure in sticking a spoke in his wheel. She never had liked him. So, he'd had no choice but to get rid of Margaret.

The dukedom needed an heir, and an heir it would have.

He glanced at the letter again. Perhaps he should make a bolt to Bath and ensure that his betrothed did not listen to gossip. He could poison Lady Aglaia against the old woman. If he avoided the Pump Room where Lady Engle held court, all should be well.

"Rogers."

Bolton's secretary appeared at the door between his study and his employee's office. "I must travel to Bath."

"Bath, your grace?"

"That's what I said. Look at my diary and arrange the trip when I have nothing else planned. I'll stay at The York."

"Yes, your grace." A few minutes later, Rogers tapped on the door. "The settlement agreements have arrived, your grace."

"Bring them here." After a brief perusal, Bolton signed them and affixed his seal. Somerset's terms were high, but if it got Bolton his heir, the price would be worth it. "I want them sent back immediately."

"I shall send them by courier, your grace."

Once his secretary had taken the documents and left the study, he leaned back in his intricately carved Moroccan leather chair. He should be able to keep the betrothal quiet. Somerset had described Lady Aglaia as a shy young lady, not prone to speaking a great deal. She had been educated at home and had not had a Season. Ergo, she had no close friends in which to confide.

The duchess would have no reason to mention the pending marriage to a stranger. Which is what Lady Engle would be to her. The woman had lived in Bath for over twenty years and knew a great many people, but the Duchess of Somerset was not one of them. In fact, he had nothing about which to be concerned. And no reason not to believe Lady Aglaia would give him the heir he needed to keep his blasted nephew from inheriting. On second thought, he should stay away from Bath as long as possible.

DAMON, MEG, AND MR. PAULET—WAS the man to always be around?—joined Laia, her mother, and her sister for breakfast the following morning.

"Your mother and Meg intend to visit the Pump Room," Damon said. "Unless you wish to go and drink the waters"—Laia shook her head. She had heard the waters tasted horrible and at this time of year, there were unlikely to be many ladies her age present—"In that case, I propose we either order the horses to be brought round, or we explore Sydney Gardens. We will do whatever you like."

Laia glanced at her sister's surprised face. Even on their birthdays they had never been given such freedom. And she knew just where she wished to visit. Sydney Gardens.

Last night, she had read the guide book the leasing agent had kindly provided, and the garden was high on her list of sites to visit. "Sydney Gardens. I read that there are shady groves, grottoes, labyrinths, waterfalls, gala nights, illuminations and public breakfasts in summer. May we see them all?"

"So that is where the guide book went to." Euphrosyne narrowed her eyes at Laia, giving her an angry look. "I searched for it for over an hour."

That sort of comment frequently preceded a squabble, but she was too old for that now. Raising her chin, she used her most grown-up tone. "You should have asked me. We could have read it together."

"We will see as much as possible this morning." Damon laughed. "But we must trust that your mother and Meg discover the dates of the gala night, illuminations, breakfasts, and what else Bath has to offer us."

Mr. Paulet dabbed his mouth with his napkin. "I have had the opportunity to visit Sydney Gardens. They are extremely interesting. I also took the time to discover the key to the labyrinths."

That was well done of him. Laia could think of nothing worse than being trapped in a maze. "When shall we leave?"

"As soon as you and Euphrosyne are ready," Damon replied.

Laia pushed back her chair. "Give me twenty minutes."

"I as well," her sister said, following Laia out of the room. "Is the guide book interesting?"

"I am not sure I would say that, but it does list a great many places to see and things to do. Would you like to look through it when we return?"

"Yes, thank you." They were half-way to their rooms when Euphrosyne said in a hushed tone, "Do you think Mama will allow us to read novels now that Father is not here to stop us?"

Laia had not even thought of that possibility. All they were allowed to read at home were improving works and newspapers. "We shall ask, but try not to be upset if she refuses."

"I won't." They reached the top of the steps. "Mr. Paulet seems to be very nice."

"Yes." Laia thought of his ready smile and twinkling eyes. Still, he had just about accused her betrothed of murder. That she could not like. Yet he gave her other things to think about as well. Did her father know how many wives Bolton had lost? "Yes, he does. I would imagine most of our brother's friends are nice."

"Perhaps we shall meet more of them." Her sister's voice was wistful, and Laia knew Euphrosyne was wishing for a London Season. A Season that would most likely never come.

Thirty minutes later, almost to the second, the foursome stepped onto the pavement in front of the Laura Place house and started up the hill to Sydney Gardens.

Laia turned around to gaze down at the view of the town. "I have never seen a place with so many hills."

"You've never seen anywhere at all," her sister said.

That was something Laia hoped would change with her marriage. "Very true."

"Come, little one," Damon said as he took her sister's hand and placed it on his arm. "Paulet, please escort Laia."

"My lady." Mr. Paulet bowed. "Escorting you would be my pleasure."

Ah. There was that smile again. This time she noticed the dimple on one side of his face. "Thank you."

Mama had made her brothers practice escorting her and her sisters, but she had always felt as if she were being dragged along. Mr. Paulet, however, adjusted his steps to her shorter ones, making strolling next to him much more pleasant than with her brothers. Particularly as they were walking up hill.

He point out his house, telling her how it had been left to him, then stopped. "You can see much of Bath from here."

Below her spread the city and river beyond. How breathtaking. No one had ever exerted themselves to ensure she was entertained before. Laia slid him a glance but he was looking at her instead of the view. Suddenly her mouth dried. He was much more handsome than she had originally thought.

CHAPTER FOUR

SEVERAL MINUTES LATER, LAIA CAUGHT her first glimpse of the gardens. Flower beds looked like colorful pillows against the green meadow. In the distance, she could see a covered bridge. "How pretty it is here. What shall we view first?"

Mr. Paulet grinned down at her. "I think we might begin with the labyrinths, and as the morning becomes warmer, we can visit the grotto."

After Euphrosyne got lost in the maze and Mr. Paulet and Laia had to go in and help her out, they explored the grotto—which was, indeed, a welcome break from the rising heat—and wandered along one of the shady paths.

Damon's stomach grumbled loudly.

"I'm for my luncheon," he proclaimed.

"When do you not wish to eat?" Mr. Paulet gave her brother such a look that Laia was hard-pressed not to laugh.

"Rarely," Damon said in a lofty voice.

"I'm hungry as well," Euphrosyne said.

Mr. Paulet glanced at Laia and sighed. "There is nothing for it. We must see these two fed. I know for a fact Hawksworth becomes a bear when he's peckish."

"To be honest, my sister is not much better." She and Mr. Paulet began to follow her brother and sister home.

He had been the perfect gentleman, helping her over small stones and dips in the paths, and telling her about Bath and the surrounding areas. Despite what she had thought last evening, she enjoyed spending time with him and was sorry her brother had put an end to their outing.

Just outside of Laura Place, they met her sister-in-law and mother coming from the direction of town. "Did you drink the waters? Were they very nasty?"

"Yes, and no." Her mother laughed. "There are a great many interesting people at the Pump Room. You may wish to accompany us tomorrow."

"Both Mr. King, who is the Master of Ceremony for the Upper Rooms," Meg said, "and Mr. Guynette, who performs the same task at the Lower Rooms, informed us there are balls twice every week and an illumination is planned four days after the next ball."

Laia and her sister would never be allowed to attend the balls, but she couldn't help but to give a little bounce of excitement about the illumination. "I never dreamt it would be so soon."

"Did you come across anyone you know?" Damon asked as he took his wife's hand, raising it to his lips.

"Indeed we did." Meg stared into his eyes for a moment and Laia felt like sighing to see them so much in love. Would she love her husband like that? "Lady Sarah and Mr. Jeremy Bellingham are here with her brother Markham."

Damon's eyes widened. "That *is* a surprise. I would have supposed Markham to be in Brighton."

"Oh, no. He doesn't like the Carleton House crowd any more than we do." Meg took her husband's arm and turned him toward the bridge to the house. "They are staying at The York while they look for a house to buy."

"Who? Sarah and Jeremy or Markham?"

"Markham is buying a house for them." Meg strolled through the door behind Mama, grinning. "You remember that Quartus told us there was a misunderstanding of some kind between Sarah and her brother? It seems they have worked it out." Meg handed her parasol and bonnet to Perkins. "We shall see them at the Pump Room tomorrow.

It is quite delightful there. I also met Lady Engle, a friend of my grandmother's. You will like her a great deal, I dare say."

Guy's ears perked up at hearing Lady Engle's name. Meg *had* been busy. The older lady's granddaughter had been his uncle's last wife, and the woman had no love for his grace at all. He would dearly love to arrange for Lady Laia to speak with the older woman. Guy wondered how many of Somerset's cronies had been present at the Pump Room and if any of them would report the meeting. Then again, none of them knew what he did about his uncle.

They were all in the hall now, and he began to take his leave of Lady Laia. "I had a delightful time this morning. I hope you will allow me to escort you to the illumination."

Her blue eyes lit up at his suggestion, making him glad he had mentioned it. "If my mother agrees, I would like it above all things."

"Guy," the duchess said, "please join us for luncheon. I intend to press you into service as one of our evening escorts."

"Oh, yes." Laia's lovely, lush pink lips widened into a smile, and damn if he didn't want to kiss her. "That would be wonderful. Please say you will."

"Of course." He could not help but to return her smile. "I live to serve. My credit will indeed rise in the company of such lovely ladies."

A light blush colored her cheeks and neck, drawing his attention to her ample breasts. Her mouth opened slightly, and it occurred to him that a gentleman had never admired her before. If they found they suited, he would, he realized, be her first for everything. And for some reason, that knowledge pleased him to no end.

He held out his arm to her. "Allow me to escort you to luncheon."

She placed her hand on his arm, warming him where

she touched him. "Thank you, sir."

"No. Thank you, my lady. I do not believe I have ever squired a more beautiful woman."

Her lips formed a perfect "O", but she recovered quickly. "I am not at all sure you should speak to me like that."

"No?" he asked, raising one brow. "Perhaps not. Or perhaps that is exactly how I should address you."

Lady Laia's cheeks reddened again, but as before she rallied. "Are you flirting with me, Mr. Paulet?"

Ah, innocent she might be, but she was no one's fool. "I am. Do you like it?"

She didn't answer until they had reached the breakfast room. "I think I do like it."

"Good. I intend to continue." And be the gentleman who showed her how to flirt.

As they sat down to a cold collation, the talk turned to other sites to be visited in the area. After discussing excursions to the ancient chapel at Farley Castle, the Roman ruins, and town of Badminton, the sisters decided to wait to visit the Pump Room and other places the guide book mentioned.

"Once we have seen all the places around Bath," Laia explained, "we will probably be so fagged we will *want* to drink the water."

"I have no doubt you are right, my dear," the duchess said. "However, I shall leave the sightseeing to you."

"But, Mama," Euphrosyne cried. "We want you to join us."

"I know you do, my love," the duchess said in her gentle way. "However, I have met some old friends with whom I would dearly love to spend time, and I must take time to look in on your brothers and sisters. Aside from that, I shall be with you in the evening for the balls and concerts."

"We're going to be allowed to go to the ball?" Laia's

eyes grew to the size of saucers. "A real ball?"

"I believe I shall host a dancing afternoon," Meg said.

Guy wanted to plant Somerset a facer. How could that old man have denied them the pleasures all young ladies should enjoy? "There are no waltzes, but will you do me the honor of standing up with me for your first dance at Lady Hawksworth's party?"

Her head swung from her mother, who nodded her permission, to him. "I would love to."

At her sister's fallen face, Damon said, "Euphrosyne, I know I am only a brother, but will you allow me to lead you out for your first set?"

Immediately, her countenance brightened. "Thank you, Hawksworth. You are the best brother ever."

"If no one objects, I shall ask Lord Markham as well as his sister and brother-in-law if they would like to join us when we ride to Farley Castle. They have just arrived in Bath as well and have not seen the sights." Meg looked at her family as they nodded, then glanced at Guy.

"That is an excellent idea." The thought of giving Lady Laia the opportunity to meet another gentleman should not have upset him the way it did. He would simply find a way to keep Markham away from her.

The corners of her lips curved up. "That is what I thought. Aside from that, we really do need another gentleman to even our numbers."

"Very true," Lady Euphrosyne agreed. "I am always left with no escort."

The excursion would also give Guy more time to come to know Lady Laia. Provided Markham did not try to cut him out. Guy really was becoming obsessed with that idea. He'd have to make it clear to his lordship where his interests lay.

He glanced at her younger sister. Perhaps Markham would be interested in Lady Euphrosyne. Her coloring was not as fair as her sister's, nor was she as beautiful, but she had a way about her Markham might like.

According to Hawksworth, she was also of marriageable age, although not as close to her majority as Lady Laia. The question was, would Somerset allow the match? Somehow, Guy could not envision Markham bolting to Gretna Green, no matter how enthralled he was with a lady. Did that mean Guy would? The thought disturbed him. A scandal, and that's exactly what it would be, was no way to help his career. He'd have to ask Hawksworth just how close to her majority his sister was.

Guy gave himself a shake. He was being ridiculous. Making matches for a gentleman and lady who had not even met each other. Imagining that he might wed a lady about whom he was not yet certain. But he couldn't seem to stop himself.

He turned his thoughts back to Lady Laia. If she and Guy were to wed, neither duke could stop them or harm them in any way, as long as she had reached her majority. Even if her father or his uncle attempted to ruin his career, he had enough power and support to weather the challenge. In fact, once his uncle had realized that Guy's politics were not the same, the man had tried to replace Guy as MP, and found he could not. If he married the lady, he had the means to protect her. And he might very well be required to do just that.

AS MUCH AS LAIA WAS enjoying Mr. Paulet's attentions, she was not certain how to take them. All she knew was that she felt a thrill of pleasure when he gazed at her, and his blue eyes seemed to simmer as they practically touched her body. When she had placed her fingers on his arm, she could not ignore his strength.

She had asked if he was flirting with her, meaning the question to be a slight reprimand, but he had turned it into something else entirely. The problem was that she did not have the experience or the knowledge to know exactly what. Laia truly wished she had more experience with men. Yet, surely her mother or sister-in-law would have said something if Mr. Paulet's behavior was not what it should be. She would have to trust their judgment. Damon, as well, liked the man, and as protective as her brother was, he'd definitely step in if Mr. Paulet crossed a line.

She pulled her thoughts to the here and now to find the very gentleman who occupied her mind was now seated next to her filling her plate with samples of meat, cheese, bread, and salad.

This time when she placed her hand on his arm, it was to stop him. "You must cease. I will never be able to eat all of it."

He glanced at her plate. "If you are sure. We have had a great deal of exercise today."

When she finished her luncheon, he asked if she would like a plate of strawberries, and she was astonished he took his time selecting the fruits and cutting them into quarters before putting the plate in front of her. "Thank you."

"My pleasure." He grinned, taking several strawberries from the bowl and popping them whole into his mouth.

Once again, Laia did not know what to think. Yet from the corner of her eye, she saw her sister-in-law's look of approval. Well, if Meg did not see anything wrong with Mr. Paulet's behavior, who was Laia, who had no understanding of men at all, to complain?

Mayhap this was the type of experience Mama had meant when she said Laia must acquire some "Town Bronze."

She glanced at her mother, but Mama was speaking

with Meg and Euphrosyne, paying no attention at all to Laia and Mr. Paulet. She blew out a small breath. As long as Mr. Paulet was putting himself out to entertain her, she might as well enjoy his efforts.

"You are not eating your fruit." His deep voice drew her out of her thoughts.

She speared a section with her fork, took a bite, and chewed. It was sweet and tart at the same time. "This is excellent. Do you know what type it is?"

He almost preened. "As it happens, I do. It is called 'chili'. It comes from my estate in Kent."

That was unexpected. For some reason, other than the house he had pointed out earlier, she had thought he was landless. "What part of Kent?"

"The estate is near Newchurch." He ate another berry. "It is very pleasant and quiet. I wish I could spend more time there."

"Why do you not?"

"Between my position in Parliament and my other estates, I hardly have time." He finished off his bowl of strawberries. "I do have several excellent stewards, but an absent landlord is a neglectful landlord. And that leads his hirelings to believe they may do what they wish."

Laia stared at him for a moment. Her father had said much the same. Unfortunately, he wasn't nearly as good-humored about traveling from estate to estate. "How many other estates do you own?"

"At last count, ten." He frowned slightly but not enough to banish his pleasant expression. "Unfortunately, they are spread all over England. There is one in Scotland as well." His eyes began to sparkle with mirth. "I am renowned in my family for taking care of my possessions. Therefore, every time someone wishes to ensure their property is cared for, they either leave it to me or give it to me." He gave her a self-deprecating smile. "I have more than enough to keep me busy without ascending to my uncle's dukedom."

Laia's face heated to the point that she knew she was bright red. Not a becoming color for her. "I . . . I . . . I mean to say I would never . . . " Oh, God. How did one confess to being wrong about him wishing the duke would never have a child?

Mr. Paulet patted her hand. "Don't swallow your tongue. Not many people know I have my own fortune. To be frank, becoming the Duke of Bolton would be a blasted nuisance."

"I see." Or at least she understood that when he had said what he had about his uncle, he was speaking the truth as he knew it.

Laia still believed that her father would not give her to a man who was complicit in the deaths of his wives. She would not broach the subject again with Mr. Paulet. To do so would either insult him or force him to slander his uncle.

Still, it behooved her to discover exactly what *had* happened to the previous duchesses of Bolton. She would speak to Meg or Damon this evening. If anyone could discover the truth, they could. And if the duke was suspect, surely her father would not make her marry the man.

CHAPTER FIVE

THE NEXT MORNING, AS LAIA waited with her family and Mr. Paulet for the other group to arrive, her brother again mentioned Lady Sarah, and this time Laia was certain she had heard the lady's name mentioned at Quartus's wedding to Anna. "Isn't she the woman Father wished to marry to Quartus?"

"She is," Damon said. "However, she was already betrothed to Mr. Bellingham."

That didn't make any sense at all. Father had no reason to go around attempting to break betrothals. "I do not understand."

Before her brother could answer, the sound of hooves on the cobblestone street reached them, and Mr. Paulet pulled the curtain in the front parlor aside. "Our fellow explorers have arrived. And, if I am not mistaken, our horses are entering the square. At least, I recognize my roan, and did Hawksworth not tell me that Lady Laia has a long-tailed gray mare?"

She went to the window. "Yes. That is my Eleanor. What a handsome fellow you have, sir."

"He has served me well. I would never have escaped Corunna alive if it had not been for him."

"Even without being told, I assumed by your bearing that you were a military man. But Mama said you served with my brother."

"We were in the same unit." He did not elaborate. "That is how we became friends."

She had read the dispatches in the newssheets and the letters her brother had sent, letting them know he was still well. Her estimation of Mr. Paulet rose now that she knew he had been in the same hard-fought battles as Damon.

"What made you sell out?"

"My father died, and I was needed at home." He flashed her a brief smile. "My mother convinced me I could serve my country better in parliament than on a battlefield. Boney had abdicated, and we had no idea Waterloo would take place."

Laia, her family, and Mr. Paulet piled onto the pavement to greet the other group. After everyone was introduced, and mounted, they set off for the ride to Farley Castle.

The day was sunny and there were no clouds in the sky to mar their pleasure. Laia rode beside Mr. Paulet for the first hour discussing politics and listening as he told her about *tonish* society and restrictions on ladies.

"That won't bother me at all. We are not allowed to go anywhere by ourselves."

"You are a rare specimen, my lady. All my sisters chafed at the restrictions and could not wait to return to the country." He grinned. "With husbands, of course."

"Of course." She returned his grin, but also wished she'd had the opportunity to attend a Season.

About half way to their destination, Lady Sarah, riding a bay mare, came up beside Laia. "This is great fun. Thank you for allowing us to join you."

"I am glad you could come." She and her sisters had been allowed only short visits with other young ladies and had no friends outside the family. She hoped Lady Sarah would be her first. "I'm glad that Meg and Hawksworth knew you."

"I cannot tell you how much I admire your brother and sister, and how grateful I am to them." Lady Sarah's countenance became solemn. "Without Quartus's and their help, Jeremy and I would have had a much more difficult time."

"I am glad they could assist you." And not only Lady Sarah, but Frank and Jenny, and Quartus and Anna as well. Meg and Damon were her only relations with the power to continuously defy Father.

"As am I." Joy filled Lady Sarah's face again. "I had heard about you and your sisters and brothers from Lord Quartus, but I never dreamed we would have a chance to meet."

Laia had never dreamed she would be in Bath and away from her father's close supervision. "I heard about you as well." She knew she should not be prying, but after what Damon said earlier her curiosity had to be satisfied. "How did you come to be engaged to Quartus when you were already betrothed to another?"

Lady Sara laughed lightly. "We were never actually betrothed. We simply allowed your father and my brother to think we were.

"It all started before my parents' deaths. They had agreed that Jeremy and I could wed, but it had to be before my twenty-first birthday. He had gone off to India, you see, and Papa wanted to ensure I did not wait for him forever. We were allowed to write to each other and had been corresponding for years, but one or two of the letters never reached me." She looked at her brother riding ahead of them and pulled a face. "For some reason, most likely because Markham and I were arguing at the time, I blamed him and never told him Jeremy was on his way home. He, quite naturally, believed that Jeremy would not arrive in time and I would lose an inheritance one of my great-aunts left me." She glanced at Laia. "I had to wed by the time I reached my majority to receive it. Your father contacted Markham and proposed that I marry Quartus. You may imagine my chagrin. However, I still did not trust my brother, and when I told Quartus I could not marry him, he assured me I could trust him with my problems. I told him about Jeremy. He and your brother and sister helped us."

Lady Sarah was fortunate she had met Quartus. "That sounds exactly like something they would do." Laia repressed a shudder at her memory of the duke's reaction. They had walked around on tip-toes for days afterward. "My father was livid."

"Yes, well." Lady Sarah shrugged as if the duke's temper was no matter to her. As indeed it wasn't. Lucky woman. "Meg thought Anna and Quartus were falling in love, and she knew your father would not approve of *that* match."

"Quite frankly, I do not understand why he disapproved. Quartus is now consort to a duchess, and they are very happy."

Lady Sarah's lips pressed together in a thin line. Then she heaved a sigh. "I should probably not say this to you, as it is not proper for me to criticize your father. However, I was told by my brother that the duke was determined to obtain my dower property, which shares a border with one of the Somerset properties."

Laia's heart dropped to her stomach then bounced into her throat, threatening to choke her. The conversation she had overheard between Meg and Damon came rushing back to Laia, and it was several moments before she could speak again. She had not wanted to believe that all her father cared about was increasing the dukedom's wealth.

Hoping for another answer, she asked, "Was that the only reason?"

"As far as I know it was." The other lady frowned. "At least that's what my brother told me, and I have no reason to disbelieve him."

As she now had some reason to doubt her father, Laia wondered if a piece of property was being traded for her and, if so, which one. Still, did it really matter? No matter her father's reasons, she was engaged to be married. Father had sent her mother a letter stating that the settlement agreements had been signed.

What choice did she have other than to wed Bolton? Her father would disown her if she attempted to jilt the duke. One of her brothers might take her in, but she would have made her sisters' situations worse than they already were. Especially Euphrosyne's. She would be the next to marry.

"Have you met the Duke of Bolton?" Lady Sarah asked. "I understand that he has been married a number of times. He is quite old is he not?"

Before Laia could respond, Jeremy Bellingham and Mr. Paulet rode up to them.

"BELLINGHAM IS MISSING HIS BRIDE." Mr. Paulet grinned as he took his place beside Laia, and Lady Sarah dropped back next to her husband. "May I bear you company?"

"Of course." Laia summoned a smile. She might as well enjoy herself while she could. Suddenly, the future did not look as happy as she had thought it would be. "Tell me, have you been to Farley Castle before? The guide books said it has relics."

The corner of one of his lips twitched. "Have you ever seen a relic, my lady?"

"No. I have only read about them."

"Then I shan't ruin the surprise."

"Have *you* seen them?" She hated surprises. Or was he was making a May game of her?

"I have seen relics on the Continent, but they were

papish ones. I doubt this chapel will have anything so gruesome."

Gruesome? Despite the warmth of the day she shuddered. "Well, of all the things to say."

She frowned at him, but his lips curved up and his eyes twinkled.

"Impossible man."

He burst out laughing.

"I shall ask my brother. He will tell me."

"No, no." He held his hand up while he brought himself under control. "The ones I saw in Spain were bones of those believed to be saints or martyrs.

Unable to hide her disgust, Laia wrinkled her nose. "Bones?"

"Yes. They were dressed in rich clothing and jewels. I greatly doubt that one would find such things in England."

"I certainly hope not." Just the idea of looking at dead people made her want to shiver.

Guy didn't think he had ever met anyone, outside of a young child, who was as open as Lady Laia. Her naiveté could not last, of course. According to Damon, the whole idea of this sojourn in Bath was to teach her what any other young lady would have learned preparing for her first Season.

Laia was well-educated, clever, and quick witted, and would soon understand that she must hide her thoughts behind a polite smile to survive. A part of Guy was sorry that he'd have to witness the change. Then again, another part of him looked forward to watching her as she navigated the social world of Bath. He had no doubt she would soon have them all—the gentlemen young and old and the old biddies—at her delicate feet.

By the time autumn came, she would be able to navigate the *haut ton* with ease. The only question was which gentleman would be by her side.

Despite the fact that he was drawn to her, any woman he wed must be able to take up the role of political hostess. Meg had been correct. In order for his career to advance, he must have a wife. A single gentleman required a hostess for entertainments that included ladies. His Aunt Harriett had acted as his hostess, but she had recently retired to the country. Was she too trying to tell him he needed to marry?

It behooved him to discover where Laia's interests lay. Although, if he fell in love with her, would it matter? Based upon the love matches he'd seen, much was overlooked or forgiven for the sake of love. Still, he should know if she was a Tory or had Whiggish tendencies. The latter would suit him well. "You mentioned that you followed your brother's progress during the war. Are you interested in politics as well?"

She glanced at him, startled. "I am, but"—her cheeks colored once more—"we—that is, my brothers and sisters and I are not encouraged to discuss our views at home." Her mouth twitched to one side. "Unless we agree with our father, that is."

No surprise there. From what he had heard, the duke did not entertain dissenting opinions from anyone on anything. Still, her answer seemed to suggest that she did not agree with Somerset. "Ah, but your father is not here. Therefore, you may express your beliefs freely and in complete confidence that you will not be betrayed."

Staring at him, she drew one corner of her lower lip between her pearl-like teeth. "I suppose I may. I have read Wollstonecraft, and Bentham, as well as John Locke, and other philosophers."

That sounded like a radical program for a young lady. "With your father's permission?"

This time when Laia blushed, it was with a guilty shrug. "No. We had a governess who encouraged our reading.

It all went well until Euphrosyne decided to argue with my father one day and used the *Vindication of the Rights of Women* as an example of him being incorrect." Laia wrinkled her nose. "The governess left shortly thereafter."

"Without a reference, no doubt."

"I assume that is what my father thought, but Mama wrote her one." Laia glanced away for a moment. "I liked Miss Rushmount and was sorry to see her go."

"Does the duke allow you to read the newspapers?" Many fathers did not.

"Oh, yes." The smile returned, and Laia's eyes were shining again. "Naturally, we do not discuss what we have read in our father's hearing. I understand that Hawksworth has become involved in supporting many of the Whig positions, even the more radical ones."

"He has." Guy should not think of her as Laia and should use her title, but he couldn't seem to do it despite the fact that it would lead to a slip he'd have trouble explaining. "Meg is becoming famous for her drawing rooms, and is an adept political hostess."

"That is not surprising. My mother said she encouraged my brother's activities. I would love to become involved in her causes." Laia's tone was wistful but eager, as if she were counting the days until she could take more of a hand in events. That would not happen if she married his uncle. "As it is, I am allowed to send only a small amount of my pin-money in support." She grimaced.

"Because of your father?" He was amazed she was allowed to support Lady Hawksworth's causes at all.

"Oh, no." Laia shook her head. " He doesn't know anything about it. Meg will not accept more. She and my mother make me save most of it. Truly, my sister and I have nothing to spend our money on at home. We are not allowed to go to the village very much."

Laia's brow wrinkled as if she were trying to figure out

a problem, and he wanted to smooth it out with his thumb.

"Meg says I may find myself in need of money in the future."

If Laia wed Guy's uncle, she might very well need funds of her own. Yet if she married him, she would never be told how to use her funds. "I think it is a wise idea. One never knows what might happen."

"Yes." She smiled. "I am sure I will find a use for it at some point."

They had fallen some distance behind the others. "You sit a horse well. Would you like to race to where the others are?"

Laia glanced around. "We won't get in trouble, will we?"

"There is no one to tattle on you here." Guy was egging her on, and he knew he should not. But she was so earnest. "If you are afraid . . ."

Her shoulders straightened even more. "On the count of three."

"One, two, three." They took off at the same time.

For a while it looked as if they'd be evenly matched, but once his gelding got it into his mind to win her mare fell behind. Still, she kept up and Guy won by only a head.

"You, my lady, are an excellent horsewoman," he said.

"Thank you, sir." Her smile was broader than he'd ever seen it. "That was exhilarating."

Hawksworth rode back to them. "Teaching my little sister tricks, are you?"

Guy raised his quizzing glass, leveling it at his friend. "Might I bring to your attention that we are not in Hyde Park? And I can think of no reason why she should not have a good gallop."

"Hawksworth," Laia said in a worried tone. "If I had known—"

"I was teasing you, Laia." He smiled at her. "Paulet is absolutely correct. There is no reason why you should not race here."

Her forehead was still creased. She really was worried about behaving wrongly. And he discovered an interesting desire to kiss her troubles away that had nothing to do with his growing lust for her. "Come, you two. We should rejoin the rest of our party."

When they finally reached the cathedral, Laia wanted to look at the relics first. As Guy had suspected, they were not skeletons covered in velvet and jewels, but old cups and other things from an earlier era.

"Well, what do you think?"

She pulled a face. "Believe it or not, I almost wish they were the relics you described. Now that I'm over my initial shock, I would like to see such things."

Guy resisted the urge to pull her closer to him. He wanted to take her to Europe and show them to her. "Perhaps someday you shall."

CHAPTER SIX

THE NEXT MORNING, LAIA WAS the first of the family down to breakfast, and she took the opportunity to read the newssheets Damon had sent to them by messenger.

The Times Laia had read many times before, but her father didn't receive the *Morning Post*, calling it nothing but useless gossip.

After pouring a cup of tea, she took a piece of toast and eagerly perused the first page. By the time she reached the court column, she had laughed over a piece on the proud hound who rode in his master's carriage, dreamed of attending the balls and other entertainments depicted, and learned who had already left Town and who remained.

When Laia got to the third page, she almost dropped her tea cup.

> *We have been given to understand that Lady Aglaia Trevor, the eldest daughter of the Duke and Duchess of Somerset, is betrothed to the Duke of Bolton.*
>
> *Lady Aglaia will be the duke's fifth wife. All of the formalities have been completed and an end of July wedding is anticipated.*

How could they possibly know anything thing about

her betrothal? She could not imagine her father sending such information to a newspaper he loathed. Nor could she think that the Duke of Bolton had sent a letter imparting such private news.

"Laia, you look as if you've seen a ghost." Her mother strolled into the breakfast room accompanied by Hawksworth and Meg. Where was Mr. Paulet? He usually came with them.

"Look at this." She handed her mother the newssheet. "Who would have sent that to them?"

"I have no idea, but I do not see anything remarkable in it." Mama handed the paper back to Laia. "Betrothals are frequently mentioned and announced. What upsets you?"

She glanced at the newssheet again, and the words, *Lady Aglaia will be the duke's* fifth *wife,* almost screamed at her. She had been quite pleased with her betrothal, but the idea of being someone's fifth wife began to sit poorly.

"Well, it certainly wasn't Bolton." Hawksworth leaned over her shoulder. "I wouldn't want anyone to be reminded that I'd already gone through four wives."

"Must you put it like that?" Laia wanted to hit him.

"Damon." Meg's tone held a soft rebuke. "Think of your sister's feelings."

"I am. Or, rather, of her health." He took two plates from the table and began to fill them from the offerings on the sideboard. "Paulet said none of them were breeding when they died."

Once again, a cold shiver ran down Laia's spine. Had the duke murdered his wives? Mr. Paulet had suggested something was not right with their deaths. She tried to keep her voice from trembling as she said, "I am bound by Father's decision."

Hawksworth shrugged. "Not under the law, you're not."

She shook her head. "I do not understand. He is my father. He may do with me what he wills."

"Yes, my dear. He is your father." Meg took the seat next to Laia's and smiled at her brother when he handed his wife a cup of tea. "However, under the law, no woman can be forced to enter into a marriage she does not want. That is not to say that family will not influence her or attempt to do so. They are exceeding good at applying pressure, as it were." Meg busied herself spreading freshly made strawberry jam on her toast. "Do you not attain your majority on the sixth of July?" Laia nodded. "In that event, you must validate the marriage contracts before your wedding if they are to take effect."

She scanned the room for her mother, who had . . . disappeared. Strange. Every time a discussion of her marriage came up, Mama was never there. "We all know what would happen if I married against Father's wishes." Of course they did. Still, Meg's and Hawksworth's steady gazes never wavered. "What do you suggest I do?"

"You?" her brother said. "Nothing. I, on the other hand, shall make some discreet inquiries into the shortened lives of the wives of your betrothed."

Laia started to speak, but Damon held up his hand. "It will most likely take some time. There is no need to worry now about anything I might discover."

Next to her, her sister-in-law breathed a sigh of relief. "I think that is an excellent idea, my love. Laia?"

"I agree. After all, we might be maligning the duke just because his wives have not been in good health." On the other hand, if the worst were true, surely Father would agree that she could not marry a man who murdered his wives.

Her brother raised a dubious brow, but said, "We might indeed." Leaning down, he kissed Meg's cheek. "I'll return in an hour or so. Will you be here, or do you have plans to go out?"

"I'm not sure yet. I must speak with Catherine." Meg

placed her hand on his cheek. "If we go out, I'll leave word for you."

Laia bit down on her bottom lip. More and more she wanted the type of marriage her brother and Meg had. But Laia had little hope she would have a love match.

GUY POURED HIS TEA, AND settled down to read the *Morning Post*, chuckling at one of the arrivals to Town. Only a few people would understand how titillating that piece of information was or who might have divulged it.

Suddenly, the sounds of someone pounding on his front door rang through the house. Blast it all. Where the devil was Pulleyn? No, that was the house in Yorkshire. Catchpole? No. He was in Suffolk. "What the hell is the butler's name?"

"Gibbs, my lord." His butler bowed. "The under-butler is attending to the door."

Under-butler? Why in Heavens did his aunt have an under-butler? Guy drained his tea cup. "Thank you, Gibbs."

"No, sir. Thank you for keeping the full staff. We are cognizant of the honor you have bestowed upon us." The servant placed a fresh pot of tea on the table.

Keeping a full staff was exactly the reason Guy couldn't remember all their damn names. He'd never been able to let any of the staff go in any of the houses he had received. Many would say he was being wasteful, but to him, keeping only a skeleton staff was false economy. All his properties were well run and maintained *because* he had them fully staffed. Not that he could let anyone go in any event. The only problem was it was deuced hard to keep track of them all. He'd have to have his secretary make a list of the senior staff for each house.

The pounding had stopped and a second later Hawksworth was ushered into the breakfast room.

"The Marquis of Hawksworth to see you, sir," the under-butler, whatever his name was, said as Hawksworth brushed past the servant.

Guy lifted a weary brow at his butler. "Perhaps some instruction as to whether or not I am home might be in order."

"Indeed, sir." The butler bowed.

"I'm that sorry, sir," the under-butler bowed.

"It would have taken more than you to keep his lordship waiting," Guy acknowledged. "You may return to your duties."

"Thank you, sir." The man bowed again and left the breakfast room.

"Do you mean to say you'd have refused to see me?" Hawksworth sat down and lifted the tea pot, as if offering Guy some as well.

"Yes, please." He put two lumps and milk into his tea. "No. But the under-butler doesn't know that."

"Point taken." His friend glanced at the newssheet. "Have you gotten to page four yet?"

Sitting up, Guy looked at Hawksworth. "Exactly what on page four do you think will interest me?"

He shrugged. "Look for yourself."

Guy turned the page and read, "Lady Aglaia Trevor, the eldest daughter of the Duke and Duchess of Somerset, is betrothed to the Duke of Bolton. Lady Aglaia will be the duke's fifth wife. Who the devil gave them that piece of information?"

His friend grinned before taking a sip of tea. "I did."

What the devil had Hawksworth been thinking? "I presume you will tell me the reason, in your own good time."

"I had an idea." Hawksworth took a piece of ham. "If it

turns out the way I wish it to, I'll tell you."

A footman brought two plates of eggs and roasted beef, still bloody from the carving. "Thank you," Hawksworth said.

Guy looked on as his friend tucked into the food. Hawksworth never turned down a meal. "Did your wife not feed you this morning?"

"No, I ate at my stepmother's house before coming here."

He would tell Guy in his own good time what he wanted and not before. Torn between irritation and humor, Guy applied himself to his own breakfast.

Finally, after another cup of tea in addition to the eggs and beef, Hawksworth wiped his mouth and said, "How well did you know Bolton's last three wives?"

"Not well at all. I spoke a few words to them at the wedding breakfasts, but never saw them again." Guy set down his serviette. "Why do you want to know?"

"I promised my sister that I would look into their deaths." The corner of one lip quirked up. "Just in the event there is something smoky about them."

The light was beginning to dawn. "And may I assume that this conversation and the subsequent vow came after *she* read the *Morning Post*?"

Hawksworth grinned. "As a matter of fact, you may."

Apparently seeing the number of wives in writing had had an effect that merely being told about them had not. Other than gathering some minor bits of information, Guy had purposefully kept away from what had gone on with the previous wives, but now he had two excuses to become involved. Helping his friend and Laia.

And, with the former Colonel Lord Hawksworth leading the charge, Guy would not be seen as making trouble for his uncle. He couldn't have planned it better himself. "His second wife's family was from someplace on the coast near Hull. He met her during her first Season. Rumor has it that she caught pneumonia and died from it."

"Her parents never questioned the coroner's report?"

"No. The doctor had been called and had verified that the girl had an irritation of the lungs, but he was not called back before she died."

Hawksworth's aquiline nose almost twitched, reminding Guy of a hound on the scent. "Who nursed her?"

"His grace." Guy fidgeted with his serviette on the table. "It was thought to be quite poignant. Cook and the housekeeper, Mrs. Dillingham, were distraught that none of their medications and remedies had worked. Cook even made her own restorative pork jelly."

"But they were not in charge of the sickroom," Hawksworth mused, staring off in the direction of a particularly bad landscape.

"They were only allowed in to help bathe her and tidy the bedchamber." Guy hadn't paid much attention to the painting before. It would have to go.

His friend's gaze never left the landscape. Guy had seen this behavior before when Hawksworth was working out a strategy. "What about his third wife? How did he meet her and how did she die?"

"She was from a family in Leicestershire. Landed gentry. Never hoped to have a Season, or so I've been told. Naturally, her family, and I assume she as well, were thrilled beyond belief when Bolton wished to marry her." Guy picked up his empty cup of tea and debated whether to call for a new pot but decided not to. If this conversation continued much longer, something decidedly stronger was called for. "Her heart stopped. Quite suddenly." He sighed. "The doctor opined that she must have had a—"

"A weak heart," Hawksworth said abruptly. "Does your uncle have an interest in plants?"

"Not of which I am aware." Guy shrugged. "That said, we are not on the friendliest of terms."

"Naturally, neither family questioned their daughters' deaths."

"Again, not that I am aware of. That was something neither Cook nor Mrs. Dillingham would have known."

"And the fourth?" Hawksworth's sharp gaze turned to Guy.

"Ah, the beauteous Sophia." Guy leaned back in his chair. "That is another story altogether."

Leaning slightly forward, his friend asked, "How so?"

"She had been sent to England for her come out from some place in Canada where her father is posted. Her father is a younger son of the previous Lord Engle. Her grandmother is the current Dowager Lady Engle. Not only was her ladyship not pleased that Bolton had turned his attention to her granddaughter, she actively opposed the wedding. Sophia, however, was one and twenty, quite beautiful, and very spoiled. In spite of her grandmother's disapproval, she decided she wanted to be a duchess."

Guy's butler, obviously anticipating they might be in need of one, brought in another pot of tea. He poured two cups.

"When she sickened with some stomach ailment, Lady Engle demanded to see her granddaughter and was refused. Finally, the duke relented, but by that time it was too late. Sophia was almost dead." He took a sip of tea. "No one knows what her grace told her grandmother, if anything, but Lady Engle was a hair's breath away from slandering my uncle."

"Or telling the world the truth." Hawksworth's lips flattened. "Where can I find her ladyship?"

"Well, there you are in luck." Guy drained his cup and placed it on the table. "She resides in Bath and can frequently be found in the Pump Room."

Hawksworth's jaw dropped. "Here? Why did I not know about that before?"

"For the very good reason that you did not ask." Guy raised one brow. "How was I supposed to know you would decide to investigate the deaths?"

"I must meet her." Hawksworth began pacing, then stopped, spearing Guy with a look.

"I cannot be seen in the Pump Room," Guy said. Still, there must be someone who could manage to meet Lady Engle and provide his friend an introduction. If only his aunt had not hied off. She was sure to have known her ladyship.

Not the duchess.

Meg. She would be perfect. "What about your wife? She is extremely well connected and must know someone who knows someone who knows Lady Engle. She may have even met the lady by now."

"You're right." Hawksworth started for the door. "Let me know if you think of anything else."

Before Guy could assure his friend he would, the man was out the door.

Nothing had been planned for the day, so he decided to go around to Laia's house and discover for himself how she was taking the announcement, if one could call it that.

Guy would be more than happy to offer any comfort he was able.

Chapter Seven

London.

BOLTON HAD LONG BEEN IN the habit of reading everything he possibly could. One never knew where he'd find an interesting piece of information. Sitting in the library of his town house in Saint James Square, he was not, however, prepared to read about his own betrothal. Rage filled him and he bellowed, "What the devil is this rubbish?"

"Your grace?" His butler came running into the library. "Is something wrong?"

"Nothing with which you can help. Leave me alone." The butler bowed and closed the door.

Bolton went back to the short announcement to make sure he had read it properly. Who would write something like that?

No, he'd been correct the first time. The question was who would give them something so outrageous to print. The paper had been very careful not to speculate on the reasons for his wives' deaths. He couldn't have hidden their passing. It was common knowledge. But to put the information in *such* a fashion was bound to catch any young lady's eye. Especially the one to whom he was betrothed. That was unacceptable. Someone did not want him to marry again. And only one person stood to gain if he did not have an heir.

Guy Paulet.

Just like his father, he had always claimed not to be interested in the dukedom, but Bolton had never believed either of them. All men must wish for the power that came with title and wealth. Still, Paulet had never done anything to stick a spoke in Bolton's wheel before. He didn't even know if his nephew knew about his latest betrothal. Chances are he was still in Town attending to his seat in the Commons.

And that was another thing. Try to do a family member a good turn and he betrays you. Guy could never be counted on to vote the way Bolton wanted. In fact, Bolton had no influence over the man at all. It was quite irritating the way Guy had managed to acquire his own wealth. It was even more irksome that he didn't owe anyone anything and voted the way he damn well pleased.

Bolton glanced at the paper again. No. As much as he wanted to believe it was his nephew, he couldn't. Someone else had involved themselves in his affairs and raised the question of his previous wives.

And he was damn well going to find out who it was.

"Kentwell." When the man entered the room, Bolton shoved the paper at his secretary. "Read that. I want the editor to attend me immediately."

"Yes, your grace. I shall see to it."

The door closed. He'd know soon who was to blame for this outrage. Someone was going to be extremely sorry.

DAMON REACHED CATHERINE'S TOWN HOUSE as the ladies were leaving the breakfast room. Focusing on his beautiful and brilliant wife, he appropriated Meg's elbow. Under the guise of giving her a kiss on the cheek, he said, "I need to speak with you."

She turned her attention to his stepmother and sisters. "I shall be with you presently. I have something I wish to say to Hawksworth." Not simply brilliant, extraordinary. She had managed to make it sound as if she were about to give him a scold. Meg led him into the front parlor and closed the door. "What did you discover?"

"I had a long discussion with Guy Paulet. He did not know the exact whereabouts of the families of Bolton's second and third wives, but the fourth has a grandmother living here in Bath."

Meg gave him a broad smile. "That is wonderful. I shall endeavor to make her acquaintance as soon as possible. Who is she?"

"Wait, that's not the best part." Damon drew her into his arms. "She all but accused Bolton of murdering her granddaughter."

Her eyes widened in surprise. "That was bold of her. What is her name?"

"Oh, Lady Engle. Did you not tell me you know the lady? From what Paulet told me she was against the marriage from the start, but her granddaughter was of age and headstrong."

"Yes, I have known *of* her ladyship for years." Meg's fine, dark brows drew together as she considered what he'd told her. "I believe I met her granddaughter, the last Duchess of Bolton, now that I think on it. It was two or three Seasons ago." She flashed him a smile. "Yes, that must be it. She was the most sought after lady of the Season until Serena Beaumont appeared. It does not astonish me at all that she accepted Bolton. What was her name?" Meg began tapping her lower lip, making Damon want to kiss her. "Sophia Whitmore. That was it. Dark hair and startling blue eyes. Quite beautiful, but spoiled."

"That sounds like her." He gave up wanting and claimed his wife's mouth. It was a long time before he spoke again.

"Will you be able to find time to speak with Lady Engle alone?"

"Of course." Meg reached up, brushing her thumb across his lips. "If you let me go, I will. At this rate, we will end up back in bed."

"Was that an invitation?" he murmured using his most seductive tone.

"No, it was a prophesy." She stepped back and shook out her skirts. "If you want me to find the grandmother, I must accompany Catherine to the Pump Room."

"What do my sisters have planned for today?" He stepped toward Meg.

"Nothing as far as I know." Wise to him, she took a step back toward the door. "I shall tend to you later." Blowing him a kiss, she turned and walked out of the room.

Damon was tempted to follow, but helping Laia find the same happiness he'd found with Meg was more important at the moment than dragging his wife back to bed.

Well, perhaps not *more* important, but necessary. Thus far, they had been able to help his brothers, Frank and Quartus, find wives they loved and who loved them in return.

If Damon was correct, Guy Paulet would be the next gentleman to fall to Cupid's arrow. If only Laia would cooperate.

MAMA AND MEG HAD DEPARTED not five minutes earlier, and Laia was wondering what she should do to occupy herself when her mother's footman handed her a note. "For you, my lady. The messenger is waiting for a response."

Euphrosyne put her book down. "Who is it from? I

wonder why Joseph did not wait for Mama to look at it."

"Mama said I could receive local correspondence." Laia opened the note, spreading the fine pressed paper on the table.

My dear Laia,

I am going shopping this morning. If you have no prior plans, I would love to have you and your sister go with me. My footman will accompany us.

Your friend,

S. Bellingham

"Listen to this, Euphrosyne. We have been invited to go shopping with Lady Sarah." Laia looked up from the letter. "Isn't that nice of her?"

"Write her back while I fetch our bonnets and gloves." Her sister dashed out of the parlor while Laia fashioned a response.

They had never been invited anywhere before. Or, rather, she had never received an invitation that had not been addressed to her mother and included her.

My dear Sarah,

My sister and I would be delighted to accompany you.

Your friend,

L. Trevor

After sealing the note with wax, she tugged on the bell pull. The door almost immediately opened. "Please take this to the messenger."

A few minutes later Euphrosyne strolled back into the room and handed Laia her bonnet. "I think I saw her carriage coming."

"It is too soon for that, but this is so exciting." She tied her hat's ribbons off to the side. "We have never been shopping without Mama."

"It is thrilling, and it really should not be more than commonplace." Her sister donned one glove. "We have been kept far too close."

Laia wouldn't argue with that. "Yes, but now that we are away from Father and have more freedom, we must be careful not to abuse it. Even Mama must be careful."

"When I marry," her sister said, jerking on her second glove, "it will be to a gentleman who will not try to rule me."

Laia pressed her lips firmly together. There was no point in telling her sister that no matter what man she wanted, she would have to take the gentleman their father selected for her. Since he had finally turned his attention to his elder daughters, it would not be long before he found a match for Euphrosyne.

With exquisite timing, Perkins knocked on the open door. "My ladies, Lady Sarah is here."

The grin on Euphrosyne's face was infectious. "We will be out straightaway, Perkins." Drawing her arm through Laia's, she began walking to the door. "Let us agree to have a good time while we can."

"Yes, let us do just that." Laia schooled her countenance. Her concern about what her sister might or might not do was no reason to ruin what looked to be a promising outing.

Sarah turned from gazing at the corner niche holding a plaster bust of someone. "This house is very nice. Jeremy and I are discussing buying property in Bath." She bussed their cheeks. "Shall we go?"

"You see," Euphrosyne whispered. "Many gentlemen treat their wives as partners."

She was thinking of their brothers and now Mr. Bellingham. "I do know that."

When they reached the footman Sarah had brought

with her, they started off toward the main part of the town. "We will go to Milsom Street first. I hear there is an excellent shop for stockings."

"We will need new stockings for the ball next week," Laia said. "And gloves. We each received the first of our new evening gowns and ball gowns and are now respectable to go out in the evening. I could not believe how out-of-date our old evening gowns were. And for some reason we had not purchased the other things we need."

"It always seems to go that way," Sarah said. "One forgets the small but very important items. I wonder what the ball will be like this evening."

As neither Laia nor Euphrosyne had ever been to a dance, never mind a ball, Laia didn't know what to say. Her sister was not so reticent. "No matter what happens, I intend to enjoy myself. Hawksworth has asked me to stand up with him, as has your brother."

Naturally, their brother would stand up with his sisters, but when had Lord Markham asked Euphrosyne to dance with him? And so far ahead of the event? Laia tried to ignore the little thought trying to intrude upon her mind that she might like to dance with Mr. Paulet, but he had not asked her to stand up with him at the assembly room ball. Her good mood faltered. He was quite handsome and probably had dozens of ladies with whom he would dance. If only one of them were her.

They spent the next three hours visiting every shop they found, even the butcher's. Madam Lamont had the most fetching bonnets. Sarah, Euphrosyne, and Laia each tried on several and came away with new hats. Laia bought three pairs of fine kid gloves, and her sister bought four pairs. They were enchanted with the clocked stockings they had seen, and made more purchases.

"I do not think I have ever had such fun." Euphrosyne smiled broadly.

"Nor I," Laia agreed.

"I must buy some handkerchiefs," Sarah said as they left one store and entered another.

"Handkerchiefs and ribbons," Euphrosyne announced.

Earlier, Meg had suspected an excursion like this would take place and had told them to send the bills to her, but Laia did not wish to ruin her sister-in-law. But an exquisite ribbon of robin's egg blue caught her eye. Surely a ribbon would not cost that much. Well, she'd buy it now, but pay Meg back.

The poor footman had run out of room in his arms to carry more packages. But Sarah had discovered that many establishments would deliver, thus freeing Laia and Euphrosyne from exercising any restraint at all on that count.

The aroma of yeast led them to a bakery. Sarah led the way in.

"Have you tasted Bath Buns?" she asked.

Both Laia and her sister shook their heads.

"In that case, you must try them."

Moments later, she bit into the caraway-covered bun, savoring the taste of sweet caraway and butter. "These are wonderful. I never would have guessed."

Not caring for caraway, Euphrosyne had originally wrinkled her nose, but bit into the one Sarah handed to her. "They are. I even like the caraway."

"Only because they are coated with sugar." Laia grinned at her sister.

It struck her that she'd not have much time left with her family. Soon she would be a wife, subject to her husband's rule as she had been to her father's. Would she be allowed to visit her mother, sisters, and brothers at all? Even if she could, it would most likely be months before it happened. She wished she knew more about the Duke of Bolton.

By the time Laia and her sister returned home, she was

more than ready to put her feet up and enjoy a cup of tea.

In the morning room, Euphrosyne set out the three fans she'd bought. "My gown is pink. Which one of these fans do you think would go better with it?"

Laia looked over the fans—one silver with a scene in muted gray, cream, and green painted on it, another with ivory spokes and a pastoral painting in green and blue, and one that was, for the most part, red. Where in heaven her sister thought she was going to carry that, Laia had no idea. The choice was easy. "I think the silver fan would look the best."

"Yes, I think that as well." Still, Euphrosyne's fingers hovered over the red fan.

Laia decided to leave well enough alone. "Will you wear your clocked stockings? They are quite elegant."

"I shall." Her sister's countenance brightened.

She would wear hers as well. It was almost a shame that she and her maid would be the only ones to see them. Laia fought down a blush. Where in the world had that thought come from?

Perkins brought in a tray with tea and some lemon biscuits and set them on the table. "My ladies, I assumed you would wish for refreshment. Would you like lemonade as well?"

The day had not been hot enough for lemonade. "No, thank you." She picked up the tea pot and poured two cups. "Tea is perfect."

He removed a letter from his jacket pocket. "Lady Laia, this came for you. Forgive me for not bringing it to you on the salver, but I thought you might not wish to wait."

That was odd. She took the letter. The blue wax had an imprint of a "P" in it. It must be from Mr. Paulet, but what could he want? Using her fingernail, she popped it open.

My dear Lady Laia,

Would you do me the honor of standing up with me for the first dance you have available? I was remiss in not requesting a set sooner, and I beg you will forgive me.

Yr. servant

G. Paulet

Goodness. Apparently, it was *de rigueur* to request a dance well in advance of a ball. Although it would make more sense if she actually *knew* any other gentlemen who would ask to stand up with her.

She glanced at her sister. "It appears you are not the only one who has been asked to dance at the ball."

"Mr. Paulet." Euphrosyne grinned. "I knew he would request a set." She pulled out the chair to the writing table and motioned for Laia to sit down. "You must answer him quickly."

"It was very kind of him, but I am sure it is only because Hawksworth is his friend."

"What a bag of moonshine." Her sister grabbed her hand and pulled her to the desk. "If that was it, he would have waited to see if you had sufficient dance partners."

"Perhaps." She sat down and pulled out a piece of paper while her sister mended the pen.

It would be lovely if Mr. Paulet had asked because he wished to dance with her. Still, she was a betrothed lady. She should be thinking of Bolton. On the other hand, she was sure betrothed ladies, even married ladies, danced with other gentlemen. Surely nothing was wrong about her accepting his offer. Indeed, Meg had mentioned that Laia could receive many offers to dance. That decided, she wrote a short note telling Mr. Paulet that she would be delighted to stand up with him.

After sprinkling sand on the letter and sealing it, she tugged the bell pull. A few moments later, the missive was off to Mr. Paulet. She should not be so excited, but she could not seem to help herself. Naturally, it would be better if the Duke of Bolton had asked her for her first dance—first without their dancing master, that is,—but he wasn't here and his nephew was. As well as other gentlemen. She hoped.

CHAPTER EIGHT

AFTER WAITING AN HOUR FOR Laia to answer his letter, Guy remembered that Hawksworth said the ladies were most likely going out. If that was the case, she wouldn't receive it until she returned later in the day.

There was no point in him waiting at the house when he could be out enjoying the day.

"Gibbs." The butler was never more than a slightly raised voice away.

"Yes, sir." Gibbs entered the room and bowed.

"I am going out. Please have Smithson bring down my hat, gloves, and cane."

"Immediately, sir." The servant left the room, closing the door behind him.

Fortunately, Guy had had the good luck to receive a well-run household with his unwanted bequest. At the rate this was going, he'd have property in every county. Bolton, wishing to increase his dukedom's holdings, had complained more than once about the property Guy had been given by relatives on the Paulet side of the family. At some point, he would have to decide whether he'd incorporate his holdings into the dukedom's. Fortunately, that decision wouldn't have to be made for many years.

In a few minutes, he was on his way out the door and down Great Pulteney into the main part of Bath.

Just as he reached Walcot Street, he met up with Lord Markham. "Good morning."

"Good morning to you." Markham fell into step with

Guy. "Do you have a destination or are you at loose ends?"

"I'm merely enjoying the day." That he had the time was a strange occurrence. "You?"

"Likewise. My brother-in-law is looking at houses, and my sister is with Ladies Laia and Euphrosyne shopping. I have it on good authority the ladies have never been shopping without their mother and then only in a small market town."

By good authority, Guy assumed the man meant Lady Hawksworth. It astonished Guy that the Trevor ladies, particularly at their ages, had not been allowed to go to their home town without their mother. "That should prove interesting."

"Oh, I dare say they shall purchase a deal of totally unnecessary and inappropriate items that catch their eyes." Markham laughed. "Much in the way of magpies. At least that's what my sister did. It will do them no harm and will help whoever ends up receiving the things they later realize they cannot use or do not like after all."

Although Guy had sisters, he'd never given much thought to their first shopping expeditions. He rather thought he'd been at school and not privy to the knowledge or interested. "I suppose they will." He tried to think of Laia going on a mad shopping tour and could not. "I wonder what there is to buy in Bath. It is not as if it's London."

"No, but that won't stop them." Markham chuckled, then sobered. "You must also remember they have never been to Town."

"I can't believe that was their mother's doing. I wish I knew what Somerset was thinking."

"He is not an easy man," Markham commented.

Naturally, Guy knew the story surrounding Lord Quartus Trevor. "Have you met Somerset?"

"No, I have exchanged correspondence with him. That

was enough for me."

With the possible exception of his wife, it appeared no one cared for the old duke. They turned down Cheep Street. "This is the way to the Pump House."

"I haven't been yet and thought I might take a look. I hear the waters are horrible, but the company is pleasant."

"I heard it's the place to be seen, and I'm not sure I want everyone and his dog"—in other words his uncle—"to know I'm in town." Although, Guy couldn't deny he wanted to visit the place.

"Walk around a bit, then leave," Markham said unperturbedly. "Aside from that, most of the *ton* is either still in Town or on their way to Brighton.

That was true. The prince regent remained in Town and parliament was still in session. Aside from that, Guy wasn't that well known to the older set who might be here for their health. "I'll give it a try."

Turning onto Salt Street, they made their way to the entrance of the Pump Room. He was surprised at how full of people of all ages it was. For some reason, he'd thought that only the old and invalided frequented the place. Instead, several fashionable ladies and gentlemen strolled the perimeter of the room. The Duchess of Somerset was seated with a group of ladies. All of them had glasses of what had to be the water. And Lady Hawksworth was in earnest conversation with an older lady. He'd wager his best horse the woman was Lady Eagle.

By this evening at the latest, Guy would be in possession of everything the dowager had said. The only question was what, if anything, he would do with it.

Bolton's hand shook with fury as he held the curt and impertinent letter he'd received from the editor of the *Morning Post*. "Can't tell me? Won't tell me is more like it.

What the hell does the rubbishing commoner mean he can't tell me?"

His secretary who'd read the note first said, "He did say the information came from a member of Lady Aglaia's family."

Not good enough. Bolton threw the missive in the fireplace. "Do you wish to seek other employment? I demand loyalty from all in my employ."

"Indeed, your grace. I have always been loyal to you. I merely sought to point out that, if it was a member of the lady's family, what can you do about it?"

Kentwell had a point. It was not as if Bolton could chastise Somerset or his family. They might even think it was strange that he cared. It galled Bolton, but he'd have to ignore the piece in the *Post* and the letter from its editor. If the announcement had come from the duke's family, it wouldn't even do any good to threaten the paper. "When am I due to travel to Bath?"

"During the second week of July, your grace."

He remembered that he had several house parties he'd accepted invitations to and he was expected to make an appearance in Brighton. "And the wedding?"

"The fourth week. I shall procure the special license shortly before you depart. Shall I continue to plan for the wedding to take place in Hampshire?"

"No, better to have it in Bath. Might as well do the deed while I'm there. I will need you to join me there so there is no point in buying the license before I depart. You can bring it when you come. The damned things aren't good for more than a fortnight." If he knew women, and by now he ought to, he'd have to spend some time courting her. Somerset obviously expected it.

Once Bolton told Somerset that the wedding would be in Bath, his duchess would have the wedding breakfast well in hand by the time Bolton arrived. "Write to the

Duke of Somerset informing him of the change."

"Lady Aglaia will attain her majority on the sixth of July. You might want to send her a gift," his secretary suggested.

"Go through the jewelry and select something suitable." God knew he had enough trinkets left from his previous wives.

"Yes, your grace." Kentwell straightened from making notes.

"That will be all." Bolton was tired of this marriage business and dealing with young ladies. Nevertheless, he needed an heir, and that was the only way to get one. "I'll be at Mrs. Peterson's house and won't be back for dinner."

His mistress had been wroth with him for not telling her he was marrying again. He patted the diamond necklace he had in his pouch. That should make her happy. If not, he'd find something that would.

The next morning at breakfast, Mama and Meg insisted that Laia and her sister accompany them to the Pump Room. "It is much more than drinking the water. Almost everyone in Bath goes to see people and be seen," Meg said. "There are also some ladies about your ages that accompany their mothers or grandmothers. It would be nice for you to become acquainted with more people."

Laia could not argue with that. Sarah was the only friend they had. "Will I have to drink the water?"

Euphrosyne scrunched up her lips. "I have heard it is horrible."

"You are not required to drink it," their mother said in a mild tone. "But you will appear provincial if you cannot discuss how bad it tastes from personal experience."

Laia and her sister exchanged looks. That answered that question. Neither of them would wish to appear any more countrified than they already did.

Laia dressed for the excursion in a new walking gown of pale blue. Her betrothal ring had been returned from the jeweler's late yesterday and was on her dressing table. Yet she had not even tried it on. Picking it up, she thought about wearing it, but set it back down. It was huge, and ugly, and did not go with anything she owned. She hated feeling childish, but there was something about the ring she could not like. Perhaps she would try it on tomorrow.

The four of them strolled to the Pump Room. It was already crowded, but Meg and Mama were hailed by a woman sitting with another matron and two younger ladies.

"Come, I shall introduce you to Mrs. Butterworth and Mrs. Applebee, and their daughters, Caroline and Margaret. Caroline Butterworth is about your age, Laia, and Margaret Applebee is just a bit younger.

"Did they not have a London Season?" Euphrosyne asked. "It is stilling time for it, is it not?"

"Not everyone can afford a Season in Town for their daughters," their mother said. "Both ladies are wives of military men. Mrs. Butterworth's eldest daughter is engaged to a baronet whom she met here earlier this year. And Miss Applebee is the youngest of five daughters. The others have all married." Mama smiled. "Bath is not such a bad place to find a mate."

Euphrosyne glanced at their mother, a considering look on her face. "No, it is not."

Once again, Laia wanted to say something to her sister about not getting her hopes up, but Mama had already begun introducing them to the other ladies.

Laia and Euphrosyne soon discovered that they had much more in common with Caroline and Margaret than Laia originally thought. Except for the butcher shop, the ladies had been to all the stores she and her sister had visited yesterday.

They discussed a massive and hideous bonnet decorated with peacock feathers all of them had seen in the window of one of the milliners. An older woman in the room was now wearing exactly that hat.

Euphrosyne asked Miss Appleby if her sisters' matches had been arranged. "No, Papa said he did not wish to marry any of us off to men we might not like."

"Indeed," Miss Caroline added. "My father said that he would not be responsible if we were unhappy in our marriages."

"Laia will be marrying soon as well," Euphrosyne said. "To Bolton."

The other ladies looked at Laia, and she wished her sister had not mentioned her betrothal.

"The Duke of Bolton?" Miss Applebee asked.

"Yes." Laia did not wish to discuss a man about whom she knew almost nothing.

"Is he not quite elderly?" Miss Caroline asked slowly, as if afraid to broach the topic.

"He is in his sixties." For the first time, Laia acknowledged to herself that she wished he were not quite so old.

"Still," Miss Applebee said, "he is a duke. How did you meet him?"

"She has not met him at all." Euphrosyne glanced at Laia. "Our father arranged the match." Her sister took a sip of the water and made a face. "I think it is quite medieval."

If Laia didn't die of embarrassment first, she was going to murder her sister. "Euphrosyne—"

"Laia, come stroll with me." Meg rose.

I will not run away. "Not yet, if you please." She turned to the other ladies. "I wish my father had not arranged a match with a gentleman I do not know, but it is my duty to obey him."

"Well said, Lady Laia." Mrs. Butterworth frowned at her daughter. "Caroline, we must be going."

Once the ladies left, Meg took Laia's arm while her mother spoke in a low voice to her sister.

"I do not know why she would have brought up my betrothal," Laia said to her sister-in-law. "She has never done anything to humiliate me before."

"Is that how you see being betrothed to Bolton?" Meg asked.

Was it? Laia had no say in the matter, and no one, even her new friends, appeared to be happy for her. Bolton had not even written to her. And she had not liked the things he had sent to her.

She gave herself a shake. "I don't know how I feel about it. Perhaps I'm simply nervous."

Her sister-in-law nodded. "You still have time."

"That is what others have said, but it is not true. Whether I wish to marry Bolton or not, I am stuck with him."

An older lady in a pink turban glanced at them, and Meg inclined her head, then gave Laia an enigmatic smile. "We shall see."

When they arrived home, Euphrosyne hurried up to Laia. "Forgive me. I did not mean to embarrass you. I just wanted you to understand how unsuitable this marriage is."

"That was not the way to go about it." Laia heaved a sigh. "And what would you have me do? If I do not marry him, it would affect you and our sisters. Father would never let you out of the castle."

"I don't know." Concern clouded her eyes. "Someone must be able to help. I want you to be happy."

"What must happen is for you to cease worrying about what cannot be changed." She took her sister's arm. "I shall be fine."

Yet she did not *feel* fine, and she could not put her finger on the reason she had become so uneasy about her coming marriage. Her father had written saying Bolton would visit her before their wedding. Yet he had not bothered to do her the courtesy of writing to her. Was he avoiding her? And if he was why would he? Laia gave herself a shake. She would refuse to allow herself to worry until there was a reason to be concerned.

Fortunately, the next time they met up with the Butterworths and Applebees, the subject was not mentioned and she and her sister were able to form friendships with the other ladies.

During the week before the assembly room ball, Laia and Euphrosyne scarcely had time to think. They were invited to dinner by both Mrs. Applebee and Mrs. Butterworth. Mr. Paulet invited their new friends as well as Lord Markham and his family to a picnic on Lansdowne. Mama, Euphrosyne, Meg, Hawksworth, and Laia drove over to visit the children. Her brothers and sisters were having a wonderful time exploring their new environs.

The evening before the ball, Sarah hosted a dinner. "It is the first time I have given an entertainment," she confided to Laia. "I do hope it all goes well. Unfortunately, I do not know any gentleman who I can ask to make up my numbers."

In the end, it had not mattered. The evening was a great deal of fun. Laia wondered what it would be like to host her first dinner. Unfortunately, when she thought of the gentleman standing next to her in the receiving line, it was not the Duke of Bolton, but his nephew, Mr. Paulet.

At all the events, Mr. Paulet flirted with Laia. She was learning to flirt back, and having much too much fun. In more quiet moments—when they were walking or riding—they discussed their families, carefully avoiding any mention of the duke. And despite her resolve, she found herself drawn to him more and more. It was difficult to remember she was betrothed to a man who had not even bothered to meet her while Mr. Paulet was being charming and attentive.

There was also more shopping to do, along with fittings for new ball gowns and morning visits. If this was what the end of the winter season in Bath was like, she wondered how much more there was to do in London.

By the night of the ball, Laia had still not heard from her betrothed, and the irritation that had begun the first day she'd attended the Pump Room grew. She was starting to wonder if she could be civil to a man who had so studiously ignored her.

CHAPTER NINE

THE EVENING OF HER FIRST ball finally arrived, and Laia stared at herself in the mirror, scarcely believing it was her. Her new gown was the color of the aquamarine ring her mother had given her for her last birthday. Bands of brilliants trimmed the neck, sleeves, and hem. Henderson, her new maid, had done Laia's hair in a complicated style of braids and soft ringlets.

Laia could not help but wonder what Mr. Paulet would think, then chastised herself for it. She should not be thinking about a gentleman other than her betrothed. Still, it would be pleasant to have a man look at her like her brother looked at her sister-in-law.

"Laia." Euphrosyne opened the door without knocking. "Look at me! Ooooh, look at you!"

"I do think I look well, and so do you." Laia smiled. Her sister was a vision in a pink gown and a white petticoat. Seed pearls adorned the neckline of the bodice and the sleeves. "You are lovely."

"You're beautiful." Her sister carefully bussed her cheek. "All the gentleman will want to dance with you.

"You as well. Do you think you'll be sitting along the sides of the room?"

For the first time, Euphrosyne's eyes did not meet Laia's gaze. Well, this was not the time to pry, but to enjoy themselves.

Then her sister did offer a comment, if not the one on her mind. "No. I think our family will make sure we have partners for every dance."

Meg strolled into the room carrying two small posies, one with yellow flowers and the other with pale pink roses, both in filigree silver holders. "I do not know why gentlemen insist on sending flowers to be carried to an event. I suppose you can put some of them in your hair, if you like."

Gentlemen? "Which gentlemen?" Laia eyed the flowers.

"Lord Markham"—Meg handed the pink bouquet to Euphrosyne—"and Mr. Paulet." She gave the other one to Laia. "I must say they were either amazingly percipient, or they went out of their way to discover what you were wearing."

Laia clutched her flowers to her breast. He had actually given her flowers and meant for her to carry them. "I could not ruin the arrangement."

"Nor could I," her sister agreed.

"In that case, you must carry them," Meg said. "If you are ready, we must dine. The balls here begin much earlier than anywhere else I've been. Damon has ordered the chairs to arrive in an hour."

Laia had wondered what it would be like to ride in a sedan chair. Yet, she'd felt sorry for the carriers holding the handles of the chair of an extremely heavy woman they had seen the other day. It was a marvel they hadn't dropped the lady.

"Will you ride with Hawksworth?"

"No, it is the custom for gentlemen to walk alongside the chairs. If they are healthy enough to do so, that is."

She wondered if Bolton would be able to walk.

When they reached the hall, she glanced around and finally found her mother in a day dress. "Why aren't you dressed?"

"I have a little bit of a headache." Mama held out her hands. "I am sure I shall feel better in the morning. I wanted to see you and Euphrosyne before I went to my room. You are both so beautiful. I wish I could be there to see your success."

"I wish you could as well." Laia hugged her mother, thinking she seemed sad somehow.

"I'm glad you came to see us in our finery." Her sister kissed Mama's cheek. "We shall tell you all about it in the morning."

"I shall look forward to hearing all about your first ball. Now get something to eat, or you will be starving before tea."

"With all the gentlemen sure to be present, I should bring a cane," Hawksworth grumbled. "And use it like Lady Bellamny uses hers."

Laia shook her head. "Who is that?"

Meg chuckled. "Lady Bellamny is an old friend of my mother's. She uses her cane to intimidate young men." Meg gazed lovingly at Hawksworth. "I do not think you will have any difficulty making sure the gentlemen behave."

"I am famished." Euphrosyne moved toward the dining room. "I was so excited I could not eat luncheon."

Soup and a cold collation were set out for them, as well as salads. "I do not know if I can eat a thing now." Laia took a sip of the soup and changed her mind. "On the other hand, this is excellent."

"Is there anything we should know about the ball?" her sister asked.

"I think you already know everything you need to know," Meg said reassuringly.

"I think this is an excellent time to review the rules," Hawksworth said, as Meg cast her eyes to the ceiling. "Do not speak to anyone to whom you have not been introduced. Do not go anywhere on your own. If a gentleman does not behave as he should, you will tell me immediately. If you turn down some poor fellow, you may not dance again. Do not dance with any man more than twice. And if either Meg or I decide you should not be introduced to a gentleman, you will not argue." He gave them a stern look. "These assemblies are not as exclusive as Almack's, and some men are in Bath visiting relatives because they cannot afford to remain in Town."

"Is that what Frank calls taking a repairing lease?" Laia asked.

"Precisely." Her brother nodded.

"From what I understand," Meg said, "the evening will begin with minuets, and after tea there will be country dances."

"It is a shame there are no waltzes." Hawksworth cast her a sultry look.

"We are acting as chaperones this evening, my love. We should not dance in any case."

"Very true. I cannot possibly perform a minuet and watch over my sisters at the same time."

"There is also a matter of watching over the items they cannot have with them when they are dancing." Meg rose, signaling for the rest of them to do so as well. "Tea will be served in the drawing room in just a few minutes." She glanced at Laia and Euphrosyne. "You should fetch your things."

They rose from the table. Laia and Euphrosyne went upstairs to collect their gloves, fans, reticules, and posies.

"Are you nervous?" Euphrosyne asked as they ascended the stairs.

"A little. I do not want to make a mistake." Laia hugged her sister. "There is nothing to worry about. We will both have a wonderful time."

After tea, they walked down the front steps, and Laia marveled at the sedan chairs. They were much more beautiful than the ones she had seen around town. And tall. She was almost afraid that the men carrying the chair might tip it over.

She was so busy looking at the equipage she jumped a bit when she heard a deep voice next to her. "You will be the most exquisite lady at the assembly rooms this evening, my lady."

Turning, she smiled. "Mr. Paulet, I did not expect to see you until we arrived at the Upper Rooms." In fact, she had been sure he would be accompanying some other lady. But he had called her exquisite, and she had not answered. "Thank you."

He placed his hand under her elbow. "How could I miss escorting you to your first entertainment?"

What to say to that? Instead of replying, she smiled again, and he smiled at her. Even under the streetlights, she could see his eyes warm, and a thrill of pleasure skated through her. "I am glad you are here."

"As am I." He placed his hand under her elbow. "Come, allow me to assist you into the chair."

"Yes, please." She had just gotten settled when she recognized Lord Markham's voice. Goodness, he must be here to escort her sister.

Had Euphrosyne known he was accompanying them? And did it truly matter? Lord Markham was perfectly eligible. Father might even approve of him. After all, he had wanted Lady Sarah to marry their brother Quartus. Therefore, the family must be acceptable. Yet, if Lady Sarah was correct, and Father wanted only land adjoining his holdings, then that was how he'd pick Euphrosyne's husband. And knowing her, there would be trouble.

"You are being quiet," Mr. Paulet said as he strolled next to the chair.

"I was just getting used to the motion," Laia lied. Now was not the time to worry about her sister. "It is different from anything I have experienced."

"I would imagine it is. Much better than attempting a

carriage on these hills or walking in slippers."

"I would think keeping one's skirts from getting dirty would be more of a problem. One can usually wear pattens to keep slippers and hems clean, but not in an evening gown."

"Sensible lady," he said in a tone of approval.

In what seemed to be no time at all, she was carried into a large hall, where the chair was set down, and Mr. Paulet opened the door.

He held his hand out to her. "My lady."

Oh, my! She felt like a princess. "Thank you, sir." Taking his hand, she stepped out of the chair. "This is extraordinary. Imagine a room just for the chairs."

"Well, one could not expect ladies to get out on the street." He grinned. "Not in Bath."

"Yes. I have heard it's considered a little stuffy, but it is the most exciting place I've ever visited."

"Even in London, those who still use chairs are carried inside." Mr. Paulet placed her hand on his arm. "Let us discover how you like your first entertainment."

They joined her brother, sister, Meg, and Lord Markham. Stealing a look at Euphrosyne, Laia noticed her sister was looking extremely pleased with herself. "How did you like the sedan chair?"

"Very well, indeed," Euphrosyne said. "I enjoyed the conversation even more."

Lord Markham had what looked to be a proprietorial grasp on her arm as they made their way into the assembly room.

"What is bothering you?" Mr. Paulet's lips were so close to Laia's ear that a shiver ran down her neck.

She decided not to tell him. Over the past week, he had become a friend, but perhaps she was worrying over nothing. Her sister deserved to have fun. This kind of visit might not happen again for her. "Nothing. I am being silly."

"I doubt that. You could be accused of being cautious." He raised a ruddy brow. "For your sister, perhaps?"

"You have found me out." Laia sighed. "I just do not want her to be hurt."

"I sincerely doubt Markham is playing with her, if that is what concerns you."

"I would be less concerned if he were." She folded her lips wondering how much to tell Mr. Paulet. "We are not free to choose our own mates."

"You are afraid she will run afoul of your father." His deep voice and his heady scent of shaving soap and man enveloped her, and she found herself moving closer to him.

"Precisely." It really was comforting being able to speak about her unease.

"It is early days, yet. Try not to worry so much until there is something to worry about."

They had reached Mr. King, the Master of Ceremony. "Good evening, my lady, Mr. Paulet. We are glad to see you here. If there is anything I can do, please ask."

"Thank you." Laia inclined her head. "What lovely rooms."

"We do try, my lady."

Once Mr. Paulet had greeted the man, they moved on into the room. It was much taller than she had thought it would be. And all the windows were far above her head. "Why are the windows so high?"

"To keep the rabble from looking in on us." His lips pressed together.

"You do not approve?" She and her brothers and sisters had not even been allowed to play with the local gentry.

"In a word, no." He slanted her a curious look. "If those who do not have what we do wish to see a world they might never know, why should they not?"

Guy watched Laia's fine, perfectly arched brows draw together. Although she and her brother had said she had studied the philosophers, she had probably never thought about putting their ideas to practice. "I do not think that merely because my ancestor or another's ancestor did a deed for a ruler"—deep pink washed over her face and neck as if she were uncertain of stating her opinion—"in whatever fashion, that makes me better than others." She had been looking off, but now focused on him. "I believe one who has been born to privilege has the obligation to help others, no matter their status in life."

He hadn't known he had been waiting for her to declare herself to be as much a Radical as he was. Now that she had, he was even more drawn to her. He wanted to discover how she tasted, not just her lips, but her breasts, and the rest of her body. Yet, she was the sister of one of his best friends. She was betrothed to his uncle. Before Guy did anything, he had to be sure of his feelings. Lust alone could take one only so far.

A few feet away from them, her sister said, "Meg, will you and Hawksworth join the set?"

"No, your brother is not fond of the minuet. He would rather waltz."

"Only with you," he replied. "Mayhap we should have a small ball of our own."

Meg laughed. "So that you and I can waltz?"

"Other people may like to waltz as well," he retorted.

"I regret I was not able to find time to plan the dancing party I had suggested." She smiled at him.

Lady Sarah and Bellingham joined their group. "We could plan a ball as well," she said.

"Then it is settled." Meg smiled up at her husband. "We shall be able to waltz."

"I would like to dance the waltz as well," Laia murmured.

"As every lady should." Guy grinned to himself. "I shall not wait to beg your hand for the first waltz we happen to come across."

Regally, she inclined her head. "I should be delighted."

Strains from the violins filtered through the air, and he held out his hand to her. "My dance, I believe."

The smile on her face as she placed her hand in his could have lit the room. "It is, and my very first dance in public."

He had not even thought about that. She must be worried. "We shall show them how the minuet is done."

Her light laughter pleased him. He hoped she was not so nervous after all.

They took their places in the line. When the dance began, her steps were sure and light. Laia didn't even falter when an older gentleman missed his step and almost ran into her. No concern showed as she righted the man and continued on as if nothing had occurred. It was as if she had been out for years.

Freed from worrying about her, he could notice the way her plump breasts rose slightly as she moved. Every once in a while, her skirts gave hints of a small waist and lush hips.

The minuet gave them time to flirt, but she was still figuring that part out. Her face glowed only with joy and happiness. That, however, would attract the other gentlemen like bees were attracted to flowers.

Pollinating. Thoughts of flaxen-haired children invaded Guy's mind. What the devil was the matter with him? He hadn't even decided if they would suit and some primitive part of him was already procreating with the lady.

He took her hand, and they twirled and skipped before resuming their places on the side while others performed the same act. The set was almost over when their gazes caught. He let out the breath he'd been holding as he'd stared into her light blue eyes and fell in love all at the same time.

His friends had been right. She was the perfect lady

for him. Now all he had to do was convince her to jilt his uncle, defy her father, and marry him in less than a month.

CHAPTER TEN

BEFORE GUY EVEN RETURNED LAIA to her brother and sister-in-law, gentlemen were queuing up to dance with her, and he could feel more behind him. He wanted to lead her right out of the door. If they'd been at a private ball, he would have been able to do just that.

He did not want to share her at all, but one more set would have to satisfy him. "Before all your sets are taken, I would like to dance the last set of the evening with you."

Her eyes widened, and for a moment he did not think she'd answer. "I would like that a great deal. I think we dance well together."

As if they had been made for one another. "I think so as well."

He left her with Hawksworth just as a young gentleman bowed to her. His shirt points were so high, Guy didn't know how he could turn his head. The popinjay would most likely step all over her pretty feet. Perhaps Guy should remove the threat before the damage was done.

Laia cast an inquiring glance at him. For a moment he couldn't figure out why. Damn, he was scowling. He needed to find something else to do until the dance when he could be with her again.

Or tea. He could escort her to tea.

Markham came up and stood beside Guy. "Most of them are a bunch of worthless fribbles, but harmless. Hawksworth will take care of any problems. I'm off to find something to drink and the card room."

Hawksworth was the proper person to act on Laia's behalf. If Guy did anything, it would cause talk. "You're out of luck. Tea is not for more than another hour and there is nothing else on the premises."

"It's as bad as Almack's," the man grumbled.

"I don't think the bread will be stale, and at least the tea is not weak." Or that is what Guy had been told.

"That's something, at any rate." Markham cast a heated look in Lady Euphrosyne's direction.

If his lordship's feeling were reciprocated by the lady, Laia had been right to worry about her sister. One never knew what the Duke of Somerset had planned for his children. If he didn't approve of Markham, it was either give up or go for the border. At least Guy had an easier road. Laia was almost twenty-one.

Thinking of that made him wonder when his uncle would make an appearance. It was not well done of him to leave Laia to her own—or rather Guy's—devices before making time for his betrothed.

Guy had better think of his course of action, as well. Laia had been steadfast in her determination to wed Bolton. Guy didn't think it was because she wanted to become a duchess. It was her sense of honor and duty to her family. Still, according to Hawksworth, she had not even been asked to agree with the match. That would change when she reached her majority and had to ratify the contracts.

One way or the other, Guy would have to find a way to convince her that, despite what her father wanted, she would be much better off with him.

He could think of only one way to accomplish that. Travel to London and procure a special license. Well, perhaps more than one. He would introduce Laia to Lady Engle.

Not at the Pump Room. The meeting must take place privately. Laia would be shocked at what she would hear, and he didn't want word getting back to either duke that they had met. Meg and Hawksworth would help him get Laia and the older lady together. He'd speak to Meg tomorrow.

Meanwhile, he must keep busy. Cards did not appeal this evening. Dancing was the only option. It would also allow him to keep an eye on Laia. He didn't recognize any ladies other than those in his own party, so he set off to find Mr. King to make introductions.

An hour or so later, Guy returned his partner to her mother, then made his way directly to Laia. A young man—callow youths appeared to abound in Bath—had just made his bow when Guy appropriated her arm. "Allow me to escort you to tea."

"I was going to ask her." The lad flushed angrily.

Guy lifted his quizzing glass, and slowly inspected the fribble from the top of his pomatumed head to his intricately tied cravat and his lavender knee breeches. "Indeed?" Guy drawled. "How unfortunate you are."

Next to him, Laia's hands covered her lips. She turned away, and her slender shoulders began to quake. The blasted woman was fighting a fit of giggles.

The youth took a step forward, and Guy's arm shot out, stopping the young man. "Don't make a cake of yourself. I am with her party."

Stepping back, the youth bowed. "Thank you for the dance, my lady. I shall hope I may escort you at another time."

"Well, done," Hawksworth murmured to Guy as the lad stomped away.

Guy turned his attention to Laia. "You abominable girl. Are you laughing?"

She mopped her eyes with a lace-trimmed handkerchief. "I could not help myself. I have heard about the use of a quizzing glass, but I have never had the opportunity to *see* how it is done." Her eyes danced with mirth. "I was truly torn between embarrassment for Mr. Hardy and admiration for your style. Then I thought about my brothers, and it was all I could do to hold back my laughter. You see, I would dearly love to see the younger ones put in their places so neatly."

Guy tucked her arm in his. "It does seem to be a rite of passage for a young man to be put in his place. I suppose we are all coxcombs when we are young and dealing with society for the first time."

"I am quite sure that is true." She nodded. "I think he will be better for the set-down."

"At least his mother has the good sense to bring him to Bath instead of Town," Meg said in a dry tone. "There is much less he can do to get into trouble here."

Guy agreed with her. Allowing green young men to run wild was one of the more idiotic things he'd seen done. "More parents should consider the option."

He kept Laia close to him as they maneuvered through the crowd. "Is your card full?"

"Yes. I am amazed at how many gentlemen wish to stand up with me." Her voice was full of wonder.

Only she could be surprised at her success. "You should not be. You are as beautiful as you are graceful."

A light blush painted her cheeks. "That is the nicest compliment anyone has given to me."

"I shan't say I am not given to flummery at times, but it is quite true. I have never had the pleasure of dancing with a lady who dances so elegantly. I am looking forward to our second dance." He had discovered that the last dance was the Scottish *figuree*. At last, he'd be able to remain with her throughout the dance and even hold her in his arms.

"As am I." She smiled. "My other partners have not been nearly as skilled as you are."

He shot her a grin. "I'm glad to see we are in accord.

We must dance together at every opportunity."

"Indeed, we must." She laughed and shook her head. "I shall be sorry to leave Bath. I've never had so much fun or been entertained so well."

If it was up to him, no matter where she was, she would always have an excellent time. "Don't despair yet. One never knows what life holds."

Laia knew exactly what her life held. Marriage to a gentleman who had not even bothered to correspond with her or come to visit her. That did not bode well for their future. As curmudgeonly as her father could be, he always treated her mother well.

If he hadn't been ready to depart for Scotland, he wouldn't have allowed Mama to leave him for so long. Yet, for some reason no one could understand, she never managed to remain in Scotland for more than a week. Something always happened to one of the children. Mayhap that was the reason they were all here where she could watch out for them. It was almost the end of June and nothing had occurred. There were no broken bones, or fevers, or even an upset stomach.

The country dances began when they returned to the ballroom. Markham had joined them for tea, but disappeared again. A middle-aged gentleman came to claim her sister for the dance while a gentleman who looked to be past fifty bowed to Laia.

Did her betrothed look like his miniature?

One or two men about her brother's age had approached, but took one look at Damon and veered off.

Sir Ralph was a good dancer. Unfortunately, the next gentleman had her skipping out of his way. Finally it was time for Mr. Paulet to claim her again.

He bowed elegantly then took her hand, placing it on his arm. "I am relieved this ends at eleven; otherwise, from the look of your sister-in-law, Hawksworth would be dragging you all home before time."

"Meg has been stifling yawns for the past half hour, and he is watching her closely."

"As he should." Laia was certain that, when Mr. Paulet married, he would care for his wife's wellbeing, and not just for the sake of the child.

Laia had danced a Scottish *figuree* before but her previous experiences had not at all prepared her to have Mr. Paulet's arms around her. The rush of excitement and the frissons of pleasure caused by his touch distracted her to the point that she almost forgot where she was in the dance.

This was nothing at all like dancing with her brothers or the dancing master. Thank Heavens for her training.

During the next move, their eyes met, and she knew he had been as affected as she. Dear God, this was not supposed to happen. She could not become attached to another gentleman. Particularly one who was so closely related to her betrothed.

For the rest of the set, Laia attempted to steel herself against his touch, but she always found herself wanting to be near him. Did she have no resolve at all? The sooner the dance was over the better, but once it had ended, she missed his touch, and had to consciously keep a distance as they strolled back to her family.

If she could just stay away from Mr. Paulet—yet how could she when he was friends with her brother? She could do only one thing: go to Meg and tell her what had happened. She'd be able to advise Laia.

She and Mr. Paulet arrived at the family grouping to discover that Damon had already called for their chairs. He hurried them into the hall where the vehicles waited. Soon Laia was seated with Mr. Paulet walking beside her. Surely he could not wish to be attracted to her. Perhaps she should mention it. But what if she was wrong? After all, she had very little experience with men. She only knew that she had never felt this way around anyone else.

He chatted lightly about everything and nothing while she responded as her breeding required. Soon she began to relax. The answer to her problem was simple. She had simply not had enough contact with the world. She was, in fact, what her older brothers would call "green." Mr. Paulet had most likely simply been flirting as gentlemen did. Ergo, the attraction was all on her side. And that would be easy enough to manage. No one need know anything about it.

In spite of her decision, Laia couldn't sleep. No matter what she did, Mr. Paulet's face and large, warm hands intruded into her dreams. She even pulled out the miniature of her betrothed and set it beside the bed so that she would dream of the duke instead. It didn't work. She still saw, not strange-looking blue eyes, but laughing eyes that begged her to pay attention. Why eyes would want her to pay heed to them made no sense at all. She was being fanciful. She turned her pillow and tried to find a more comfortable place for her head. Eventually, she fell asleep.

By the time she woke, bright sunlight streamed through the crack in the curtains. Laia was tempted to roll over and close her eyes, but her sister rushed into the room. "Laia, you would not believe the number of bouquets that are in the parlor and drawing room."

She rubbed her eyes before pushing herself up. "Bouquets?"

Euphrosyne sat on the side of the bed. "Yes, and poetry. We have each received about the same number." She pulled a face. "All of it horrible drivel, but just think of a gentleman making the gesture. They have been arriving for hours."

Surely the morning could not be so far advanced that . . . "What time is it?"

"Almost nine. Breakfast is being brought up to you, so

you must rise now."

"Yes, of course." Laia never slept this late. "Why didn't my maid wake me?"

"Mama said to let you sleep." Euphrosyne left the bed and headed to the door. "She also said we are to expect visits from the gentlemen later today during her visiting hours."

I do not wish to see more gentlemen. I'm having enough trouble with two already.

"I should have stayed in bed." Laia had a strong urge to pull the bedcovers over her again.

"You are still in bed," her sister pointed out. "Mama expects you in the morning room in an hour."

"An hour?" She groaned.

"Yes, and you will want to see the flowers and read some of the poetry." Euphrosyne practically skipped out of the room.

Three quarters of an hour later, Laia made her way down the stairs and into the drawing room. Her sister had not exaggerated. Dozens of bouquets filled the room. There were probably no blooms left anywhere else in Bath.

As she gazed at the display, one bunch of red roses caught her attention. She reached for the card, but knew before she opened it who they were from.

Mr. Paulet.

> *To the most beautiful lady in Bath*
> *My dear Lady Laia,*
> *Thank you for the dances and conversation.*
> *I beg you will allow me to call on you today.*
> *Yr devoted Servant,*
> G

Her heart began to beat faster and butterflies took up residence in her stomach. This short missive was much better than any poetry she could have received. It proved that Mr. Paulet felt as strongly for her as she did for him.

And that was . . . that was a disaster.

Tears started in her eyes. No matter how she felt about Mr. Paulet or him about her, she couldn't marry him. Her father would be furious if she did not wed Bolton. Laia didn't care so much for herself. She would be beyond his reach, but he would forbid her mother and younger sisters and brothers all contact with her. He'd lock her sisters up. Euphrosyne especially. If she had any chance at all of marrying Lord Markham, Laia refusing to marry Bolton and instead wedding his nephew would ruin it. In fact, Father might even insist Euphrosyne marry Bolton in Laia's stead.

She could not do that to her sister.

As if called, Euphrosyne strolled into the room, going immediately to a bouquet of pink flowers. They would be from Markham. But this time Laia couldn't fault her sister, not when Laia was forming an attachment for a gentleman after her father had already promised her to Bolton.

What a mull she had made of things.

"Markham has already written Father asking permission to marry me."

Laia's jaw dropped. She quickly shut it again. "That is wonderful."

"Neither of us thinks he will allow us to wed." Her sister's round jaw firmed. "We might go to Scotland instead."

She could not believe what she'd just heard. "Scotland?" Euphrosyne nodded. "You would risk a scandal?"

"We would be chaperoned by Sarah and Jeremy."

Laia dropped into a chair. "But what about our sisters?"

"Father is never going to allow any of us to marry for love. What we do will not change that. How could he be harsher than he already is? We cannot go into the town alone, we cannot walk outside of the garden by ourselves. Even when we are in the garden we are watched." Euphrosyne took Laia's hands in hers. "If I could change any of that by marrying whom he chooses, I would. But, I cannot, and neither can you. All you will do is sacrifice yourself for nothing."

She stared into her sister's militant eyes for the longest time. In the background, the door opened and closed. Was Euphrosyne right? After all, the family did not need Laia to marry for money or position. Father wanted something, but it was not vital to the happiness of the rest. And Bolton had shown no interest in her at all. Could she wed where she loved? Would Mr. Paulet even ask her?

Laia took her sister's hands and gently squeezed them. "You must follow your own road, as I shall follow mine." She gave Euphrosyne a rueful smile. "Wherever that leads me."

CHAPTER ELEVEN

GUY ARRIVED AT THE HOUSE Hawksworth had rented shortly after ten o'clock the next morning. When he followed the butler into the breakfast room, Meg had just poured a cup of tea and was reading a newssheet. Hawksworth was doing the same.

Oh, for domestic tranquility. Guy could easily imagine this exact vignette with Laia and himself.

"Mr. Paulet," their butler intoned.

"I wondered who was disturbing our peace." Damon put down his paper.

"I'm sorry to bother you this early, but I need help."

"This is interesting." Meg slowly lowered her newssheet. "Guy Paulet almost never needs help. Please, take a seat. Have you broken your fast?"

He should have known she would bring up his rejection of her aid for one of his charity projects. What was worse, she'd been correct. He should have accepted her help.

She poured him a cup of tea.

"No, I came straight over here."

"Whatever it is can wait until you have sustenance. One always thinks better on a full stomach. If you do not believe me, ask my husband."

Hawksworth filled a plate for Guy, and Meg pushed the toast toward him. After he'd finished half his food and another cup of tea, he said, "It's Laia."

One of Meg's dark brows rose. "Laia?"

Drat and damn. This is what he got for calling her by

her name in his head. "Lady Laia."

"Too late for that." Hawksworth leaned back in his chair and grinned. "Does this mean you have decided to marry her?"

Guy wanted to run a finger beneath his collar. "Yes."

"Excellent," his friend said. "How do you plan to go about courting her?"

"That is not the complicated part." He was tempted to rake his fingers through his hair in frustration. "First I have to convince her that she is not going to marry my blasted uncle."

"That might not be as difficult as you believe." Meg's eyes had a sly look. "I have a plan to do just that."

Now what was she up to? "If you are thinking of bringing Lady Engle into this, please reconsider. I've given it much thought. The problem is that she has no direct proof."

Apparently undaunted, Meg continued, "I had tea with her the other day, and there is one piece of information she had not previously divulged. Bolton planned to divorce Sophia. He had two men who would swear to having conjugal relations with her. Her illness began after she refused to cooperate with a divorce."

Guy shook his head. "It's not enough."

"For the Lords, probably not. But to convince Laia"—Meg's brows rose again—"it will be sufficient."

If he could have thought of another way to turn Laia away from marriage with his uncle, Guy would have taken it, unfortunately, he could not. "Very well, then. We can try it. I want to be there."

Meg's smile reminded him strongly of a cat who'd caught its prey. He was glad she was on his side. "I suggest you make the most of tomorrow night's illumination."

"My lord, my lady." The butler entered the breakfast room. "Lady Aglaia to see her ladyship."

"Meg"—Laia stood in the door as if frozen, her gaze on Guy—"Forgive me. I did not know you had company."

He took in her worried expression and wanted to go to her, hold her in his arms. "I was just leaving."

"No." A dull red colored her cheeks. "I mean . . ." She stammered to a halt, but her eyes never left his.

Before he knew it, he had risen and started toward her. Hawksworth coughed, stopping Guy, but his and Laia's gazes held for a few seconds longer.

"Show Lady Laia to my parlor," Meg instructed. "I shall join you in a few moments."

"Yes, my lady."

After the butler left with Laia, Meg stood and shook out her skirts. "There is no time like the present."

Hawksworth poured Guy another cup of tea. "You might as well remain. I doubt this will take long."

Guy wouldn't have left in any event. If he had his choice, he'd never leave Laia.

LAIA PACED MEG'S SMALL PARLOR waiting for her sister-in-law to appear. Fortunately, she did not have to wait long.

The door opened and Meg glided in, her sharp blue gaze on Laia. "I take it you would like to discuss something with me?"

Taking a breath, Laia nodded. Earlier, she had thought she had fallen in love with Mr. Paulet. After seeing him again, she was certain she had. "I have come to a decision."

Meg sank onto the loveseat and motioned to the chair next to it. "Please, have a seat. Shall I ring for tea, or have you had your fill?"

Mama always said tea helped any crisis, and this was

definitely a huge one. "Tea would be wonderful."

Not able to pace, Laia fidgeted as she never had before. The fringe on her shawl seemed to fascinate her as did the pearl ring on her right hand. Finally, the tea tray arrived, and Meg poured.

Once the door closed behind the servant, Meg said, "Now then, how can I help you?"

Laia turned her cup in the saucer, before taking a quick drink and setting the cup back down. "I do not wish to marry Bolton."

"Because you are in love with Guy Paulet?"

She wasn't sure she was ready to tell anyone of her feelings, but this was Meg, and Laia knew her sister-in-law would never betray her trust. "That is one reason." She took another sip of tea. "The other is that Bolton has shown no interest in me."

Meg poured them both another cup of tea. "Mr. Paulet aside, I think you are making a wise decision. It has come to my attention that Bolton wished to divorce his last duchess when she did not become pregnant. When she refused, she began to sicken and eventually died." Meg's lips firmed for a moment. "I think the reason he has no children is due to his inability to procreate. Neither Damon nor I wish you to be his next victim."

Suddenly, what Mr. Paulet had said made sense. "Will Damon tell Father?"

Her sister-in-law shrugged. "Most likely. Yet, although I hate saying it, I am not sure it will matter. Damon has discovered that Bolton has a property your father wants."

Sarah was right as well. Rage welled up in Laia as it never had before, and her hands began to shake. "So I am to be traded for land to a man who might be a murderer?"

"Not if I have anything to say about it." Meg's calm, steady voice soothed Laia's nerves. "And I believe I shall have a great deal to say." She rose from the loveseat. "Now,

I am almost certain there is a gentleman who would very much like to see you."

Laia stood as well. "What will you do?"

"Damon and I shall discuss the matter. We will let you know what we decide." Her sister-in-law started toward the door then stopped. "He received a copy of the settlement agreements from your father's solicitor."

"That's how he knew about the property." Of course it was. He would have read the contracts before giving them to her.

"Indeed." Meg opened the door. "Shall I tell Guy to come to you?"

"Yes." Laia nodded. "Yes, please."

Seconds after she closed the door, it opened again. Mr. Paulet strode in and gathered her into his arms. "I hope you don't mind, but I have an urgent need to kiss you."

Before she could acquiesce, his lips met hers. He swept his tongue into her open mouth. *Oh, my! Who knew a kiss could be like this?* Laia touched her tongue to his, and he made a growling sound and pulled her tighter against him. She threw her arms around his neck.

He slanted his mouth, deepening the kiss, and Laia couldn't help but moan with pleasure. She could happily remain here all day, and longer. One of his hands slipped to her derrière. She should protest, but his caresses burned though the muslin and linen, making her bottom and nether parts tingle.

Then he broke the kiss. He touched his forehead to hers. "Forgive me."

"No. I wanted you to kiss me." Laia cupped his cheek, pressing her lips to his.

"I'm not making myself clear." His lips broadened into a smile. "I do not want forgiveness for kissing you, but for doing it before I declared myself."

"Mr. Paulet—" He touched his fingers to her mouth.

"Guy. You may call me Mr. Paulet when we are in public, but please call me Guy in private."

She had always had a fondness for the name Guy, and she was glad it was attached to a gentleman she loved. "Then you must call me Laia."

"In my mind, I have called you Laia since shortly after we met." Her face heated again, and she stared into his molten silver eyes. "It took me a while longer to figure out I loved you."

She felt as if she were standing on a cloud. To think that she had found a man who loved her as she loved him. It was almost too good to be true. "You said you had something to say to me?"

"Come, let us talk." He led her to the loveseat. Once they were settled next to each other, he put his arm around her. She leaned her head against his shoulder. "I should be down on one knee, but then I couldn't hold you. Laia, I would like more than anything in the world to marry you. Will you have me?"

"Yes." She said the word without thinking, ignoring the consequences. "I would love to be your wife." She turned her head and Guy kissed her again. "How will we manage it?"

He let out a sigh. "I'm not sure. I only know that we will. No one will take you away from me."

"That is how I feel as well." She snuggled closer to him, praying that they could marry.

"When shall we have the wedding?" Guy nuzzled her hair and kissed her again. "Do you wish for a large wedding breakfast?"

Impossible man. Laia grinned to herself. "Here am I worried that something will stop us and you simply want a date."

"If the army taught me anything, it was to have a battle plan."

"And am I a battle to be won?" she asked in a flirtatious tone.

Yet his eyes didn't twinkle with pleasure. They turned hard and serious. "I expect someone, either your father or my uncle, possibly both of them, will try to stop us."

Laia bit down on her lower lip. Father had attempted to stop her brothers. "Let us marry on my birthday."

Guy seemed to relax a little. "We will require a settlement agreement of some sort. To protect you and our children."

Whatever her dowry had been, she doubted she would receive it. "I might come to you a pauper."

"If you do"—he shrugged—"I have wealth enough for both of us."

"I would like to see the property that was so important my father would ignore the talk about Bolton." She had tried to be fair and think that perhaps her father had not known about the duke's other wives, but she could not do it. Her father knew almost everything that occurred.

Guy lifted her onto his lap. "You are not the only one in your family to discover what Somerset is. It has nothing to do with you."

Then why did she feel like her value as a person had been decreased? "No?"

"No." Damon strolled into the room accompanied by Meg. "Our father cares only for the dukedom. That does not reflect on you, or me, or Frank and Quartus. It will not reflect on our other brothers and sisters. Your mother loves you enough that she wrote to Meg and told her what had happened."

Her brother slid a look at Guy, and he lifted Laia off his lap. So much for cuddling with her new betrothed.

Kentwell strode into Bolton's study. "Your Grace, I have

news of Mr. Paulet."

Bolton glanced up from the books he'd been working on. "And?"

"He has been seen in Bath in the company of the Marquis of Hawksworth and his family. Including Lady Aglaia." His secretary cleared his throat. "Escorting Lady Aglaia to events and around Bath. Only in the company of her family, however."

"Need I ask how you came by this information?" Kentwell might be only the youngest son of an earl, but his family was well connected.

"My mother via my aunt, who received a letter from my grandmother, who was in Bath taking the waters. She recognized him due to his resemblance to his late father."

In other words, to Bolton himself. Although Kentwell, knowing how Bolton felt about his nephew, would never mention that.

Damn Paulet! Bolton had suspected he would somehow involve himself with Bolton's betrothed. "Cancel my engagements. I shall travel to Bath as soon as possible."

"Yes, your grace. I'll send a messenger to the York."

"And get that special license. As long as I'm there, I may as well get married."

"Immediately, your grace."

Bolton watched with satisfaction as his secretary dashed out of the study. The next time a seat in the Commons came open, he would have Kentwell stand for it. At least one of his seats would vote the way he wished.

For the moment, he must decide how to deal with his nephew and his betrothed. Nothing Kentwell had said indicated that an attachment was forming between the two. That Paulet was frequently found in Hawksworth's company was not out of the ordinary. Still, Bolton always trusted his intuition, and it would be better to discover what, exactly, was going on.

He could not afford to lose Lady Aglaia. His chances of finding another suitable lady to marry were not good.

As it was, Bolton didn't depart for Bath until the following morning. It irritated him that his tolerance for travel had diminished with his age, making it necessary to spend the night on the road and delay his arrival.

Kentwell had informed Bolton that an illumination was planned for the evening of his arrival, and Hawksworth and his sisters were likely to be present. That would give Bolton time to observe his betrothed and probably his nephew without them knowing he was present.

The next day he arrived at The York in Bath and gave instructions that no one was to know he was present. The illumination was held that evening in Sidney Gardens.

It took Bolton almost an hour to locate Guy Paulet's party. He recognized Hawksworth first. With him was a woman Bolton assumed was Lady Hawksworth, and three ladies and three gentlemen. One of whom was his nephew. He watched the party until he became bored, but could see nothing wrong with Paulet's behavior or that of the lady he squired.

A journey to Bath for nothing. He'd return in the morning via the property he was supposedly giving up for this bride.

CHAPTER TWELVE

TALL STRUCTURES—MUCH LIKE THE ONES in Vauxhall—lit with hundreds if not thousands of candles illuminated sections of Sidney Park. Lanterns were strung in other areas, and the bright lights left parts of the park even darker than they would usually seem. Orchestras played and people began to dance.

"I've never seen anything like this," Laia marveled next to Guy.

"Next Season I'll take you to Vauxhall. It is even grander, and you will be able to see the Catherine Wheel as well." Since they had arrived, he'd kept propriety in mind and not shown her the love he was feeling. By this time, all of Bath would know about her betrothal to his uncle. They needed to limit any talk.

"I have heard of a Catherine Wheel. How wonderful it would be to see one." She looked up at him, her face glowing with happiness. "Oh, Guy, I would so love to see London!"

"You will not only see it, but you will have an elegant townhouse in which to live when Parliament is in session. You will also have the opportunity to host political parties." He held his breath. She wanted to be politically active, but did she wish to be a political hostess?

"That is perfect. I will ask Meg the best way to go about it." They had reached another of the towers, and she stopped to gaze at it while he let out the breath.

How had his life become so wonderful? His mother

would say—*Drat!* How had Guy forgotten about his mother? He'd have to write her first thing in the morning. She would never forgive him if he married Laia and did not tell his mother first. They still had a few days, but he'd better send the letter by messenger. Having Laia in his life right now was fraught with difficulties, but they would all be worth it.

Their party strolled the gardens for another half hour or so. Then Hawksworth said, "Meg is getting tired. I'm afraid I will have to shorten our evening.

"I am ready to leave," Laia said, even though Guy knew she wasn't.

"I am as well," her sister agreed.

Markham joined them as they made their way to Laura Place. What Guy wouldn't give to be able to take Laia back to his house tonight.

Soon. At least he knew he'd be able to marry the woman he loved.

The next morning, he joined Laia and her brother as they drove to view the property Somerset wanted. The Duchess of Somerset took the opportunity to ride with them and visit her younger children.

Meg and the duchess were already seated in the coach when Guy assisted Laia up the stairs. Keeping his voice to a whisper, he asked, "Does your mother know about us?"

She shook her head. "At least I do not think she does. Yet it has occurred to me that she might not wish to know certain things."

Knowing Somerset's reputation, that would be wise. He wanted to kiss her again, but that had not been possible since the first time. "I'll see you when we arrive."

Three-quarters of an hour later, after leaving the duchess at Roselands, Guy pointed out an old, rambling

Elizabethan manor house nestled in a copse of trees. Across a nearby meadow, a tall tower rose as if guarding the house.

Guy helped Laia down from the coach. "This is it."

"It is beautiful." She turned and gazed. "How long has it been in your family?"

"According to my secretary, not more than a century. It came to us through a marriage. I'd forgotten all about it until I received the details. Then I remembered my father bringing me here once or twice when I was a child." He glanced down at her. "It's much newer than the house. I think it was my great-grandmother's father who decided he should have a castle, but he was talked into settling for the tower."

She looked at him in surprise. "Believe me when I tell you that castles are not all that comfortable."

"I've been in enough old houses not to argue." He held out his arm, and she tucked her hand into the crook of his elbow. "Shall we inspect the castle, my lady?"

"Lead the way." Laia looked over her shoulder. "Damon, are you coming?"

"I'll meet you there." He smiled, but Guy had seen that look before. It usually meant Hawksworth expected trouble.

Guy glanced around. Finally, he saw where the grass had been crushed as if a coach had run over it, but there were no signs that an intruder was on the grounds. It could have been one of the caretakers in a wagon.

He and Laia were almost to the tower when she twirled into his arms and kissed him. "I cannot believe how lucky I am to have met you."

Drawing her closer to him, he brushed his lips across hers, but she was having none of it, and pulled his head down until their mouths melded. "I can't believe how lucky I am to have found you."

Several long moments later, they continued their stroll.

The folly had two round towers attached to a shorter, square center building. Mullioned windows had been added to the center building and long narrow openings to the towers.

Laia gazed up at it. "It looks as if it has rooms."

"As I recall, there are no chambers, but it is certainly large enough for them." Guy scanned the windows for any sign that someone was in the tower.

"Perhaps your ancestor either lost interest or could not afford to finish it."

He grinned at her serious expression. "Or perhaps he just wanted to be able to look at the view from the top."

"It must be wonderful. How far can one see?"

"I truly do not remember. I was more interested in the wooden swords my father brought to play with. Do you wish to go up?"

"Yes, of course." Her smile lit her beautiful face as if he were giving her a treat.

The door swung open on well-oiled hinges, giving way to a hall and a massive wooden staircase. When they reached the top landing, he opened the door for her.

Laia stepped through, and a shrill scream rent the air. He rushed through the door to find her several feet away. Bolton held her against an opening in the turret.

"Lady Aglaia, I assume," his uncle said in a voice so soft and pleasant that bumps rose on the back of Guy's neck.

She swallowed, cutting a furtive look his way. He prayed she'd shake her head, instead she asked, "Who are you?"

"Do you not recognize your betrothed, my dear? I thought the miniature I sent you quite did me justice."

She winced as the duke's fingers dug into her arms. Laia was struggling to present an impassive mien, but her breathing was rapid and one eye began to twitch. She had to be terrified.

Bolton pointed a pistol at Guy. He had to figure out a

way to get her away from that madman. "Let her go."

"Do not come any closer, Nephew." His uncle's grip on her arm tightened. "You would not wish the lovely Lady Aglaia to fall from this height."

Light footsteps sounded from the stairs. It had to be Hawksworth. Hopefully, he'd brought a weapon. If Guy could keep his uncle talking, the blackguard might not notice they were about to have company.

Laia closed her eyes for a second, and her chest heaved as she took a breath. "Why are you doing this?"

Void of all expression, Bolton glanced at her. "The opportunity presented itself. You really should not make love in public, my dear. Anyone could see you." Bolton's eyes speared Guy with hatred. "I am not surprised you would play me false."

Laia began to inch along the wall away from the space to the safety of the brick turret, ever so slightly edging Bolton toward the empty space at the same time. Most women would have had hysterics. Despite her fear, she was keeping her head about her.

"I could not allow you to murder her ladyship for failing to breed."

Laia was almost there. If Guy could keep his uncle's attention, perhaps she would succeed. Still, more was needed. He had to get Bolton away from Laia, and Guy knew of only one way to accomplish that. "None of your wives have quickened. Not even your mistress has born you a child. It cannot be due to the inability of all of them. The fault is yours."

Bolton's face mottled red with rage, forgetting the pistol, he lunged toward Guy.

The crack of a pistol sounded near Guy's ear.

Bolton stopped. His body canted back. He toppled over the ledge.

In a blink of an eye, Laia was in Guy's arms, tear

streaming down her cheeks. "Are you hurt? Did he hit you?" Before he could answer, her hands and eyes were searching for a wound. He stroked her back as she slumped against him, burying her head in his shoulder, giving in to her emotions. After several moments, she said in a shaky voice, "I was never so frightened in my life."

"You're safe now. It was Hawksworth's weapon you heard." Guy murmured, stroking her back as he attempted to replace some of the warmth she'd lost.

"But you almost got yourself killed." Laia leaned back and punched him. "What were you thinking? Don't you ever do anything like that again!"

Guy started to laugh as she pummeled him harder. "Sweetheart, I was never at any risk. Even if he had fired, he was always a horrible shot."

"Paulet was giving me a chance to shoot the bounder." Hawksworth said as he stilled Laia's fists. "If you don't cease, Paulet will think he's marrying a mad woman."

"Never." He kissed her forehead, then tilted her head up and found her lips. "I've never seen a braver lady."

Hawksworth harrumphed, strode to the turrets, and looked over. "At least your former betrothed won't be able to kill anyone else. He's dead."

That got her attention. "How can you be sure?"

She started to pull away from Guy, but he wasn't going to let her go. "There are rocks on that side of the tower. It will not be something you want to see."

She began to shiver.

"Let's go."

"The horses are waiting." Hawksworth grinned at Guy. "You'll have to carry her with you on your horse until we get back to the coach. Take her home. I'll have the magistrate called."

Guy shook his head. "I should be the one to do that."

"No, you should not, your grace. The less you have

to do with your uncle's death, the better it will be for everyone." Hawksworth's eyes cut to Laia.

He was right. If the whole truth got out, they'd have a scandal on their hands. That was not the way to start a marriage.

GUY BURIED HIS UNCLE THREE days later. Several days after that, the magistrate found that Bolton had died from his fall from the tower. Later that day, Guy wrote the Duke of Somerset.

"YOUR GRACE, HER GRACE SENT this by special messenger." Belling hurried into the Duke of Somerset's study in his Scottish castle. "There is also a letter from the Duke of Bolton."

"Give me her grace's missive first."

Belling handed Somerset a letter written in his duchess's hand. "I wonder what this is about." He took his knife and slid it under the seal.

My darling,

There is no good way to tell you what I am about to write. The former Duke of Bolton attempted to murder Aglaia and is now dead. Fortunately, Hawksworth and his friend, Mr. Paulet, now the Duke of Bolton, were present and saved her. Hawksworth, not the current duke, shot him, and he died from the fall he took.

Apparently, the former duke was also privately accused of murdering at least one of his wives. Therefore, I am pleased with the result. I know you could not possibly have guessed what the devil was up to or you would not have betrothed our daughter to such a monster.

You may wish to know that the current duke has asked Aglaia to marry him, and, knowing you desired a match with Bolton, she agreed to wed the current duke. If you should choose to attend the ceremony, it will take place one week after her birthday.

I expect you will receive a letter from the Duke of Bolton in a day or so.

Your devoted wife,

C.

Somerset scowled as he open Bolton's letter.

My dear Somerset,

I assume you have received your wife's note. Since that was sent, I have discovered that the property the former Duke of Bolton was to have given to you is part of the dukedom's entail, and thus, cannot be legally sold or conveyed to you.

You will be pleased to know that I have decided to honor the agreement that your daughter, Lady Aglaia, marry the Duke of Bolton. With the exception of the property, and an increase in the funds I have made available for my future wife and children, the settlement will remain the same.

Bolton

"Damn and blast the blackguard to Perdition!" Somerset pounded his desk and watched with some satisfaction as his secretary jumped.

That Aglaia marry a man of whom he had not approved was in no way acceptable. Somerset had a right, a duty, to increase his holdings and the marriages of his children were the only way to achieve that.

The Fates, though, seemed to be against him. How the

devil could he end the betrothal and not cause a scandal? His usual methods wouldn't work.

"There is a new Duke of Bolton, and he has discovered that the last one was ready to cheat me. The property I wanted is entailed."

"A new duke, your grace?" Belling's voice was slightly faint.

"Indeed. It appears that I was mistaken in the last one's character." Somerset ground his teeth. No one must know how furious he was about this turn of events. "Hawksworth has taken care of the matter for me. Lady Aglaia shall marry the new duke. I wish to depart within the next two days for Somerset. I shall journey to Bath the day before the wedding."

Belling's lips moved as if he wanted to speak.

"Open your budget, man."

"Do you not mind that she shall marry a man you haven't met?"

Of all the idiotic questions. Of course, he minded. *Damn Hawksworth and that harridan he'd married.* Somerset had no doubt his traitorous eldest son was in the thick of this new betrothal.

Hawksworth delighted in defying Somerset at every turn. If there was a way out of this mess, he'd find it. The only problem was that he had to ensure his daughter's reputation was unharmed. That made things much more difficult. "I know the current duke's reputation, and he's a friend of my son. Aside from that, one duke or another, what does it matter?"

CHAPTER THIRTEEN

"AND THIS IS THE MASTER'S bedchamber." Guy held out his hand, inviting Laia into the room.

Since the former Duke of Bolton's death, Guy, Laia and the others had eschewed public entertainments. That, however, had meant he and she had not been able to spend much time together. Fortuitously, his housekeeper had asked when the future duchess would inspect the house, giving Laia the perfect opportunity to finally be alone with her betrothed.

He opened the door from Laia's future rooms into a room where a massive bed took up most of the space.

"Your aunt slept in this?" She dragged her gaze from the bed to him.

"Ah, no. I found this disassembled in the attic. Her bed didn't fit me," he said a little sheepishly.

She allowed her attention to be distracted—as it was a great deal—by his tall, broad frame. "Is it comfortable?"

"I find it to be extremely comfortable." A wicked glint came into his eyes. Thanks to a conversation with Meg, Laia now knew what that particular look meant and a great deal of other useful things as well. Mostly, her sister-in-law had said to follow her instincts and not be embarrassed.

Trailing her hand along the walnut footboard and on to the mattress, she raised one brow in what she hoped was a sultry glance. "And if one wished to be certain?"

"God help me. I was going to wait until our wedding night," Guy groaned, and it was all she could do to stop from giggling.

Laia didn't know, or care, who moved first, but she was in his arms. Exactly where she wished to be. His firm mouth crushed hers. Whenever he had kissed her before, he had never gone beyond stroking her derrière. This time, with one hand he pressed her to him so that she felt the hard ridge of his member. His other hand cupped her breast. Frissons of pleasure speared through her from her breasts to her mons, and she wiggled against him.

"I have been thinking, dreaming, about this for weeks." His lips moved to her neck, and her nipples turned into hard buds waiting for his attention.

Her bodice sagged as he released the buttons on the back of her gown from their moorings. She let her gown and petticoats fall. Guy unlaced her short stays, and they joined the rest of her garments in a puddle on the floor.

"My God, you're beautiful." He'd stepped back, and his eyes traveled over her.

"You, on the other hand, have too many clothes on." She unraveled his cravat and pulled it off as he divested himself of his jacket and shirt.

For a few long moments, she could only stare at his chest. Dark, reddish curls covered his muscles and tapered down his flat stomach. When she spread her fingers over his torso, he groaned. Then she traced the path down to his pantaloons and unfastened the buttons of his placket. Just as she had been told it would, his member sprang ready into her hand.

"You are going to be the death of me," he growled.

She landed on the bed and was promptly stripped of her shoes and stockings. "Blast it all! Boots should not be this difficult to remove."

Laia took the time to admire his tight bottom. A second later, first one then the other boot hit the rug with soft thuds. Picking her up, he placed her head gently on the pillows, and began taking out her hair pins before running his fingers through her hair.

"This is like silk." Guy's lips moved over hers, then down her body, sipping and licking until she was on fire. "Your whole body feels like the softest, finest silk, and you taste of apricots." He moved her legs apart, and finding her center, licked.

Something inside her broke and warm waves of pleasure engulfed her. Then he was on top of her, his member at her entrance. "I am told this will hurt the first time."

"I've been told the same thing." Laia clutched as much of Guy as she could reach to her. "Do not stop."

He plunged into her. She inhaled at the sharp pain, and he stopped. "Give it a minute."

By forcing her body to relax, she could focus on how he filled her and the pain lessened. As if her hips knew what to do without her direction, they lifted, inviting him to move again.

Guy kissed her as he thrust slowly, and soon the pleasure she had felt before returned, and the tension grew until she convulsed around him. Guy thrust twice more and called her name.

Collapsing to her side, he pulled her close to him. "I wish we could stay here forever."

Laia snuggled even closer, and laid her head on his chest. "I know what you mean."

CHAPTER FOURTEEN

GUY COULDN'T BELIEVE LAIA WAS his. Her silvery blond curls fell down her back as she moved to gaze into his eyes. Plump breasts tickled the side of his chest, and his cock began to harden again. He'd have to get her out of this bed. It was too soon to make love to her again. He just had to keep reminding himself it would not be long before they could stay in bed all day if they wished.

His valet's discrete knock came on the door. "Your grace."

"Yes, Smithson." Beside him, Laia's eyes widened.

"I am sorry to inform you that her ladyship's mother is in the drawing room." He coughed. "She is being served tea, while we look for you."

"Thank you." Guy looked at Laia. "What's a quick lie?"

"We're in the attics." Her brows lowered as she frowned. "I've found something and will be down soon."

"That should do it." He kissed her forehead.

The second his valet left, she sprang out of bed. "Help me with my clothing, then I will help you."

In a shorter period than he'd thought possible, she was dressed and putting the hair pins in a knot high on her head while he was still trying to tie his cravat in a respectable manner.

Laia's light laughter rang out as she helped him into his jacket. "I wonder what she wants."

"To make sure we are not doing what we were doing, is my guess."

"You are most likely correct." She cupped his cheek and kissed him, then groaned. "No, she is here because we are to have tea with friends." Twirling, she looked at herself in the mirror. "I should do."

Standing behind her, he couldn't resist bringing his hands up under her breasts, then slipping his fingers down over the soft swell of her hips. "I have to agree."

"I can see that once we have wed, I will never get out of the house."

Guy nuzzled her neck, pressing his lips along her jaw. "Not for at least a month. I do intend to take you on a honeymoon."

Leaning back against him, she sighed. "That sounds like a lovely idea."

FOUR DAYS LATER, LAIA WAS in a bedchamber at Roselands dressing for her wedding, which would be held in the small chapel attached to the house.

"Are you nervous?" Thalia, Laia's second youngest sister, asked.

"No, I am marrying the gentleman I wish to wed." Something she had not thought would ever happen. Considering Father had arrived demanding she return home .She had been shocked that her father had not refused his consent, but then Mama had pointed out that it would have reflected poorly on Father and might have ruined Laia. Being betrothed to two Dukes of Bolton and failing to wed one of them would have caused a scandal. Laia had a feeling there was more to it than that, but this was not the time to question fate

"Well, I think his grace is very handsome," Mary, the youngest, commented.

"Yes, he is." Handsome in looks and actions. Laia glanced in the mirror and watched as Smithers, Laia's maid, put flowers in her hair.

"I wish Mama, Meg, and Lady Phillip would get here soon." Thalia turned a broach over and over in her hands.

Laia glanced at her right hand, where a modestly sized sapphire flanked by smaller diamonds circled her ring finger. It was beautiful and fit her exactly. Soon it would be on her left hand.

Lady Engle had the ruby ring. It had been her granddaughter's.

"Here we are." Mama swept into the room. "Thalia, you may begin."

She handed the broach to Laia. "This is borrowed. It belongs to the dukedom's jewelry and must be returned." Then her sister whispered in a grave tone. "I think you should be able to keep it, but then it couldn't be borrowed."

Trying not to let her lips twitch, she replied in the same tone, "Very true." She turned to her youngest sister. "Mary."

She handed Laia a handkerchief embroidered with whitework on the edges and pulled a face. "This is new. I meant to give it to you for your birthday."

"That's all right, sweetie." She kissed her sister's cheek. "I did not give you much time."

Lady Phillip Paulet, Guy's mother, stepped forward, bussed Laia on her cheek, and handed her a necklace of gold filigree set with sapphires, pearls, and diamonds. "This is old, and you will be allowed to keep it. Welcome to the family, my dear."

Smithers fastened the necklace around Laia's neck.

"And these are blue," Meg said as she rushed into the room. "I was afraid I'd be late." She handed Laia sapphire-tipped hair pins.

A few moments later, after her maid had replaced aquamarine-tipped pins with the new ones, they left the room and made their way to the hall, where her father waited.

Laia curtseyed to him. "Father, I am glad you could be here."

"You have done the family credit by accepting the current Duke of Bolton." Despite her father's words he looked as if he'd eaten a lemon. "I trust you will be an obedient wife."

Standing behind her father, Meg rolled her eyes.

"I will be just as his grace would like me to be."

From the corner of Laia's eye, she saw Euphrosyne grin, then cover her lips with a handkerchief. Lady Phillip pressed her lips together. Laia had not known her mother-in-law long, but she knew that her ladyship had not approved of Father's statement.

"We should be going," Mama said.

They made their way into the chapel, entering by the side door. The rector of the nearby church stood talking to Guy and Damon. Something must have alerted the man to women's presence, as he stepped back and opened his prayer book.

Guy's gaze captured hers as she strolled forward, and the rector began the ceremony. They each said their vows in firm voices and exchanged heated looks when he promised to worship her body. It was not until the ceremony was over that Laia realized she had not vowed to obey him.

Taking her arm, Guy escorted her to the register, and whispered, "I see that you realized something was missing."

"Your doing, I suppose." She picked up the pen.

"There was no point in having you make a promise you could not and should not keep." She signed the page and handed the pen to him.

"How very modern of you," she commented as he signed the register as well.

Guy placed the pen down and turned to her. "A

marriage should not mean bondage for the woman."

Laia's heart swelled with joy. "Have I told you lately that I love you?"

Guy drew her into his arms while Meg and Damon signed the book as well. "I will never tire of hearing it."

"I love you."

AUTHOR'S NOTES

I hoped you enjoyed the third book in The Trevors. Those of you who have read my series The Marriage Game will recognize Damon and Meg and the Duke and Duchess of Somerset. If you are reading my books for the first time and wish to know more about my stories and me, visit me on *www.ellaquinnauthor.com*.

Not much is known about the summer season in Bath. The list of entertainments is accurate, as well as the fact that the waltz was not danced at the assembly rooms. I could find no description of the illuminations, although it seemed to me that the planners were likely to copy other places that had illuminations.

It is true that relics differ in England and on the Continent. Churches in Germany and France really do have skeletons dressed in silk, satin, velvets, and jewels.

And finally, you'll notice, if you care about that type of thing, that I didn't capitalize "your grace." After discussions with some English authors and a bit more research, it appears that lower case is correct.

Married By Twelfth Night

Book Four of The Trevors

CHAPTER ONE

Late June 1818, Somerset Castle

"OH, MY LADY," LADY EUPHROSYNE Trevor's maid whispered excitedly. "Her grace's maid told me to pack. We're going to Bath!"

"Bath?" This had to be the strangest and most wonderful thing that had happened to Euphrosyne in her life. "Why?"

"Lady Laia is to be married," Turner said, "and her grace wants her to have some experience getting on."

Not only strange but sudden. "Do you happen to know whom she will wed?"

Laia appeared in the doorway, hands clasped at her waist, her smile broader than Euphrosyne had ever seen it. "The Duke of Bolton."

The recently widowed Duke of Bolton. Euphrosyne remembered reading about the duchess's untimely death. She also recalled the woman had been his fourth wife. "Isn't he quite old?"

Laia's smile wavered and a worried look entered her eyes. "I do not wish to discuss his age. After all, Father is much older than Mama."

Euphrosyne decided not to press the issue. There was no point in upsetting her sister, and they *were* being allowed to go to Bath because of the betrothal. "As long as you are happy, that is all that matters."

"We shall have so much fun! There are assemblies, and

parks, and all sorts of things to do there." Laia settled on the window seat next to Euphrosyne's favorite chair. "I have never been so excited!"

"Who else is going with us?" She prayed her father was not. The Duke of Somerset was never in a good mood, and she avoided him as much as possible.

"Mama, the younger children, and the twins."

"That will be fun." Of her brothers and sisters still at home, only their thirteen year-old twin brothers, Decimus and William, had seen anything of the world, and that was due only to their being at Eton.

The following day, her father left for a tour of his estates, and a mere four days later, under clear skies, Euphrosyne and her family began their short journey to the spa town. They went first to Roselands, a modest family estate only a half hour from Bath. Thalia, their third sister, who was seventeen and too young for the entertainments in Bath, would remain there until the wedding with Mary, the youngest sister at eleven, and the twins. The children were accompanied by their nurse, nursemaids, tutors, and governess, and soon the house seemed to be teaming with people.

By the time Euphrosyne, her mother, and her sister arrived at the town house in Laura Place, it was almost time to dress for dinner. After descending to the pavement, Euphrosyne gazed up at the house that was part of a long row of town houses. The narrow house had four floors, including attics, and cellars. At least one would not become lost trying to find the dining room.

"Let us find our chambers and prepare for dinner." Mama shook out her skirts and smiled. "Then I have a surprise for you."

The butler opened the door, and Euphrosyne followed her mother and sister into the hall and up the stairs. She found her bedroom in the back of the house. Turner had already unpacked the trunks and put out a gown appropriate for dinner.

Throwing her gloves, reticule, and bonnet on the bed, Euphrosyne turned her back to her maid for help in getting out of her travel garments. "Please be quick. My mother said she has a surprise."

"I'll be a quick as I can, my lady, but you must allow me to turn you out properly, or her grace will let me go without a reference." Turner handed Euphrosyne a wet cloth. "Wipe your face while I unfasten your gown."

Less than forty minutes later, voices floated up the stairs as Euphrosyne descended. One deep voice in particular made her hasten her step, and when she entered the drawing room, she found her eldest brother and his wife. "Meg, Hawksworth! This is wonderful. I never dreamt you would be our surprise."

"Now, that's what I call a proper welcome!" The Marquis of Hawksworth twirled Euphrosyne around before setting her feet back on the floor.

"We've missed you." She gave her sister-in-law a quick hug. "Thalia, Mary, and the twins are at Roselands. Will you visit them as well?"

"Of course we will." Meg kissed Euphrosyne's cheek. "We have missed all of you as well."

Her father had barred Hawksworth and Meg from Somerset Castle. That they were here must have been the work of Mama.

The small drawing room already seemed crowded with people when her mother's butler, Perkins, intoned, "Mr. Guy Paulet."

A gentleman who bore a striking resemblance to Laia's betrothed entered the room.

"Who is he?" Euphrosyne whispered to her sister-in-law.

"Oh, merely a friend of ours who just happens to be in

Bath." Meg strolled forward to greet the newcomer, and Euphrosyne followed suit.

She was surprised to discover that her mother already knew Mr. Paulet. Even more interesting was the look he gave her sister when they were introduced.

Just happens to be in Bath? My foot. She could almost smell a conspiracy in the air. Paulet was the family name of the Duke of Bolton. *Good God!* The man was the Duke of Bolton's heir. Apparently, Euphrosyne wasn't the only one not pleased with her sister's betrothal.

Mama held out her hand. "Euphrosyne, I would like to introduce Mr. Paulet. Guy, my second daughter, Lady Euphrosyne."

Euphrosyne curtseyed, and he bowed once again. "Delighted, my lady."

"Thank you." She glanced at her brother. "I am always happy to meet my brother's friends." Leaning toward Mr. Paulet a bit, she said, "We do not often get to do so."

Her sister-in-law pressed a glass of lemonade into her hand. "Come. Let us have a comfortable coze until dinner is served."

Mr. Paulet had drawn Laia aside, engaging her in conversation. Euphrosyne took a sip of lemonade. "What are you up to?"

"Why"—Meg's eyes widened—"would you think I am up to anything at all?"

"I know who Mr. Paulet is, and I have the feeling you are no more in favor of this betrothal than am I."

"Let us say I have some concerns." The tone she used was considerably drier than before.

"You can count on me to help." Unlike Laia, Euphrosyne believed their father had nothing in mind but his own benefit when he'd selected Bolton. "I would not let Laia know what you are about. She can be extremely dutiful and stubborn."

"That's what Hawksworth said." She cut a glance at Laia and Mr. Paulet. "We'll take things as slowly as possible. But what about you? Will you use this time to cast around for a husband?"

Frankly, Euphrosyne had been so thrilled to leave Somerset Castle for this small bit of freedom, she hadn't given her plans much thought. But why not look for a husband? "If I find someone I would like to wed. And of whom Father would approve. Unfortunately, I am not near enough to my majority to completely ignore his wishes."

A shrewd look appeared on her sister-in-law's face. "As my grandmother Featherton always says, where there is a will there is a way. Even though the path might not be easy."

Or it might be close to impossible. "Let's first see if there are any eligible gentlemen in Bath." She grinned. "Other than Mr. Paulet." Euphrosyne finished her lemonade. "The first thing I want to do is see the sights. The leasing agent gave us a guide book. I plan to read it before retiring."

"Please do. I have never been to Bath before, but I hear there are many sights."

Yet, later that evening, when she went to fetch the guide book from the morning room to take to her sister's room so that they could look at it together, it wasn't anywhere to be found. She went to the library, but it wasn't there either. She was pleased to discover several novels, however, to help her while away the time.

THE FOLLOWING MORNING, HAWKSWORTH AND Mr. Paulet joined Laia and Euphrosyne for breakfast.

"Your mother and Meg intend to visit the Pump

Room," her brother said, taking two more pieces of toast. Euphrosyne was glad she'd claimed her pieces. Hawksworth went through food like a horde of locusts. "Do you wish to go and drink the waters?"

Even at nineteen, she couldn't help but make a face. The waters had a reputation of tasting horrible. She'd also heard that the season in Bath was over, so she would probably find few ladies of her age with whom to speak.

"In that case," Hawksworth continued, "I propose we either order the horses to be brought round, or we can explore Sydney Gardens. It is your choice."

Euphrosyne's jaw dropped open, and she snapped it shut. Only on their birthdays were they ever given a choice of what to do. Even then, they were restricted to the grounds. The problem was that without benefit of the guide book, she did not know what there was to see.

"Sydney Gardens," Laia said. "I read that they have shady groves, grottoes, labyrinths, and waterfalls, gala nights, illuminations, and public breakfasts in summer. May we see them all?"

"So that is where the guide book went to." Euphrosyne narrowed her eyes at her sister. "I searched for it for over an hour last night."

"You should have asked," Laia said in her I'm-the-elder-sister tone, which usually set Euphrosyne's teeth on edge.

Well, her sister wasn't getting away with it this time. She raised a brow. "Indeed? I did not ask because it did not occur to me that you might have taken it and not offered to share."

At last her sister looked contrite. "I apologize. You're right. I should have told you I had it."

"We will see as much as possible of Sydney Gardens." Hawksworth laughed. "But we must trust that your mother and Meg discover the dates of the gala night, illuminations, breakfasts, and what else Bath has to offer us."

"I have had the opportunity to visit Sydney Gardens," Mr. Paulet said. "They are extremely interesting. I also took the time to discover the key to the labyrinth."

Euphrosyne would rather attempt to conquer the labyrinth without a key. Still, her sister would like his preparedness.

"When shall we leave?" Laia placed her serviette on the table.

"As soon as you and Euphrosyne are ready," Hawksworth replied.

She pushed back her chair. "Give me twenty minutes."

"I as well." Euphrosyne followed her sister out of the room. "Is the guide book interesting?"

"I am not sure I would say that, but it does list a great many places to see and things to do. Would you like to look through it when we return?"

"Yes, thank you." They were half-way to their rooms when an idea struck her. "Do you think Mama will allow us to read novels"—negating the necessity to hide the one she had found—"now that Father is not here to stop us?"

"We shall ask, but try not to be upset if she refuses."

"I won't." Euphrosyne would simply keep her book at the bottom of her wardrobe. If only she hadn't mentioned novels in the context of love matches to their father, he wouldn't have taken them away. Deciding to test her sister's interest, she said as casually as possible, "Mr. Paulet seems to be very nice."

"Yes." Laia's brows drew together slightly. "Yes, he does. I would imagine most of our brother's friends are nice."

"Perhaps we shall meet more of them." Now that there might be a possibility of meeting a gentleman, Euphrosyne wondered if Meg and Hawksworth had invited another of their friends to Bath, and Euphrosyne would meet him soon.

Thirty minutes later, almost to the second, the foursome

stepped onto the pavement in front of the Laura Place house.

"Come, little one." Hawksworth took her hand and placed it on his arm. "Paulet, please escort Laia."

"My lady." Mr. Paulet bowed. "Escorting you would be my pleasure."

Euphrosyne grinned to herself. He was charming and handsome. At this rate, her sister would be sure to find Mr. Paulet preferable to the duke. They started up the hill to Sydney Gardens.

They were within sight of the gardens when she stopped to look down at the view from whence they'd come. The city seemed to have been designed in a plan and dotted with gardens. "It's beautiful here." It was still early, and not many people were about. She turned her attention to the Sydney Gardens. Paths wandered between colorful flower beds. "What shall we do first?"

"I think we might begin with the labyrinth," Mr. Paulet offered. "As the morning becomes warmer, we can visit the grotto."

"There are also a castle folly and a scene with automatons," Hawksworth added.

"I'd like to see those first." Euphrosyne was glad her brother had mentioned them. If the labyrinth was extensive, it might take a long time to work it out, and they might miss the moving figures with their ingenious clockwork mechanisms.

Her sister nodded.

"Very well," Mr. Paulet agreed.

When they did get to the maze, try as she might, Euphrosyne could not find her way out and suffered the ignominy of being rescued by Mr. Paulet and Laia.

After that, they explored the grotto, and wandered along one of the shady paths until Hawksworth's stomach grumbled loudly.

"I'm for my luncheon," her brother proclaimed.

"When do you not wish to eat?" Mr. Paulet groaned and gave Hawksworth a disgusted look that made Euphrosyne want to laugh.

"Rarely," Hawksworth retorted in a lofty tone.

His stomach was not the only one complaining. Just the loudest. "I'm hungry as well," she said.

Mr. Paulet glanced at her sister and shook his head. "There is nothing for it. We must see these two fed. I know for a fact Hawksworth becomes a bear when he's peckish."

"To be honest, my sister is not much better." Laia sighed, and Euphrosyne was hard pressed not to stick her tongue out at them.

She tugged Hawksworth's arm. "Let them straggle behind if they wish. I'm for my luncheon."

As they were about to mount the steps to the house, they met her sister-in-law and mother coming from the direction of town. "Did you drink the waters?" Euphrosyne asked. "Were they very nasty?"

"Yes and no." Her mother laughed lightly. "The Pump Room has many interesting people, including some young ladies. You may wish to accompany us tomorrow."

"Both Mr. King, who is the Master of Ceremony for the Upper Rooms," Meg said, "and Mr. Guynette, who performs the same task at the Lower Rooms, informed us there are balls twice every week and an illumination is planned four days afterward."

Euphrosyne prayed that they would be allowed to attend the balls.

"Did you come across anyone you know?" Hawksworth took his wife's hand, raising it to his lips.

"Indeed we did." Meg stared lovingly into his eyes.

That was what Euphrosyne wanted when she married. To love her husband and have him love her.

"Lady Sarah and Mr. Jeremy Bellingham are here with

her brother Markville."

"That's a surprise," Hawksworth said. "I would have supposed Markville to be in Brighton."

"Oh, no. He doesn't like the Carlton House crowd any more than we do." Meg took Hawksworth's arm. "They are staying at The York while they look for a house to buy."

That put whoever Markville was at political odds with Euphrosyne's father, who supported the monarchy in everything. This Markville interested her just for that reason. "Who are Sarah and Jeremy and Markville?"

"Your father wanted your brother Quartus to marry Sarah. Jeremy is her husband, and the Marquis of Markville is her brother. Markville is buying a house for them," Meg said to Hawksworth as she strolled grinning behind Mama through the door. "You remember Quartus told us there was a misunderstanding of some kind between Sarah and her brother? It seems they have worked it out."

Meg handed her parasol and bonnet to Perkins. "We shall see them at the Pump Room tomorrow. It is quite delightful there. I also met Lady Engle, a friend of my grandmother's. You will like her a great deal, I dare say."

Mama invited Mr. Paulet to join them. As they sat down to a cold collation, the talk turned to other sites to be visited in the area. After a good deal of discussion, they decided on excursions to the ancient chapel at Farley Castle, the Roman ruins, and the badminton court. Euphrosyne was more than happy to put off sampling the waters, although she very much wished to meet Sarah, Jeremy, and Markville.

The rest of her family wanted to go on horseback, but Euphrosyne knew her mother would require a carriage. "Hawksworth can hire a barouche for you if you wish."

"Thank you for the thought." Her mother's clear blue eyes smiled. "However, I shall leave the sightseeing to you."

"But, Mama, we want you to join us," Euphrosyne

pressed, but Mama, in her own gentle way, was every bit as stubborn as the rest of them.

"I know you do, my love," she said in a firm tone. "However, I have met some old friends with whom I would dearly love to renew my acquaintance, and I must take time to look in on your brothers and sisters. Aside from that, I shall be with you in the evenings for the balls and concerts."

"We're going to be allowed to go to the ball?" Laia's eyes grew to the size of saucers. "A real ball?"

Yes, yes, yes! Euphrosyne's prayers were coming true! The way this was going she might even find a husband.

"I believe I shall host a dancing afternoon," Meg said.

Mr. Paulet turned to Laia. "Will you do me the honor of standing up with me for your first dance at Lady Hawksworth's party?"

Her head swung from her mother, who nodded her permission, to him. "I would love to."

As happy as Euphrosyne was for her sister, she couldn't but wish she had a gentleman with whom to dance.

"Euphrosyne, I know I am only a brother, but will you allow me to lead you out for your first set?"

"Thank you, Hawksworth. You are the best brother ever." Still, she hoped that by the time of the dance, she would have met at least one other gentleman.

CHAPTER TWO

CHARLES, MARQUIS OF MARKVILLE, FOUGHT to keep a scowl from forming as his sister Lady Sarah Bellingham read the invitation aloud.

"I, for one, would love to take this excursion to Farley Castle," she said. She turned to her husband, smiling brightly. "Do you not agree, Jeremy?"

"Yes, of course, my love." Although it was not yet mid-afternoon, he pressed a glass of claret into Markville's hand. Bellingham was a perceptive man.

"And"—she waved the papers she held in the air—"if I am reading this correctly, Meg requires our assistance."

Markville would rather not have anything to do with the Marchioness of Hawksworth's schemes. She and her husband were the most interfering pair Markville had ever met.

At Sarah's pronouncement, even her doting husband appeared nonplussed.

Markville had no doubt Hawksworth, the Duke of Somerset's heir, and his wife were engaged in arranging someone's life. Then again, as much as Markville hadn't liked their interference in his family, it had turned out for the best. Sarah was happier than he'd seen her in years.

The Hawksworths had decided to become involved in politics as well, and Markville had the feeling that before long the couple would be a force to be reckoned with. Not that he objected to their causes, which were the very ones he supported. He simply wished his sister had confided in him instead turning to Meg Hawksworth in order to effect Sarah's marriage to Jeremy.

"Very well." He smiled to himself at his sister's grin. "I suppose we might as well go out and see the sights." It would also give him an opportunity to exercise Samson, his three-year-old black stallion.

The following morning, they rode to Laura Place and were met by Hawksworth's party on arrival at the door. Markville was surprised to see Paulet and intrigued to see him escorting an ethereal-looking young woman with silvery blonde hair. She must be one of Somerset's daughters. Then he noticed another young lady with the same hair color, but there was nothing otherworldly about her. Even though their features were similar, energy emanated from the lady's every move. Her bright, light-blue eyes sparkled as one small foot determinedly touched the pavement as if she were setting out to conquer the world. Even her pale-blue nankeen habit seemed to shimmer.

"Good morning, Markville." Lady Hawksworth smiled at him. "Euphrosyne, allow me to make you known to the Marquis of Markville. Markville, my sister-in-law, Lady Euphrosyne Trevor."

As he bowed, he admired her graceful curtsey. "My pleasure." How old was she? Surely she was out. "Were you not in Town last Season? I am sure we would have met."

"No."

Her cheeks colored slightly, not with shyness, but with barely subdued anger, Markville suspected.

"I should have been out last year, but our father decided none of us needed a Season."

Well, that was plain speaking. He liked her better for it. "What a pity." Her eyes flashed for a moment. When she turned toward a white horse, he approached her. "Allow me."

"Thank you." Lady Euphrosyne reached up for the

saddle, clearly expecting him to cup his hands for her foot. Instead, he clasped her waist and lifted her onto the horse. Eyes wide, she stared at him. Now he had her attention. "That was"—she cleared her throat—"unexpected."

For reasons he could not understand, Markville wanted more.

He didn't know how strong her reaction was. Her breathing was steady, and the lace ruff hid any sign of her pulse. Only her eyes and words showed her surprise. Did she have a great deal of countenance, or was she cold? With a father like Somerset, Markville wouldn't have been surprised at the latter, but there was something in the spark of her eyes that made him think she was anything but made of ice. Not to mention the energy he'd observed earlier.

He'd learned this morning that her sister was betrothed to Bolton, of all the hideous choices. Who did her father have in mind for Lady Euphrosyne? Not Markville. He had no land with borders that marched with Somerset's holdings, and that was main qualification as far as the duke was concerned. Markville could barely take his eyes from the lady when, in fact, he would be better off staying away from Lady Euphrosyne.

She expertly guided her horse after her brother's. Quickly mounting Samson, Markville followed and soon drew up beside her. "I understand from my sister that this is your first time in Bath."

"Other than my brothers' weddings, it is my first time away from Somerset." A current of anger ran beneath her pleasant tone. "If it were not for my sister's betrothal, we would not be here at all."

Guilt struck him that he had even considered agreeing to Sarah's marriage to Lord Quartus, one of Lady Euphrosyne's many brothers. Not that there was anything wrong with Lord Quartus, but it would have left him in the duke's control and placed Sarah there as well. Even if Quartus could have broken from his father, he would have had no means of support.

They crossed Great Pulteney Street and headed toward Claverton Down. "What have you planned for your visit here?"

Her polite smile finally broke into one that touched her expressive blue eyes. "A great many things. According to the guide book, there will be illuminations and open-air breakfasts. My mother said there will be balls and dances at the assembly rooms." She heaved a sigh. "I have never been to a ball or a dance. And, of course we shall have more outings like this one." Her short, straight nose wrinkled. "I suppose at some point I must taste the waters."

He couldn't help but laugh. "Truth to tell, I have been avoiding them myself."

"But one would not wish to be thought provincial." Her nose wrinkled even more.

"Perish the thought." Markville wanted to be present when she tasted the water, if only to see her expression. Damn. He'd been a fool to agree to the excursion. She had immediately intrigued him, and it wouldn't do either of them a bit of good. "If my sister finds a house soon, I suppose she will wish to entertain."

"I'm glad she is a friend of my sister-in-law's." Lady Euphrosyne glanced behind her and he followed suit. Sarah was in close conversation with Lady Laia, who did not appear happy. "I have a feeling we shall be spending more time together."

"As do I." That was, after all, the only way Sarah would be able to assist Lady Hawksworth in whatever plan she'd hatched.

"Do you know much about Farley Castle?" Lady Euphrosyne asked, drawing his attention back to her.

"I do. My maternal grandmother lived here for several

years, and my sister and I used to visit. It was built in the fourteenth century by the Hungerford family, who had several ups and downs over the centuries. In the end, the final owner was beheaded by King Henry VIII, and the castle fell into ruin."

"Well, the owner's end is not surprising," she said. "King Henry seemed to go about beheading anyone who disagreed with him."

"You and my sister are in agreement on that point. It is fortunate our regent does not have the same power."

She gave him a searching look. "Are you friends with Hawksworth?"

More acquaintances than friends. "Why do you ask?"

"I thought you might share some of the same ideas." She lifted one shoulder in a shrug. "He once gave me a copy of Wollstonecraft's *A Vindication of the Rights of Women*. Our governess at the time considered it to be an excellent piece of philosophy." Lady Euphrosyne grimaced. "My father did not agree."

That didn't surprise Markville in the slightest. Yet Somerset didn't strike Markville as the type of parent who would interest himself in his daughter's studies. "How did he discover the book?"

Her softly rounded chin firmed. "He made a pronouncement that I did not consider to be just, and I argued with him." Once again, her magnificent blue eyes burned with the unfairness of it all. "He discharged my governess without a reference and burned the book. He also refused to allow Hawksworth to visit again."

"Nothing like a scorched-earth strategy to endear one to one's family and others."

Lady Euphrosyne nodded, her gaze steady. "He must attempt to annihilate anyone who does not do as he wishes. Fortunately, Mama wrote an excellent reference for Mrs. Williams and made sure she was paid the next year's wages."

He thought he knew the answer to his next question, but that didn't stop him from asking, "Have you argued with him since?"

"Yes." Her already erect spine straightened. "Although, I am careful that no one other than me will be punished." She urged her horse to a trot. "I'd like to enjoy the day. Shall we race to the willow?"

"As you wish."

Lady Euphrosyne whispered in her horse's ear and they were off like a shot.

"Come, Samson. We must at least make a showing."

Markville need not have worried. His stallion seemed determined to catch up with her mare. Yet only that. The horse had no inclination to pass the ladies. Actually, neither did Markville. Lady Euphrosyne was an interesting woman. And despite recognizing it was a bad idea, he wanted to know her better.

Euphrosyne couldn't believe Lord Markville's huge horse hadn't passed her and Estelle. Once man and beast had caught up, they seemed content to ride alongside. If only she knew whether they were merely displaying good manners or if it could be a sign of something else. Perhaps he was a gentleman who, like her brothers, preferred a partnership with a wife. Laia would scoff, but was it not true that most single ladies and gentlemen regarded one another as potential mates? After all, despite Wollstonecraft's arguments to the contrary, what kind of life did a lady have if she remained single? Not one that Euphrosyne wanted. It would keep her under her father's boot for the rest of her life. Why not see if she and Lord Markville would suit? As a peer he required an heir. Therefore he needed a wife. If she was right about his philosophies, he might be for her.

There was only one way to find out. She would ask him when the race was over.

When they reached the willow, she gave him a curious look. "Why did you not pass me? You have the stronger horse."

He flashed a grin that displayed straight white teeth. The man was definitely handsome. Was his mind as pleasing as his person? Parliament had recently been dissolved. That was a good topic for exploring whether he objected to a woman discussing the next government, and what his own views were on the matter. It was all to the good if his beliefs matched with hers.

"I can assure you that it was not my decision," he said. "I like to win as much as the next man. I believe Samson wishes to be on better terms with your mare."

"I cannot blame him. She is a beauty." Euphrosyne stroked her horse's neck. "Do you think the Whigs have a hope of gaining control of Parliament now that it has been dissolved?"

"As much as I hope we will, I'd be surprised if we did more than gain a few seats."

His dark brows drew together. So, this was a point of concern for him.

"At the moment, there is too much fear among the landed gentry that we will end up like France," he added.

The Whigs supported the contentious position that the common man should be allowed to vote. Needless to say, her father staunchly believed that God gave the peerage and the King the right to rule. A position with which she did not agree. In fact, Euphrosyne would like women to be able to vote. Yet, only the most liberal thinkers, such as Hawksworth, agreed with her. "What do you think of the idea that women should be allowed to vote?"

Euphrosyne held her breath as his gray eyes focused on her in a way they had not before. "I think it will, unfortunately, be a very long time before they are emancipated. However, that is not the only thing that must change for women."

"I completely agree." She decided to charge on. "Property laws for married women must change as well. The ladies will never be able to achieve equality in their marriages if they do not."

"Very true. I take it you wish a marriage of equals."

"I wish for partnership in a marriage."

The corners of his well-shaped lips tipped up. "As do I."

For some reason, her neck and cheeks began to heat. Who knew that merely obtaining information could make one blush? Mayhap it was time to change the subject. "Do you think the Duke of Clarence's marriage will produce the heir we need?"

Markville's lips twitched as if he would burst out laughing. "One can only pray. The royal dukes seem much better able to produce off-spring outside of marriage than within."

"Am I being too direct? I have never actually made conversation with a gentleman I wasn't related to before." Not that it mattered. She did not know how to be anything other than what she was.

"No." Gazing at her, he slowly shook his head. "At least you are not too frank for me. I have simply never before met a young lady like you. You are extremely well informed."

This matter of making conversation was much more difficult than Euphrosyne had thought it would be. "I do not know how to take that."

This time the corners of his nicely formed lips tipped up. "Take it as a compliment. You are an intriguing woman."

Her cheeks warmed even more, and Euphrosyne wondered how red she'd become. "Thank you." As she did not know what else to say next, she continued with the conversation they'd been having. "Prinny is actually the only example in heir producing we have thus far. But with two of the royal dukes now married"—the Duke of Kent had wed on the same day as his brother—"perhaps one of them will soon have an heir."

Lord Markville cracked a laugh. "I sincerely hope you are correct." He pointed ahead of them. "In the distance you can see Farley castle."

"The guide book said it was mostly ruins and had a ghastly story about the Lady Tower. Do you know if it is true?"

"It is. Poor Lady Elizabeth Hungerford was almost starved to death by her husband, the first Baron Hungerford, before he was executed."

"I read that he also attempted to poison her." Euphrosyne shivered at the delightfully morbid story. "I must see the castle."

"You should also know," he said in a dry tone, "that the lady went on to marry and lived, it is believed, a happy life."

"Oh, pooh." Euphrosyne was not going to be put off by a happy ending. "That does not negate the evil that was done to her there."

Unfortunately, the guide book had been correct about the condition of the castle. When they arrived, there was not much of the tower to see. Half of the wall was gone and all the floors. "I must say, I am disappointed."

"Come, I'll show you the crypt. It is much more impressive."

The burial room beneath the chapel was very interesting. The room was musty and damp, lending an atmosphere of being in a dungeon. Some of the figures on the tombs had death masks, and one could easily imagine them in life. She couldn't believe he had actually brought her here. Her father wouldn't have allowed her to see it. "You're right.

This is much better. We have a large tomb at Somerset where all my ancestors are buried, but my father maintains that it is not suitable for ladies."

"In that event, I sincerely hope this satisfies your taste for the gruesome." Humor tinged his voice, and she suspected he was making a game of her.

She shifted her gaze to him. The look in his eyes now wasn't at all humorous. Instead, he seemed to be searching her for something. "Yes, it does. Thank you for escorting me."

"It was my pleasure. I forgot how fascinating I found the crypt." He heaved a sigh. "I was allowed to view my family's remains, and they are not nearly as interesting."

"No death masks?" She took his arm as they climbed the shallow stone stairs back to the main floor of the chapel.

"Unfortunately, not." Tilting his head to one side, he lowered his brows. "My house had several notable personages. I have always wondered why we don't have any masks."

"It does seem unfair." She enjoyed seeing him like his. Less the marquis and more the man.

"I have to agree." He smiled down at her. "I should see if I can remedy the problem."

He sounded so sincere she couldn't help but laugh and was pleased that he laughed with her. She would definitely like to know him better.

CHAPTER THREE

MARKVILLE'S CHEST TIGHTENED WHEN HE heard Lady Euphrosyne laugh. It was as if he'd been waiting all day to hear her express some joy. She was an interesting mix of naïveté, maturity, and an innocence he rarely, if ever, saw in a lady of her age. She did not attempt to flirt with him or engage him in strained conversations about himself or show an exaggerated interest in him like most of the young ladies he'd met during the last Season. Eventually, she would have to learn how to go on in the *ton*. Yet, even on such a short acquaintance, he knew she'd easily navigate the dangers of Polite Society without losing herself when the time came. He could imagine her holding French style salons, and political dinners. Of course, she would first need to be married. He set a slow pace up the stairs, wanting to learn more about her before sharing her with the rest of their group. Even so, the short flight of stairs was not long enough to meet his needs.

His sister awaited them in the chapel.

"Have the masks changed much?" Sarah screwed up her face in disgust.

"Not at all." What *had* changed was his appreciation of them. Markville had enjoyed sharing the death masks with a lady who was as drawn to them as he was.

Lady Euphrosyne laughed lightly. "They were quite interesting. What is there to see here?"

"The medieval painting is of interest." He led her to a work beside a stained glass window. "What do you think?"

"It's beautiful." She glanced up at him, her eyes glowing with happiness. It was hard to believe such a simple thing could mean so much to her. "Thank you."

"You're welcome. I am happy to show you about." Ignoring what he knew of her father, he started making plans in his mind to guide her through more of Bath and the surrounding area. What harm could there be in spending a little more time with her?

"Is everyone ready to ride to the inn for luncheon?" Hawksworth's tone suggested it was not a question at all, but a command.

"Yes, of course." Lady Euphrosyne tucked her small hand in the crook of Markville's arm. "We are coming."

After a substantial luncheon—during which Markville learned that Lady Euphrosyne had a healthy appetite—the group started back to Bath. For a while, the ladies rode together, making plans to visit the shops. Hawksworth and Paulet were off to the side engaged in a discussion when Jeremy came up next to Markville.

"I'm glad to see you're enjoying yourself more than you thought you would." His brother-in-law glanced at Sarah.

"Yes, I am." He *had* been rather curmudgeonly, and he'd been unable to make out why. The mood had started during the Season, and, despite everything going well, he'd been unable to shake it off. Now, after seeing his sister and brother-in-law together along with Hawksworth and his wife, Markville rather thought he was missing something, or someone, in his life. "Is it my imagination, or is there some matchmaking going on?"

"Between whom?" Jeremy's tone was too innocent and uninformative for nothing to be occurring.

Markville arched one brow. "I was referring to Paulet and Lady Laia."

His brother-in-law didn't even flinch. "Indeed. It's early days, but I believe there is hope in that direction."

Jeremy's tone hadn't changed, but Markville got the feeling the man was leaving something out.

"And is Sarah, perhaps, thinking of another match?" Markville wouldn't put it past his sister to encourage him and Lady Euphrosyne. Although, why he cared he didn't know. He liked Lady Euphrosyne, but her father was a different matter, and she was not close enough to her majority to make her own decisions. He also did not wish to be pushed into something for which he was not ready. Not that anyone could make him dance to their tune. And it was past time he looked at starting his nursery. Damn. Even to himself he sounded contrary. Was he so set in his ways that he was afraid of changing them? Or was this just another example of him being difficult?

His brother-in-law studied him for a while. "I shall not deny that my wife wants you to find the happiness we have found. Yet, as she had not met Lady Euphrosyne before today, she could hardly have decided to match-make."

That put him in his place. "You make a good point. I must apologize."

"I'm not saying she won't do it"—Jeremy cracked a laugh—"just that she didn't start out the day with that intent."

That made Markville grin. "It's not as if I've had a great deal of luck on my own."

"As Sarah would say, you have simply not met the right lady." Jeremy glanced at the Lady Euphrosyne. "In the event you require any assistance, we will be happy to oblige." He inclined his head. "I believe I shall retrieve my wife."

When Markville reached the ladies, positions shuffled and he was once more riding next to Lady Euphrosyne.

Why shouldn't he see if they got on together? All his life he'd been cautious, always concerned that every part of his and his family's life was in order. And where had it got him? He was close to thirty years of age and had no wife or children in his nursery. Except for the lady now riding beside him, he hadn't even been more than ordinarily interested in a female. Oh, he would have married the Duchess of Wharton if Lord Quartus hadn't beat Markville to it, but it would have been out of duty, the need to have a wife, not out of love. And why *shouldn't* he have a love match if he wanted one?

If he fell in love.

Perhaps all this time he had been looking for the wrong things.

Samson sidled closer to Lady Euphrosyne's mare. "Have you planned out your time in Bath?"

"Only part of it. We are attending the ball next week." The corners of her lush pink lips curled up. "Your sister has been telling us about the stores in Bath. It is a sad fact of my life that I have never been shopping without my mother, and we do not even live near a large market town. It is only a small one some half-mile or so from the gates."

Markville fought to keep his jaw from dropping. From a relatively young age, his sister had had the run of the fairly good-sized market town near his main estate. The hell with Lady Euphrosyne's father. Markville was going to do everything he could to see that she experienced everything she wished to while she was here. "I'm told that while the stores are not as extensive as in Town, they are quite good."

Her open countenance displayed all her joy. "That's what Sarah said. I am looking forward to visiting them." Lady Euphrosyne's smile faded. "Whenever my mother decides we may go."

He hoped that would be soon. Although, try as he might, he could not summon enough interest in shopping to suggest her accompany her. Still, Bath had other sights. "As you are attending the ball, I shall beg a dance from you if I may."

Her eyes lit up, and she smiled again. "I would greatly enjoy standing up with you. Thank you."

There was a breakfast a few days after the ball at Sidney Gardens. If he could convince his sister to act as his hostess he could get up a party and invite Lady Euphrosyne and her family to accompany them. He'd have to find out if Bath had something akin to the Grand Strut in Hyde Park. If there was, he could ask her to accompany him. For the first time, it forcibly struck him why the London Seasons existed. It was extremely difficult for a bachelor to plan entertainments when he could not host them for mixed company without a female being in charge of it. He had never given it much thought before, but one did not attend Lord So-and-so's ball. One attended Lady So-and-so's ball, or musical evening, or Venetian breakfast, or any other event. And he would have to address the issue of gaining permission for Lady Euphrosyne to accompany him to anything. Perhaps he should offer to go shopping.

Over tea, later that afternoon at the hotel, he held his cup out to be refilled and turned to his sister. "Have you thought about inviting Ladies Laia and Euphrosyne to go shopping with you one day?"

"Shopping?" Sarah gave him an arch look.

"Yes, indeed." He took a sip of tea. "You have extensive knowledge of the stores. It would be helpful to them if you showed them your favorite ones."

Still regarding him, she set her cup down. "Yes, I think that can be arranged. We have a house to see early tomorrow. There is no reason why I cannot invite them to go shopping later in the morning. They are both very nice ladies."

"Yes, indeed." Something tickled his throat and he cleared it. "Er, I could accompany you."

Her lips began to twitch, and he hoped she didn't laugh at him. "My dear brother. As much as I love you, you would be decidedly de trop when it came to selecting some of the items, such as stockings, that will be needed."

An image of Lady Euphrosyne in nothing but stockings and garters invaded his mind, making him very glad he was sitting down. "I hadn't thought. You are correct. Thank you. Send your bills to me."

"Now there is an offer I shall not refuse!" Sarah brought her cup up, hiding her mouth, but her eyes were bright with mirth.

"I shall see you at dinner." He left the parlor before his sister lost her countenance. Still, it felt good to do something for Lady Euphrosyne. Even if it was as simple a thing as shopping. Although, as much time as ladies spent in the occupation, perhaps it wasn't such a meaningless activity at all. And he was glad his sister had agreed to help him. Now all he had to do was get rid of this cock-stand.

THE NEXT MORNING, EUPHROSYNE WENT over everything Lord Markville had said to her and what she had said to him. She had the feeling he was used to much more sophisticated ladies, but he'd been kind and fun to be with. She wondered when she'd see him again. If she saw him at all. Despite talk about shopping and other excursions, no actual *plans* had been made. And she and her sister would have to ask Mama before they could do anything. Euphrosyne did not even know what a gentleman who was interested in a lady would ask her to do.

Once again, Meg and Hawksworth joined them for breakfast. They departed before Euphrosyne could draw Meg into a conversation.

Euphrosyne and her sister were in the morning room when a footman presented her sister a letter.

"Laia, who is it from?" Euphrosyne put down the book she'd been pretending to read. "I wonder why Joseph did not wait for Mama to look at it."

"Mama said I could receive local correspondence from ladies." Euphrosyne suppressed the urge to lean over her sister's shoulder as Laia opened the note, spreading the fine pressed paper on the table.

"Listen to this, Euphrosyne. We have been invited to go shopping with Lady Sarah." Laia looked up from the letter. "How very nice of her."

Nice? It was above all things wonderful! But would their mother let them go? If they accepted the invitation before asking, surely Mama would not stop them. "You respond to her, and I shall fetch our bonnets and gloves."

"Yes. I'll do just that." Laia pulled out a piece of paper.

Euphrosyne hurried out of the parlor. No time had been mentioned, but it was better to have their bonnets, gloves, and reticules at hand when Sarah arrived.

It took longer than Euphrosyne had thought it would to decide which of her two hats to wear. Then she sent her maid to fetch a bonnet and gloves for her sister, and picked up her own.

Oh, and she must ask her mother if they could go. She hurried to Mama's room, knocked, and entered Mama's parlor. She was seated at her desk.

"Good morning." Euphrosyne waited until her mother put a piece of paper down.

"Good morning." The look her mother gave her was encouraging. "Do you need something?"

"Yes. Lady Sarah sent an invitation asking if Laia and I would like to go shopping with her this morning. May we?"

"Of course." Mama smiled. "I see no reason why you should not." Opening a drawer, she drew out a wooden box, unlocked it, and handed Euphrosyne several coins, and a few bank notes. "For larger purchases, you may have the bills sent to me."

She had never had so much money before! Naturally, she would give half to her sister, but still, to have such freedom! Going back to her bedchamber, she counted out the money and divided it up between her reticule and her sister's.

Before returning to the parlor, she glanced out the windows in the front of the house, just as a carriage made its way toward the town house. Could it be Sarah so soon? Euphrosyne must hurry in the event it was.

Dashing back into the morning room, Euphrosyne handed Laia her things. "I think I saw her carriage coming."

"It is too soon for that, but this is so exciting." She tied her hat's ribbons off to the side. "We have never been shopping without Mama."

"It is thrilling, and it really should be common." Euphrosyne pulled on her gloves. "We have been kept far too close."

"I agree." Her sister nodded. "But now that we are away from Father and have more freedom, we must be careful not to abuse it. Even Mama must be careful."

"When I marry"—Euphrosyne donned her other glove—"it will be to a gentleman who will not try to rule me." What would Lord Markville be like as a husband? He had tried to make his sister do as he wished, but, from what she'd been told, he'd wanted to ensure she would not lose her inheritance. It wasn't his fault Sarah thought he was trying to keep her from Jeremy. That had all been a misunderstanding. And now he was buying them a house.

Her sister's lips pinched together as if she would make a comment.

Just in time to forestall a lecture about the duke choosing her husband, Perkins knocked on the open door. "My ladies, Lady Sarah is here."

"We will be out straightaway, Perkins." Euphrosyne drew her arm through her sister's and began walking to the door. "Let us agree to have a good time while we can."

"Yes, let us do just that." Laia lifted her reticule. "This is heavier."

"Mama gave us money for shopping."

They reached the hall, and Sarah turned from gazing at the corner niche holding a plaster bust of someone. "This house is very nice. Jeremy and I are discussing buying property in Bath." She bussed their cheeks. "Shall we go?"

"You see," Euphrosyne whispered to her sister. "There are many gentlemen who treat their wives as partners."

"I *do* know that," Laia responded waspishly.

Sarah sent the carriage back to the hotel and the footman Sarah had brought waited for them on the pavement, and they started off toward the main part of the town. "We will go to Milsom Street first. There is an excellent shop for stockings."

"We will need new stockings for the ball next week," Laia told Sarah. "And gloves. We each received the first of our new evening gowns and ball gowns and are now respectable to go out in the evening. I could not believe how out-of-date our old evening gowns were. And we have found we need other things as well."

"It always seems to go that way," Sarah said. "One forgets the small, but very important items. I wonder what the ball will be like."

"No matter what happens, I intend to enjoy myself," Euphrosyne said. And speaking of the ball, she wondered how many dances she would have. "Lord Markville asked me to stand up with him at the ball."

Her sister gave her a disapproving look. Well, Laia might believe she should obey Father, but Euphrosyne did not. Not if he was going to pick husbands who were more than twice her age and had already gone through four wives.

They spent the next three hours visiting every shop they found, even the butcher's. Madam Lamont had the loveliest bonnets. Sarah, Euphrosyne, and Laia each tried on several and came away with new hats. Euphrosyne bought four pairs of gloves. Then she discovered some beautiful clocked stockings and purchased several pairs of those. At one store, a red fan caught her eye, and she decided she could not leave the store without it.

"I do not think I have ever had such fun." Euphrosyne smiled, even if she was rapidly spending all of her money.

"Nor I," Laia agreed.

"I must buy some handkerchiefs," Sarah said as they left one store and entered another.

"Handkerchiefs and ribbons," Euphrosyne said. The selection far exceeded what she could find at home.

The poor footman had run out of room in his arms to carry more packages. But Sarah had discovered that many establishments would deliver, thus freeing Euphrosyne from exercising any restraint at all. After all, Mama had said to send the bills to her, and Euphrosyne's purchases would have to last for a long time.

Down the street, they found a bakery that smelled so good they had to stop. Sarah led the way in.

"Have you tasted Bath Buns?" she asked.

Euphrosyne exchanged a look with her sister, and they shook their heads.

"In that case, you must try them."

She was disappointed to find they had caraway, and turned up her nose at first, but decided to try the bun and was glad she did. "They are excellent. I even like the caraway."

"You like them only because they are coated with sugar," her sister said.

"I shall not deny that I have a sweet tooth." She finished the confection, then wiped her hands on her handkerchief.

Upon arriving home, she sent all her purchases except her fans to her bedchamber. Once she and her sister were seated in the morning room, she unwrapped the fans, opened them, and set them on a low table.

"My gown is pink. Which one of these fans do you think would go better with it?" One was silver with a scene painted in muted gray, cream, and green. Another had ivory spokes and a pastoral painting in green and blue. The last one, her favorite, was red. That was the one she wanted to carry.

Laia made a point of looking over the fans. Her eyes widened when she saw the red one. "I think the silver fan would look the best."

"Yes, I think that as well." Or rather, that was the one she knew she should carry instead of the bold red. Still, she could not stop her fingers from going to the red fan. Someday she would have a gown to wear with it.

"Will you wear your clocked stockings? They are quite elegant."

"I shall." She'd never had such beautiful stockings before.

Perkins brought in a tray of lemon biscuits, tea, and a letter for Laia. "Her grace said to give you this."

Euphrosyne waited for her sister to open the missive.

Her sister glanced at her. "It appears you are not the only one who has been asked to dance at the ball."

"Mr. Paulet." She was thrilled for her sister. "I knew he would request a set." She pulled out the chair to the writing table and motioned for Laia to sit down. "It is a shame Meg changed her mind about the dancing party. You must answer him quickly."

"It was very kind of him, but I am sure it is only because Hawksworth is his friend."

"What a bag of moonshine." Euphrosyne pulled her to the desk. "If that was it, he would have waited to see if you had sufficient dance partners."

"Perhaps." Laia sat down and pulled out a piece of paper while Euphrosyne mended a pen and handed it to her. "Now tell him you accept."

Euphrosyne could hardly wait for the ball and her dance with Markville. But the way Laia had responded, Euphrosyne might have to spend more time encouraging her sister's interest in Mr. Paulet than focusing on her own gentleman.

CHAPTER FOUR

MARKVILLE JOINED HIS BROTHER-IN-LAW IN the parlor as Sarah was leaving. She kissed Jeremy lightly on the lips, and Markville's thoughts went immediately to Lady Euphrosyne. Would she engage in such wifely behavior?

"Please go back to the last two houses and look at them again," she told her husband. "I cannot decide between them."

"I'll make a list of their best and worst features. Then we may continue our discussion this evening."

"Yes." She placed her palm on her husband's cheek.

Why was Markville all of a sudden noticing every loving gesture she made?

"That will be just the thing I need."

Jeremy's gaze remained on her as she left the room. "I suppose my day is now spoken for. Would you like to join me?"

"Thank you for asking, but I'm going to finish my correspondence and take a stroll around town." Where Markville just might come across Lady Euphrosyne.

"Very well. Wish me luck." His brother-in-law picked up his hat, gloves, and cane. "Hopefully, she will make a decision soon."

"Good luck." His sister's usual method of making a decision between two things was to purchase them both.

About an hour later, Paulet hailed Markville. "Good morning."

"Good morning to you." Paulet fell into step. "Do you have a destination or are you at loose ends?"

"I'm merely enjoying the day. You?"

"Likewise. My brother-in-law is looking at houses, and my sister is with Ladies Laia and Euphrosyne shopping. I have it on good authority the ladies have never been shopping without their mother and then only in a small market town."

Paulet looked appalled. "That should prove interesting."

"Oh, I dare say they shall purchase a deal of totally unnecessary and inappropriate items that catch their eyes." Markham laughed remembering the things his sister had bought on her first solo excursion to the shops. "Much in the way of magpies. It will do them no harm and will help whoever ends up receiving what they later realize they cannot use or do not like after all."

"I suppose they will." Paulet was silent as they strolled on. "I wonder what there is to buy in Bath. It is not as if it's London."

"No, but that won't stop them." Markham chuckled, but then a related thought not only sobered but angered him. "You must also remember they have never been to Town."

"I can't believe that was their mother's doing," Paulet said. "I wish I knew what Somerset was thinking."

Markville remembered the negotiations in which he'd engaged on Sarah's behalf, and stories he'd heard since then. "He is not an easy man."

Paulet cut Markville a curious look. "Have you met him?"

"No, but I have exchanged correspondence with him." Terse letters that should have warned Markville not to betroth his sister to the man's son, which thankfully came to naught in any event. "That was enough for me. What is the duchess like?"

"Gracious, caring, warm. In short, everything the duke is not." They turned down Cheep Street. "This is the way to the Pump House."

"I haven't been yet and thought I might take a look," Markville said. "I hear the waters are horrible, but the company is pleasant."

"I heard it's the place to be seen, and I'm not sure I want everyone and his dog to know I'm in Bath."

Markville glanced at Paulet. What was he hiding?

"I have wanted to visit the place, though," Paulet added.

"Walk around a bit, then leave." *I've become too suspicious*, Markville told himself. It was probably nothing. "Aside from that, most of the *ton* is either in the country or in Brighton."

"You're right. I'll give it a try."

Turning onto Salt Street, they made their way to the entrance of the Pump Room. Markville was glad to see a crowd. It showed not everyone followed Prinny to Brighton. For the most part, the waters were not as fashionable as they used to be, but the place was still full of people of all ages, as it always had been. People still promenaded around the edges of the room, while servants ran to and fro fetching glasses of water for those who wished to drink it.

Lady Hawksworth was speaking with old Lady Eagle. She'd been a friend of his mother's. After she was finished with her conversation, he'd greet her. In the meantime, he took his time surveying the room and ascertained that neither his sister nor Lady Euphrosyne was present. They were most likely still shopping.

When he did next see his sister, he should attempt to discover what plans he could convince her to make that would include Lady Euphrosyne. Lady Engle was now in conversation with another lady. He would speak to her some other time. "I've seen enough. Will you stay and taste the waters?"

"No, I'm ready to go as well." Paulet strolled out with Markville.

"I have been thinking that my sister might like to put together some events that include Hawksworth's family between now and the evening of the ball."

"That's a very good idea. And perhaps I shall arrange a picnic at Lansdowne." Paulet frowned. "As long as Hawksworth doesn't mind me asking his wife to be my hostess."

"Under the circumstances, he'll no doubt agree." Markville was glad his sister had offered to help him. Otherwise, he might have trouble spending time with Lady Euphrosyne. As they reached the point where their paths separated, Markville said, "I shall see you soon."

Jeremy arrived at the hotel at the same time Markville did. "How did it go?"

"I think the house on Laura Place must suit her better. It is closer to town than is Upper Camden Place. The appointments are elegant, and it has a large garden." His brother-in-law pulled a face. "How did that sound?"

"I'd leave out the part about it must suit her." Markville chuckled. "Sarah is liable to take it as a command."

"You're right. I shall focus on the elegance of the rooms and the easy walk to the center of town as well as the view."

"What view?" Entering the room, Sarah removed her bonnet and placed it on a chair.

"From Laura Place." Jeremy kissed her cheek. "Would you like wine or tea?"

"Wine sounds delightful. Have you decided on the house in Laura Place?"

"It is for you to make the final decision, but I must say, I think the house is more elegant."

Markville buried his nose in a newssheet and pretended

not to listen to the couple discuss the property.

"We could move in as soon as the staff was hired," Jeremy added. "The house in Upper Camden Place would need some renovations before we could live there."

"I think you are correct. Laura Place is a better choice for us," she said. "I particularly like that it is on the corner."

Laura Place would suit Markville well. He'd be able to see Lady Euphrosyne much more often. He set down the paper and rose. "If that is your decision, I shall arrange for the purchase immediately. I must admit, I am tired of living in a hotel."

"Perfect. I shall have my maid visit the employment agency," his sister said.

When he returned from the estate agent's office, he was pleased to find himself alone. He needed the opportunity to think. If he wanted to know Lady Euphrosyne better, he had to find ways to spend more time with her. Perhaps a ride tomorrow morning would be in order, although she would naturally require a groom.

Refusing to second-guess himself, he pulled out a piece of paper and began writing.

Dear Lady Euphrosyne,

Would you do me the honor of going horseback riding with me tomorrow morning at eight o'clock?

My servant will await your reply.

Yr. Servant,

Markville

The missive was a bit formal, but they didn't know each other well. The suggested hour was early, but she mentioned that she liked morning rides. He sanded the letter and sealed it.

Hearing his valet in the dressing room, he called, "Smithson, I have a letter to be delivered."

"I shall see it done straightaway, my lord." Smithson took the letter and bowed.

"Send one of my footmen and have him wait for an answer." Normally, Markville would have sent a groom, but he wanted the servant in livery to make a better impression. Not so much on Lady Euphrosyne—he didn't think she would care—but with the duchess.

The door closed, and his valet's steps moved rapidly down the corridor. Now the waiting began.

Euphrosyne was in the morning room reading when Mama entered.

"Euphrosyne." Her mother handed her a letter that had come. "Lord Markville has invited you to go riding tomorrow morning."

The invitation was short, but the writing was in a bold, commanding hand that gave Euphrosyne more information about his lordship than she'd had before. A delightful thrill raced through her. "May I go?"

"I do not see a reason for you not to accompany him if you wish."

"Thank you, Mama." Sitting down at the small cherry desk, Euphrosyne wrote a short reply accepting his invitation. After sealing her letter, she gave it to the footman outside the door. "Please give this to the messenger."

She went back to her book, but it failed to hold her attention. The only problem with knowing when she would see Lord Markville was waiting for morning to come.

Not long afterward, Meg sailed into the room. "I would like to invite you to dine with us tomorrow evening."

"That would be lovely." Mama motioned Meg to the place on the sofa next to her. "Is that the only reason for your visit?"

"No, I have had a letter from my grandmother that is full of news."

Mama rang for more tea, and she and Meg settled in for a comfortable coze. Euphrosyne, not being particularly interested in talk about people she would most likely never meet, slid out of the room. Surely she could find something to speed the hours until tomorrow.

The next morning, sun streamed in the room as Euphrosyne woke. Thankfully, it looked to be another lovely day. Now that she thought of it, this summer had been the warmest and driest one she could remember.

Her habit was already spread out across a chair. She glanced at the clock and found she had an hour before Lord Markville would come for her.

"My lady." Turner entered the room carrying a tray with tea and a sandwich on it. "I thought you might want something to eat before you go riding."

"Thank you." Normally, Euphrosyne would have toast to keep her until she broke her fast with her mother and sister. Today, she would probably require more sustain her.

At five minutes until the hour, she was ready to go and tempted to look out the window. Instead, she began to pace. Then, just as the clock struck the hour, Lord Markville plied the knocker.

Seconds later, she was informed of his arrival. Keeping in mind the books she had read that made mention of how a lady should greet a gentleman, she made her way sedately down the stairs.

And just like in the stories, he gazed up at her. A slight smile curved his well-molded lips as he moved to take her hand. "Good morning, my lady."

"Good morning, my lord." Euphrosyne grinned before remembering to incline her head like a sophisticated lady would do. "Shall we be off?"

"As you wish." He settled her hand on his arm. "I looked at a map and thought we might ride toward Charlcombe."

"That sounds lovely." Not that she knew where Charlcombe was. Still, she was certain she'd enjoy the ride.

They made their way through streets crowded with tradesmen and crossed the Pulteney Bridge as she had done on the walk to Sidney Gardens, but then they turned right instead of left. Soon after leaving the town, they found a place to canter.

"I'll race you to the tree," Euphrosyne called, not waiting for him to start. Moments later his black was keeping pace with Estelle, and Euphrosyne remembered what he had said the other day. "He does appear as if he is happy to run alongside her."

Markville's gray eyes turned silvery and intent. But what did that mean? "He does. I believe there is a stream close to here. Shall we find it and give our beasts water?"

He had obviously studied the map well to know about a brook. Then again he did say he had visited Bath in the past. "Have you been here before?"

"No. When we had outings, Lansdowne was the preferred place. I thought it too far away for an early morning ride." They walked the horses a little way into the woods to find the brook. "Here it is."

The stream raced over rocks and wasn't suitable for easy watering of the horses. "It's pretty, but we would have to lead them into it for them to drink," Euphrosyne said.

"It was an idea." He glanced up at the sky, just discernable through the green canopy of leafs. "We should probably start back."

As far as Euphrosyne was concerned, the ride had been much too short. As if Lord Markville agreed, they ambled slowly back to the road, talking as they went.

"Do you have only the one sister?" What would it be

like to not be overrun with brothers and sisters? Not that she would give any of them up.

"Yes." He grinned. "And she was a surprise. My mother had great difficulty conceiving and carrying babies. I think that was the reason Sarah was allowed to choose whom she wished to wed."

Euphrosyne shook her head, not understanding.

"My mother wanted her to marry a gentleman who, like my father, would love her even if she did not conceive."

"Ah. I do not know what my father would have done if my mother had difficulty bearing children." He probably would not have been as kind as Lord Markham's father. "Fortunately, for her it has not been a problem."

"I cannot imagine what it would be like to have a large family." He stared off into the distance if he was trying to fathom it. "Do you get along with all your brothers and sisters?"

"For the most part." She thought of the twins and smiled. "I have twin brothers I would gladly give away at times. The only ones at home, if you do not consider the time they spend at Eton, are the twins, Decimus and William, and my three sisters."

"Where are the others?"

"Well, you know about Hawksworth." She smiled at Lord Markham. "Frank married an American and is in the Colonies helping to run her father's shipping company. Quartus married the Duchess of Wharton earlier this year. Sextus is in Russia at our embassy. Quintus in the army and Octavius is in the navy. I have only seen Octavius a few times. He left when he was twelve and rarely comes home. Septimius was to have been in the clergy, but is now a secretary to Lord Stanstead. He would like to run for Parliament someday. Nonus is studying law. One of my brothers died before I was born. Would you like to have a large family?"

For a few moments he didn't answer, then said, "I would like to have as large a family as my wife wishes."

Once more Lord Markham showed himself to be a gentleman who might wish his wife to be a partner. "I do think a lady's preferences should be taken into consideration."

"As she is the one to do most of the work, I agree." He laughed. "I have an aunt on my father's side who had six children and declared that was enough."

"Six seems like a reasonable number," Euphrosyne said. Much better than fifteen. Although her mother never seemed to mind. "What do you do when you aren't in Bath?"

"My life is boring," he said in a sorrowful voice. "I look after my estates and my investments, and attend Parliament."

"Yet in those occupations, you have the opportunity to do a great deal to help others." With only one estate, her brother and sister-in-law were already making a difference.

"Taking care of my people is the part of estate management my father stressed. Trying to get laws enacted to help the rest of the people is harder." They rode for a while in a companionable silence. "I would like to travel to Europe at some point."

"I would love to go to Europe." If only she could marry a man who wished to travel. "I have read so much about the grand cities in France, Austria, and Italy."

He glanced at her sharply, causing her breath to stop. "You should be able to visit them."

Euphrosyne held his gaze. "So should you."

Perhaps they could see them together. Perhaps they could create a better world for people together.

CHAPTER FIVE

MARKVILLE COULDN'T TEAR HIS EYES away from Lady Euphrosyne. Despite her blackguard of a father, he was going to court her. Hell, he was going to marry her if she'd have him. He had wondered briefly if his attraction to her was to save her from the duke. If any lady required rescuing she did, but that would *not* be a good basis for a marriage. Now he knew he was simply entranced by her. She cared about the same things he did, and she had an adventurous side that called to him. He wondered what their children would look like. He could feel her at his side as they grew old.

He didn't want *her* to marry *him* in order to escape her father. How would he know what she felt for him? He'd never been able to tell what women thought or felt.

When they reached the main road back into Bath, they picked up their pace. He had to spend more time with Euphrosyne. Perhaps then he'd know.

In the meantime, it felt good to think of her by her name.

"My sister and brother-in-law have decided on a town house and will be moving to it soon. I'm sure she will wish to celebrate by having a party." Said sister was going to tease him mercilessly about him arranging events for her to host. "I am certain she'll want you and your family to attend."

"I am almost positive my mother will agree." Euphrosyne's face shone with happiness. "Where is the house?"

"At the other end of Laura Place." He flashed her a grin. "We shall be neighbors."

Her smile widened. "That will be wonderful, and it will make it very easy to arrange outings." A blush rose in her cheeks, and she lowered her eyes. "If that is something you would like."

He saw nothing merely polite or hidden in her expression. She did wish to spend more time with him. "I would like nothing more."

When they arrived in Laura Place, he quickly dismounted and went around to Euphrosyne's side. Markville would be damned if anyone but him would help her down. The moment he clasped his hands around her small waist, possessive feelings surged through him, and he wanted to hold her against him and never let her go.

Not hiding her reaction to him, she sucked in a breath, and her eyes widened as he slowly lowered her feet to the ground. "Oh, my."

Still, it didn't hurt to make sure. "May I call on you again?"

"Yes." Her voice was breathy and warm, caressing his cheek. She pulled her bottom lip between her teeth. "We are going to the Pump Room this morning."

He escorted her the short way to her door. "Odd." He lowered his voice so that only she could hear him. "I believe I shall be there as well."

"I look forward to seeing you." The door opened, and he stepped back as she strolled into the house.

By the time he arrived at the York, his sister and brother-in-law were finishing breakfast.

"Oh, there you are." Holding a piece of toast, Sarah waved him to a chair. "I have hired a butler, housekeeper, and cook and put them to work. They are responsible for hiring footmen and maids. I expect that to be accomplished today. I plan to complete our move into Laura Place tomorrow. I hope to host a dinner party in three day's time." She finished her toast and took a sip of tea while he filled his plate from the dishes on a sideboard. "What do you think of that?"

That he was relieved that he did not have to ask her to plan a party. "About the move or the dinner?"

"Both."

"I am impressed by how quickly you are managing everything." And how much easier it would be to see Euphrosyne. Still, three days was too long. Perhaps he could convince Paulet to hold the picnic he had mentioned between now and then.

"Excellent. What are your plans for today?" Sarah applied herself to a soft boiled egg.

"I thought I would visit the Pump Room, then take care of some other business." Such as finding Paulet. Markville had been remiss in not discovering where the man was staying. "I assume you will be busy at the town house."

"Indeed. Not that there is much for me to do, but I wish to make sure my senior staff has a good start."

After his sister and brother-in-law left, he read the newspapers, but couldn't seem to concentrate. Finally, he decided it was time to go to the Pump Room and look for an opportunity to stroll the room with Euphrosyne. But when he arrived, she was sitting with her mother, sister-in-law, two matrons, and two young ladies, and he did not feel as if he should interrupt. He couldn't hear their conversation, but at one point, her sister appeared to take umbrage at something one of the women had said.

Striding quickly toward the party, he bowed to the duchess. "Your grace, if Lady Euphrosyne does not object, may she stroll the room with me?"

The duchess, who had been regarding her younger daughter with an exasperated eye, nodded. "That sounds like a wonderful idea. Thank you, my lord." Turning to Euphrosyne, the duchess said, "Euphrosyne, Lord Markville has asked if you would like to take a stroll with him."

She gave her sister a worried look, then smiled at him. "Thank you. I would like that."

As soon as they were far enough away not to be overheard, he asked, "What is the trouble?"

"Bolton." Even keeping her voice low, she practically spat the name. "I cannot think she will be happy, and I made a comment I should not have." Her brows came together as she gazed up at Markville. "I do not know how to make her see she must call off the betrothal. Our father will be furious, but Meg and Hawksworth would help her."

He wanted to take Euphrosyne's cares away, but the only thing he could do was offer support. "If your brother and sister-in-law are involved, you may leave it to them to arrange things to Lady Laia's benefit."

The concern on Euphrosyne's face remained. "Do you truly think so?"

He almost laughed. The way they had managed to make the last two weddings happen was nothing short of brilliant. "I would wager on it, and I am not one for gambling."

"That's good then." The line between her eyes disappeared. "I shall apologize to Laia. I should not make her feel worse."

"You are close?" He wished he hadn't wasted time attempting to be a parent to his sister. She hadn't needed one, and his behavior had strained their relations.

"Yes. We are the nearest in age and have always been together." Euphrosyne glanced toward her sister again. "Despite our differences, I would not wish to be estranged from her."

They had just reached the duchess and Lady Hawksworth when he saw Paulet amble in with Hawksworth. Markville caught Paulet's eye. "My lady." He bowed to Euphrosyne. "I hope to see you again soon."

Curtseying, she answered, "I hope so as well."

He strode quickly up to the other gentlemen. After greetings were exchanged, he said, "My sister has found a town house and is planning a dinner party in three days. Can I convince you to hold your picnic between now and then?"

Hawksworth's shoulders shook, and he glanced away. Ignoring him, Markville focused on Paulet.

"I think that can be arranged." Although his lips twitched, at least he didn't break into laughter. "Hawksworth," Paulet commanded, "attend to the conversation. I shall require your wife to act as my hostess. Do you have an objection?"

Hawksworth swiped a hand down his face, and when he turned, only his eyes showed his mirth. "I think she will be delighted."

"Thank you." Markville knew that he had practically asked for interference by seeking the favor of the picnic with Euphrosyne's brother present. Yet Markville knew the duke, and interference might be exactly what was required. "I shall wait to hear from you." He glanced at Euphrosyne and saw that the ladies were preparing to depart. "I'll bid you a good day, gentlemen."

Euphrosyne tried to think of different ways to apologize to her sister, but finally decided to just say it without any roundaboutation.

When they arrived home, she hurried up to Laia. "Forgive me. I did not mean to embarrass you. I should not have commented on what was said, I just wanted you to understand how unsuitable this marriage is."

"That was not the way to go about it." She gave an exasperated sigh. "What would you have me do? If I do not marry him, it would affect how you and our sisters are treated."

"I don't know." Euphrosyne brushed off that concern. Markville thought Meg and Hawksworth would help stop the marriage, but Laia had to agree not to wed the man as well. Euphrosyne tried again. "Someone must be able to help."

"What must happen is for you to cease worrying about what cannot be changed." She took Euphrosyne's arm. "I shall be fine."

Harrumph. Perhaps she should leave it to her brother and sister-in-law. After all, she had other things to occupy her thoughts. Lord Markville was becoming very interesting, and she would rather spend her time deciding how she felt about him. If they could spend sufficient time together, mayhap something would come of it. She already liked him very much. Euphrosyne did not wish to wait until their father chose a match for her.

Euphrosyne needn't have worried about how long it would take to see Markville again. The next day both Mrs. Applebee and Mrs. Butterworth—the ladies Euphrosyne had been introduced to in the Pump Room—issued dinner invitations for successive evenings. Lord Markville and his family attended, as did Hawksworth, Meg, and Mr. Paulet. The day following Mrs. Butterworth's entertainment, Mr. Paulet invited the little group they had formed to a picnic on Lansdowne. Then Sarah invited them all to a dinner at her new house and planned another dinner the evening before the ball.

At every event, Markville singled her out. They walked and talked about everything from art to politics and gardening.

"Do you play an instrument?" Euphrosyne asked.

"Not well." He gave her a rueful grin. "I had a piano instructor, but I always found something I'd rather be doing than practicing."

"You sound like my brothers. They always managed to avoid practicing." Which Euphrosyne thought was very unfair as she and her sisters never managed to elude practicing.

"I take it you play?"

"Yes. The piano and the harp." Until she'd discovered that she would not have a Season, she had looked forward to playing for someone other than her family. "And I sing."

"Now that is one thing I can do." He seemed quite pleased with himself. "I have been told I have an excellent voice."

"We should find out if we sing well together." She had never been able to sing with any gentlemen other than her brothers. It would be nice to have a husband with whom one could sing. Was she truly thinking about him as a possible husband? Well why not? She enjoyed being with him, and missed him when they were apart. For the past week, they had been together every day, and she awakened looking forward to being with him. And lately she kept thinking about what it would be like if he did more than merely tuck her hand in the crook of his arm. What if he held her and kissed her?

"I'm sure my sister will want music after dinner."

When he glanced at her, she could swear that his eyes warmed, as if he were thinking of how he would like to hold her. "Would you like that?"

"Yes." Perhaps they could sit on the piano bench together where their legs would touch briefly as he turned the pages for her. A pleasurable frisson shot through her. "Yes, I would like that very much."

Two nights later, before the ladies left the gentlemen to their port, Sarah suggested that they have music before tea was served. When it was time for Euphrosyne to play, she chose the piano, and Lord Markville immediately offered to turn the pages for her. The reality of singing two duets with him and the constant touch of his body against hers, lighting fires that scrambled over her skin and through her veins, exceeded all her expectations. It even surpassed all the books she had read, and by the end of the evening she was sure she had fallen in love. The problem was finding out how *he* felt about *her*.

That night, as Turner readied Euphrosyne for bed, she wished she had someone to confide in. Unfortunately, it could not be either her sister or mother. Even if Lord Markville wanted to marry her, there was Father to consider. Would he entertain a proposal from Lord Markville? What would she do if her father refused to allow her to marry him? She was still three years away from her majority.

Euphrosyne climbed into bed and waited while her maid closed the bed hangings, leaving a crack to admit the morning sun. Meg was the only person with whom Euphrosyne could discuss her feelings. Hopefully, her sister-in-law and Hawksworth would join them for breakfast the next morning, and she could speak with Meg then.

Waking early, Euphrosyne rang for her maid and dressed for the day. Sometime during the night, it came to her that she could not talk with Meg about Lord Markham here in the house. They must go for a walk or repair to her house. But Laia would want to accompany them.

Euphrosyne was thankful after all that Meg and Hawksworth chose to break their fast in their own house.

As soon as possible after finishing breakfast, Euphrosyne fetched her bonnet and gloves. Making sure her sister wasn't in the hall, she dashed down the stairs and said to the footman on duty, "If anyone asks, I am going to see Lady Hawksworth."

"Yes, my lady." The servant bowed.

A few minutes later, Euphrosyne was ushered into her sister's parlor. Meg rose and came forward. "Euphrosyne"—

her sister-in-law bussed her cheek—"I'm delighted to see you. Would you like a cup of tea?"

"Yes, please." She removed her bonnet and sat on a cane-backed chair. They chatted about the weather and the ball that evening until Meg's butler brought in a tray with tea and biscuits.

Once the door closed, Meg said, "How can I help you?"

Euphrosyne took a sip of tea, swallowed, then took a breath. This was more embarrassing than she'd thought it would be. "I have fallen in love with Lord Markville, and I do not know if he feels the same about me."

Meg set her cup down. "I think I can safely say that he feels exactly the same as you do."

"But how do you know? Has he said anything?" Euphrosyne caught herself chewing her bottom lip.

"My dear, sister"—Meg laughed lightly—"it is the way he looks at you, as if he would like to carry you off. The way his eyes follow you, always making sure he knows where you are. Only men in love do that."

"Are you certain?" Euphrosyne so wanted her sister-in-law to be right.

"As certain as I can be." Meg picked up her cup again. "The only question is whether he will ask your father for permission before he proposes."

Euphrosyne almost groaned. "What if Father refuses him?"

Her sister-in-law stared at her for a few moments. "In that event, you will both have to decide if you will defy the duke."

"As my brothers did." The euphoria she'd been feeling fled. Defy Father. Was it as easy as that? Merely a decision to be made? Or was it much more difficult? Yet it wasn't her choice alone. Markville would have to wish to marry her without her father's blessing. Perhaps without a dowry. "Thank you. You have given me much to consider."

"Don't be too concerned yet. Your father might decide in his favor. After all, Markville is extremely eligible."

That made her feel better. "Yes, he is, isn't he?"

Meg nodded.

"I had better be going. I left word I would be here without actually asking if I could come."

Rising, Meg said, "Let me know if you wish to speak with me again." She came around the table and took Euphrosyne's hands. "I am always here for you."

"Thank you." Despite Markville's eligibility, she could not be easy. Euphrosyne had never yet won a battle with her father. On the other hand, she had never fought a battle this important.

CHAPTER SIX

AFTER SEARCHING THE HOUSE, MARKVILLE finally found his sister on the terrace. "I must speak with you."

"What is it?" Sarah set aside the book she was reading. "You do not look like yourself. Are you all right?"

"Yes. No." He'd never cared, never loved a woman before Euphrosyne. And he was much more nervous than he thought he would be. "It's just that I have decided to propose to Euphrosyne, and I need your help."

"My help to propose?" Sarah's brows rose, and she looked as if she thought he was insane.

"I'd like you to ask her to come here." He didn't dare do it at her house. They would never be allowed to be alone, and he did not yet have her father's permission. Perhaps he was uneasy because he knew he should obtain that first. He'd never done anything so precipitant.

"I hope you know what you're about." No matter her skepticism, she went to the desk, scratched something on a piece of paper, sealed it, and called for a footman.

"What does that mean? I thought you liked her." After all he and his sister had been through this year, he did not want another rift between them. Nevertheless, he would marry Euphrosyne—if she'd have him—regardless of Sarah's wishes.

"Oh, Markville." She hugged him tightly. "I think she is perfect for you. I am just thinking about her father."

As was Markville. First, he would make sure of

Euphrosyne's feelings for him, then he'd deal with the duke. "When did you ask her to come?"

"As soon as she is able." Sarah frowned. "It is not like you to flout propriety."

"No." And if it were any other man but Somerset, Markville wouldn't ignore what he could only think of as a sense of decency. "But I have a strong feeling this is what I must do."

"Very well." She hugged him again. "I wish you luck. Although, I do not think you'll need it with Euphrosyne."

Several minutes later the same footman brought back a response. Sarah opened it. "She will be here within the next half hour."

"That will have to be good enough." He wanted a brandy, but this was not the time to start drinking. He must remain sober.

Markville posted himself in the back parlor and paced. His sister had promised to bring Euphrosyne to him as soon as she arrived, and he'd heard sounds from the front of the house. She had arrived at least two minutes ago. What was taking them so long?

Suddenly the door opened and Sarah stepped in with Euphrosyne. "I believe my brother has something he wishes to say to you."

Euphrosyne started at him, uncertainty clouding her beautiful blue eyes.

Not wanting to alarm her further, he stepped quickly to her, took her hands, and searched her face. He was as sure as he could be of her feelings toward him, but what if he was wrong? "Euphrosyne, my love."

"Markville." She gazed at him, her gaze earnestly meeting his. "Do you truly love me?"

"God, yes." He took her in his arms, holding her tightly against him.

"I'm very glad." She snuggled into him. "Because I love

you too, but I've been too afraid to be the first one to say it."

"Never be afraid again." He closed the distance between their lips. She'd never been kissed before, and he wanted her to enjoy it. He planned to spend a great deal of time kissing her. Lightly, he brushed his mouth across hers, feathering the corners of her pink lips, caressing her long slender neck with his thumbs, before fitting his lips to hers.

The kiss was sweet, innocent, something he'd never experienced before. How lucky he was that he'd found her. She slid her arms over his shoulders, and he began to burn with need. He'd never wanted a woman as much as he did her. When she opened her mouth on a sigh, he slid his tongue in, exploring and begging her to play. Her tongue tangled with his, and, despite her innocence she matched him step for step. Just as she would do in their marriage.

He drew back, just enough to break the kiss.

Her fine, dark-blonde brows signaled her confusion.

"I have a question I must ask before we continue." He took a breath. "Will you marry me? I find I cannot think of my life without you in it. I haven't approached your father yet, but I will."

Her happy face convinced him he was in heaven. "Yes, yes, I'll marry you! I don't care what he says. I cannot image being with anyone but you."

Euphrosyne pulled Markville's head down, kissing him again. God, he was going to love being married to her.

His hands roamed over her body, unable to touch her enough. He wanted to mark her as his, to make sure she knew she belonged to him as he belonged to her. Tilting his head, he deepened their kiss. When his hand caresses her derrière, she slipped one hand down and stroked his. Their breath became ragged, and once again, he stopped.

"If we keep this up, I'll take you here and now. You

deserve better than that." If only they could be wed soon. He raked a hand through his hair. "I must write your father. Or perhaps I should visit him."

She shook her head. "He is touring the estates. What if he says no?"

His chest tightened. It was entirely possible her father would refuse his offer. He hoped what she had said before was the truth. She would marry him with or without her father's permission. It might come to that.

"We'll find a way." He held her closer, breathing in her lavender scent, now mixed with musk. "But as much as I expect you have reason for concern, I must give him a chance to accept or refuse me." Markville would write the duke today, but now that he had found her, no one would take her away from him.

Markville held Euphrosyne close to him as if he'd never let her go. Her love for him expanded so much she thought her heart would burst with bliss. This was the happiest day of her life in a lifetime that would be full of love and joy. If only they did not have to involve her father. If only Markville were a little less honorable. Yet, would she love him as much if he were not? She wished she could say something trite like of course my father will accept your offer, but she knew the duke would do what he wanted. Even if any other father would be delighted to accept an offer from Markville, her father might not.

He pressed soft kisses on her neck. "If only we could tell the world that we are betrothed, I would claim every one of your dances this evening."

That would be lovely. "Even if another gentleman asks me and I must accept, I will not enjoy the dance nearly as much as if it were you." A light scratching came on the door. "Is it safe to come in?"

She grinned at her betrothed. "I suppose Sarah will have to be told."

"I suppose she will. At least I know she'll keep it to herself." He pulled a face. "Well, she'll probably tell Jeremy."

Euphrosyne wanted to tell her sister, but should she? "We can tell Meg and Hawksworth. They might be able to help us."

"Yes." Markville slowly nodded. "We should do that, and soon."

"After the ball." There was no time before then.

"Are you still in there?" Sarah's exasperated voice came from the other side of the door.

Trying not to laugh, Euphrosyne touched her forehead to Markville's broad chest. "You must answer her."

He kissed the top of her head, before saying, "Come."

As the door opened, she turned to greet her soon-to-be sister. "You may be the first to wish us happy."

Flying forward, Sarah embraced Euphrosyne and Markville. "I am so very happy for you! I had begun to despair of my brother finding a lady he could love." Stepping back, Sarah glanced from Euphrosyne to Markville. "But what of the duke? Shall we fly to Gretna Green? Jeremy and I will chaperone you."

"No." Markville squeezed his sister's shoulder. "I shall write him today."

Sarah gave them a dubious look, prompting Euphrosyne to say, "If he refuses, we shall accept your offer."

"Very well." Sarah hugged them again. "Euphrosyne, a footman came with a message that you are to return home to go shopping for the things you and your sister need before this evening."

She glanced at a clock on the fireplace mantle. "Oh, my goodness. I did not realize the time." Standing on her tiptoes she touched her lips to Markville's. "I shall see you this evening."

"Until then, my love." Drawing her into his arms again, he kissed her firmly. "I'll walk you home."

"Do you think that is wise?" She never knew what her father might hear from the staff. Although he would know soon enough that she and Markville wished to wed.

"I think it will be fine." He tucked her hand into the crook of his arm.

The rest of the day passed at a snail's pace. Even shopping seemed to drag on. Finally, it was time to dress for the ball. When Turner finished, Euphrosyne stared in the mirror, amazed. The pink and white ball gown had seemed almost childish when she had seen the drawing, and she had not looked in a mirror during the fittings, but the gown was anything but a child's. Seed pearls interspersed with brilliants adorned the sleeves and the neckline, which was much lower than she'd remembered. Her maid had threaded a strand of pearls and pink quartz in Euphrosyne's hair. She wore earrings and a pink quartz pendant set in platinum around her neck, gifts from her mother. "I look like a princess."

"You certainly do, my lady." Turner smiled.

"I'm going to see how my sister is doing. I'll come back after dinner for my things." She reached Laia's room and opened the door without knocking. "Laia, look at me! Ooooh, look at you!"

"I do think I look well, and you look lovely." Laia smiled.

"You're beautiful." Euphrosyne carefully bussed her sister's cheek. "All the gentlemen will want to dance with you." Especially, Mr. Paulet, she hoped. Her sister deserved more than an old duke.

"Do you think we will be sitting along the sides of the room?" Laia's worried eyes met Euphrosyne's.

Afraid that her sister would discover her secret, Euphrosyne lowered her lashes. "No. I think our family will ensure we have partners for every dance."

Thankfully, before Laia could ask any unwanted

questions, Meg strolled into the room carrying two small posies in filigree silver holders, one with yellow flowers and the other with pale pink roses. "I do not know why gentlemen insist on sending flowers to be carried to an event. Although, I suppose you could take them out and put some of the flowers in your hair, if you like."

Gentlemen? "Which gentlemen?" Laia asked, frowning at the flowers.

"Lord Markville"—Meg handed the pink bouquet to Euphrosyne—"and Mr. Paulet." Meg gave the other one to Laia. "I must say they were either amazingly percipient or they went out of their way to discover what you were wearing."

Laia clutched her flowers to her breast as if someone might take them from her. "I could not ruin the arrangement."

"Nor could I." Euphrosyne could not believe Markville had not let on at all that he was sending her flowers. How wonderful of him to have discovered the color of her gown. She would simply have to find a place to put them when she was dancing. "We had better go down to dinner."

The choices were light. White soup, roasted chicken instead of one with a sauce, fresh *haricot vert* with a light butter and lemon sauce, small boiled potatoes, salad, and poached fish. She managed to do justice to the meal despite the butterflies that had taken up residence in her stomach.

"It is a pity there are no waltzes." Hawksworth cast Meg a sultry look.

Euphrosyne realized Markville had looked at her exactly the same way earlier. How were they going to hide their feelings for each other? Or would they be able to?

"We are acting as chaperones this evening, my love," Meg responded. "We should not dance in any case."

"Very true." One of Hawksworth's brows rose. "I cannot possibly perform a minuet and watch over my sisters at the same time."

Euphrosyne harrumphed. If any man attempted to take advantage, Markville would protect her.

"There is also a matter of looking after the items they cannot have with them when they are dancing." As Mama had not joined them, Meg rose, signaling for the rest of them to do so as well. "Tea will be served in the drawing room in a few minutes." She glanced at Laia and Euphrosyne. "You should fetch your things."

They rose from the table. Laia and Euphrosyne went upstairs to collect their gloves, fans, reticules, and posies.

"Are you nervous?" Euphrosyne asked as they ascended the stairs. She had been, but the more she considered the evening, the less anxious she became.

"A little, but only because I do not want to make a mistake." Laia's sister embraced her.

"There is nothing to worry about. We will both have a wonderful time."

Euphrosyne's thoughts were filled with dancing with Markville. Even if there were no waltzes, it would be wonderful.

"Yes, we will."

After tea, they walked down the front steps, and Euphrosyne could not help but admire the elegance of the sedan chairs. They were much more stylish than the ones she had seen elsewhere around town. The paint was unblemished, and they appeared to have been fitted out inside in velvet. They were so tall she could have worn a turban with feathers and not been concerned about them being harmed.

Looking more handsome than ever in breeches and a dark blue jacket set off by a snowy white cravat, Markville stepped out from the other side of one of the chairs. "Allow me to assist you into your chair, my lady."

"It would be my pleasure." She placed her hand on his

arm, feeling the strength in it. If anyone could convince her father to allow their marriage, he could. The light caught his waistcoat, causing her to admire the small pink flowers on vines. "I like your waistcoat."

"I hoped you would," he said in a low voice. "Even if we cannot make our betrothal known, I wished to do something to show that we belong together."

She, too, wished they could tell everyone of their engagement. "You do not like keeping this secret, do you?"

"No." His jaw tightened, and his mouth set into a thin line. "There is something about it that is not honorable." They had reached the chair, and he brought her fingers to his lips. "I sent the letter today. Still, I shall feel better when I speak with your brother."

She would feel better when they were married. "I would like to be present when you see Hawksworth."

"If he allows it, then I agree." Markville's palm cupped her cheek. "I am at a disadvantage."

"You are not." Hawksworth would understand. She was sure of it. "When would you like to marry?"

"Soon." Markville gave her a passionate look, and she wanted him to take her in his arms. "I would also like you to call me Charles. No one else does."

"Charles." She tested the name, enunciating as she said it. "It suits you. But if I am to call you by your first name, you should call me by mine."

"Gladly. It is one of the most beautiful names I have heard."

The chairs were carried into a large room and set down. Charles helped her out, and she saw that Mr. Paulet had escorted Laia.

After shaking out her skirt, she asked, "How did you enjoy the ride?"

"Very well, indeed." Particularly the talk of marriage, even it was short. "I enjoyed the conversation even more."

But not as much as she would enjoy dancing with Charles.

"Shall we go up?" He held out his arm.

"Of course." She placed her hand on his sleeve, and they followed her brother and sister-in-law up the stairs. As they entered the ballroom, his arm tightened. "Is anything wrong?"

Giving his head an imperceptible shake, he smiled at her. "It just occurred to me that I do not want you to stand up with anyone but me, and you must."

Nor did she wish to dance with another man. "Perhaps no one else will ask me."

"I would not wish that for you, my love. This is your first ball and you should enjoy it. We shall have the rest of our lives to dance together. Tonight it will have to be enough that I have your first set and the supper dance."

And that was one of the reasons Euphrosyne loved him. Even if he wasn't happy about the situation, he wanted her to enjoy herself. "I shall make sure to have fun. Your sacrifice should not be in vain."

"Minx." His eyes twinkled with laughter. "You'll break hearts tonight."

But never his heart.

CHAPTER SEVEN

THE MINUET WAS THE MOST unsatisfying Markville had ever danced. He didn't like being separated from Euphrosyne, and caught himself scowling at every man who touched her hand. The worst part of it was that he knew the feeling probably wouldn't go away after they married. For the first time he understood why Hawksworth tried to keep all his wife's dances for himself.

As Markville knew would occur, the moment he returned Euphrosyne to her sister-in-law, gentlemen, young and old, began vying for a set with her.

He sidled up to her brother. "May I come to see you tomorrow? There is something I'd like to discuss. Lady Euphrosyne would like to be there as well."

The man glanced at Euphrosyne then nodded. "Is eight too early for you?"

"Not at all." Although it was a strange hour to have a meeting. Unable to remain and watch as most of the gentlemen in Bath attempted to flirt with his betrothed, jaw clenched, he strolled away as unconcernedly as possible.

Several moments later, he came across Paulet, who appeared to have the same idea as Markville about getting away from the frustration of having to watch their women dance with others. "Most of them are a bunch of worthless fribbles, although harmless," Markville said. "Hawksworth will take care of any problems. I'm off to find something to drink and the card room."

Paulet nodded, but his gaze remained riveted on Euphrosyne's family.

"Care to come with me?" Markville asked.

Finally he dragged his eyes from Lady Laia. "You're out of luck. Tea is not for more than another hour, and there is nothing else on the premises."

"It's as bad as Almack's."

If this were a private ball, Markville might be able to steal Euphrosyne away for a bit.

"I don't think the bread will be stale, and at least the tea is not weak. Or so I have been told."

"That's something, at any rate." Markham's attention was drawn to Euphrosyne being led to the dance floor by a young man. This was going to be a very long night. "Still, there ought to be a place a gentleman can hide."

"Oh, there's a card room." Paulet barked a laugh. "It will not be what you are used to."

"No matter. I find I must do something to while away the time." And not watch his love with other men.

Paulet raised a brow. "Is it that serious with you?"

For a second, Markville considered revealing that he had written the duke, but he did not want Paulet to say anything to Hawksworth until Markville had a chance to speak with the man. "I have hopes in that direction." From the corner of his eye, he saw her dancing. Thank God the balls ended early in Bath. "I'm for the card room."

Paulet chuckled. "I believe I'll join you."

Well, they made a fine pair. "I'm happy to have the company."

Not being a gambler, Markville was glad to find the stakes weren't high, but the game was interesting enough to keep him occupied until he could be with Euphrosyne again. When he found his way back to her, she was surrounded by a cadre of hopeful-looking gentlemen.

"My lady." He bowed. "I believe this is our dance."

Euphrosyne's polite smile broadened into a real one—or at least he thought it did—and she curtseyed. "You are correct, my lord."

Fortunately, the country dance enabled him to spend more time touching her. It wasn't as satisfying as a waltz, but it soothed his ragged nerves. He had to marry her soon.

THE FOLLOWING MORNING, MARKVILLE ARRIVED promptly at Hawksworth's residence and was escorted to the breakfast room where he, his wife, and Euphrosyne were drinking tea as racks of toast were set on the table. The sideboard was laden with dishes.

"The Marquis of Markville," the butler announced.

"Markville, well met." Hawksworth inclined his head.

"We shall want more tea," his wife said, coming to greet Markville. "Please help yourself if you have not already broken your fast."

"Thank you, but I ate a while ago." In fact, he'd been up for hours. "A cup of tea would be welcome."

Euphrosyne grinned and indicated the chair next to hers. Hawksworth sat at the head of the table, his wife on the side opposite Euphrosyne. By the time they had discussed the weather, the tea arrived. Lady Hawksworth dismissed the footmen and poured.

"I cannot remain long," Euphrosyne said. "The rooms are already filling with flowers, and Laia will want me there to open the cards with her." She touched his arm. "Yours were the most beautiful. Thank you."

"It was completely my pleasure." Once they were

properly betrothed to be married, he could give her pearls and precious gems.

Hawksworth drained his cup and held it out to be refilled. "I take it you wish to discuss marrying my sister?"

Markville placed his cup on the table and took Euphrosyne's hand. "Yes. I wish to wed Euphrosyne, and she returns my regard. I have written to your father, but I am not sure that I will receive the response we want."

"We rarely get what we want from him." Hawksworth rubbed a hand over his forehead. "My advice to you is to take her to Scotland."

Euphrosyne's fork clattered to the dish.

That was the last thing Markville thought he'd hear. That her brother would suggest such a thing was shocking. "That would be—"

Hawksworth held up his hand. "I know, but unless you have something he values—property bordering one of the Somerset estates to be precise—the chances of your suit being accepted are slim."

"Are you positive?" Euphrosyne asked.

Hawksworth nodded. "I am."

The only land in Markville's family that met that criteria now belonged to his sister's husband and was now entailed. "I have nothing."

"Surely Sarah and Jeremy would accompany you," Lady Hawksworth added. "You can avoid some of the scandal by being chaperoned."

Euphrosyne glanced at Markville, a frown on her beautiful face.

"Sarah already offered." He had seen how the *ton* treated couples who eloped, and it wasn't with kindness. "I cannot do anything that would harm Euphrosyne's reputation."

"In that case"—Hawksworth rose—"you must excuse me. I have some pressing business. I wish you luck, but cannot help you. Let us know if you change your mind.

My sister will be in Bath until Laia's wedding. After that, I don't know what will happen."

"Thank you." After kissing Euphrosyne's hand, Markville stood and bowed. "Make no mistake, I fully intend to wed Euphrosyne. However, I hope such drastic measures will not be needed."

Lady Hawksworth gave him a doubtful look, and Euphrosyne appeared worried. "Yet, if it does come to that, I will do as you suggest."

"We have taken you aback, but do not underestimate the duke," Lady Hawksworth said. "He cares nothing about the feelings of his children. And he will use any method to get his way."

"Thank you, again." He inclined his head. "But I must attempt gain her hand in an honorable fashion."

Markville only prayed he was doing the right thing by not immediately fleeing with Euphrosyne.

Euphrosyne watched her Charles leave the room with her brother. "I did not know my situation was so dire that you and Hawksworth would counsel us to elope."

"I wish I could give you more hope of being able to wed Markville honorably." Meg handed Euphrosyne a plate of toast. "On the other hand, I do understand why he feels he must make the effort. Perhaps we could plan for you to leave directly after your sister's wedding if your father will not accept Markville's proposal."

That was an excellent suggestion. If she and her sister-in-law made the plans, then Charles would be certain to agree if Father refused to accept the match. "We would have to involve Sarah and her husband."

Meg spread marmalade on a piece of toast. "Do you think she would keep it a secret from Markville?"

Euphrosyne did not want to start her marriage with

Charles keeping secrets. "I would not ask it of her. As I think of it, I'd tell him that if my father has not answered by the wedding or refuses his consent, we shall elope."

Her sister-in-law nodded distractedly. "My suggestion would be to sail to Scotland.Your father will expect you to travel by coach. As long as the wind is in the right quarter, a ship is faster."

"Thank you. I must return home. Mama and Laia will be up soon."

"We shall see you later today."

Euphrosyne was finishing a soft boiled egg and her third piece of toast when her mother entered the breakfast room. "Good morning, Mama. Laia is not yet up?"

"Good morning. Let her sleep a little longer." As she went to her seat, the butler brought a pot of hot chocolate. "Have you had a chance to see all the flowers?"

"I looked at them earlier. I never expected to receive so many." She had not expected them even from Charles.

By the time she and her mother had finished eating, and she'd had an opportunity to read some of the poems sent along with the flowers, she decided to fetch her sister. Laia should at least see the bouquet Mr. Paulet had sent. Perhaps they would all elope.

Smiling brightly, Euphrosyne opened the door to her sister's bedchamber. "Laia, you would not believe the number of bouquets in the parlor and drawing room."

She blinked then pushed herself up onto one arm. "Bouquets?"

Euphrosyne perched on the bed. "Yes, and poetry. We have each received about the same number." She grimaced when she thought of some of it. "All of it horrible drivel, but just think of a gentleman making the gesture. They have been arriving for hours."

Glancing at the window, Laia frowned. "What time is it?"

"Almost nine. Breakfast is being brought up to you, so you must rise now."

"Yes, of course. Why didn't my maid wake me?"

"Mama said to let you sleep." Euphrosyne left the bed and headed to the door. "She also said we are to expect visits from the gentlemen later today during her visiting hours."

Laia groaned. "I should have stayed in bed."

"You are still in bed." Euphrosyne had never seen her sister so attached to her bed. "Mama expects you in the morning room in an hour."

"An hour?" Her sister collapsed back against her pillows.

"Yes, and you will want to see the flowers and read some of the poetry." It suddenly occurred to her that Charles would be one of the gentlemen paying a call.

She went to the music room and began to practice some new duets she hoped to be able to sing with him. An hour later, she decided to fetch the flowers he'd brought and take them to her bedroom. Laia was in the drawing room standing next to the bouquet Mr. Paulet had sent, staring at a card.

Had she fallen in love with the gentleman? Mayhap if Euphrosyne told her sister about Markville, it would encourage her to choose Paulet. "Markham has already written Father asking permission to marry me."

Her sister's jaw dropped. "That is wonderful."

"Neither of us thinks he will allow us to wed." Despite what she'd told Charles, she couldn't keep what might happen from Laia. "We might go to Scotland instead."

"Scotland?"

Straightening, Euphrosyne gave a short nod.

"You would risk a scandal?"

Perhaps it wouldn't be quite that bad. "We would be chaperoned by Sarah and Jeremy."

Laia dropped into a chair as if stunned. "But what about

our sisters?"

Hawksworth and Meg had confirmed that the duke cared nothing about her or her sisters. It was time Laia heard the truth. "Father is never going to allow any of us to marry for love. What we do will not change how he treats our younger sisters. How could he be harsher than he already is? We cannot go into the town alone. We cannot walk outside of the garden by ourselves. Even when we are in the gardens, we are watched." Euphrosyne took Laia's hands in hers. "If I could trust he would pick a man different from himself and my life would change for the better by marrying whom he chooses, I would. But, I cannot, and neither can you. All you will do is sacrifice yourself for nothing."

She locked gazes with her sister. Finally, Laia gently squeezed Euphrosyne's hands. "You must follow your own road, as I shall follow mine." Her sister gave a travesty of a smile. "Wherever that leads me."

That afternoon, Euphrosyne experienced her first morning visits. Even her mother, however, couldn't tell her why morning visits took place in early afternoon. As Euphrosyne had been told to expect, all the single gentlemen who had danced with her at the ball appeared at one point or another. Yet, the only man she wished to see was Charles. His eyes touched her as he lounged against the fireplace mantle while she put off a young man who wanted to go walking with her. Mr. Paulet came as well, and the smile he shared with her sister made Euphrosyne hope he was making progress with Laia.

A few days later, Euphrosyne and her family, except for her mother, attended the Illumination that transformed Sydney Gardens.

Thousands of lights lit temporary buildings, and fireworks were to be held later. "Is Vauxhall like this?" she asked Charles.

"Something in the same vein. At Vauxhall, there is a building for dancing." They secluded themselves under the branches of a large tree, and Charles took the opportunity to draw her into his arms. "I shall take you, and you will decide."

"I wish I could dance with you now." She wished they could find a place to be alone where they would not be interrupted or be discovered and create a scandal.

He pressed his lips against hers and smiled. "I received a letter from your father as I was dressing this evening. He says he will meet with me during your sister's wedding breakfast."

On the day after the ball, Laia and Mr. Paulet had—to Euphrosyne's utter shock—become engaged. "Does that mean my father knows she is not going to wed Bolton?"

Charles's brows lowered. "That is a very good question, and one to which I do not know the answer. I shall speak with Paulet. Your father might still be expecting her to wed the duke."

But the next day, while Laia, Hawksworth, and Mr. Paulet were visiting the property that was to have been turned over to Somerset upon Laia's marriage to the duke, the Duke of Bolton attempted to murder Laia, and Hawksworth killed him. Making Mr. Paulet the new Duke of Bolton.

CHAPTER EIGHT

"BUT WHAT DOES ALL OF this mean for us?" Euphrosyne asked.

Markville wished he knew the answer. They had gathered at Hawksworth's house with her sister, the new Duke of Bolton, Hawksworth, and Meg—as Markville had been asked to call her—several days after the inquest finding that Bolton died accidently from a fall. No one wanted the scandal that would have occurred with any other result.

"I wish I could tell you," Paulet replied. "I had to write Somerset and tell him that the property my uncle promised was entailed."

"It is a shame your uncle did not allow you to have anything to do with the dukedom." Meg rubbed her forehead. "That is not going to make Somerset happy. Have you heard yet whether or not he will agree to *your* wedding?"

"Catherine"—meaning the Euphrosyne's mother—"wrote telling him that Bolton had kindly agreed to honor the betrothal, and Somerset agreed to it," Hawksworth said. "But that was before he discovered the land was entailed."

Laia—Markville had also been invited to call her by her first name—glanced at each of them. "What is the length of time one must mourn an uncle?"

"It varies from three weeks to three months, depending upon one's relations with the uncle." Meg glanced at Bolton. "However, I do not see why you could not be married during that time if it is a quiet ceremony attended only by family and close friends."

"In that case," Laia said, "I suggest we plan to wed in three weeks." She raised one brow. "No matter what my father says."

After she had discovered that the old Duke of Bolton had murdered his last three wives, she had lost all sense to duty toward her father.

Euphrosyne sighed. "Markville, you have not heard anything further from him?"

She knew he had not. He would have told her. "Unfortunately, no."

"I realize you wish to meet with him," Hawksworth said. "But I propose you make plans to take Euphrosyne to Scotland directly after the wedding ceremony. Especially after he was informed the old duke had planned to cheat him and he can no longer have the property he planned to acquire for Laia's marriage. The chances he will allow Euphrosyne to marry without it benefiting the dukedom are slim."

Laia looked at Bolton, and he nodded. "We shall accompany you."

"That way I can make the arrangements, and no one will be the wiser."

"Do you have an objection?" Euphrosyne's eyes searched Markville's.

He had many, but none of them were as important as spending his life with her. "Not at all."

THE MORNING AFTER BOLTON'S MOTHER arrived at Roselands, Meg caught up with Euphrosyne as she was going to her bedchamber. "I found the most delightful folly when I was out walking yesterday."

Euphrosyne had either walked or ridden over most of the property, but that had escaped her. "Where it is?"

"To the south. If you go through the garden, there is a gate to a path that goes along the river. Not more than ten minutes will bring you to a bridge over the river, and just on the other side is a cottage nestled in a glade. It reminds me of something out of a fairy tale."

That was strange. She was certain she had been told that . . . "Are you sure it doesn't belong to the neighboring estate?"

"Quite sure. I looked at the estate map when I returned." They had reached the corridor where their rooms were located. "Hawksworth and Bolton are coming here this morning to review something about the settlements with one of your father's solicitors. Markville will accompany them. While they are busy, you and Markville should go see the folly. It's magical."

That would at least give Euphrosyne and Charles some time alone while the others attended to wedding business. "What a wonderful idea. Thank you."

"They should be here anytime." Her sister-in-law grinned, probably because she would see her husband soon. "I'll see you later."

Euphrosyne changed into a walking gown and waited until she heard the sound of carriages coming up the drive. Her sister and sister-in-law were entering the hall from the back of the house as Euphrosyne came down the stairs. She joined them, and the three went outside to greet the men. Soon they were heading toward the morning room.

Charles bent his head so that only she could hear him speak. "I have not heard further from your father. Therefore, I assume he still wishes to meet with me."

It had been several weeks now, and, after what her brother had said, she'd lost what little hope she had that her father would agree to her marriage. Not that it mattered. If he refused, she and Charles would be on their way to Scotland. "Let us take a stroll. Meg told me about a folly she discovered."

He gave a terse nod. What a toll this must be taking on him. "I am happy to be able to spend some time with you."

"Even two days has been too long. I do not know why we had to come to Roselands so soon."

The moment they were behind a large hedge, concealed from the house, Charles drew her into his arms. "God, how I've missed you."

His warmth surrounded her, and his scent made her giddy. "Kiss me."

"Gladly." He lightly brushed his lips across hers before claiming her.

Euphrosyne reveled in the feel of him as his tongue swept into her mouth and danced with hers. The sound of a gardener on the other side of the hedge made her break the kiss. Putting her finger to her lips, she took his hand and led the way toward privacy via the gate to the river path. She had been given so much freedom since they'd been in Bath she did not dare risk behavior that would result in her liberty curtailed.

She held Charles's hand as they ambled along the path and over the bridge. "How have Hawksworth and Bolton been?"

"Your brother's been a bear since Meg came to stay here, and Bolton's not any better." Charles let Euphrosyne's hand go and wrapped her arm around her waist. "Then again, neither have I have been very good company."

His words filled her heart with a sense of love and joy she'd never experienced before. "I do not like that you haven't been happy, but I do like that you've missed me."

"You are everything to me." Pulling her into his arms again, he claimed her lips, and it was several long moments before he broke the kiss. "Look over there. I think we've found the folly."

She turned around and saw what he was looking at. Surrounded by a stone wall and a garden displaying a riot of color, the cottage could not have held more than two rooms. It was built from the same white stone as the wall. Bright-blue shutters framed the windows on either side of the door, and lace curtains peeped out from the inside. "Oh, it's beautiful!" Taking his hand she walked toward the gate. "I wonder if the inside is as pretty as it looks to be."

Charles opened the door, standing back for Euphrosyne to step in.

"Oh, my." The walls had been plastered and painted white. But what caught her attention was a large bed hung with pale-yellow silk curtains at one end of the large room. At the other end was a fireplace with a kettle, a square table, and four chairs. A picnic basket rested on the table. In the center of the room stood a small sofa and two stuffed chairs covered in flowered chintz, and three small cherry tables. "It is very elegant."

"It is extremely well kept."

He was right. Everything was spotlessly clean. She glanced at the bed and swallowed. She would not be surprised if the sheets were fresh. Meg had sent them here deliberately. The only question was, did Euphrosyne have the courage of her convictions? She did not doubt Charles, and she could not doubt herself. In any event, they would be married soon.

Turning, she gazed up at his deep gray eyes and knew his thoughts were the same as hers. "Yes."

His gaze heated, turning his eyes to silver. His hands were anchored on her waist. "You have to be absolutely certain."

The decision was not difficult. "I love you with all my heart, and I will never leave you."

"You have become my world." He brushed his lips across hers. "I'll never let anything or anyone tear us apart."

Pulling the ribbon on her bonnet loose, she removed her hat and tossed it onto a chair. "I would have you make me your wife."

"As I'll be your husband." He took her hand. "Our marriage bed awaits."

Thank the Lord she had listened from an adjoining room when Meg told Laia what to expect. Needing to do something, Euphrosyne pulled off her gloves, and began to untie Charles's cravat as he unfastened the ties at the back of her gown. When he cupped her breasts, her fingers faltered. "That is like nothing I've ever felt."

"Good." His voice was a low growl. He yanked his jacket and waistcoat off, leaving them in a heap on the floor before pushing her gown down over her shoulders and hips. His lips captured hers, and her petticoat was the next to slide down. Then her stays joined the growing pile on at their feet. "Drat." Charles quickly gathered their clothing, laying it carefully over the sofa. "Now where were we?"

"I must remove my half-boots."

He glanced down at his own boots, and grimaced. "I wanted this to be romantic for you."

Euphrosyne couldn't help but to laugh. "It will be much more romantic without our shoes."

"I cannot argue with you."

When he rose from taking off his boots, he drew his shirt over his head, and her mouth dried. She had never seen a male chest before. Dark-sable hair lightly covered his upper torso and dipped down toward his pantaloons. Unlike her nipples, his were almost brown. Spreading her fingers, she touched him, marveling at the difference between the soft curls and the hard muscle of his chest.

"You're beautiful." Wanting to see all of him, she undid

his falls, and the hard ridge that her sister-in-law had called a manhood sprang into her hand.

Yet before she could do anything more than touch it, Charles swooped her into his arms. "If you keep that up, I won't last, and I intend this to be good for you."

He placed her gently on the bed and feathered kisses over her neck as, inch by inch, he peeled down her chemise. When he licked her already hard nipples, she thought she'd come off the bed. Nothing had ever felt as good. Rolling one tight bud between his fingers, he drew the other into his mouth and frissons of pleasure speared through her. Heat coalesced at the apex of her legs, and her hips lifted.

"Soon, my love." Charles moved one hand, leaving her breast bereft, but he placed it on her mons and rubbed. The tension rose and Euphrosyne writhed, trying to get relief. Then his finger was inside her as he rubbed faster. "Come for me. Let go." Just when she thought she could not stand any more, she flew apart, and he entered her with one smooth stroke. "Put your legs around me. I'm sorry for the pain."

She couldn't deny it hurt, but soon the pain began to fade, and he started to move inside her. Cupping her cheeks, he kissed her deeply, his chest hairs abrading her breasts, making her whole body more sensitive to him, as if fires had been lit. Soon the tension she'd felt before began to rise, and this time she welcomed the tremors. Crying her name, he thrust into her twice more before collapsing off to her side, bringing her with him.

Markville held Euphrosyne as close to him as he could. He'd never considered how different the act of sexual congress would be with a woman he loved. The experience was much more than physical. It was as if his soul had melded with hers. Nothing, no one would take her away from him. He would not allow it.

"I love you." He stroked her fine curls, wondering how long they could remain here.

"I love you, too." Her face was alight with joy, and his heart tightened. He must be the luckiest man in the whole of England if not the world.

"Are you ready to depart after the wedding if need be?" After this, he could not take any chances.

She searched his eyes. "You know I will. With your sister and husband and my sister and husband accompanying us, surely we will not have to worry as much about propriety."

"I'm not certain how much that will help."

He'd been told yesterday that a ship had been arranged.

"To be honest. I do not care what people think."

Only because she had never been in Polite Society and had no idea how cruel it could be. "We shall make it work."

"Yes, we will." She shifted. "I wonder what is in the basket."

"I almost forgot how much you enjoy food." He ran his hand over her flat stomach. She was one of those people who could eat what they wanted, but one day her stomach would grow big with his child. He could already have planted the seed. His cock started to harden again, but it was too soon. She needed time to recover. "I'll go look."

Opening the basket, he found flasks and napkins. He uncorked one of the bottles. "Lemonade, and it feels like the napkins are wrapped around sandwiches."

Slipping out of the bed, Euphrosyne walked naked to him, pulled out a chair and sat. "Let's eat."

They arrived back at the house none too soon. The curricles were being brought around. The two skirted the drive and went through the gardens to the morning room.

"That was close," he said.

"I wish you did not have to leave so soon."

Drawing her to him he held her, never wanting to let

her go. He wanted to take her with him now, but that would be selfish. She'd worry her family. "I wish I did not have to leave at all." He kissed her softly.

OVER THE NEXT TWO DAYS, it proved impossible to be alone with Euphrosyne. Somerset arrived and Markville sent a note asking for a meeting before the wedding. He did not receive a reply.

The evening before the wedding, he dined with Jeremy, Bolton, and Hawksworth. Markville asked Hawksworth, "What is your father waiting for?"

"He is playing with you." Hawksworth took a sip of wine. "I strongly advise you not to meet with him. Leave as soon as possible after the wedding."

Something inside Markville urged him to do exactly that. But blast it all, he wasn't a barbarian. Both the duke and he were peers. They were civilized men.

"I'd do as the man said," Jeremy commented. "He knows his father best."

"That's a fact," Bolton agreed. "If the duchess hadn't been able to convince the old man that Laia would be ruined if she didn't marry me, this wedding wouldn't be taking place."

"Lord Markville." Jeremy's butler entered the drawing room carrying a letter on a silver salver. "This just came for you."

Markville took the note. "It's from Somerset." He popped open the seal and shook out the letter. "He confirms that he will meet with me after the wedding breakfast."

Hawksworth set down his glass. "I suppose you will do what you think is right. I'll see you in the morning."

"I'll walk out with you." Bolton rose and turned to Jeremy. "Thank you for a good evening."

Markville noticed that none of gentleman had wished him luck. Was he being foolish believing that the duke would treat him fairly? He gave himself a shake. All would be well. It had to be. Surely the duke had some shred of human decency Markville could find in their meeting to appeal to.

The next day, he couldn't take his eyes off Euphrosyne as she attended her sister. It wasn't until the wedding breakfast that he was able to speak with her. "I am meeting with your father after we are done here."

"Finally." She smiled. "Do not let him rob you. He does have a reputation of hard dealing."

"I would give him everything I had to be able to marry you with his permission." He'd attempted to find a property with a common border along the dukedom's lands, but had no luck.

"In that case," she said tartly, "I sincerely hope that the majority of your property is entailed."

"Lady Euphrosyne," said one the many footmen her father had brought.

"Yes?"

"Your sister, the Duchess of Bolton, would like to speak with you. I would be happy to take you to her."

"Yes, of course." Euphrosyne threw Markville a grin. "I shall see you soon."

A few moments later, he was asked to join the duke in the study. The butler announced Markville, and he entered the room. Somerset, seated behind a large walnut desk, stared at Markville with a cold eye. A sliver of apprehension crawled up his spine, making the hairs on the back of his neck rise. Nevertheless, he bowed. "Your grace."

"Lord Markville, I am refusing your request to marry Lady Euphrosyne." He opened his mouth, but the duke stayed him. "I don't need to hear about how eligible you are or how much you regard my daughter. I am sure you will be acceptable for some other lady, however, it is my duty to increase the wealth of the dukedom, and you have nothing to offer me."

This was not what Markville had hoped for, and he was glad he had made other arrangements. Still, the refusal pricked his pride. Fighting to maintain a well-bred drawl, he said, "Your daughter's happiness and the life I can give her is not enough? She will want for nothing. I would even be willing to settle an amount on her."

"Money, bah! What do I care about that or how she feels about a marriage? Land is real wealth. It's enough that Lady Aglaia's marriage brought me nothing. That will not happen with Euphrosyne. She will be wed to someone appropriate within the next few months."

Rage like Markville never felt before surged through him. It took all his will power not to reach across the desk and throttle the old cur. This was it. He'd leave with Euphrosyne tonight if not sooner. "I would like to see her before I depart."

Having already lost interest in Markville, the duke looked down at his document. "She has already left. You will not see her again."

"You will understand if I do not wish you a good day." Markville turned on his heel. Behind him, the vile cur was cackling. Markville would find Euphrosyne and marry her, and this time, he didn't care what he had to do to have her in his life. He'd been a fool not to listen to her brother, but he'd not be a fool again.

Hawksworth and his wife were in the hall when Markville got there. "He said she's gone."

"I know. She'll be back at Somerset before this evening." Meg placed her hand on his arm. "We are preparing to depart." She headed out the door, leaving him no choice but to accompany her. When they reached the drive, he saw his curricle. "Listen to me. You cannot go after her now. He has a small army surrounding the coach. Do not doubt he's ordered them to shoot you if you interfere. We shall find a way for the two of you to wed. For right now, try to have a little patience."

"I am afraid I am out of that particular virtue, my lady." She patted his arm. "Trust us. We have some experience dealing with Somerset."

"Do as my wife says and keep us informed as to your whereabouts." Hawksworth slapped Markville's back. "I should have been more forceful in making my suggestion."

"It wouldn't have mattered." The anger he'd felt at the duke was now turned to himself. "I was bound and determined to be honorable."

"Being honorable is not in Somerset's bones." Hawksworth helped his wife into the coach. "You'll hear from us soon."

Meg was right about Euphrosyne being guarded, Markville discovered. More than half the footmen had departed. They would be keeping Euphrosyne captive. Well, he might not be able to stage a rescue on the road, but he could try to rescue her from her home.

CHAPTER NINE

EUPHROSYNE HEADED TOWARD THE HALL, surprised the footman was following her. "I do know the way. You may go back to your duties."

"I am tending to my duties." He took hold of her arm.

The nerve of the man! "Unhand me."

"I'm sorry, my lady, but you are to depart immediately. The duke's orders."

This could not be happening! "I wish to say farewell to my brother and sister-in-law. Where is my mother?"

"She will follow later. I'm afraid you must leave now."

She struggled but was unable to break his hold on her. No one but the coachmen and outriders were around. *Where is everyone? Drat, in the back of the house. The only way they'd hear me is if I screamed.*

She opened her mouth to do just that, but she was lifted up and shoved into the coach. Her scream was lost in the rumble of the wheels on gravel and the sound of horses.

"Oh, my lady." Turner fluttered her hands. "I never would have imagined they'd treat you this way."

"You are here. Did you know we were to leave immediately?"

"Not like this." Turner shook her head. "After you went to the wedding this morning, I was told to pack your clothes, but I assumed that we'd be going with the duchess in the morning." Turner wrung her hands. "If I'd known this would happen, I would have told your mother."

Now that Euphrosyne thought about it, Mama would

not have been able to help. "They wouldn't have allowed it." The duke—she would no longer think of him as her father—had planned it to a nicety. Euphrosyne glanced at her maid. She wanted to trust the woman, but couldn't bring herself to put her maid's livelihood at risk. Not only that, any new maid her father would hire would be more gaoler than servant. For now, she would keep her own counsel and look for ways to escape. "It is not your fault. Do you know the name of the footman?"

"Sittle, my lady. He's one of his grace's men." Meaning that even if she had something with which to bribe him, it would be useless.

As her maid stared out the window, Euphrosyne thought she saw tears in the woman's eyes.

No matter what, the duke would not get away with this.

She had been home only for a few days when she heard her name being called as she crossed the courtyard.

Charles! He'd come for her. She rushed toward the portcullis, shouting, "Markville! I'm here."

Oh, my God no! They're lowering the portcullis. Hiking her skirts, she ran as fast as she could. She could make it, even if she had to duck and roll under the thing.

From behind a hand grabbed Euphrosyne, pulling her back. "You are not allowed to go out, my lady. The duke's orders."

She stared at Charles. He and his men were fighting the duke's thugs. Then the drawbridge was raised, and she lost sight of him. Why had she and her brothers and sisters thought it was such a wonderful thing that the old defenses still worked? They should have sabotaged them years ago.

She began walking the ramparts. Charles returned every day for a week, but the drawbridge remained closed, and all they could do was stare at each other until she was not even allowed that. The next time she went to climb the stairs, the door was locked.

Somehow she had to get out of this castle, but every time she tried to sneak into the muniment room to look at the old castle plans, hoping to find a secret tunnel—there had to be at least one—the door was locked. She attempted to climb the high walls, which had for hundreds of years protected the castle and its gardens, and that had not been at all easy in a gown. It became impossible after her father assigned another footman to guard her door when Sittle was taking his rest. A rest she ensured was much deserved. Even though she was confined to the buildings and grounds, they were extensive. She rode and walked for hours, many times eschewing luncheon. Each night, she dropped into bed exhausted from trying to tire her keepers.

The only bright spot was that Charles was persistent in trying to gain access to see her and talk to her father.

One day after Charles had left, her maid entered her chamber. "My lady, I received a letter that had a missive for you enclosed."

Euphrosyne scrambled off the window seat. "How? I mean, who do we both know who would write you?"

"Lady Hawksworth's maid has asked that I pass notes to you." Shaking her head, Turner shrugged. "I will, of course."

"Letters from my sister-in-law?" Meg must know that all her correspondence, even from Laia, was read before Euphrosyne received it.

"Yes. They are about"—her maid lowered her voice to a whisper—"Lord Markville."

Oh, God, how she wanted to involve Turner further in this, but she could not put the maid at risk. "Write her back telling her you cannot deceive the duke. If anyone reads your letters, they will believe you to be loyal to him."

Relief showed on the woman's face. "I would do

anything for you, but thank you, my lady."

"I shall find a way out of this difficulty without harming anyone." Except, perhaps, Sittle. Euphrosyne went back to the window seat, pulling a warm woolen shawl around her shoulders. Advent was just a week away. "You may go."

If only she'd had the foresight to train pigeons to carry messages.

Once the door closed, she placed her hand on her stomach. It wouldn't be long before the world—or at least everyone in the castle—knew she was carrying Charles's child. Perhaps then her father would allow her to marry him.

A few days later, Euphrosyne received a summons to attend the duke. After making her way to his study, a room that seemed as cold as the man himself and had never boded well for her, she waited until she was announced, but refused to wait submissively further for him to notice her.

Taking one of the dark leather chairs in front of his desk, she gave him to the count of thirty before saying, "I was given to understand you wished to speak with me. If you are not prepared to do so, I shall return later."

The duke's head jerked up like a puppet's on a string. "Impertinent miss. Of all my children, you are the most impudent." Her father waved his hand as if he was warding away something distasteful. "Fortunately, you will not be my problem much longer. I am arranging a match for you."

Her breath caught, and before she could stop herself, she said, "Markville?"

"No." Somerset glared at her. "Absolutely not! The two of you make me sick with your maudlin sentimentality. I suppose I should be glad he doesn't have an army at his command, or he'd be laying siege. One would think he had better things to do than moon after you." For a moment, she thought he'd spit. Which was a ridiculous notion. He'd never do anything so human. "I am in negotiations with three dukes. You will wed one of them."

She would not. "No." Euphrosyne clenched her hands into fists. "I am carrying Markville's child, and I shall wed him."

The duke's eyes grew colder, if that was even possible. "Pregnant. You've hidden it well." Without taking his gaze off her, he drew out a paper. "That, however, makes my choice easier. You will have the honor of marrying the Duke of Ross. He's riddled with the French pox, and detests the cousin who would inherit. Therefore he requires an heir. Don't worry, he won't touch you until you give birth. Now leave me."

Biting her cheek, Euphrosyne rose and left the room, her spine straighter than it had ever been, as if nothing were amiss. It was time to take drastic measures.

HAWKSWORTH HANDED MARKVILLE A GLASS of wine while Meg shook out a letter. "You'd better sit."

He didn't know why he'd been summoned, but they'd better get to the point fast. The message to come here had arrived as he was setting out for Somerset, again. Somehow he had to make the duke allow his marriage to Euphrosyne.

Meg's lips flattened. "Euphrosyne is with child."

Good God! He'd never even considered, or thought . . . That, of course, was stupid. He should have known it would happen. He did know it might happen. Truthfully, he'd wanted Euphrosyne to bear his child. Hawksworth snatched the wine out of Markville's suddenly slack fingers. "I have to go to her. Somerset must be made to see reason."

"You won't get within five miles of her before he slams

that blasted drawbridge shut on you again." Hawksworth raised one black brow. "Not after the commotion you caused the last time. Though, I must admit hiring a band of traveling actors to make as much noise as possible all night and day long was a brilliant idea.

Markville had been shocked to discover that Somerset Castle still had both inner and an outer walls set with spikes, not to mention a functioning drawbridge. The damn place was impregnable. "I don't suppose you know of any secret entrances."

"I do," Hawksworth said. "But he knows about them as well."

Meg poured a glass of wine for herself. "The one thing you are doing is costing Somerset a great deal of money."

What did any of that matter? Nothing had worked! "She is pregnant with *my child*! I must get to her."

"Speaking of that, the *only* thing stopping me from breaking your nose"—Hawksworth glowered—"is that I know you love her and want to marry her. And"—he glanced at his wife—"I know that you were not given much choice. If it were my wife, I'd not be able to resist."

"I will wed her." Markville grabbed the glass back from Hawksworth and swallowed half of it. "He will have to allow the wedding now."

Lady Hawksworth shook her head, her expression bleaker than Markville had ever seen it. "He plans to marry her off to Ross."

"Ross! He can't. That old goat is full of the French pox."

"And doesn't want his cousin to inherit the dukedom. Euphrosyne is his one chance to change his heir." She glanced at the letter again. "They are leaving in two weeks for the duke's estate outside of Edinburgh. The wedding is planned for Twelfth Night."

The idea that that old roué would even lay a finger on her arm made Markville want to commit murder.

Preferably on the Duke of Somerset. "If she is carrying anyone's heir, it's mine."

"I think we all agree on what should happen." Lady Hawksworth head swiveled toward the door. "Oh, good. They have arrived."

Markville felt as if he were going mad. Dealing with Somerset was like dealing with some medieval war lord. "Who has arrived?"

Hawksworth re-filled his and Markville's goblets then lifted his glass. "The cavalry."

His butler opened the door, then stepped aside as two older ladies swept into the study. "The Duchess of Bridgewater and Viscountess Featherton."

"Thank you, Saunders." Lady Hawksworth's visage lightened. "Grandmamma, Duchess"—she held out her hands—"I am so glad you could come."

"Of course we would be here for you." The smaller lady with silver hair kissed Lady Hawksworth's cheeks. "Now, pour us some wine and we shall discuss how we can assist you."

"First, allow me to present Lord Markville. It is he and Hawksworth's sister Lady Euphrosyne who require your help. Markville, my grandmother Lady Featherton and her good friend the Duchess of Bridgewater."

The duchess inclined her head. "Pleased to meet you, Markville."

"I as well." Lady Featherton said. "You poor dear. I hear Somerset is involved."

"We're glad you agreed that Meg should ask for our aid," the duchess said.

He hadn't, but there was no point in mentioning it. He had no other ideas.

"Yes, indeed." Lady Featherton nodded. "We have been giving your difficulties some thought."

They repaired to a long table set off to one side of the

room, and Lady Hawksworth explained that, although he was perfectly eligible and he and Euphrosyne were in love, and she was now in a delicate condition, her father was determined to marry her to Ross.

"I always knew Somerset was a cur." The duchess scowled before taking a sip of wine.

"He was never pleasant, even as a young man," Lady Featherton agreed. "But that is neither here nor there. Now that this has become urgent, we must come up with a plan that will enable Lord Markville to wed Lady Euphrosyne." Lady Featherton and the duchess exchanged a glance and a nod, then her ladyship smiled brightly at all of them. "Fortunately, we know just the woman who can help. Lady Theodora Grantham."

Lady Hawksworth tilted her head then nodded. "Didn't she arrange Kit and Mary's wedding?"

"She did, indeed," the duchess said. "She and her husband have a town house in Charlotte Square in Edinburgh's New City. Although she is English, she has been there for years and is very well connected. Her father is the Duke of Gordon."

That sounded good. But how the lady could help was beyond Markville's understanding. He needed to hire a troop of former soldiers and save Euphrosyne.

"I shall write to her explaining the problem," Lady Featherton said. "And have it sent tonight with the mail coach. It is faster than a private messenger would be." She looked at him. "You must be prepared to travel north as soon as we hear from Lady Theo."

The duchess focused on him as well. "I suggest you position your horses along the route to Edinburgh."

"Oh, yes!" Lady Featherton smiled at him. "You will not want to waste time waiting for teams. I do not suppose you have an unmarked traveling coach?"

"Er, no." He'd never needed one.

She nodded knowingly, "In that event, you may borrow ours."

Surely once they were married there would be no need for subterfuge. Markville shook his head.

"My dear man, you will want to be far away from Somerset's reach before he knows who exactly was involved in spiriting his daughter away. I would wager my diamonds you are being watched."

"Watched?" The words came out sounding like he was choking. "There has been no indication."

"You have shown you will not willingly give up Euphrosyne," Hawksworth said. "Somerset probably started having you followed after the first incident." He took a sip of wine. "That's the reason I instructed you to leave from the back of your club and come here via the mews." Again a brow was raised. "You did do that, did you not?"

It had never occurred to Markville that the duke would have him followed, and he'd been strongly tempted to ignore the instructions. Thank God he had not. "Yes, but if I am being watched, he'll know I'm going somewhere. My carriage is being readied to depart in the morning."

"Do you have a property between London and Scotland?" the duchess asked.

He did. "Yes, and it is fairly close to the Duke of Gordon's main estate in Hull."

"Perfect." The viscountess clapped her hands. "We will send our coach to you there. That way when you leave from there, no one will know it is you."

"Just a moment," Hawksworth said frowning. "Which estate is that?"

Had the man had Markville's holdings investigated? Hawksworth must have done. Then again, it was his sister Markville was going to marry. Come to think of it, Somerset had probably done the same thing. "It's a new property. I bought it from a gentleman who wished to move to Italy and had no heirs."

"In that event"—Lady Hawksworth said—"do not go there. Keep it a secret for now. You will most likely have need of it after you wed Euphrosyne."

"Then where—"

"Your holding near Peterborough." Hawksworth nodded as if reassuring himself it was the right decision. "You can just as easily switch coaches there."

"It also has the benefit of being in the opposite direction of Somerset," the duchess said.

Markville felt as if he'd lost control over his life. It was becoming as lurid as one of those novels his sister liked to read. Still . . . "Is all this subterfuge really necessary?"

Four sets of brows rose, followed by incredulous looks.

"You poor boy," the duchess said. "Do you still have no idea of what Somerset is willing to do?"

"Remind me to tell you the stratagems involved to ensure my marriage as well as those of my brothers." Hawksworth took a drink of wine. "My father is ruthless. In order to win, you must be able to fool the fox."

"Laia's wedding was easier only because Bolton attempted to harm her, and Hawksworth was forced to kill him," Meg reminded Markville.

He drained his glass of wine. Whatever it took to make Euphrosyne his wife, he'd do. Including murder her father if necessary.

Chapter Ten

EUPHROSYNE AND HER MOTHER HAD no sooner arrived at the Duke of Ross's house than his sister Lady Emily Stewart insisted on taking them on morning visits. "My brother will understand." The soft burr underlying Lady Emily's tone was almost imperceptible. "You must come to know our society here in Edinburgh. Even though he has a vote in the Lords, he prefers Edinburgh society and rarely attends." The lady's amber eyes seemed to estimate Euphrosyne. "I trust you will not miss English society."

Euphrosyne was glad she could answer truthfully. "Not at all."

Sittle handed her into the coach after her mother and Lady Emily. They had left Somerset so quickly that Euphrosyne did not know how Charles was to find her. Once she settled her skirts, she asked, "Where are we going?"

"We have been invited to Lady Theodora Grantham's tea." Lady Emily's lips formed a moue. "She is English, but has been with us for so long we barely remember it."

Deciding to ignore the not so veiled insult to her countrywoman, Euphrosyne smiled brightly. "How lovely. I am sure she will be helpful in showing me how to go on."

"I am sure she will be happy to aid you in any way possible." The other woman's lips relaxed so that she no longer looked as if she'd been sucking a lemon.

As her mother took up the conversation with Lady Emily, Euphrosyne applied herself to attempting to memorize the route from the Ross estate to Edinburgh. It was fairly straightforward until they turned at a crossroad with a tavern by the name of the Sheep Heid Inn and the route became much more complicated. Her ladyship helpfully pointed out Holyrood Palace and Cannongate hill before they emerged into what was the New City.

Fortunately, the Duke of Ross did not own a castle. And, other than a wall bordering the front of the property, there did not seem to be one enclosing the estate. Good. It would be easier for her to escape when the time came.

"I will take you to visit the old town later." Lady Emily straightened her bonnet as they pulled up in front of a large corner town house.

It had taken less than an hour to make the drive, but Euphrosyne knew that attempting the distance on foot would take much longer. Resisting the urge to touch her gently swelling stomach, she was determined to make her escape as soon as possible.

"Euphrosyne." Her mother's voice reminded her of her duty.

"Coming." They climbed shallow steps to an open door. The house was much larger and more ornate than the town house in Bath.

A butler bowed and footmen stepped quickly over to collect their cloaks and gloves. "If you will please follow me?" the butler said.

She took in the ornate plaster picked in pale blue paint and the small paintings with gilded frames. Even with the formal decoration, the house seemed more like a home than her own did. They entered a drawing room situated half-way down the corridor. The butler intoned, "Her Grace the Duchess of Somerset, Lady Euphrosyne Trevor, and Lady Emily Stewart."

A tall, elegant lady near Mama's age glanced up sharply. Her gray eyes met Euphrosyne's, and the lady moved toward them. "Welcome." Taking Lady Emily's hands, the lady bussed her cheek. "Emily, it is so good to see you. Please introduce me."

"Your grace, Lady Euphrosyne, this is our hostess Lady Theodore Grantham. Theo, the Duchess of Somerset and her daughter, my brother's betrothed."

Lady Theo smiled as she greeted them. "I am so happy you have joined us. Emily, if you will introduce her grace to our friends, I shall make Lady Euphrosyne known to the younger set." Lady Emily opened her mouth, but Lady Theo continued, "You cannot expect her to have no friends her age."

Euphrosyne hid her smile as Lady Theo drew her away toward a group of younger matrons.

"I must be quick. Keep a pleasant smile on your face. You must in no way let anyone know what I am about to tell you. There is a gentleman here who is very anxious to see you again. I believe you know of whom I speak."

For a bare second, Euphrosyne lost her breath. Charles. He'd found her. "He's here? In the house?"

"Indeed. You will not see him today. Perhaps not for a few days, but all will be well."

They had arrived at the group of ladies. "Thank you."

"Lady Euphrosyne." Lady Theo broadened her smile. "I'd like to introduce you to Lady Maitland. Lady Euphrosyne is the Duke of Ross's betrothed."

One by one she was introduced to the other women present. Although, many of the ladies quickly covered their distaste for the coming marriage, a few of the younger ladies audibly gasped and did not even offer their felicitations. Well, it was no worse than what she was feeling. At least now she knew the marriage would never happen. The only question was how soon Charles could rescue her.

When it was time to leave, Lady Theo bent as though to kiss Euphrosyne's cheek and whispered. "You will hear from me soon." She straightened and addressed Lady Emily and Mama. "I hope you had a pleasant time. Your grace, I am more than happy to introduce you to my modiste if you are in need of anything."

"Oh, but I was going to take them to Mrs. Kennedy," Lady Emily objected.

Lady Theo raised one blonde brow. "My dear, Emily, I know you are devoted to Mrs. Kennedy, but you must admit that Madame Aufroy's fashions are more stylish."

"Thank you, both, for your suggestions." Mama gave them each a diplomatic smile. "I see no reason why we cannot visit both dressmakers."

"Yes, indeed." Euphrosyne copied her mother's expression. "I think that is an excellent idea." The more time she was able to spend in town the greater her chances of escaping.

"Yes, of course." Lady Emily smiled again. "You will most likely require the services of both modistes for your trousseau. I understand that you do not have a competent dressmaker near your estate."

"How very true." Euphrosyne linked arms with her mother. "I shall greatly enjoy the shopping in Edinburgh. How lucky you are to live nearby."

Every minute until she heard from Lady Theo would seem like days.

THE FOLLOWING MORNING, AS EUPHROSYNE and her mother were breaking their fast in her mother's parlor, a note arrived from Lady Theo.

Mama's maid handed her the letter opener, and she

popped slit open the seal. "It appears that Lady Theo has made an appointment for you with her modiste at eleven o'clock this morning."

"I did not expect it to be so soon." Euphrosyne's heart began to thud so hard it was amazing no one heard it. It was all she could do to maintain her countenance. Perhaps she would learn more about how her escape would be made. "As much as I appreciate Lady Emily's offer, I think the cut of Lady Theo's gown superior."

"It was more stylish." Mama sighed. "We still must visit the other dressmaker. You do not wish to get on the wrong side of Lady Emily. I have the feeling she is not at all pleased with being supplanted as the mistress of this house."

"You are probably correct. She has had charge of the duke's houses for many years." Not that the lady had to be concerned. Euphrosyne would not be here that much longer. "I should dress. It is already past nine."

Setting down the letter, her mother rose. "I suggest you bring your maid. In addition to our visit to Lady Theo's modiste, we shall take the time to do some other shopping while we are in town."

"As you wish." Euphrosyne looked forward to making her father's guard follow her around in a more difficult setting. She would also make him carry packages, regardless of the accompanying maid.

When Euphrosyne entered her bedchamber, Turner was supervising a housemaid cleaning the room. "I have an appointment with a modiste this morning, and then I will do some more shopping. I would like you to accompany me."

"Of course, my lady." Her maid went to the wardrobe and took out a light blue cashmere gown and a Prussian blue wool spencer that Meg had sent. Euphrosyne was happy that its design made her pregnancy less noticeable. "I have a list of items you require. I shall bring it with me."

Shortly after the appointed time, they arrived at the shop on the Royal Mile across from St. Giles Kirk—as she'd been told it was called instead of church.

A small bell rang as she, her mother and their maids entered. Sittle took up a place on the street to the side of the door.

"Your grace, my lady, welcome," Madame Aufroy, a small woman with dark hair greeted them. "Would you care for tea or coffee?"

"Tea would be lovely." Mama sank onto a sofa. "My maid has several items she must purchase. Perhaps one of your assistants could advise her as to which stores are better."

"*Mais naturellement*, your grace." Madame signaled to a woman who had been straightening up a counter. "I shall send Marie with her." Before they were out the door, Madam turned to Euphrosyne. "Please, come with me. I must take your measurements."

She followed the modiste into a good-sized closet warmed by a small tiled heater. Another woman began to undress Euphrosyne. The tension and excitement she'd been feeling ebbed, leaving her slightly depressed. She'd so hoped she would learn something more about her rescue, but it did not appear as if anything of moment would occur today.

"Elsie, you may go. I will call if I need you," Madame said. Once the door closed, she addressed Euphrosyne in a low voice. "I will take your measurements as planned. Then we will spend one hour selecting fabrics and designs. After which you will beg some time to visit St. Giles to pray. Sit in the first pew and wait."

Euphrosyne's heart began to race. "Will I see Lo—*him*?"

The older woman smiled. "I think you can be sure of that."

Euphrosyne selected several beautiful fabrics in velvet

and cashmere as well as the gowns into which they would be fashioned, yet the clock moved at a snail's pace.

Finally, the modiste signaled for the samples and fashion plates to be removed. "I believe we have had a productive day." She inclined her head to Mama. "Your grace, I hope to have everything to you within a week. Fortunately, this is a slow time of year, and many sempstresses are looking for work."

"At Christmas?" Euphrosyne was surprised to hear that.

"The Scottish do not celebrate Christmas like the English do. They save their parties for the new year."

Euphrosyne noticed her mother's maid and the other woman had returned, each bearing packages. "Mama, I would like to visit the church across the street. I need a few moments to myself."

"That is a very good idea." She took Euphrosyne by her shoulders and drew her closer. "Do what you must, and remember that I love you."

"I shall." Her mother's eyes filled with tears, but the next second they were gone, and the placid countenance she showed the world was back. "I love you, too."

"My lady," Madame Aufroy said, "the front door to the church is always open. Whereas the side doors are frequently locked. You should enter that way."

Euphrosyne held back her own tears. "Thank you."

"Euphrosyne, take Turner."

"Yes, Mama." The maid followed Euphrosyne out of the shop and across the street. Sittle fell in behind them.

When they reached the thick, old-fashioned, wooden doors, her maid stopped. "Would you like me to accompany you inside?"

"If you would not mind sitting a few pews behind me, yes." Euphrosyne glanced at the footman. She didn't know what exactly would happen, but whatever it was he would be decidedly *de trop*. "Please wait here. I shall not be long."

"My orders are never to let you out of my sight when you are not with her grace." He was absolutely her father's man.

Closing her eyes, she sighed. "Have it your way, but you will remain at the back of the church."

Doing as she'd been instructed, Euphrosyne made her way to the first pew, bowed her head, and waited. She had just finished the Lord's Prayer when a door opening echoed through the church, and a young man followed by Lady Theo, a gentleman Euphrosyne did not know, and Charles strolled from an inside door located to the side of the choir into the transept. Her heart must have stopped because she couldn't catch her breath.

Before she could rise, he was with her, drawing her into his arms. "My love, we don't have much time."

Boots rang on the stone. "Stop! I command you in the name of the Duke—" A sickening crack sounded, and Sittle collapsed to the floor. Behind him stood an old man holding a club.

"Is he dead?" Even her whisper seemed loud.

"Ach, nay." The old man shook his head sadly. "More's the pity. I canna abide interfering Englishmen." A grin split his weathered face. "Present company excepted, o'course."

"Good job, Shamus," the other gentleman said.

Lady Theo nodded. "Yes, well, let us get this wedding done. Lady Euphrosyne, if you do not mind, my husband, Lord Titus, will give you away."

"That would be perfect." *This is truly happening. I'm going to marry Charles!*

They took their places in front of the vicar. Reluctantly, she dropped her hand from Charles's arm and placed her other hand on Lord Titus's arm, only to have her hand returned to Charles a few moments later. This time it was for the rest of her life.

The service was much shorter than in any of the other

weddings she had attended. She was pleased that her voice was strong when she said her vows, and Charles held her gaze until the vicar reminded them they had to sign the register.

"Lady Theo requested that you sign a separate register as well," the vicar said. "It is not usually done, but I understand your father is difficult."

"That is one way of putting it." Euphrosyne glanced at her ladyship. "Where will you put it?"

"We are traveling to my father's main estate for Christmas. I shall give it to the rector there for safekeeping."

Shamus took the second register and nodded. "I tied yon Englishman up and put him next to the door. I wanted to douse him with whisky, but Lord Titus didn't want the man losing his position."

A laugh burbled up in Euphrosyne, but she managed to tamp it down. "That was very kind of Lord Titus." She looked at her maid, who'd been standing silent. "Do you wish to come with me?"

"If I may, my lady." Turner grinned. "The idea of living in Scotland never really suited me."

Lady Theo removed her bright scarlet cloak and bonnet, handing them to Euphrosyne. "Wear these until you are in the coach. It is as close to the door as we could manage, but in the event anyone is watching, we do not want him to see you."

"Where will we go?" Turner helped Euphrosyne don the bonnet.

"Back to my house for the night." Lady Theo unwrapped a package tied in brown paper, drawing out an identical red cloak, while Turner folded Euphrosyne's cloak and wrapped it in the emptied paper. "Tomorrow we will all travel south to my father's estate before the weather sets in."

"My coach is at a small inn off the London road."

Charles took the paper package and wrapped Euphrosyne in the red cloak. "I shall send our wedding announcement with the mail, but we'll remain at the Duke of Gordon's estate until I'm sure you are safe."

"Believe me"—Lady Theo glanced at Euphrosyne over her shoulder—"there is no love lost between my father and yours. He was more than happy to help us."

"I think he also owed Lady Featherton a favor." Lord Titus laid the other red cloak across his wife's shoulders.

"My sister-in-law's mother?" Euphrosyne was confused. How had she become involved?

"Meg's grandmother," Charles said. "She is a fascinatingly scary old lady. I now know where your sister-in-law comes by her scheming."

"We'll tell you all about it on the way home," Lady Theo said.

CHAPTER ELEVEN

MARKVILLE COULDN'T BELIEVE EUPHROSYNE WAS finally with him again, finally his wife. But this wasn't over yet. It was Scotland, and contrary to England, their marriage had to be consummated. He wanted to rush her to the waiting coach, but forced himself to make the short walk from the side door to the carriage at a steady pace. Nothing must appear strange. They knew of the one footman who had already been felled, but Hawksworth had warned there could be others.

Markville assisted Euphrosyne into the coach, then joined her. "Almost there."

She snuggled next to him. "How will Lady Theo and Lord Titus get home?"

"We are collecting them from the back of a store." The carriage turned down two narrow streets, then stopped. "Here we are."

Lady Theo and her husband came out of the store and entered the carriage. "There is no sign the coach was followed, but two men were watching the kirk. It will not be long before your father knows you are gone."

Euphrosyne nodded. "What happens next?"

"Next we take you to the mews behind our house, and you will enter through the garden. No one knows Markville is staying with us, so your father has no reason to search for you here. In the morning, you will enter the coach from the mews."

"My maid." Euphrosyne sat up, tension radiating from

her. "How will she join me?"

"We've been very canny about protecting her." Lord Titus smiled slyly. "She could not come with us without causing talk. Therefore, she will find the guard your father set on you and raise the alarm. She will then rejoin your mother and her maid, but instead of leaving with them, Shamus will fetch her from the alley in back of the modiste."

She glanced at Markville. "My mother knows, doesn't she?"

"She wrote to Meg and told us what was happening." If it had not been for the duchess, he wouldn't be here now.

A line marred Euphrosyne's forehead, and he wanted to smooth it away. "Does the duke not read her correspondence?"

"We don't know. However, it doesn't matter. She writes in code." He laughed when her jaw dropped.

"*Code?*"

"It was hard for me to believe as well, but it is, apparently, not as uncommon as one might think."

Euphrosyne smiled up at him. "I'm very glad she did. Thank you for rescuing me."

"I wish I could take the credit. My role as a hero has been severely limited. I have done nothing more than do was I was told to do."

"And by ladies at that." Lady Theo chuckled.

"Ah, well." His beloved wife grinned. "Sometimes that is for the best."

He would have liked to at least have punched someone.

Later that day, after he'd made love to her slowly, making certain she knew he was happy about the baby, they slept with his hand wrapped protectively on her stomach. Their child. They would not be able to hide how far along she had been when they'd finally married, but it didn't matter. Not to him. And if anyone had the audacity to comment, he'd make sure everyone knew Somerset was responsible for the delay.

Shortly before dawn the next morning, her maid and his valet awakened them.

"Turner." Euphrosyne yawned. "We have no clothing, you and I."

"Not to worry, my lady." The maid averted her eyes from the bed. "We have been well taken care of. I don't know how it happened, but all of our clothing arrived this morning, and his lordship brought another trunk for you."

His wife glanced at him. He didn't know either, but he could guess. "I think Lady Theo's and Lord Titus's people have been busy."

The one part Markville had planned was their procession south to Hull. Before he'd left for Scotland, he'd sent letters to friends he knew along the way. Instead of traveling covertly, as Somerset would expect them to do, they lodged with friends, most of whom were peers. Each time they stopped they were greeted with a warmth he had not expected, and enthusiasm for his marriage to Euphrosyne.

By the time they reached Hull, half of England would know he and Euphrosyne were married, making it almost impossible for her father to do anything other than accept the marriage.

They spent the first night at Howick Hall with Earl Gray. The next day, when they stopped for luncheon, Euphrosyne said, "Charles, why are we advertising where we are? I thought we did not want my father to be able to find us."

"My love, he won't find out where we have been until after we are in Hull. He will be expecting us to be traveling by ourselves and staying in out of the way coaching inns. I would own myself surprised if his men ask about two carriages traveling together and visiting private estates. You will notice that we are not stopping at inns along the way for more than a quick bite and a change of horses. This way, by the time we do arrive in Town, everyone and their dog will know you are married. Those who for some reason have not been informed will see it posted in the paper."

Euphrosyne had been worried, but the answer seemed to erase her fears. "That was an excellent idea."

"I'm glad you approve."

The Ross Estate outside of Edinburgh

"WHAT THE DEVIL DO YOU mean she's gone?" The men Somerset had watching Euphrosyne blanched. "How the hell did she get out of your sight?"

Three of the men looked toward Sittle. "As I told her grace, Lady Euphrosyne went into the church. While she was praying, Lord Markville, another gentleman, a vicar, and a lady came out of a room. I was running to get her ladyship when I was hit on the head. When I came to, I was tied up and everyone was gone. Her ladyship's maid found me and went to tell her grace." He shuddered. "Her grace had everyone running everywhere looking for Lady Euphrosyne, but she disappeared."

"Disappeared, hell." Somerset couldn't believe Markville had found her. Not only wouldn't he get the land he wanted next to the Somerset holdings in Scotland, but what in damnation was he going to tell Ross? "You three"—he pointed at the men who were supposed to have been helping Sittle—"are sacked. You should have been watching all the doors in that blasted church. Get out of my sight." The three men bolted out of the room. "Sittle, we need to find her."

"Yes, your grace. I have already sent grooms out to

taverns and inns. I'll join them tomorrow. They must be heading to one of Lord Markville's estates." The man paused. "I don't know how the team watching his place near Peterborough missed him leaving."

"They will be dealt with shortly. This sloppiness is inexcusable. Did you question the maid?"

"Yes, your grace, but she was hysterical, and I couldn't make any sense of what she was saying. The housekeeper gave her a sedative. I'll talk to her again in the morning."

"At least I don't have to worry about Ross's questions. He's eating opium again."

Somerset noticed his servant had nothing to say to that. If the duke kept indulging, they could depart with him being none the wiser. The only person he had to explain himself to was his duchess. If she even cared to listen to him. Knowing her, she already had all the information he did. He knew that she'd publically excoriated Sittle for losing Euphrosyne.

Four days later, the butler brought him the London Times.

> *Lady Euphrosyne Trevor, daughter of the Duke of Somerset, and the Marquis of Markville in Edinburgh on the 17th of December.*

"Sittle, tell her grace we are going home."

May 1819

EUPHROSYNE HAD BEEN SURPRISED TO see how many members of her family were present for the christening of hers and Charles's son, Charles Fredrick Damon, Earl of Hartwick. The only one missing was Laia, who had given birth to twin boys a few weeks before

Euphrosyne.

"He is precious." Mama held her eighth grandchild. Meg had given birth last September, and Quartus and his wife had had twins in autumn. Mama might never see Frank and Jenny's twins in America.

"It will be nice that he has cousins near his age." Charles hadn't left her side during the birth, and was always willing—much to Nurse's consternation —to take care of the baby.

Even Sarah, who had given birth two months ago, was here.

"Mama, where does Somerset think you are?" Since she had made her vow last year, Euphrosyne never called or thought of him as her father. What real father would do what he had tried to do to his daughter?

"He knows I am here." She smiled gently. "He is well aware that no matter the circumstances, I will not miss the christening of any of my grandchildren. Except Frank and Jenny's, which could not be avoided. They are planning a trip to England next spring."

"It will be wonderful seeing them again." Euphrosyne still found it hard to believe that her mother, a seemingly placid woman who never contradicted her husband, had a network of friends and allies ready to assist her. Chief of whom were Meg and Hawksworth, but Mama also knew Meg's grandmother, and the Dowager Duchess of Bridgewater, and numerous other people. And Mama knew codes, which she used regularly, not only to remain in practice, but so that if the duke read her letters, he'd be none the wiser.

Tears sprang to Euphrosyne's eyes. "Thank you for making sure Charles and I married."

"My dear, dear, child. I could do nothing less. It was clear the two of you were deeply in love and belonged together." She smiled ruefully. "I only wish I'd known what Somerset planned to do at Laia's wedding. That was a miscalculation on my part that I will not make again."

Euphrosyne believed that wholeheartedly. She glanced at her mother. "We read that Ross had died. Who was the cousin?"

"His land-steward. He and Lady Emily were very much in love. He asked for her hand several years ago, but Ross refused to allow the marriage. They wed privately a few days after her brother's death."

"No wonder she didn't like me." The absurdness of the situation struck Euphrosyne. "She would have been more than happy to help me escape."

"Indeed she would have." Mama took the baby and cuddled him.

"I wonder which of us will be next," Euphrosyne mused.

Charles joined them, handing her and her mother glasses of champagne. "Whoever it is, we will be there to help them if they need it."

"Yes." Euphrosyne stood and held up her glass. "I want to thank everyone for your support and making sure that Markville and I were able to marry. We will pledge our assistance for the next of our brothers or sisters who require it."

"Here, here!" Charles slipped his arm around her waist. "I knew it. I knew you were going to be a dangerous woman to cross."

AUTHOR'S NOTE

I hope you enjoyed the continuing saga of The Trevors. Those of you who have read *One Duke Or Another*, the third in the series, will understand the references to the Duke of Bolton and his death more fully. For those of you who have not yet done so, enjoy! Unfortunately, the length of this book did not allow me to fully delve into all the particulars.

Likewise, if you have read *Miss Featherton's Christmas Prince* (The Marriage Game Book #8) you'll already have been introduced to the Duchess of Bridgewater and Lady Featherton. Lady Theo and Lord Titus were first introduced in *A Kiss for Lady Mary* (The Marriage Game book #6). I hope you enjoyed their return.

As always, I studied old maps of Bath and Edinburgh. Sidney Gardens was built to be like Vauxhall.

The stories of the Trevors are initially released in box sets. As I receive the rights back, I make them available as single titles. The first book, *A Promise of Love*, is free if you sign up for my newsletter at www.ellaquinnauthor.com. The second book, *It Takes a Hero*, is at your favorite e-retailer. The third book is in *The Scoundrel Who Loved Me* box set, available on Amazon. I'm working on making each of these novellas available in print.

Made in the USA
Monee, IL
21 September 2020

43099758R00267